GENESIS

LEGENDS ONLINE BOOK ONE

JONATHAN YANEZ
ROSS BUZZELL

CONTENTS

STAY INFORMED

Get A Free Book by visiting Jonathan Yanez' website. You can email me at jonathan.alan.yanez@gmail.com or find me on Amazon, and Instagram (@author_jonathan_yanez). I also created a special Facebook group called "Jonathan's Reading Wolves" specifically for readers, where I show new cover art, do give-aways, and run contests. Please check it out and join whenever you get the chance!

For updates about new releases, as well as exclusive promotions, visit my website and sign up for the VIP mailing list. Head there now to receive a free copy of *Shall We Begin*.

http://jonathan-yanez.com

Enjoying the series? Help others discover *Legends Online* by sharing with a friend.

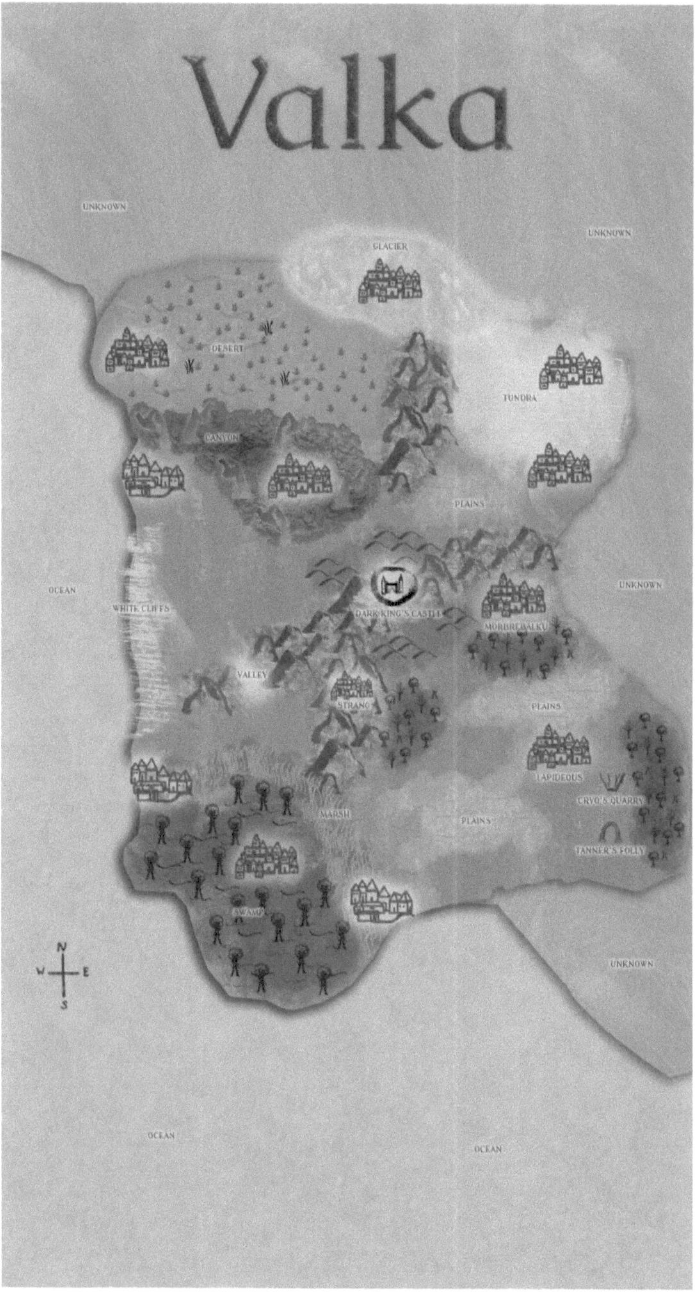

Valka
UNKNOWN
GLACIER
UNKNOWN
DESERT
TUNDRA
CANYON
PLAINS
OCEAN
WHITE CLIFFS
DARK KING'S CASTLE
UNKNOWN
VALLEY
STRANG
PLAINS
LAPIDEOUS
CRYO'S QUARRY
MARSH
PLAINS
TANNER'S FOLLY
SWAMP
N
W
E
S
UNKNOWN
OCEAN
OCEAN

1

GOOD MORNING VIEWTUBE

THE OLD CAR'S brakes squeaked as Ray came to a stop in front of BranCo Industries. Grabbing his handheld video camera, he opened his car door. It started to sag ever so slightly. After stepping out, Ray lifted the door in an effort to close it.

Pressing the "lock" button on his car fob out of habit, he heard no beep. It hadn't worked for months now. Ray smirked at his old, beat-up car. He'd owned it since high school, and fifteen years later, it still served him well. They'd been through hell and back together, only the car showed more of that adventure than he did.

Ray glanced at an enormous hangar-like building before him with a BranCo Industries logo plastered on its corner. A high fence with razor wire encircled the structure. The logo was a shield with a cross in the middle. An armed guard approached as Ray walked up to the fence's gate. Ray eyed the man's rather large weapon and laughed to himself.

These guys take their games really seriously! he thought to himself. *Do they really need firearms or do they just like wearing them because it makes them feel cool?*

Ray reached into his jacket pocket, pulling out a formal invitation for a site visit. The guard took one look at the paper and grunted, waving Ray into the fenced off area around the structure. Ray gave a sigh of relief. He was by no means a small guy and was more than capable of handling himself, but compared to the guards that patrolled this facility, he seemed to be a shrimp.

Standing before the hangar-like structure was a Japanese man dressed in an expensive suit that probably cost more than Ray made in a month. The man offered Ray a warm smile.

Oh crap, am I supposed to bow? Ray wondered. *Is that racist?*

Ray stopped short of the man with an awkward half-bow that he hoped was sufficient.

"Mr. Matsimoto, it is an honor to be here."

To Ray's relief, Mr. Matsimoto bowed back. Ray stood head and shoulders above the man, but while Ray had height on him, Mr. Matsimoto had billions on Ray.

"The honor is mine," Mr. Matsimoto said with another warm smile. "Your reputation precedes you and we feel with your viewership and track record, the worries about our new product will be laid to rest."

Mr. Matsimoto's accent was thick, but Ray was able to understand him just fine. Holding his camera up, Ray flipped open its viewing screen.

"Would you mind if I did a live stream of your facilities?" Ray asked.

Mr. Matsimoto motioned for Ray to enter their facilities.

"Please, be our guest." Mr. Matsimoto replied.

Ray pulled a jerry-rigged selfie stick out of the inside of his jacket and attached his camera to it. Ray synced the camera to his ViewTube account for a live stream, noticing that out of his fifteen million subscribers, almost two hundred thousand were online. Holding his stick out, Ray framed himself with the BranCo Industries facility set as his backdrop, making sure to get their logo in the picture.

"Good morning, Sunbeams! I'm Ray Robbins coming to you live from sunny southern California at BranCo Industries, where I will be taking you on a tour of the newest step in video gaming technology. With me is CEO Hiro Matsimoto, who would like to fill us in a little bit about what I will be showing you today."

Ray swiveled his camera to Mr. Matsimoto, who gave a toothy smile and waved.

"Good morning. Today, you will be seeing the newest innovation in video gaming technology. We have designed a completely immersive virtual experience from the ground up. But telling you about it is the boring part. I will let Ray show you." Mr. Matsimoto kept his intro brief while waving for Ray to follow.

Ray kept his camera rolling as they entered the facility.

"Mr. Matsimoto, what kind of games do you have lined up for your players?" Ray asked as they entered the significantly darker building. "I'm sure they'd love to know as much as you're willing to share."

"Right now, it is an RPG with the most advanced A.I. programmed for the NPCs so that no two playthroughs are the same," Mr. Matsimoto continued as they wound through a maze of hallways. "It's something truly remarkable, if I do say so myself."

"And how is the immersion?" Ray added to his list of questions.

"We have a day-to-year system integrated into our games. One real world day is equal to one year in game. We are constantly tweaking to enhance that mechanic for our three levels of immersion," Mr. Matsimoto responded. "In game, where there is no difference from a Virtual Reality set, immerses where you put on a motion-capture suit and move on a track pad and life."

Life. Now that sounds like an interesting setting. It piqued Ray's interest.

"And what does the 'life' setting do?" Ray's words were tentative, not wanting to push too far too fast.

Mr. Matsimoto waved Ray forward as they approached a set of double doors.

"Why don't you find out?" Mr. Matsimoto teased as he pushed the double doors open.

Ray stepped into a much larger room. Ray's jaw hit the floor so hard, it could have registered on the Richter Scale. A sense of awe washed over him as his gaze, and his camera, followed the miles of wire that fed from all corners of the room into a singular reclined chair.

It reminded Ray of the bed used by the bad samurai guy in one of Hugh Jackman's hero movies before his character's powers were stolen. Ray's heart pounded in his chest out of excitement.

Never before in his thirty-three years had he seen anything remotely close to this. Like a child on Christmas Day, Ray looked over at Mr. Matsimoto for permission to approach. The businessman nodded, complying with his visible wish.

"What is this thing?" Ray marveled.

Ray climbed the small platform the gaming system sat on and ran his fingers over the cool interface.

"I am the Neural Gaming Interface, or N.G.I. for short. Would you like to run a demo?" a robotic voice called out from speakers hidden within the room.

Ray panned his camera around. His viewership spiked to nearly a million people viewing, with hundreds of thousands of likes and comments on his live feed. Ray waved one of the guards over to him. Mr. Matsimoto nodded, allowing the smaller of his personal bodyguards to approach Ray. Ray handed the camera off to the guard.

"Okay, just keep me in frame, and if Mr. Matsimoto or one of your techs wants to talk about what is going on, then go ahead. There's no such thing as too much information," Ray exclaimed.

As Ray climbed onto the cool recliner, he felt it contour and morph around him before changing to a temperature at which he hardly felt the contouring device around him. A light beamed down from the ceiling as a technician spoke in the background. Ray's heart pounded so hard in his chest, he hardly noticed what the technician was saying.

"We are now scanning Ray's body for automated projection into our virtual world. On 'life' level immersion," Mr. Matsimoto explained, "the scans even duplicate an individual's brain waves to aid in complete immersion. Mr. Robbins, you may feel a novel sensation. It is completely normal."

Ray nodded as he closed his eyes. The moment he did, white words that read "LOADING" seemed to project onto the inside of his eyelids. A strange tingling sensation washed over his body. After several moments, Ray could swear he felt a breeze on his face, something that should have been impossible inside of a closed-off hangar bay. A small blip of light crested on the horizon before growing brighter and brighter with each passing second. It was a sunrise.

Ray took several steps forward. His brain told him everything he was seeing was digital, but his eyes were struggling to differentiate reality from the game.

'The white of the clouds, the blue of the sky, my goodness those God-rays! This place is AMAZING!" Ray thought to himself.

He took in the sky before him. A slight tickle ran over his hand, causing Ray to look down. He was standing in a field of waist-high grass. Taking in a deep breath, he could even pick up its scent, just like the wild grass in the field behind his house back home. Ray jumped a few times, and gravity pulled on him just as it did in the real world. He jogged, then ran, then sprinted to the point of exhaustion.

Stopping to catch his breath, Ray noticed a soft blue blinking at the bottom right of his field of view. After not moving for several seconds, the blue bar refilled automatically. As it filled, Ray was able to catch his breath, and his heartbeat slowed. His muscles ached less and less with every passing second.

'Stamina bar, nice mechanic!' Ray thought to himself.

A notification filled his vision, accompanied with a soft "PING," which read:

Magic is of great use in this game. Try casting a frost spell.

To use the spell FROST, hold out your hand and focus your mana into your palm. Let the mana flow freely in order to continuously cast the spell. FROST will continue to flow until you either drop your hand or run out of mana.

Ray nodded, impressed with the mechanics thus far. Obeying the instructions, Ray stretched out his arm and visualized ice forming in his palm. After several seconds, a sensation of cold gripped his hand, accompanied by the sound of frozen wind blowing.

A wave of snow, ice, and visibly chilled air rushed from his hand, coursing over the grass before him. A green bar appeared in the lower left hand corner of his screen. The bar drained at a consistent rate. Once it was empty, the frost spell sputtered out like his car did that one time he ran out of gas in the middle of the desert.

A soft breeze blew through the grass, causing the blades that had been touched by his magic to shatter and fall to the ground instantly.

Wow that was realistic; kudos to whoever coded that! Ray thought to himself. *This place is amazing. I'm freaking out right now.*

He took a step forward, intending to test out some more mechanics. His foot slipped out from under him as Ray stepped on the ice he had just made, causing him to land face first in the cold, frozen grass.

He felt the impact, pain lacing through his body the same way it would if he experienced a fall in real life. A red bar appeared in between the green and blue. It dropped down slightly. A soft "PING" and a message showed up.

Falling damages the player, reducing the health you have.

Health regenerates over time while outside of battle, items or spells are needed to restore health while engaged with an enemy. If your health reaches zero, you will die and respawn at the last town you visited. You have a set amount of times you are allowed to die. All loot and carried items aside from armor and weapons will be left where you died.

Players may retrieve their loot, but be quick. Bandits may get there first.

As he pushed himself off the ground, the sensation of pain faded from his fall. His health increased. As much as he'd hate to die in most RPGs, at least he would get to keep what he had with him upon respawn. A sick little part of him kind of liked the idea of losing loot as a punishment.

The hair on the back of Ray's neck stood on end and goosebumps cascaded over him. He wasn't quite sure why as he looked around at the beautiful paradise that surrounded him. Something seemed off, not with the game or anything inside. He heard the echoes of voices in his head. They were far away, but he recognized Mr. Matsimoto's voice. "No! Not again, I thought we fixed this! Get him out of there!"

His disembodied words echoed in Ray's mind. Ray whirled around.

"Guys, what's going on? Mr. Matsimoto, can you hear me?" Ray yelled.

"There is a cerebral feedback loop. We can't pull him out!" a technician's voice rang out, rife with terror.

"It's going to blow!" another voice screamed.

Ray spun around just in time to see a wall of fire rip across the beautiful grassland and slam into him. The force of the blast sent Ray flying. The concussion forced the wind from his lungs while heat seared his skin, causing agonizing pain to ripple throughout his body.

Ray's vision was blurred as the blue of the sky, the green of the grass, and the fiery red of an explosion all whirled together before all combining into one color: brown. Ray slammed into a hard, rough surface with so much force, it rendered him unconscious.

2

SLIDERS

RAY'S HEAD THROBBED, and his vision filled with spots.

What the hell did I just hit? he thought to himself.

Raising his hands against the rough exterior of what felt like a tree, Ray tried to open his eyes. They were swollen shut. In a bit of a panic, he ran his tongue along the inside of his teeth and found they were all there. He'd be a monkey's uncle if four years of braces and three of headgear were going to go to waste in the blink of an eye, even if it WAS in a video game.

Ray turned around and sat at the base of the tree that stopped him so abruptly. He had no idea what to do. His eyes were swollen shut. He didn't have access to whatever menu he seemed to before. Waiting was his best option, and hopefully, after the swelling went down, he'd be able to log out of the game.

Memories of people screaming about a problem, an explosion, teased at his resolve.

"No reason to freak out," Ray said to himself out loud. "Maybe it's a part of the game. Even if it wasn't, they'll get it under control."

Ray held his hands up to his face, cleared his mind, and tried to conjure his frost magic in an attempt to quicken the pace that his swelling went down. Following what the tutorial suggested to him, Ray grew impatient. He was unable to summon his magic.

With only the bustle of the wind dancing through the grass, everything else was quiet. After several frustrating moments of failure to summon his frost magic, Ray dropped his hand and leaned his head against the tree. The same tree that first beat him now was acting as a support for him. Footsteps filled Ray's ears. He tilted his head, listening for whatever direction they were coming from.

"By the gods." A woman's soft voice filled the silence.

Her footsteps sped up as she approached Ray. From the sound of it, she dropped to her knees beside him. He felt her cool hands cup his warm face.

"What happened to you?" she asked, her words tense with concern.

Ray wouldn't lie. The sensation of her hands on his skin made him want to let out an audible moan of relief. It reminded him of when he got sunburn as a child and his mother would rub cool ointment on the burns to relieve the pain.

"I was caught in some kind of explosion and was thrown into this tree. Do you know of anyone who can help me?" Ray pled.

Reaching up, his hand gently hooked against her elbow. Her skin was soft, almost silk-like. It made his heart race. Ray had a bad habit of fumbling over himself in the presence of women, and even though she was an NPC most likely, she felt real.

"I know a few healing spells, but they can only go so far. You'll have to take care of the rest," she responded, her voice as soft and light as a feather.

Without another word, Ray felt a pleasant warmth flow into him, most likely from this woman. He felt the swelling of his face go down. Just as his vision began to clear so he could lay eyes on his healer's face, a window blocked her from his view.

You've been in an accident. As a result, you are rather repulsive.
Thanks to this healer, she has given you a chance to fix your

ugly mug. Move the sliders from left to right in order to change your appearance from play dough to something more palatable.

Ray blinked. The menu had disappeared. In front of him stood a model of a default character. It was similar to his natural look, but it had a larger nose and his eyes and lips weren't quite right. Reaching out, Ray brushed his fingertips over the sliders next to his avatar.

Custom characterization, nice touch with the reasoning to need it. I would have preferred not to have been turned to mush in the first place, though, Ray thought to himself as he toyed with the sliders.

He squared off the jaw a little more to match his own before making his avatar's nose just a little smaller. Next was his eyes. He'd always liked his eye color, a bright hazel that faded from blue to green. The details were astounding, as every little fleck of his iris was included.

As he moved to hair color, a smirk tugged on his lips. He couldn't help it. Grabbing the color wheel, he whipped his hand around, changing his hair to hot pink. It was not something he ever kept in his RPGs, but he always liked to make his character look goofy before locking them in for the duration of the game. Picking long, flowing hair, Ray imagined a little dance he used to do in college. Immediately, his avatar danced his memorable little jig.

This made him laugh. Ray spent the next several minutes tweaking his character to look exactly like himself. Pausing for a moment, he looked over his avatar's form, which was dressed in tattered cloth. *Am I really that scrawny?* Ray thought as he got a good look at his slim physique. Quickly, he rubbed the slider for "physique" to the right a little over halfway across its track. This caused his avatar to fill out and appear like a world-class athlete.

Ray looked over his "creation" once more. Everything seemed to fit perfectly. Looking down at the button that read "accept,"

Ray focused on it. The button clicked in, and another window popped up and read:

Are you sure you'd like to lock in your choice?

Once you begin your adventure, you will be unable to change your appearance again.

Let's Pretty Up | Let's Do This

Ray focused on the "let's do this" option. It greyed out, causing Ray's health gauge to fill completely. Once it filled, his vision cleared, revealing the woman who healed him. Ray's stomach leaped into his throat.

"I-ugh—so you come here often?" Ray said, already mentally kicking himself. "I mean—thank you."

"You're welcome, dear," she responded while pulling on his arm to help him to his feet.

She wasn't objectively hot like Kate Beckinsale or even especially sexy like a Victoria's Secret Model. She had a classic beauty to her, almost like she was modeled off of the perfect blend of Audrey Hepburn and Marilyn Monroe.

'Yaowzer!' he thought to himself, or did he whisper it out loud—he couldn't quite tell. She let off a little giggle nonetheless.

"Welcome to Inopia, traveler. What is your name?" she asked.

Another menu, this time in the corner of Ray's vision:

You may name your character whatever you wish. Remember, once you make this choice, you may not change your name through the duration of the game.

Under the menu was a blinking cursor indicator for his name. A sly grin formed on his face as he ran through the same names he usually did, like Gant the Giant Slayer or Dracon the Conqueror. He even juggled the idea of using Kippers for a moment before relenting, as always, to a name that had deep meaning to him.

"Illume," he said softly.

The name typed out in the window before he was prompted to confirm. As he focused on the confirmation, it clicked away before the name menu disappeared entirely, allowing the NPC to take up his full field of view.

"I am Illume," was all he managed to get out.

Illume kicked himself. He wanted to say something grand like *I am Illume, Lord of Light, righter of wrongs, defender of the weak.* But nope, he was rendered to just a stammering, whimpering man in the presence of such a classic beauty.

The NPC handed Illume a map. Upon his acceptance of her gift, a menu prompt kicked in on the corner of his view. When he glanced at the prompt, a large square took up his field of vision. The brief excitement he felt for an opportunity to see how large the world was, was quickly snuffed out.

It didn't take long for him to realize the entire map was covered in the dreaded "Fog of War" and that his tiny ping sat in the bottom right hand corner of the map. A circle was clear around an arrow that, as he rotated, spun wildly on the map.

"I am venturing to lands to which you cannot follow. You will need supplies. I would strongly suggest going to Tanner's Folly just west of here," her melodious voice cooed over the translucent map before him.

The moment she said "Tanner's Folly," an image of a house seal formed on the map. It had grey outlines, but the face of a golden retriever is unmistakable. As he focused on it, the words "Tanner's Folly" became translucent under it. When he turned his gaze back to his little arrow, the words disappeared.

Blinking twice, the map retracted out of his field of view as he saw the NPC walking away. Her light blue dress flowing in the breeze reminded him of the only woman who managed to look past his nervous fumblings long enough to actually date him. It brought a smile to his face before she disappeared into a thick, dark woods.

Recognizing a natural boundary when he saw one, Illume knew he was unable to follow and turned his attention west. He was tempted to venture off track, but if his favorite RPG taught him anything, it was that if a player ventured away from the area they were directed, a giant often showed up to launch them into space.

Activating his map once more, Illume oriented himself to face west so that his little cursor was pointed directly at Tanner's Folly before returning it off screen. He was tempted for a brief moment to try and exit the game, but he really wanted to see what the first encounter was like, resolving he would log out as soon as he got to Tanner's Folly. Illume began his journey west.

The distance between Illume and Tanner's Folly on the map was about half an inch, which meant nothing until he knew how large the world was. After walking for roughly an hour, he pulled up his map to see that.

Yay! I'm halfway there! he sarcastically thought to himself.

It wasn't long before Illume saw a wooden cart on a road. He took off in an all-out sprint toward the cart. His stamina bar became visible and started to drain. It drained significantly faster than it did in the tutorial stage and ran out before he got to the cart.

Gasping for breath, Illume cursed his fit body for not having the attributes that typically came with such a physique. He moved to a saunter, allowing his stamina to regenerate to near full by the time he reached the cart.

Illume's stomach dropped as he realized that the cart was abandoned. A soft buzzing of flies filled the air as they landed on what appeared to be bloodstains. Illume looked around. The road's dirt was wet with someone's blood. The cart was stained too.

He was no doctor, but he knew that this much blood must have resulted in a fatal wound. Reaching out, he touched the red substance; it was sticky and partially dry. Crouching, Illume wiped his hand against a tuft of grass at the roadside, relieving it of the blood.

There was no horse, but the leather strips that used to bind the creature to the cart appeared to have been cut free. Illume was astounded by the realism of the game. He could actually feel the tackiness of the semi-coagulated blood. The stench of molded iron burned his nostrils, undoubtedly from the viscera cooking in the sun for most of the morning.

Whatever happened here, he desperately needed to get some form of protection. Circling around the back of the cart, Illume found a trunk that had clearly been pried open. Lifting the lid, he glanced inside. Most of its contents were gone, aside from a set of leather armor bunched up in the corner.

Reaching down, Illume grabbed the armor. The moment he did, numbers became visible on the armor itself:

Leather Armor Set
Body Armor: +20
Weight: +3
Worth: 100 Polis

Leather Boots: +5
Weight: + 1
Worth: 20 Polis

Leather Bracer: +5
Weight: +1
Worth: 20 Polis

Leather Helmet: +10
Weight: +1
Worth: 45 Polis

Matching Armor Bonus: +3

Total Armor Weight: +6
Total Armor Rating: +43
Total Armor Worth: 185 Polis

"Sweet action!" Illume murmured to himself.

Grabbing the armor, he put it on. Surprisingly enough, it fit! A small notification faded in at the top right of his vision that read "+18 Polis." It faded out just as quickly. As he glanced down at his waist, a smirk formed on his lips. Whoever robbed this cart wasn't very thorough. They missed a money pouch that had been fastened to the armor.

Glancing back into the trunk, Illume saw a book whose cover was tattered but whose pages appeared still intact. Reaching for it, Illume felt a cold chill over his hands upon clasping the book.

When he opened the book, he saw the inside cover read "Gods of Ice Vol. 1." Instantly, the book turned into solid ice and shattered as frost traveled up Illume's arms. Feeling as if he's being frozen to his core, Illume staggered back. His brain hurt like the worst brain freeze he'd ever had times a thousand.

Falling back, Illume landed on his butt, causing the ice that had built up around him to shatter off. The sounds of flutes whistled through the air as the words *"Frost Spell Learned"* floated across his vision before disappearing completely. A soft icy blue ping caught his attention from the corner of his eye. He focused on a page that appeared with the title:

Destruction Magic:
There are many schools of Destruction Magic you have learned frost.

Frost: Deals 5 points of damage and costs 3 mana per second.
Cost: 1 Skill point.

You have 5 points available to start with. Spend one to activate frost?

Yes! | No!

Illume selected yes. The sound of water freezing filled his ears as the knowledge of casting frost seemed to imprint itself into his mind. Curious as to what the rest of his points could go to, Illume stood and brushed himself off before rifling through the menus to find his attribute/skill trees.

Attributes:
Health: 120 regenerates 1% of max health per second while not in battle.
Mana: 150 regenerates 3% of max mana per second while not in battle.
Stamina: 120 regenerates 5% of max stamina per second while not in battle.
Weight Capacity: 6/500, +10 per skill point added to stamina.
Survival: Unique skill, player has 70% resistance to cold attacks.
Charisma: +20, drops to +10 when in the presence of women.

"SERIOUSLY?! Come on. Cut me a break, will you?" Illume grumbled at the "Charisma" footnote. He continued to read.

Strength: +18 Below average for male humans.

"Ball buster!" he murmured yet again.

Dexterity: +20 average for a human.
Intelligence: +20 average for a human.
Constitution: +20 without armor rating, average for a human
Wisdom: +28 With age comes wisdom, above average for a human +30 mana

"Now that's more like it!" Illume cheered to himself before

adding a single point into wisdom, two into constitution and one into dexterity.

New Stats:
Dexterity: +21
Intelligence: +20
Constitution: +22
Wisdom: +29 +10 mana. Mana pool 160

Illume glanced once more into the trunk. There wasn't anything else inside. Moving past the cart, he nearly tripped as he kicked the handle of a sword buried under the road's dirt, probably from the fight that had taken place. Reaching down, Illume picked it up.

Iron Sword:
Single Handed
Base Damage: +8
Weight: +10
Worth: 20 Polis

Being armed was always better than being vulnerable. Illume held his new weapon firmly. It was dinged and had clearly seen numerous battles, but he saw it like having a gun in the real world. It was better to have it and not need one than need one and not have it.

With a final glance, Illume did not notice anything else he could take with him. Before him was a small wooded area, and judging from what he'd managed to clear thus far from the map, Tanner's Folly was probably just on the other side of the woods.

Moving forward, Illume followed the main road through the forest without incident. There were rustling noises that sent a chill down his spine. Undoubtedly, this would be a great place to come back and grind later in the game, but right now, as a level 1 scrub, it was more important that he got to Tanner's Folly first.

About an hour later, the scent of fire filled Illume's nostrils as the trees began to thin. He increased the pace, jogging slightly, being careful to move just slow enough not to eat into his stamina bar.

Upon reaching the woods' edge, Illume discovered the burning scent's source. Tanner's Folly, a small town made mostly of wooden structures, was on fire and under attack from the same raiders he could only assume attacked that cart.

A soft *PING* filled Illume's ears as the words *"New Quest Added"* scrolled across the screen. As he focused on those words, his quest log opened with only one quest available for him titled *"SAVE TANNER'S FOLLY."* Illume's fingers gripped his new, damaged sword tightly before he charged at the raiders' flanks.

3

TANNER'S FOLLY

ILLUME RAN AS FAST as he could to the burning town, keeping a close eye on his stamina bar in the process, stopping any time it reached the halfway mark in order to let it recharge. After four of his little burst runs, he passed through the broken gate of Tanner's Folly. The wooden walls smoldered now, as they had been charred. Bodies lined the cobblestone streets and the stench of burning flesh stung his nostrils.

His fingers gripped tightly against the iron sword in his hand. His free hand dropped in temperature. Illume felt ice begin to form around his fingers. Judging from an anvil outside of the skeleton of the first building to his right, Illume assumed that was the town's forge. Screams for help rang out as flames licked over the building's straw roof.

Running toward the screams, Illume approached the front doors. A shovel handle barred the door shut. Drawing back, Illume slammed his sword into the shovel handle. It chipped the wood but did not break. After striking his sword into the shovel several more times, it finally broke.

He pulled the door open to be greeted by a plume of black smoke billowing into his face, stinging his eyes. A woman lay on the floor with a beam of smoldering wood pinning her leg down as parts of the roof fell in around her.

Throwing his hand up, Illume unleashed a torrent of frigid air and ice into the structure, not only extinguishing the flames but also stabilizing the roof. His mana bar fell to ten percent.

Charging into the building, Illume could tell he wouldn't be able to free the woman under his own power. Hoping the coders knew what they were doing when they accounted for physics, Illume slid his sword under the beam and pushed with all his might. The extra leverage lifted the pillar just enough to allow the woman to free her leg. Helping her to her feet, Illume supported her as both exited the forge.

"They headed to the hold. Our governor is there! You must protect him!" she yelled, pointing to a large structure in the center of town. "I'll be fine, go!"

Another soft PING rang in Illume's ears. In smaller letters, the words *"save the governor of Tanner's Folly"* faded in and out at the top center of his vision, a sub-quest.

Without wasting any time, Illume took off running toward the center of town, passing buildings that were either burning or already a pile of cinders. Bodies were strewn across the ground. Some were civilian. Others, based off their armor, were guards. A handful appeared to be bandits, as they were armored but not uniformed.

Movement caught the corner of Illume's eye. He came to a sliding stop just as a massive battle axe slammed down into the ground before him. As he turned his attention toward the bandit holding the axe, his heart skipped a beat.

The bandit was enormous, standing a full head taller than Illume's already impressive six foot one. No helmet sat on his ratty raven-haired head and thick leather armor stood between Illume and his opponent's squishy flesh.

The bandit attempted to pull his axe from the ground but was unable to do so. Illume took advantage and wound up to slash at his head with his sword, only to be interrupted by the bandit's massive fist slamming into his face.

A small portion of Illume's health bar dropped as he staggered back, seeing stars. Illume focused on his target once more. There were arrows protruding from his armor and small slashes here and there, showing he'd been in several fights. A red bar, similar to his own, faded into existence at the top center of Illume's vision. To his relief, it was already over half empty.

This didn't change his opponent's tenacity, though, as he yanked his axe from the ground. He prepared to strike at Illume once more. Throwing his left hand out, Illume engulfed the bandit in a torrent of ice. The bandit's health dropped, but nowhere near as fast as Illume's mana. Illume sidestepped a vertical swing from the axe before changing his frosty focus to the axe head until his mana ran out.

With all his might, Illume swung his sword down onto his opponent's weapon, the frost doing its job, resulting in his handle shattering. Roughly a third of Illume's stamina disappeared with that single power attack. Using his momentum, Illume took a page out of Leonidas' book and attempted a 300-style kick to this fighter's chest. Illume ended up staggering backward as the bandit only growled.

Leonidas looked so much cooler doing that! he thought to himself, embarrassed at his feeble display of a physical attack. *Need to work on that one for next time.*

Illume's opponent responded by bashing the remaining wooden handle of his axe across Illume's face. Another portion of his health dropped. He now had a little over three-fourths health.

A volatile stinging sensation erupted throughout his cheek and across his face, but his opponent's powerful attack left him vulnerable to a counterattack. Illume took full advantage of probably his only chance and thrust his iron sword forward, planting it hilt-deep into his opponent's armpit.

The attack was accompanied by a bone-chilling squishing sound as the bandit's warm blood sprayed onto Illume's arms.

The spattering of crimson blood splashed across his face and even into his mouth.

Illume's stomach instantly turned and he released his sword before staggering backward, leaning forward and vomiting all over the ground of Tanner's Folly with some of it splashing onto his deceased foe.

"Oh God! I'm so sorry!" Illume cried out.

Not because he'd just killed the man but because parts of his lunch had spattered all over the deceased's face. Illume took several deep breaths, pulling himself together. The reality of this world was near impossible to differentiate from the reality of his own. Even the acidic taste of vomit burned his throat and mouth.

He noticed the scan managed to pick up part of the sandwich he'd had for lunch. Stepping over his mess, Illume retrieved his weapon. The heavy armor looked like it would offer more protection, but speed was what saved him in this fight, so he decided not to take the armor. A red vial caught Illume's eye, dangling off the bandit's waist. As he grasped it, an item description appeared, hovering over it.

Potion of Minor Healing
Restores 20 health
Weight: .03
Worth: 10 Polis

Popping the cork off, Illume guzzled the potion. He choked down the liquid while keeping an eye on his health. It rapidly filled nearly all the way, with only a sliver that wasn't restored.

Dropping the rounded bottle, Illume spotted a coin purse. Illume had never plundered the dead in video games. He thought it as bad form, even in a virtual world. Hitting someone twice in the face was just as bad, which made taking the coin purse just a little more forgivable. *"25 Polis added"* appeared in the corner of his vision before he continued on.

Changing his moving style, Illume crouched and walked with

the "heel to toe" method, which allowed for each step to be completely silent. He moved from cover to cover, keeping just off the main road. As he approached the main hold, a soft drum-striking sound filled his ears. *"Sneak increased."*

Illume's head swiveled around as he looked frantically for whomever was in his vicinity. Sneak couldn't increase unless someone was nearby to be sneaking around. He saw no one before glancing around the corner of a house. A bandit stood facing a small piece of burning wood, peeing on it.

Animal skins were draped over his body as his armor. Everyone knows that hide armor is the worst kind in RPGs. This gave Illume the advantage. He sneaked up on the man. A two-handed battle axe sat leaned against the house Illume was hugging. It had to belong to this bandit. As silently as he could manage, Illume leaned his sword against the structure. He reached out and grabbed the leather-bound wooden handle of the two-handed weapon, lifting it off the ground.

Iron War Axe Two-Handed
Damage: +18
Weight: +23
Worth: 50 Polis

Illume could feel a dark grin form on his lips. Near twenty damage! His attention turned to the man before him. He had full health, but that didn't mean much when you've been decapitated. Illume wound up and swung the axe with all his might. He managed to hit the bandit and a multiplier appeared briefly in the top left of his screen. *"Sneak attack x 3 damage."* The attack caused nearly all of the bandit's health to disappear. It also made him fall to the side and into a burning log. Catching fire, the flames finished him off.

Illume noticed his stamina bar didn't drop; that must not have been considered a power attack, then. Slinging the axe over his shoulder, he retrieved his sword from its resting place with his right hand. He was now several steps away from the hold, whose front door had been axed in. He continued to move silently up the hold's steps, smoldering rubble on either side. Voices echoed from inside; some were scared, others were demanding.

"Give us the key to your vaults, old man!" one individual roared.

Illume moved closer, peering around the shattered doors. Inside was a bandit wearing metal armor, unlike anyone he'd seen alive or dead so far. He was probably the leader. He stood on a flight of stairs that led to an elevated throne. The bandit held a bloodied old man by the collar and struck him in the face, hard.

"I told you our vaults are empty. We haven't a thing," the old man gasped through his own blood. "Please, please take whatever we do have, but spare the lives of our people."

Illume clenched his teeth. There were two other bandits inside. No way he'd be able to take on all three of them as a level one scrub. While he moved, the acronym W.W.I.D. (What would Iceman do) played on a loop through his mind. That was when he saw it. Both bandit guards were standing below two massive iron chandeliers.

Sneaking into the structure's main hall, Illume followed the chains back to a single hook that held both iron structures in the air. "*Sneak increased*" popped up again as he approached the hook.

Gently grasping the chain with his left hand, Illume channeled his frosted powers into it, causing it to grow brittle before finally snapping under the chandelier's weight. The sounds of whipping chains filled the hall before a deafening crash was accompanied with the distinct sound of two watermelons hitting the ground from a rather great height.

Opting for another sneak attack, Illume poked his head out from behind the pillar, only to be greeted by the sight of an arrow mere inches from his face. He withdrew, allowing the projectile to narrowly miss him. Illume took a deep breath and dashed out from cover in the opposite direction.

Another arrow whizzed by him as the bandit leader stood tall on the steps, his bow raised high. Illume threw his left hand out, casting frost on the steps, freezing them solid. The old man slid away from the bandit chief, while the bandit chief himself slipped and fell on his back, sliding down the steps as well. Illume noticed him nock another arrow in mid-slide.

Illume took full advantage of the situation. Redirecting himself, he dropped his sword and changed to his two-handed axe as another arrow whistled past him. Covering the gap, Illume lifted the axe over his head, and with all his might and half his stamina bar, Illume drove his weapon into the bandit leader's chest.

The blow forced the bandit leader to drop his bow. His beaten breastplate gave way but he only lost a third of his health. There was an awkward moment when both men locked eyes.

"Hi," Illume said, not coming up with anything better as he tried to pull his axe free from the bandit chief's chest.

Illume strained to free the axe, to no avail. The bandit leader took advantage, resulting in a sharp pain howling through Illume's side.

Looking down, Illume discovered the bandit chief had driven a dagger between the protective pieces of his armor, resulting in half of his health vanishing. Illume staggered back, each man leaving his weapon in the other.

Grabbing the blade, Illume ripped it out. *"You are now bleeding"* faded in on the upper left corner of his vision. Illume placed his hand over the wound and froze it shut. *"You are no longer bleeding"* replaced the previous notification.

Steel Dagger: Bloodlust
Damage: +5 on armor +15 on unarmored.
Weight: +2.
Worth: 300 polis.
Bleed effect enchanted on item: +10 damage if a target is struck where there is no armor they will obtain a bleeding effect.

Illume gripped his blood-soaked weapon tightly. It was cool that they had an enchanting system but not cool that he was on the receiving end of such a nasty little bite. By the time he was finished reading the description, his opponent had already risen back to his feet and pulled Illume's axe from his chest, dropping it to the ground.

The chief let out a primal roar, charging at Illume. Illume threw his hand up, releasing a torrent of ice at his opponent. His mana was roughly three-fourths full. Illume kept a close eye on his mana, ignoring the life bar of his opponent. He stopped casting as his mana bar was drained to only a third full.

Looking back at the chief, he saw his health bar read half full. The chief was also right on top of Illume. A jarring sensation rattled Illume's body as he was lifted off the ground and driven back into a pillar, dropping his health even more.

The bandit chief grabbed Illume by the throat and squeezed. Illume had flashbacks of when he was held underwater as a boy by the school bullies. This caused all logic to and tactical awareness to flee from him, leaving only instinct. He struggled to breathe but was unable to.

He tried to stab the chief several times with the dagger, but his opponent's armor was just too thick. Illume reached out and pushed against the bandit chief's face in a desperate attempt to free himself, but no such luck. His health bar drained rapidly.

As his vision began to go dark, Illume used the last of his mana to unleash a torrent of ice out of his left hand and into the bandit chief's face. To his relief, Illume was dropped free just as the last of his mana ran out.

Falling to the ground, Illume coughed several times, catching his breath before realizing what he managed to do. Before him lay the headless body of the bandit chief. On the ground, spinning slowly, was his head, frozen solid.

I love cryomancy, Illume thought to himself. *I love this game.*

He stood to his feet with a bit of a wobble. Grabbing the bandit chief's head, he walked outside, where nearly a dozen bandits descended on the hold.

Fear quickly turned to courage as an idea unfolded in his mind. Fighting in his already weakened state wasn't an option, but maybe he didn't have to. Illume held their former leader's frozen head out with an upturned palm.

"You will leave Tanner's Folly at once or you will suffer the same fate!" Illume roared in his best attempt at sounding intimidating. Then, just because he couldn't help it, he added, "The Cryomancer cometh!"

Replicating a move that one of his favorite characters executed in a game he used to play, Illume punched the back of the bandit chief's head, causing it to shatter into hundreds of little pieces while screaming internally to himself in a deep announcer voice, *"FATALITY! Illume wins!"*

The spectacle was violent and grotesque enough that the other bandits dropped their weapons. One of them even peed himself a little before they all fled in terror. Illume was relieved to watch as they left. His health bar was so low, he could hardly see any red. He didn't want them to witness what he was about to do next. Illume's vision blurred and darkness closed in around him. He lost consciousness, falling to the ground.

4

HOME BASE

COMING TO, the first image Illume saw was Tanner's Folly's governor. He began to speak as Illume's health regenerated. Ignoring the governor, Illume glanced to the side, opening his menu, and selected to save his game.

That was more than enough of a demonstration for BranCo Industries to get his glowing recommendation. He loved his experience, from the added drama at the beginning when there was something wrong with the game to the ice decapitation.

When he selected "quick save," a wheel of dots rotated for several seconds before disappearing. Moving to the main menu, he stopped as his vision rested on "quit game." Illume's heart sank. It was greyed out. He attempted to select it, but nothing happened. He tried once again, feeling panic's icy hands wrap around his heart. Still nothing. As he focused wholeheartedly on his selection, a window popped up:

Unable to quit game at this time. Please continue.

Illume gave off a groan, refusing to lose his cool. There had to be an explanation for this. Maybe he was going to have to finish the game to get out? He exited out of the menu, focusing on the governor and finally allowing what he was saying to reach him.

"I am no longer able to protect my people. You are now the governor." His voice was somber and slightly slurred through his swollen face.

"I'm WHAT!?" Illume blurted, pulling himself to his feet.

The radiant pain in his face dissipated once his health fully restored. A trumpet sounded, filling Tanner's Folly. From the lack of reactions from those gathered, Illume assumed he was the only one that heard it.

Save Tanner's Folly: Completed
Save Governor of Tanner's Folly: Completed

Congratulations! You completed a quest against low level bandits while others did most of the heavy lifting!

Level Up Available, use this to git gud!

A secondary menu appeared in Illume's field of view. The world around him seemed to pause, allowing for him to read it.

Level Up grants 5 points for attributes.
Level Up grants 1 point for skills.

Leveling automatically fully restores health, mana, and stamina.
Points will not disappear or be automatically allocated.
They will stack on themselves until player manually assigns both skill and attribute points manually.

Illume decided to hold off on the leveling up for now. It could provide a strategic opportunity later in the game. Turning his attention to the governor and raising an eyebrow, he finally tuned in to the old man's speech.

"As our new governor, the resources of Tanner's Folly are yours to command. A portion of our market will go to your private coffer, our blacksmith will forge you the best weapons and armors we come across, and you will have a manor in which to live, so long as you remain strong enough to protect the people." The governor's voice was informative; he seemed to have little grief over the loss of his people.

"What is your name?" Illume asked.

"I am Balathor," the old man responded.

Illume looked among the burning rubble of Tanner's Folly. Several people appeared out of the smoldering woodwork. The only building that still stood complete was the town's blacksmith and that was only because of his ice. Once it warmed up, the final building was destined to collapse as well.

"Balathor, tell me about Tanner's Folly," Illume commanded.

"Tanner's Folly, population formerly two hundred, currently eighteen. Infrastructure, non-existent, burned to the ground. Financial worth, minuscule. Rebuild required." Balathor's voice changed to something more informative as he spoke.

Illume nodded. The town was a pile of cinders. Rebuilding with this few people here would not be possible. Standing at the highest point of Tanner's Folly, Illume turned his gaze to the horizon. They were on a plain, low flatlands.

"Where can we rebuild?" Illume asked.

Balathor reached into his cloak, retrieving a small parchment, and handed it to Illume, who swiftly took the yellowing paper. When he opened it and looked inside, a soft hum filled the air.

Map Extended.
The world map is covered in the fog of war.
The only way to clear out the fog is by adventuring and discovering the land for yourself or by purchasing or finding maps.

Instantly, the information was replaced by his world map.

Nearly all of it was still fogged out. Illume focused on his little cursor, causing the map to zoom in on his location. A small portion had been cleared out; by his estimates, a ten-mile radius. Most of what was visible are plain lands, save one small hill on the edge of his cleared zone, next to a lush forest. The hill was titled *"Abandoned Quarry."* Closing the map, Illume began to walk, waving Balathor to follow, which he did.

"Tell me about the abandoned quarry to the north," Illume requested. As they traveled, Illume inspected the different kinds of armor and weapons that were strewn around. None of them were great, but they all could have been sold for something.

"It's just that, a rock quarry that was abandoned," Balathor responded.

Illume rolled his eyes and let out a frustrated sigh.

"I gathered as much. Why is it abandoned and who abandoned it?" Illume's voice had a bite to it. "Sorry, it's been a crazy day for me. Please tell me more."

"The city of Lapideous, sir! It lies to the west, three days' travel. They abandoned it because they found a quarry that was much closer." Balathor's words were hurried as he spoke.

A wide smile formed on Illume's face. Quarries typically had extremely deep trenches dug in around them, meaning their first layer of defense was already laid. A ping rang out as a new quest presented itself. *"New quest: Safely escort survivors to the abandoned quarry to start a new town."*

Kneeling down, he grabbed a golden chain that housed a blood-spattered diamond and removed it from the body of a dead raider. As he held it to the light, the diamond shined brightly despite the blood. A spark of hope flared within Illume, as this was the most beautiful stone he'd ever seen. Turning to Balathor, Illume tossed him the necklace.

"I will send you and your pick of nine people to go with you to the abandoned quarry. There I want you to start setting up camp, using the quarry's ditches as a defense, and move what is salvageable from here to there." Illume had a certain command to his voice that surprised even him.

Illume pulled out the map once more. It looked like part of the forest he'd come through moved close enough to the quarry that harvesting resources would be made easy. Illume closed the map to see Balathor with a look of concern on his face.

"Of course, sir, and what of the other nine?" Balathor asked.

His face screwed up in a look of utter horror. "Are they to be left behind? Are we to be abandoned and cast out in our darkest hour? Are we to be forsaken?"

Illume looked upon the downtrodden faces of the handful of survivors that stood before him, one of which was the blacksmith. Illume turned to the horrified face of Balathor.

"Don't be so dark. They will come with me. I will want whoever partakes in trade or selling of goods. People who know how to haggle to get the best price for what we are going to be selling. I will also need two strong men to accompany me to help protect our group." Illume called out to the survivors. "We're going to rebuild your homes. You have my word on that."

Several unassuming individuals raised their hands, calling out that they used to run the shops there and would be able to fetch high prices. Two burly men covered head to toe in armor, who looked exactly like one another, volunteered to join the group. After several moments of silence and Illume gazing over those who'd survived, the blacksmith reluctantly raised her hand.

"Fine, I'll go too. I may be able to trade some of this crap for what we'll need for a forge!" Her tone was one of reluctance.

Illume nodded, satisfied with the volunteers.

"Good! Now let's start stripping these bandits of armor and weapons. Any gold you find, you may keep. Any jewelry or gems come with us for trade. Burn their bodies but bury your dead. Anything of value you wish to keep, keep. The rest comes to Lapideous with us." Illume's voice was soft yet strong as he spoke. "If we work together, we'll be done before the sun sets."

Immediately, the crowd dispersed. Illume continued to walk

amongst the burning city. Survivors looted the bodies of the raiders and tossed them on the still smoldering fires.

"I want four piles. Armor in one, weapons in another, precious resources, gems, jewelry and the lot in a third, with the final being things we don't need, but that are still valuable enough to trade," Illume called out while joining his people in work.

Illume pulled off a set of cheaply made leather armor and tossed it to the side.

"Balathor, tell me, how will this new settlement work?" Illume asked.

Balathor, keeping several paces behind Illume and covering his nose and mouth with the corner of his lavishly adorned robe, responded, his face a mask of disgust as he saw the dead bodies being thrown into the fires.

"Along with the perks I already mentioned, you will be re-enforced whenever needed by whatever warriors we can spare. However, this will depend on you. As our governor, it is your responsibility to go out and recruit people to your settlement. The higher quality the person, the better your settlement will become."

Balathor's tone continued to be informative as he spoke as if he was reading off a printed piece of paper. "The more you expand, the greater your perks will be. I will warn you, as I have learned, it is sometimes better to go with quality over quantity. The base will revert back to its default of 100 maximum occupants. You will be able to recruit ten for level one and an additional eleven now that you've reached level two, resulting in a maximum of one hundred and twenty-one settlers."

Illume nodded in agreement. It made sense.

"So what if I were to bring in a few low-level mercenaries as town guard but hire one high-level mercenary or military officer to train them. Would they get better?" Illume asked, pulling a sword that was in worse shape than his from a corpse and throwing it to the side before taking the sheath as his own.

"Yes, they would, but be careful; the higher level a recruit is compared to you, the less likely they will be to stay loyal to you and not a former master. As you can see, I learned that lesson the hard way." Balathor motioned to the burning rubble around him. "Now despair and ruin have fallen over our fair city. We have been thrown into the gutter of fate like—"

"I'm just going to stop you there before this gets more depressing," Illume said with an upturned palm. "We're going to be okay. Glass half full."

Over the next several hours, bodies were burned and buried and the piles of tradable items grew higher and higher. Illume sent out the blacksmith and one of the twin brothers to retrieve the cart he came across at the beginning of the day.

They returned an hour later with not only the cart but two horses as well. They explained they ran into one of the mounted bandits, and the other horse was just grazing near the cart.

Some of the residents managed to repair a second broken cart, resulting in a juddering, lopsided mess. As they loaded the two carts with as much as they could carry, a little lumber included, Illume noticed the sun beginning to move down in the sky.

Eager to keep the game moving on, Illume hunted down Balathor, only to find the older man sitting at the entrance of his hold eating an apple. Not even really eating, more like nibbling at the fruit.

"Balathor, can we make it to the quarry by nightfall?" Illume asked.

Balathor looked at the sky, took another dainty nibble, and shook his head.

"Not likely. With our loadout, it will take a significantly longer time to reach our new camp. There are things far worse on the roads at night than bandits, I would suggest waiting until dawn." Balathor's voice had a distinct lackluster tone that frustrated Illume.

Leaving Balathor behind, Illume took it upon himself to inspect what little defenses Tanner's Folly had left. As he walked the edge of the town, he saw most of its walls had been rendered useless by massive burned out holes within them. Home structural integrities were compromised, leaving no safe place to hold out the night. Circling back around, Illume stopped at the forge. Outside stood the blacksmith, gathering her things.

"What's your name?" Illume requested.

This caught her attention. She glanced at him, revealing her golden eyes. This made his heart race.

She's just an NPC, she's just an NPC, she's just an NPC! Illume screamed to himself in an attempt not to make an idiot out of himself for once. *Oh no, here come the sweaty palms again.*

"I am Nari, blacksmith of Tanner's Folly and indebted to you," Nari responded softly.

Her voice was like silk dancing in the air. It nearly caused Illume's knees to buckle at the prospect of having an "indebted."

"And you are Illume, the cryomancer. We owe you a great deal," Nari spoke in a hushed tone.

"You know it, baby!" Illume blurted out as a soft coin-dropping sound rang out, accompanied by a small banner on the top left.

Trophy Earned.
Name: Dumbass
Type: Bronze
Requirements: Embarrass yourself so badly to a member of the opposite sex that they consider killing you in an attempt to spare you from your own humiliation.
It would be a mercy really.

He instantly kicked himself, that those words had just erupted from his lips. A deep burning bloomed across his cheeks before he bolted off toward the hold as swiftly as his legs could take him.

"For the living sake of Mr. Freeze, get yourself together, man!" Illume whisper-screamed to himself.

Feeling like a complete and total nerd, Illume passed the twin soldiers. He couldn't really tell them apart but took a wild guess and pointed to one of the men.

"We are postponing our trip until first light. I want you to round up everyone and get them inside the hold," Illume commanded before turning his attention to the other brother.

"You, help get the carts inside the hold. Once everyone is inside, we are going to barricade ourselves in." Illume's voice was slightly more tender as he continued to speak. "You're doing a good job. I can't tell you apart yet—I'm just going to be honest with you on that—but both of you are good men."

The twins branched off and executed the tasks they were assigned. Approaching the hold, Illume saw a young boy struggling with a chest. Leaning down, he offered the boy a friendly smile. The boy couldn't have been more than twelve.

Grasping one end of the trunk, Illume hoisted his side up, surprised with how heavy it was. Neither said a word, Illume still slightly too humiliated to attempt small talk, while they approached the hold. As they entered, they passed Balathor, who was still sitting and eating.

"Don't mind us, Balathor, we're only trying to hold up for the night." Illume's voice dripped with sarcasm.

"Oh, I won't, sir," Balathor responded with a genuine tone. "Have you tried the chicken? Once you're done moving that chest, you really should."

Illume was beginning to realize why Tanner's Folly was left vulnerable in the first place. Entering the hold, Illume set down his side of the trunk before making his way through the damaged yet still standing building. Using his icy blasts, Illume put out smoldering embers and small flames, each plume of his cold magic hardly taking any of his mana away.

Townsfolk piled into the hold. Illume used this opportunity to search everywhere else and ensure that they were, in fact, safe. Searching each nook and cranny, Illume discovered no hidden threats. Upon returning to the hold's main hall, he saw Balathor standing next to his former "throne."

"Everyone has arrived, sir, and are settling in for the night. I have made sure that the bodies of your victims have been removed as to not upset our people," Balathor proclaimed as if he had just saved the day.

Illume shot Balathor a cold glare.

"They were not victims, or do I need to remind you what they were going to do to you before I interceded?" Illume's voice was as cold as his eyes.

Descending the steps, Illume could see Nari out of the corner of his eye. Intentionally, he took the path that kept the most distance between them and did not look at her directly.

Looking at hot chicks is like looking at the sun, Illume reminded himself. *You get a glimpse but never look directly at them.*

"Okay, everyone, settle in for the night. We leave at first light. I'll take the watch," Illume said. "If anyone has questions, I'm here to answer them."

Illume approached the destroyed doors. Holding his hand out, he summoned a blast of ice to seal the gap. Illume glanced at his mana meter just as it emptied. With the last vestiges of his magic sputtering out, Illume cringed to himself. The door was unimpressively only a third of the way sealed, leaving plenty of room for potential attackers to get in.

Illume waited for his mana to recharge. His back to the townsfolk, a line by one of his favorite actors, Robert Downey Jr., played in his mind. *Performance issues aren't uncommon... One in five.*

Thinking how humiliating this was for him, Illume felt a soft tug at his free hand, turning his attention over. The boy he'd helped get his trunk into the hold offered a large blue vial to Illume. Reaching out, Illume took the vial, thanking the boy before examining it.

Philter of Limitless Mana

Fully restores mana, increasing mana regeneration by 300% for ten seconds.

Weight: +0.5.

Value: 500 polis.

Illume hesitated for a moment. This wasn't a cheap gift. Not sure if he should take something so valuable from the boy, Illume glanced back at him. The young, bright-eyed boy nodded for him to continue.

Without a word spoken, Illume pulled the vial's cork free and drank it, nearly spitting it back out. The philter's taste was bitter, worse than one of those green Warhead candies his sister used to force him to eat.

Choking down the rest of the philter, Illume felt a burst of energy strike him out of nowhere. He cast his ice spell once again, only this time, his mana did not run out.

One, two, three… Illume counted while working on plugging the hole, reaching the final portion. His mana began to fall. Just for good measure, Illume continued to cast "frost" until his mana was completely empty, leaving a thick wall of ice in place of a once glaring weak spot. The coin sound rang out once more, accompanied by the notification:

Trophy Earned
Name: Put a Cork in it!
Type: Bronze
Requirements: Use your magic to completely block a hole…That's what she said!

A tinge of curiosity tugged at his mind. He wondered how many trophies there were and if he could get a platinum. Steam whirled from the wall, dancing to the ground as his trophy notification vanished. Now that his town was safe for the night, Illume decided to test out a new mechanic.

Entering his menu, Illume selected a button that read *Wait,* focusing on it. A slider popped up with a zero on one side and a twenty-four on the other. Illume slid the cursor over until it reached eight before hitting "confirm."

5

BOOTS ARE MADE FOR WALKIN'

TIME PASSED RAPIDLY after Illume confirmed his wait on the translucent screen. In the background, his ice wall melted, looking like one of those time lapses on the Discovery Channel. Having an option to cancel his waiting, Illume was ready to stop at any moment should a threat appear. His timer reached zero. Everything returned to a normal speed. The townsfolk began to rustle as they awoke.

An orange hue overtook Illume's ice block, indicating that it had grown thin enough to shatter. As he looked around, Illume's vision landed on his old battle axe. It still lay where the bandit chief dropped it. Approaching his former weapon, he grasped it, lifting it off the ground.

Iron War Axe Two-Handed
Damage: +18
Weight: +23
Worth: 50 Polis

Axe in hand, Illume approached his structure. Drawing back, he swung his weapon as hard as he could. Nearly all of his stamina bar vanished upon his attack. As iron met ice, Illume's wall shattered into hundreds of pieces, some large, others small, but his axe brought down the entire ice wall. Kicking the pieces of ice away, Illume slung his axe onto his back before turning to face his new people.

By now, most had either woken up or were already prepared to leave. Everyone save Balathor, who was still asleep on a patch of hay, a luxury no one else was afforded. He had his right thumb in his mouth, suckling at the appendage like a small child.

Illume approached Balathor and gave the bottom of the man's foot a kick. The longer he was in this old man's presence, the more Illume disliked him. Illume said old; Balathor was maybe fifteen to twenty years older than him. He still had some fight left in him. Balathor rocked awake, thumb still in his mouth. He looked at Illume, who nodded at the hole he'd just made in the wall.

"We're moving out," Illume informed him. "Get ready."

Illume left Balathor to take his thumb out of his mouth and get up on his own accord. Illume approached the warrior twins.

"What are your names?" Illume asked.

"I am Abdelkrim," responded the man on the left. Illume noted a slight green to his blue eyes.

"And I am Halfdan," the other responded. Illume noticed a slight brown to his blue eyes.

"Abdelkrim… Can I call you Abe, because that's a mouthful?" Illume asked with a laugh in his voice.

"You are our governor. If Abe is easier for you, then you may call me that," Abe responded in agreement.

Illume nodded to both men to follow, making his way over to the boy that provided him with the mana philter the night before. He gave him a hand lifting his trunk up, helping him carry it outside to the carts.

"Thank you for your help last night. May I ask your name?" Illume requested.

"I am Khal, son of the potion maker." The boy's voice was soft, almost sad.

"Where is your father?" Illume asked as they exited the building, approaching one of the carts.

"He was killed in the attack," Khal responded.

Illume helped the boy set his chest on the cart of things to keep.

"And your mother?" Illume asked once again, knowing what the boy's response would be.

"She died giving birth to me," Khal once again responded.

Illume's heart broke for the boy. Turning his gaze to several motherly-looking women, Illume led Khal to them.

"Ladies, may I request that you take care of Khal here for me, at least until I have a chance to find a good place for him to stay?" Illume didn't trip over his words, as these women had a good twenty to twenty-five years on him.

Immediately, the women brought him under their wings, asking Khal how he's doing, what they can do for him, and overall acting like mothers. Illume turned his attention to the carts. Nari had already hooked up both horses, and from the looks of it, managed to fix the wobbly cart's broken wheel. She noticed Illume staring and waved. Illume felt his cheeks grow hot as he waved back. He was happy she was an NPC and that no REAL person bore witness to his humiliating crash and burn.

"ABE!" Illume shouted.

"Yes, sir!" he responded from the far side of the other cart.

"You take point! Halfdan, you take the rear, I'll cover the middle," Illume ordered.

He noticed Balathor just leaving the hold, clearly thinking they would wait for him.

"Everyone move out!" Illume commanded.

Abe took point. He had his hand on his sword as he led the first cart, accompanied by three people, down the main street of the burned town. Illume fell into the middle with several others, while the second cart took up the back with Halfdan manning the rear. Illume noticed that most everybody had found a weapon to carry with them in case of another attack.

"Hey!" Nari's voice rang out.

Illume's stomach turned as he heard her footsteps approach from behind him. Her hand fell on his shoulder as she moved in next to him.

"Oh! Uh—hey there. How'd you sleep?" Illume asked. *How'd you sleep? What are you, her mother!?!?* Illume screamed at himself.

"I didn't. I noticed you dropped this, thought you might want it back," she responded.

Nari held up an ornate sheath with a dagger in it. Illume reached out and took the weapon.

Steel Dagger: Bloodlust
Damage: +8 on armor +18 on unarmored.
Weight: +1.
Worth: 600 polis.
Bleed effect enchanted on item: +13 damage on non-armored targets. +3 damage on armored.

"I noticed it had a poorly sharpened edge and that its handle was made cheaply, so I gave it a few upgrades. Everyone needs a dagger and that is your trophy." Nari's words were laced with passion.

She clearly had a knack for forging. Illume had a knife collection in the real world, but not one nearly as ornate or beautifully forged as this.

"Thank you," Illume whispered.

Nari gave him a powerful pat on the back.

"You're welcome. Now if you'll excuse me," Nari replied before she made her way to the cart holding the weapons and inspected them. "I have inventory to take."

The caravan exited Tanner's Folly. As Halfdan took the last steps out of the city limits, its sign and sigil broke and fell to the ground. Abe led the townspeople on a dirt path that stretched nearly as far as the eye could see, straight ahead. On their right were the woods Illume crossed, which were more like a full forest that stretched just as far as the path does.

Looking to his left, Illume noticed plains of golden-green grass dancing lazily in the soft, cool breeze. This brought a smile to his face while he strapped his dagger onto his back, tucking it under the lower portion of his back armor. Without breaking stride, Illume opened his menu and selected "quick save." After his game was saved, he noticed that the button for *quit game* was still greyed out.

Man, this game is fun, but how much do I have to play to be able to exit? Illume asked himself, knowing there was no way for him to answer the question. *Maybe this is all the tutorial still?*

"Where are you from, Illume?" a man's voice questioned.

Illume turned to see one of Tanner's Folly's peasant men approaching him, a sword strapped to his back. His hair was long and nappy and his clothes were mere rags, but he looked strong and capable. The man caught up to Illume while they walked.

"I am from the lands in the east, lands that are VERY far away from here. What is your name, and what was your occupation in Tanner's Folly?" Illume asked, not breaking his stride.

"I am Andreas. I am a farmer. I have surveyed the lands around the quarry, they are crude and unworked, but if you get me twenty good men, I can make them fertile enough to feed an entire city. We could even bring cattle and more horses to the city, which would give us more to trade." His voice was tinged with hopefulness.

"I can promise nothing, but when I get to Lapideous, I will offer the work on your farms to as many people as I can. How would you like to be the head of agriculture? You seem smart, as a farmer undoubtedly knows how to work land and with a business approach to it nonetheless," Illume offered.

Andreas rendered Illume a beaming smile.

"Of course I accept!" he belted out in excitement. A wind chime filled the air.

Civilian Assignment: Agriculture
Civilian: Andreas
Occupation: Farmer
Special Ability: Green Thumb; Andreas is able to grow any crop in any condition few other farmers can make that claim.
+15% Crop yield, +15% Cattle breeding, +15% Quality of meat, +15% polis for higher quality products.

The sound of a coin dinged once more.

Trophy Earned.
Name: Like a Glove
Type: Silver
Requirements: Assign someone to a position they are perfectly suited for within your city.

Andreas fell back to a beautiful woman with a bulging belly before offering her a kiss in celebration.

"You have chosen wisely," Balathor announced. "Your town will be far more prosperous with the proper people in a role that is best suited for them. Had you chosen Halfdan to be the head of your agriculture, for example, these would have been your stats," Balathor continued as he waved his hand.

Civilian: Halfdan
Occupation: Guardian
Job Assigned: Farmer
-10% Crop yield, -10% Cattle breeding, +8% Quality of meat, -10% polis for lower quality products.

"As you can see, you must choose wisely, otherwise, your town will be stunted, as mine was." Balathor's tone was informative more than anything else.

"That's why Tanner's Folly burned? Because you assigned the wrong people into the wrong positions?" Illume asked in shock.

Balathor nodded. "Among other things, but that is why we were defeated by low-level bandits." Balathor's voice trailed off as his eyes fell to the tree line.

Illume followed Balathor's gaze to see ten bandits descending on them. Illume drew his battle axe.

"RIGHT FLANK!" he roared.

Immediately, Abe and Halfdan took positions between their people and the bandits.

"Get the carts together, move into a group!" Halfdan bellowed.

Several other townsfolk separated from the pack, having donned the armor of their attackers and arming themselves as best they could. One had a sword and shield, another wielded a war hammer. Illume stepped to the line, standing between Abe and Halfdan. Nari moved in next to him, a long, thin straight sword in each hand.

As he watched the bandits descend, an idea flashed across his mind. If it worked once, why couldn't it work twice? Throwing his hand out, Illume blasted the ground with a torrent of ice, making it slick on two sides, leaving a funnel of non-frozen grass for the bandits to run through.

Two took the path while one on either side slipped and fell, sliding down into the blades of the townspeople. Being outmatched, the funnel gave the townspeople at least a two-on-one advantage.

With eight closing in, Illume threw his hand out once more and managed to create a small block of ice about shin height before his mana ran out, resulting in the spell sputtering out.

Keep an eye on mana! he reminded himself. Drawing back his axe, Illume threw it just as one of the bandits hit the ice block and tripped forward. Half of his stamina disappeared upon release, but his axe found its mark, causing the helmetless head to be split nearly in two. The bandit's health bar fell so low that he must have had only one hit point left as the words *critical surprise combo strike 10x damage* faded into view.

"Don't let them separate us," Halfdan growled.

Illume drew his sword as he scanned his targets. All the bandits seemed to be trained on him. Taking several deep breaths, Illume planted his feet, keeping his sword low as he took a crouched position. *Please let the larping I did in college pay off!* he yelled inside his own mind as he dove forward just as the bandits were within striking distance.

Hitting the ground, Illume rolled forward just as several swords and axes slammed into the soft, grassy dirt behind him. Spinning, Illume slid to his feet, turning his attention to one of the bandits as three were stabbed in the back by the villagers. Their health bars falling to below half, one even dropped to his knees and held his hands up while screaming, *I yield! I yield!*

The yielding bandit was kicked to the ground by Halfdan as he brought his two-handed great sword to bear against another bandit, who was able to deflect the attack.

Illume leaped into the fray as the clashing of metal on metal and the screams of the bandits left to the townsfolk rose into the air. Immediately, Illume engaged in combat with one of the bandits who still had full health. The bandit was strong, but Illume was fast, ducking, dodging, and side-stepping any attack cast upon him.

Waiting for an opening, the bandit moved in for a thrust. Illume stepped to the side. Using his free hand, he grabbed his attacker's wrist and pulled him forward. With a powerful swipe of his axe and a spray of red mist, the bandit's arm fell to the ground. *You have incurred bleeding* appeared in the corner of his screen as the bandit's health drained just like his blood.

Illume turned, jumping back as an axe fell straight for his head. Less than a foot from impact, one of Nari's swords stopped it. She slid between both men and swiped with her other sword, cutting his leather armor clean in two. Illume took the advantage and ran his sword into the bandit's un-armored gut, removing three-fourths of his health. Abe brought his war hammer to bear, knocking his head to the side, caving in the bandit's helmet, resulting in a spurt of blood. The rest of his health disappeared as his lifeless body fell to the ground.

A quick glance at his stamina bar told Illume it was empty. He expected as much as a wave of fatigue hit him. It was no large matter as the tables had turned with Abe, Halfdan, and Nari killing one each, plus the two dead by the townsfolk in addition to the yielder and the two Illume had taken care of himself. There were only two left and they were armed with weapons that didn't look like they were sharp enough to cut a piece of fruit, let alone armor.

"Drop your weapons," Illume barked. "I mean it."

Nari, Halfdan, and Abe all fell in, surrounding the last two bandits. Immediately, the bandits discarded their weapons and fell to their knees.

"We surrender!" they both yelled as fast as they could.

Illume approached both men and aimed his sword at one of their throats.

"Why did you attack us?" His words had a visceral bite to them.

"We were commanded to under pain of death!" one of them stuttered, trembling in fear.

Illume noticed the other wetting himself. With a sigh, he sheathed his sword, shaking his head in disappointment.

"Who threatened you?" Nari growled.

The sound of her voice going dark sent butterflies dancing in Illume's gut. The bandits looked around at the bloody remains of their compatriots.

"Please, have mercy!" the piss-soaked bandit begged.

"Look, I am just a merchant, he's a cook. We were given a choice, join or be killed like our villagers. We joined, we had nothing to do with Tanner's Folly, and we haven't harmed anyone, I swear!" The dry one's voice was pleading.

Illume didn't feel that he was lying; a ping rang out as a quest was presented. *Side Quest: Spare the bandits and bring them into the fold, or don't. It's up to you if you want their blood on your hands.*

Illume rolled his eyes at the passive-aggressive nature of the quest.

"Neither of you are permitted to wear armor or bear arms at any point. Should either of you try anything aggressive against my people, you will be executed in a manner chosen by them. Do I make myself clear?" Illume decreed in a guttural tone.

Side Quest Complete:
You spared the cook and the merchant.
At least your people will eat well, you bunch of gluttons!

Both men instantly pulled their armor off, sliding hidden daggers from their boots and tossing them to the side.

"We accept and will gladly join you!" they spoke in unison.

"Get them up, Nari. Bind their hands and keep one of your blades in each of their backs until we make camp. I don't want any more bloodshed from our people." Illume surprised himself; he managed to speak to her without turning into a total mess.

Turning to face his caravan, Illume felt a sharp pain in his throat and his vision flashed. Standing at the side of the weapons cart was the bandit that yielded. Armed with a bow, he fired another arrow into Illume.

Illume's heartbeat pounded in his ears as the second arrow pierced his shoulder, causing him to fall to his knees. Through his blurred vision, he saw both the bandits he'd just spared leap into action and stab the other bandit to death.

Falling back, Illume noticed his health bar nearly gone and falling fast. His eyes rolled to the back of his head as he started to lose consciousness, only for the action to activate the skill screen.

Level Up Available
Use This To Git Gud!

Attributes:

Health: 120 regenerates 1% of max health a second while not in battle.
Mana: 160 regenerates 3% of max mana a second while not in battle.
Stamina: 160 regenerates 5% of max stamina a second while not in battle.
Weight Capacity: 40/500, +10 per skill point added to stamina.
Survival: Unique skill, player has 70% resistance to cold attacks.
Charisma: +20, drops to +10 when in the presence of women.
Strength: +18 Below average for male humans.
Dexterity: +21 average for a human.
Intelligence: +20 average for a human.
Constitution: +22 without armor rating, average for a human
Wisdom: +29 With age comes wisdom, above average for a human +30 mana

Instantly, Illume selected to level up. He had two skill points to play with and five attribute points. Illume chose to add two attributes to *Charisma* for the sole purpose of not tripping in front of Nari again. One point went to *Strength,* wanting to get to average at least, one in *Wisdom* and one in *Constitution.*

New Stats:
Charisma: +22 drops to +12 around women
Strength: +19 increases damage done with physical weapons.
Stamina: +170 +10 weight capacity.
Wisdom: +30 +10 mana. Mana pool 170

Overall Stats:
Health: 120 regenerates 1% of max health a second while not in battle.
Mana: 170 regenerates 3% of max mana a second while not in battle.
Stamina: 170 regenerates 5% of max stamina a second while not in battle.

Weight Capacity: 40/510, +10 per skill point added to stamina.
Survival: Unique skill, player has 70% resistance to cold attacks.
Charisma: +22, drops to +12 when in the presence of women.
Strength: +19 average for male humans.
Dexterity: +21 average for a human.
Intelligence: +20 average for a human.
Constitution: +22 without armor rating, average for a human
Wisdom: +30 +10 mana.

You have two skill points would you like to use them now?

Yes | No

Illume selected YES. Pulling up his skill tree, Illume cycled through the many different skills available to him. The speech tree looked good, but he had more pressing matters to tend to. Cycling through the armor tree, he liked the stats provided under light armor, but given his current predicament, he selected to put one point into "Tank," giving himself 20% protection when he wore heavy armor. *Heavy Armor Level 1 reached!* scrolled across his screen.

Archery, weapons combat, both single and two-handed, were enticing, but he chose to keep scrolling. Currently having no use for sneak or alchemy, he jumped over those without a second look before slowing down on theft for a brief moment.

Illume was never really a thief and it could be a fun mechanic to explore. Ultimately, he decided to move on, passing over healing, since he knew no healing spells, leaving only Destruction Magic left.

Selecting the Destruction Magic skill tree, Illume realized he was already at "level 1" for destruction. *Magic deals 25% more damage, costs 3 mana per second. Price: 1 skill point.* Illume noticed there were two slots available for skill points and immediately placed his last remaining skill point into Destruction Magic. *Destruction Magic Level 2 reached!* scrolled across his screen.

Now that his leveling was complete, the menu vanished, bringing him back to the game. The pain in his throat and shoulder vanished as the arrows disintegrated. All of Illume's health, mana, and stamina restored completely. Illume pulled himself to his feet, groaning in mild discomfort as he did.

The entire town stared at him in confusion and awe; some even had a hint of terror in their eyes. Illume offered a smirk and a shrug.

Illume pointed forward as Nari finished binding their prisoners.

"Let's keep moving, shall we?" Illume suggested as the caravan continued down the road. "I leveled up!" he declared with a laugh. "Wow, that was close."

Although he seemed nonchalant about nearly dying, Illume realized what a mistake that could have been. He rubbed at the phantom pain in his neck where the arrow struck him.

Eyes open, Illume coached himself. *If you didn't have the level up option waiting in the wings, you'd be dead.*

As they came to a cross in the road, a sign pointed to the west reading "Lapideous." Balathor approached Illume, standing by his side.

"So will you be leaving us, sir?" he asked, his voice slimy.

Illume shook his head, pointing onward to the quarry.

"It is far too dangerous for me to leave you now. I will accompany you to the quarry and help set up camp." Illume's voice was resolute.

Custom Bow: Folly's Bow
Base Damage: +10
Weight: +3
Worth: 400 polis
This bow was custom made for the hunters of Tanner's Folly. Assembled in a lost style Folly's Bows automatically cause a critical hit with multipliers depending on where they strike.

Illume gathers a quiver full of iron-tipped arrows from the cart.

Arrows: Iron Arrows
Base Damage: +2 Worth: 1 polis

Approaching the corpse of the bandit that shot him, Illume leaned down, wrapping his fingers around the black bow's leather grip. Lifting the weapon, Illume was surprised at how light it was, given the length of each limb and how they curved out nearly two and half feet in either direction.

Placing the quiver on his back, Illume slung his new bow over it. Repeating their scavenging, Illume decided not to take the battle axe back. It cost too much stamina each time he used the weapon. So he placed it in the cart for trade. However, he retained the sword. After setting fire to the corpses, his townsfolk continued to press forward, staying in one large group. From the fork in the road, their journey was only a few more hours.

As he approached the quarry, a smile formed on his lips. It was even better than he could have imagined. A massive hill with the sides gouged out offered a plateau on top larger than Tanner's Folly was. A single, easily defensible piece of earth was left to allow the stonemasons to shave off whatever top was left of this hill.

Catching sight of the abandoned quarry, everyone increased their pace and ran as quickly as they could towards it. In no time, the survivors reached the land bridge's base and stopped.

Illume brought up the rear, his stamina bar consistently depleted, with the words of Yoda ringing in his ears. *How embarrassing HOW EMBARRASSING!* Illume kicked himself for not working out more in the real world. Perhaps he would have been better suited for the physical rigors of this world if he had.

All his townsfolk turned to face him as he approached, taking a step back to make a path for him. Illume approached the land bridge. It was just wide enough to accompany the carts; anything larger would have fallen off. His eyes danced over the white stone that stood before them, around them, and even below them in the trenches dug by the years of mining.

"You're our leader. Lead us to our new home," Rani whispered to Illume.

Heart racing, palms sweating, and his breath uneasy, Illume took his first step up the land bridge. Adrenaline surged as he got closer to the new home for his people. As he passed over the land bridge, his gaze scanned the filed-down hilltop that is perfectly even. The sound of his people following him filled his ears as they came to a stop behind and around him.

"People of Tanner's Folly, welcome home," Illume whispered.

"We are no longer of Tanner's Folly," Halfdan informed Illume.

"No, we are now the people of Cryo's Quarry," Abe added.

Illume nodded to his men.

"Scout around the edges. If this is the only way in and out, then set up camp on the far side and use what resources we have to build a spiked defense on the land bridge. Balathor!" Illume called out. Balathor slid off the cart, where he was hiding under some blankets as everyone else, even the children, had walked.

"Yes, sir?" he asked.

"First thing tomorrow, I want you and four other men to scout the forest. I don't want any surprises from other bandits. Harvest lumber and build lodging for people. At first light, the people who work the market will be joining me to Lapideous to sell what we've scavenged and recruit more people to help build our little town."

Quest: Safely escort survivors to the quarry complete!

6

LAPIDEOUS

AFTER CHECKING ONCE MORE, to no avail, to see if he could exit the game, Illume entered the wait mode once again. It was an easy way for him to keep an eye on his surroundings while everyone else got some much needed rest. The night passed without incident, and as the sun rose and his clock dropped to zero, Illume felt the effects of waiting instead of resting for the first time.

He didn't feel tired, more like a little butter spread over too much bread. When he turned to face his townspeople, the world seemed to have a slight lag tugging at it. After nearly a minute, everything snapped back to normal. A notification menu appeared in his vision:

> *Waiting is great and all but don't discount a solid eight hours. Waiting for too many nights may trigger a bug we are attempting to fix resulting in a game crash. Nobody wants that.*

Illume closed the menu while wondering what would happen if the game were to crash with him still inside. Illume was approached by Balathor and Nari along with half of the townsfolk and their cart meant for trade.

"Do you think you and this woman have what it takes to defend these people all the way to Lapideous?" Balathor sneered.

Illume arched his brow, wanting to reach out and slap the old man. For a "mission critical" NPC, he was coded to be quite the jerk. Next thing Illume expected was for Balathor to ask if Illume *gets to the cloud district often, of course you don't.* Which was a great way for Illume to practice with his new bow.

"Balathor, I don't want to hear it. Just make sure what I directed gets done. We will be back in a few days," Illume commanded.

Balathor pushed past Illume, accompanied by Halfdan and Abe. Illume grabbed Abe by the shoulder and stopped him.

"Keep an eye on Balathor. Something about him doesn't sit right with me. If he tries anything, detain him. You'll be in charge until I get back if that is the case," Illume whispered.

Abe nodded in obedience before making his way behind his brother. Several strong townsmen followed behind with their second cart loaded with axes. Illume proceeded to move out with his little group as well, leaving five behind to tend to the camp. Three were capable men while Khal worked on an alchemy set with one of the women staying behind to tend to the boy.

Illume took point while he assigned Nari to bring up the rear of his group. The trip to Lapideous went without incident. Each step of the way, Illume gazed at the white fluffy clouds, the brilliant blue sky. He was awestruck by the gold rays that burst through the clouds to the ground.

The plains of green grass and golden wheat gave a serene peacefulness to this land. Memories flooded back to the times Illume and his brother stole their grandparents' four-wheeler and tore around their farm. He laughed to himself, remembering how badly they had scared the cows and how furious their mom was. Simpler times.

At night, Illume and Nari set up camp for the others, having packed plenty of food to last their trip. No one had to hunt for game and everyone settled in peacefully for the night, with Nari taking the first watch and Illume taking the second. For the next two days and nights, it was more of the same: walking, setting up camp, eating, then sleeping. *God, I wish they had fast travel!* Illume screamed inwardly as they continued to walk.

On the horizon, a glint caught his eye. As he squinted, the image came into focus. A massive city made of pure white stone. He could swear it looked just like a free-standing Minas Tirith. The curve of its defensive wall had to be a quarter mile in diameter at least. Illume glanced back at his people, all of whom had huge smiles on their faces.

"I'm assuming that is Lapideous?" Illume called out. Most everyone nodded.

As if a carrot on the end of a stick, the sight of Lapideous, just out of reach, encouraged everyone to pick up the pace. Before what Illume assumed is ten A.M., they reached the gates. Standing at attention were two men in golden white armor unlike anything Illume had seen before. They were fair-skinned and had copper-golden eyes. Slits in the sides of their helmets allowed for pointed ears to protrude just slightly into view. The guards stepped in front of Illume, blocking his path.

"Who are you and what is your business in Lapideous?" one of the guards asked.

"I am Illume. I bring items for trade from Tanner's Folly," Illume replied, glancing back at his people.

"Tanner's Folly is a trade town. Why do you need to make such a long trip to trade here?" the other guard asked, his voice slightly more stern.

Crap! His charisma must have still not been high enough; that, or with Nari so close, his charisma might still be suffering the whopping ten point drop.

"We mean no trouble," Nari's voice responded.

Illume could have sworn he saw a hint of recognition in one of the guards' eyes. Nari made her way to Illume's side and gently placed her hand on his shoulder. His heart beat so hard, he worried it would cause his body to shake. *Little puppies, little puppies, little puppies!* Illume screamed to himself in a failed attempt to calm himself. Since he was a dog person, they always helped him relax.

"Tanner's Folly was burned to the ground. Had it not been for this man, we would have all perished. We were here simply to trade what we can, for what we can, so we can rebuild." Nari was smooth, her voice flirty yet serious and her tone slick like the skeevy politicians back home.

It worked! The guards stepped to the side, clearing a path for Illume and his people.

"Were those elves?" Illume asked as they passed through the gates.

"Elves are hired as guards and security. They have an affinity for magic and their natural speed and agility make them perfect for protecting others. They find it a sacred duty!" Nari explained as they entered the city.

Illume let out a surprised huff. It was nice to see elves portrayed not as racist or pretentious for once. Illume turned his attention to the white stone around them. He saw humans, orcs—with their massive stature, green skin, and differing tusk lengths—dwarves, and elves all moving freely around the city. Some were in fancy, high-end clothing, while others were in garments not much different from the rags he had been wearing upon entering the game.

Stepping forward, Illume attempted to get an orc's attention. They passed him by as if he weren't there. Next, he moved on to a dwarf—same thing. Even humans ignored him. It was starting to feel like his ninth-grade Sadie Hawkins dance all over again.

"Excuse me?" a sweet voice rang out.

Turning, Illume noticed a woman approaching him. She wore a gold and white dress with similar patterns to those on the guards' armor.

"Welcome to Lapideous. Is there something I can help you find?" The human woman offered Illume a soft smile.

"Uh, yeah… I uh… hmm." Illume tried to speak, but only strange noises left his lips.

"Yes, we are looking for the market?" Nari stepped in. "Excuse my friend. He is new here."

"Of course! If you follow the wall of the city behind you about five hundred paces, then turn left, you will be at the market," she responded, using an open palm to direct them without losing her smile. What was she? A Disneyland employee?

"Thank you," Nari said softly as Illume felt her grip his arm tightly, whipping him around. Nari's voice was sharp. "Are you some kind of idiot? You seem like a capable man, but you completely shut down whenever a cute girl bats her eyes at you."

"Not an idiot," Illume murmured. "At least I didn't say anything embarrassing."

Pulling away from Nari, Illume walked backward, throwing two thumbs-up and leaning back.

"Ehhh!" He tossed the quote at her, as if she would get it, before turning and making his way to the market.

"Dear Illume… you suck! Sincerely, Illume!" he whispered to himself as he thought on how very much NOT the Fonz he'd become.

Glancing over his shoulder, Illume noticed his people were following. He was happy he didn't have to tell them to do so, as anything that came out of his mouth right now would have been a garbled mess.

Quest started: Sell your wares

The words scrolled across his field of view.

Quest started: Recruit people for your town scrolled across as well.

Quest started (optional): Speak to a woman without being a bumbling idiot!

Was the game yelling at him? The optional quest seemed a bit passive-aggressive to him, but it had a point.

Houses were built right into the stone buildings. People were coming and going, children of all species playing together, and the occasional patrol marching through the streets. Illume got a sense that this place was designed to be truly peaceful. If history told him anything, the nicer the façade, the worse the underbelly. He just hoped that they could get out before anything went dark.

7

MARKET

A SOFT MURMUR reverberated off of the city's rounded wall that stood nearly fifty feet high adorned with battlements and defenses that would have made Tolkien proud. As Illume moved forward, the murmurs grow louder and louder with each passing step. When he came to a clearing of buildings, Illume's jaw hit the ground. A massive market sprawled out before them. Storefronts, tents, and tables with goods scattered on them packed the clearing so tightly, they didn't need oil to be sardines.

Contrary to first glance, the market wasn't as chaotic as it first appeared. In the far right corner, under the shade of tents and the shadows of buildings, were farmers and gardeners with livestock, crops, and flowers. Next to them were the butchers and chefs selling meats, flour, and loaves of bread. From there, the booths changed to skins and furs, then to leathers, then armor. Nari stepped forward, her eyes locked on the weapons and forges section.

"I'll be over there," she murmured with a smirk before walking toward the dwarven stalls.

Illume turned to the rest of his townsfolk.

"Okay, sell everything you can, buy what we'll need, and only what we'll need. Be as frugal as you can. We'll need it to hire more people," Illume assured, his voice soft.

He had a boss that was a super hard-ass; no one liked working for her and their performance suffered greatly. He always told himself if he were ever in charge, he would lead by example as opposed to command and he would have a gentle hand where he could. Loyalty garnered better results than fear.

Moving to the back of their cart, Illume grabbed a few trinkets and some jewelry.

Gold Necklace
Weight: +.05
Worth: 175 polis

Silver Garnet Ring
Weight: +.75
Worth: 250 polis

Gold Necklace of Exhaustion
Drains target of 1 stamina per second upon contact.
Weight: +.5
Worth: 500 polis

Leather Pouch
Weight: +3
Worth: 150 polis

Illume slung the pouch over his shoulder. Grabbing pieces of broken iron and a few ingots, he tossed them in the sack along with two pieces of leather.

Iron Shard x8
Weight: 3 x 8
Worth: 5 polis x 8

Iron Ingot x 6
Weight: 1 x 6
Worth: 15 polis x 6

Leather x 10
Weight: 2 x 10
Worth: 25 polis x 10

His pouch pulled heavily to his right as he set off into the market, moving to the opposite side of the forgers where the jewelers were. Starting off with the gold necklace, Illume was initially offered only 60 polis for it. Knowing its worth was 175 polis, he moved to another vendor, this time a woman. She offered 10 polis for it. Illume stuttered and kicked himself as he walked away.

Illume moved again. This time, the merchant offered 120 polis for it. Illume hesitated, knowing it was worth more, but his gut told him that was all he'd be getting. Making the agreement, Illume handed over the necklace as the vendor handed over the polis. Thinking he'd found a vendor he could bargain with, he offered the silver garnet ring and was instantly offered 75 polis.

Sighing, Illume shook his head, wondering if his charisma mixed with his low level rendered a lower percentage of success and a lower rate of trade when selling goods. *'This is going to suck!'* Illume thought to himself as he continued to bounce around from vendor to vendor, some offering a decent price; others, primarily women, straight up laughing him away.

Getting lucky, he stopped by the last vendor, a massive orc who looked like he'd taken on entire armies by himself and won. Surrounded by ornate little decorations made of glass, metals, and stone, the monstrous man spun a small wheel that was stuck on a tiny golden windmill. His hands looked like they could crush steel, yet they were gentle enough to not even tarnish the gold he held.

Illume watched as he set down the windmill; he had a sad

look on his face, making the tusks that protrude from his lower jaw look nowhere as intimidating as they were supposed to be. As Illume approached, he realized this orc's table had no one around it.

"Slow day today?" Illume asked, looking at a few of his stone carvings.

The intricacies in the stone were mind-blowing.

"Always slow for Urtan," the orc grumbled.

"Why is that?" Illume asked as he moved on to another carving, this time of glass in the form of a dragon.

"Urtan is outcast of his family." His voice was soft, almost sad.

Illume looked at the mountain of flesh before him. Usually, he'd be running in fear at the sight of this being. He only felt peace in Urtan's presence.

"And why is Urtan an outcast?" Illume asked.

"Because Urtan does not wish to follow in father Burtan's footsteps. Urtan would rather be sculptor than senator. For that, Urtan is outcast." Urtan beat his chest as he proclaimed to be a sculptor. This caused the beads of his necklace to bounce off his bare green chest.

"Why does that affect your sales?" Illume continued his line of questioning as he looked at another ornate piece, this time of jewelry.

"Urtan's father is powerful in this city. People don't wish to upset him, so they don't shop." Urtan waved his hand over his wares.

Illume held out the ring to Urtan.

"What will you give me for this?" he asked.

Urtan took the ring and examined it closely. Shaking his head, he handed Illume back the piece of jewelry.

"Urtan does not have enough to buy such a piece." His tone was resolute.

"Okay, then, how about a trade? I will give you this ring in exchange for the little dragon figurine." Illume lifted the little dragon.

"That isn't fair trade," Urtan replied, shaking his head. "Urtan only makes fair trade."

Illume nodded his head as an idea formed.

"Okay, how about this? I give you this ring, you give me this dragon, AND you join my people near Tanner's Folly," Illume proposed.

"Smoke billows from Tanner's Folly, it burns," Urtan protested, shaking his head.

"That is true, but I have a group of people who are forging a new town and we could use someone with your eye in our market. What do you say?" Illume offered the ring in one hand and held out his other hand to the giant to shake.

"Urtan supposes he could sell the ring to start new." Urtan had a hint of hopefulness in his voice.

After snatching the ring, Urtan grasped Illume's forearm and gave it a powerful shake. A trumpet of triumph filled the air.

New Key Member Added
"Urtan likes pretty things!"
Name: Urtan
Species: Orc
Career: Master Sculptor, Excellent Shop Owner Urtan is a giant teddy bear and once you have his loyalty, it is for life. However, don't make Urtan angry. You would not like him when he's angry.

A soft chime followed.

Speech
Level Up
All speech stats increase by 2%.
You're going to need all the help you can get.

Illume furrowed his brow. How did his speech level up automatically, but he had to allocate points to his other stats? Hoping this wasn't a "pity level," Illume opened his menus in an attempt to figure out what was going on. The "quit game" was still greyed out, he noted. Filing through, he found nothing to shed light on the phenomenon. Shaking his head, Illume pursed his lips, not appreciating the freebie.

Urtan packed as Illume moved on to sell the final necklace. There was no luck on the jeweler's side so he moved over to the forgers. Shopping it around, Illume only got offered 300 polis for the necklace. He even offered trading the necklace for goods and services, but everyone shot him down. A boisterous laugh overtook the sounds of the crowd and the hammering of metal.

Following the sound, Illume saw Nari laughing with a dwarf. He made his way toward her as she took several steps away from the dwarf. Meeting him just out of earshot, Nari shoot Illume a fake smile.

"What are you doing?" she asked, her words laced with frustration.

Illume presented the necklace.

"I'm trying to find a buyer for this, and someone who can forge me a new weapon out of the resources we have," Illume replied.

Nari snatched the necklace from Illume, appearing to be hurt at his statement. Reaching out, she yanked his bag off his shoulder.

"If you want something smithed for you, come to me. Don't go someplace else!" Nari shook her head.

Does she actually sound hurt?

Nari marched over to her new dwarf friend, holding out the necklace and opening the bag. She turned and pointed at Illume. He offered a wave. The stocky bearded man, or was it a woman, waved Illume over. As Illume approached the dwarf, he looked Illume up and down intently.

"I'll make you a deal: that sword, your armor, the bag, and the necklace. I'll give you 1,200 polis and I'll give Nari here access to my forge. What do you say?" the dwarf, who spoke in a soft voice, asked. The female dwarf held out her hand.

Reaching out, Illume gave the dwarf a firm handshake. He had to hand it to her, Nari was very good at this. Unstrapping his armor, Illume let it fall to the side. Unsheathing his sword, he handed it over to the dwarf, handle first. Now wearing only a tattered tunic and his dagger, Illume had to admit he felt rather naked.

"Now why don't you find us some lodging and we will meet you later?" Nari spoke sweetly. Illume had been on the receiving end of that enough to know it was not meant to be sweet.

"Okay. Oh, by the way, Urtan will be joining us on our trip home," Illume added.

"Who's Urtan?" Nari asked, confused.

Illume pointed to the behemoth, who stood head and shoulders above even other orcs as he made his way through the crowd.

"That big guy!" Illume retorted.

Moving back into the crowd, Illume made his way to Urtan, finding it much easier to walk right behind him.

"Urtan, do you know of any place I can buy rooms for myself, my companion Nari, and eight other people to stay the night?" Illume shouted over the noise of the crowd.

"No need, Urtan has room for new friends." His voice was brimming with what Illume could only assume was hope.

Illume followed Urtan around the outer edge of the city.

"Urtan, do you know of any farmers or former soldiers that may want to move out of the city?" Illume looked around as he spoke.

No one seemed to notice he was dressed in rags, or they just didn't care. Urtan let out a laugh.

"You cannot afford guards and soldiers. Urtan knows a few farmers whose lands have become infertile. Urtan is sure he can persuade them to join you. Why build a town from scratch when your people could move into here?" Urtan asked.

Illume wasn't sure why no one suggested moving to Lapideous. Judging from the appearance, however, the survivors of Tanner's Folly would not have been able to make enough to live on, much like Urtan.

"I guess they feel that it would be easier to start from nothing and build something of their own. Most of my people are older women. We have a few children and a farmer, but overall, I think they don't want to have to struggle for the rest of their lives to make a living. Starting from the basics guarantees some hard times, but after that, things will be looking up." Illume's response surprised even him.

Urtan nodded as he came to a stop at a rather large house with a guard at the door.

"I guess that makes sense. Faltar, it is good to see you, my friend. Would you be so kind as to go to the market and inform a woman named Nari of our whereabouts? Urtan will be having guests tonight," Urtan requested. Without hesitation, Faltar, an orc guard, moved the same direction from which Illume had come.

Entering Urtan's home, Illume was shocked at how bare it is. The floor plan was wide open, but the minimalist decor reminded him of something straight out of a Swedish house. There was plenty of room for his entire party, and better yet, he got to hold on to some of his coin. Urtan disappeared for several moments before returning with a large cloak.

"Urtan gives you this. It may be too big for such a puny human, but at least you won't be naked." Urtan laughed at his own words.

Illume took the cloak and threw it around his body. It was surprisingly heavy.

"Thank you, Urtan," Illume added.

"You are welcome. Urtan go to sell his ring. There is a tavern around the corner should you wish to drink." Urtan walked to his front door.

The orc pointed to his left before turning right, his ring in hand. Illume followed the path Urtan had disappeared from, seeing his wares all sprawled out on a bed made of stone. Immediately, Illume backed out, feeling as if he'd invaded Urtan's privacy by entering his room.

His town would need a tavern; perhaps a quick scout could reveal an amateur brewer looking to make a name for himself. Leaving Urtan's house, Illume followed his directions. It wasn't hard to find the tavern. A building much dirtier than the rest, it had smoke billowing from its chimneys. The loud sounds of men singing erupted from every window and door that was open.

Making his way in, Illume was taken aback by how dark it was within the tavern. Sitting at the bar, he waved down the barmaid. Moving to speak, Illume half expected just mumbles to come out.

"Uh, yeah, hi! How are you? I'm good." *GET TO THE POINT!* "Do you know of anyone who is looking to brew in a new little town?" He couldn't tell what was worse, the mumbling or sounding like a Ted Bundy wannabe.

"Don't mind that guy. He's joost a bet shay." A young man sat on the stool next to Illume.

Half expecting to see a drunk Irishman next to him, Illume was surprised by the dark, slender man wearing tight form-fitting clothes, his appearance unlike anything he'd seen to date in a fantasy game or movie.

"Ahm Trillian, bat ye can call meh Trill and I'd like to offer ye a drank." The light-haired man set a small pile of coins down on the bar and offered Illume a sly grin.

8

A NIGHT TO REMEMBER?

ILLUME TOOK A DEEP BREATH, his eyes bursting open as the stench of feces stung his nostrils. Soft oinking filled the air as Illume pushed himself out of a pit of mud, covered head to toe in the slick brown stink. His head throbbing, Illume looked around to get his bearings.

It was dark, but the light of the full moon reflected Lapideous' strong white walls. Illume was just outside the city. A familiar sound blasted Illume's ears, making the throbbing in his head spike. Was he hung over? Words scrawled across the top of the screen.

Level Three Reached
5 Attribute points available. 1 Skill point available.

Then again it rang out.

Level Four Reached
5 Attribute points available. 1 Skill point available.
Speech Level Up x 2
All speech stats increased by 4%.
Now able to put skill points into Haggling.

Congratulations, you MIGHT be getting there!
Hand to Hand Combat Level Up
Now able to put skill points into skill One Two Punch.
Better luck next time!

Pickpocket Level Up x 2
Now able to put skill points into skill Pickpocket.
Now able to put skill points into skill Bad Form.
Butterfingers!

Sneak Level Up x 3
Now able to put more skill points in Sneak.
People won't be able to hear you when you fall this time.

Heavy Armor Level Up x 2
Now able to put more skill points into Tank.
Lucky you.

Each level and unlocked skill made Illume's head throb even more. He let out a groan and fell to the ground as a trophy notification popped up.

Trophy Earned.
Name: Liver of Steel
Type: Bronze
Requirements: Drink three consecutive people under the table.
You're not an alcoholic, more like a booze enthusiast.

Trophy Earned.
Name: Takin a Piss.
Type: Silver
Requirements: Prank a guard and steal their armor.
You've got a set of brass ones on you.

Trophy Earned.

Name: Black and Blue
Type: Bronze
Requirement: Win your first fist fight.
Good job on this one actually.

"Oh God, what happened?" Illume whimpered to himself, kicking himself with a deep-seeded regret. He'd told himself he'd only have one drink, and the next thing he knew, he was waking up from a blackout. Concern tugged at the back of his mind that this was how alcoholism started for his father and perhaps history was repeating itself.

"Wat an amazing night that was!" Trillian's Irish accent rang out.

Illume looked to see the man who'd bought him a drink sitting on a fence post.

"What did you do to me?" Illume asked with a whimper to his voice.

Pulling himself to his feet, Illume got bombarded with more notifications.

3000 polis added

Elven Heavy Armor: Guardian
Defense: +35
Weight: +10
Worth: 0 polis (Stolen)

Elven Heavy Boots: Guardian
Defense: +14
Weight: + 5
Worth: 0 polis (Stolen)

Elven Heavy Gauntlets: Guardian
Defense: +14
Weight: +5

Worth: 0 polis (Stolen)

Elven Heavy Helmet: Guardian
Defense: + 19
Weight: +5
Worth: 0 polis (Stolen)

Guardian armor increases Stamina by 10 for each piece worn, +30 added for a set bonus. Does not affect carry weight.

Spear: Guardian Pike
Damage: +15, +20 against mounts.
Weight: +10
Worth: 0 polis (Stolen)

Guardian Pike deals 20 additional damage to stamina and mana. 33% chance of critical strike.

"I did noothin to you, my friend. Boot I have ta say, you dadn't dassappoint. I saw your fighting at Tanner's Folly, I saw it again on your way to tha quarry. And after your feats last night, I wash to offer you my sword. You are going places and I really feel as if I can teach you a lot." Trill's voice came off as if he were making jokes.

Looking around, Illume found the pike buried deep in the mud. Retrieving the weapon, Illume put the pike at Trill's throat.

"You drugged me. You made me a thief, maybe even a wanted man. And most of all, my people probably don't know where I am and are searching for me! Give me one reason not to run you through," Illume growled.

"I'll give you two!" a powerful voice rang out from the dark.

Gliding out of the shadows, into plain view of the full moon's light, a man with long black robes stood before Illume and Trill.

"And who are you?" Trill asked.

"I am William. I have a certain… pull with the law of Lapideous. Should you spare this man's life, I will ensure all charges you face are dropped and you will be able to have several of my kin to join your little village." William's voice was as smooth as silk.

"How do you know about that?" Illume managed to squeeze out.

"My dear boy, I keep my fingers on the… PULSE of this city. I know all kinds of things." William's tone changed as if he thirsted for power and knowledge.

Illume lowered his weapon. Having all charges dropped was always a good incentive and having a few extra hands was never a bad thing either.

"And what is it that you want in exchange?" Illume demanded.

William moved closer to them. Something about his movements were far too graceful to be a normal person's. This was highly unsettling for Illume.

"My brother and his family are being hunted in the woods just over that ridge." William nodded to a small ridge a few hundred yards away. "Should you stop his would-be assassins, capture or kill, it matters not to me, then I will be sure that you are cleared of all crimes." William had a slight plea in his voice as he named his terms.

"And why do I need him?" Illume asked once again.

"Because the ones who came with you will surely perish should they enter the forest with you. Without him, you will too. This one also entertains me to no end. Do you accept?" His pale skin pulled tight over a crimson eye, causing his brow to arch.

New Quest:
Save Victor and his family from hunters.
(Optional: Turn in bounties for illegal hunters)

Illume sighed. Reaching out, he took William's hand and gave it a firm shake.

"Fine. We'll go and find your brother," Illume agreed.

"Now wait just a bloody second, I nevar agreed to thas!" Trill interrupted as he hopped off his post.

Illume turned his attention to Trill for a split second.

"You don't get a vote. I'm missing most of the night because of you. You're going to help me fix it." Illume's sound of command was so palpable, it startled even him for a moment.

Turning his attention back to William, he found the man was gone. Illume glanced down to the mud. There were no footprints where the man once stood. This intrigued him, but there was no time to investigate.

"Get moving, Trilly," Illume growled.

"I'd kindly appreciate it if you'd not call me Trilly," Trill confessed.

"And I'd kindly appreciate it if you'd not get me hammered and turn me into a thief!" Illume retorted, mocking Trill's accent.

"Good point. Hey, that was pretty good! A lattle more practice and you'll be able to fool my people in no time," Trill called to Illume as he marched toward the crest before him, then to the forest beyond.

9

HUNTER OR HUNTED

MOVING over the hill's crest, Illume finally got a good look at his stolen armor in the moonlight. By this time, most of the caked-on mud had dried, removing the armor of its shiny white and gold quality. For a brief moment, he was happy for waking up in the pig sty.

Taking a deep breath, Illume let his gaze fall on the dark forest before him. A chill ran down his spine as it reminded him of the nightmares he'd have as a child of monsters twisting themselves out of the woods behind his house to consume him.

"So what do you thank, you ready to move in?" Trill asked as his hand moved to a straight sword that was fastened tightly to his back.

"Not yet," Illume responded softly.

His gut screamed that he would need as much help as he could get. Illume attempted to activate his level up screen, but a firm THUD against his chest stopped him. Dropping his vision, Illume saw a book being held against his chest by Trill.

"Af you're doin' what I thank you're doin', then you're going to need all the help you can get." Trill's tone had a hint of sincerity.

Taking the book, Illume held its cover to the moonlight. Time had worn the leather cover that had an unearthly blue tint to it. Underneath a symbol of frost read *Enhanced Ice*. Accepting the book, Illume opened its pages. Just like before, the book dissipated into a flurry of cold and light that flowed into him.

Chills ran through his bones as he felt like his body was being frozen from the inside out. The strange part was there was no pain that usually accompanied cold like this. As his body's temperature returned to normal, Illume's left hand frosted over, then his right hand.

Enhanced Frost Learned
Frost Magic deals 25% more damage.

"Thank you," Illume whispered before looking up.

His level up screen activated. Cycling through his skills, Illume noted all the new abilities he'd unlocked in his blacked-out state. Upon seeing that, Illume instantly put one skill point into *Tank,* enhancing his defense. Cycling through, he put his final skill point into *Enhanced Magic,* maxing out his new ice skills.

Moving on to *Attributes,* Illume decided to put three attribute points into *Strength,* another three points to *Constitution.* Two points go to *Dexterity,* with the final two making their way into *Wisdom.*

New Attributes:
Health: 150 regenerates 1% of max health per second while not in battle.
Mana: 190 regenerates 3% of max mana per second while not in battle.
Stamina: 160 regenerates 5% of max stamina per second while not in battle.
Weight Capacity: 540, +10 per attribute point added to strength.
Survival: Unique skill, player has 70% resistance to cold attacks.
Charisma: +22, drops to +12 when in the presence of women.
Strength: +22 average for male humans.

Dexterity: +21 average for a human.
Intelligence: +20 average for a human.
Constitution: +22 without armor rating, average for a human + 10 health
Wisdom: +31 +10 mana

New Skills:
Tank: + 40% heavy armor protection
Advanced Destruction Magic (Ice): + 50% More damage

The frosty ash from his book floated to the ground while Illume's fingers tightened around his pike. When he glanced over his shoulder, a wave of relief washed over him, seeing his bow and several arrows slung over his back. Unearthly howls erupted from the forest before them, causing Illume's mouth to go dry.

"Are you ready, Trill?" Illume fought through tense vocal cords to speak.

"Of course I am. Lat's go do thas thang!" Trill cried out in confidence.

Trill pulled his sword from his back. Its handle was as black as a starless night sky while the blade was slender, about three feet long and straight with one edge sharp. The moonlight gleamed off of his weapon, showing how it was just as pure and pale as the full moon itself. Illume wouldn't lie; he lusted after Trill's weapon a little bit, always having wanted a straight sword of such refined beauty.

Illume turned his attention back to the woods as a woman screamed. Both men took off sprinting as fast as they could, Illume's encumbrance causing his stamina bar to deplete faster than usual, making it a little over halfway to the woods before Illume's stamina ran out. Slowing down to catch his breath, Illume held his pike out to Trill, who took it from him.

"Hold this; we'll probably need some range," Illume said between labored breaths.

Upon releasing his weapon to Trill, Illume pulled his bow off his back and notched an arrow. Growing up, he'd play with bows and arrows with his siblings while their dad would be passed out in front of the TV. He was a decent shot, but his brother and sister were better. Illume and Trill reached the forest's edge by the time Illume's stamina bar was fully regenerated.

Both men were crouched as they moved through the ever darkening woods until it was so black that only four patches of light from torches could be seen a few yards to nearly a hundred yards off.

"Why don't you grab my shoulder. I'll lead us through thas devil's sphincter," Trill suggested.

Illume chuckled at his vivid choice of words. Releasing the string of his bow, Illume grabbed Trill's shoulder.

"You can see in the dark?" Illume whispered.

"Sort of. My people were able to use magic to ensure that we can see better in low light. Af it's pitch black, we can't see shite," Trill responded with a whisper.

Illume kept a tight hold on Trill as they moved forward in the darkness. Illume ducked when Trill ducked, he stepped sideways as Trill stepped sideways. Both men moved surprisingly swiftly through the darkened woods thanks to Trill's unique little skill.

"By the bloody gods! Thas isn't right," Trill nearly whimpered.

"What is it?" Illume questioned, worried they'd just stepped into a trap.

Illume felt Trill grab his hand and pull him forward. Reaching out, Trill pulled aside a bush.

"That right there, that's not right!" Trill exclaimed.

Illume's jaw dropped. A little girl, no more than six years old, had chains holding her hands against her chest, crossed at the wrist. A mask was fastened tightly over her face with a muzzle-looking instrument over her mouth. A piece of cloth was tied so tightly over her eyes, that even in the low light of torches, Illume could see the outline of her eye sockets.

A soft coo came from the girl. Illume could tell it was her crying, but the muzzle greatly hampered that. Four men stood on each side of her, each holding a chain that was attached to a collar around her neck.

The longer Illume observed, the more he noticed there was something off about these "hunters'" chains. They seemed to be made of silver. Turning his attention to the men, he saw their clothes were shiny and their collars were high; under their jaw bones, more silver.

"What are we facing here?" Illume demanded in a hushed tone.

"Hunters, thay track down outcasts, capture tham, and sell tham to the slave trade in the great desert. I've never seen tham venture thas far south because thay all have considerable bounties on their heads," Trill responded.

"What condition do they need to be in for their bounties to be cashed?" Illume asked.

Illume was never a greedy man, but now that he had potentially hundreds of people to take care of, he could use all the coin he could get his hands on.

"At's even trade, dead or alive. Parsonally, I thank we should find out who the hall sent tham so we can cut off their access to thas land at the source." Trill's voice had a hint of rage in it.

Illume pulled a second arrow out of his quiver. He'd taught himself a trick shot his brother and sister could never manage to master. Drawing the bow, Illume took aim.

"I couldn't agree more. I'll take the two in the front, you take the two in the back," Illume whispered as the hunters moved once again.

Illume released his two arrows. A sharp sting tore through his fingers; the feathers sliced him. Illume's health bar became visible. Both arrows found their mark, impaling the hunters' hands, causing them to drop their hold on the girl's chains.

Illume's pike flew out of the bush at breakneck speed and skewered one of the rear guards like a boar. The only thing heard from him was the deforming of his metal armor as he was run through. Trill leaped from the bush like a wild animal and slashed at the fourth hunter, causing his grip on the chain to falter as well, freeing the girl.

Illume notched another arrow as his two targets drew their swords. Illume managed to stick his second arrow into the guard's hand; it was hard to miss at such a close range. Holding his bow by the middle, Illume slammed the recurve into the first hunter's head, sending him falling backward. *Hunter crippled* scrawled itself across the upper left hand corner of Illume's screen.

As the first hunter fell, the second hunter rose up with an overhead swing of his sword. Illume swiped his bow to the side, deflecting the attack into the ground. Arching his bow across, Illume caught the hunter with his weapon's other side, hooking under his chin, sending him falling back as well. *Watching movies so DOES teach you things!* Illume laughed to himself, having learned that exact move from one of Orlando Bloom's most notable roles.

Turning to face Trill, Illume was tackled to the ground by the other hunter. Taken by surprise, Illume ended up dropping his bow while falling to his back with the hunter on top of him. The hunter attempted to stab Illume in the face with the arrow that was still stuck through his own hand, but Illume held his arm up as best as he can. Blood poured from the hunter's hand onto Illume's face and into his mouth, causing him to gag.

"Oh God! No way this is sanitary!" Illume screamed while trying to move from the path of dripping blood. "A little help here!" Illume cried out, looking over at Trill.

Trill had already killed his two men and freed the girl. He crouched, watching with his head tilted to the side and giving Illume a thumbs-up.

"I believe in you, you got thas!" he tauntingly encouraged.

"Oh screw you!" Illume responded, thankful he put the extra attributes in strength.

Reaching, Illume grabbed the arrow from the hunter's hand and yanked it free before stabbing him in the throat repeatedly.

With each jab Illume delivered, the hunter's health dropped, eventually to zero. Blood bathed Illume and his stolen armor. Had it not been for the mud hiding all the gore, the scene would have been truly grizzly.

Illume staggered to his feet; he hadn't noticed the struggle had depleted his stamina almost completely. The second hunter began to rise to his feet. Sword in hand, he swung it in stylish flurries in a clear attempt to be intimidating. Illume smirked, draining all of his mana into his hand.

When he opened his palm, a blast of concentrated ice impaled the hunter with hundreds of tiny shards. The hunter's health bar steadily dropped until the hunter himself did the same, shattering into several pieces in the process.

"I could have been killed! You son of a..." Illume was cut off by Trillian as he covers the little girl's ears, mouth open in shock.

"Language! Thar are lattle ladies present!" he responded.

Archery Level Up
Enhance Strike, now available for skill points.
Focus, now available for skill points.
Reinforced Shot, now available for skill points.
Not Quite Legolas!

Illume smirked at the taunt. At least he'd gotten somewhere. Illume kneeled in front of the little girl.

"We aren't going to hurt you. We were actually sent to help your family. Where are they?" Illume asked softly.

The little girl cowered away from him and burrowed her face into Trill's chest. Trill shrugged confusedly at Illume.

"It's okay, lattle one. Why don't you tall me where your family is so myself and this nice man can halp protect them." Trill didn't even try to accommodate the girl's young age with his tone.

Apparently, it worked. She pointed deeper into the woods. Trill released the girl, made his way over to one of the hunters, and retrieved their sword, offering the handle to Illume.

"What do you say we hunt some hunters?" Trill offered with a smirk.

Illume grasped the hunter's sword, opting to leave his stolen pike impaled in the other hunter.

Silver Sword Refined
Damage: +10
Weight: +4
Worth: 600 polis
This higher quality forged sword is made of hardened silver damage doubles when wielded against undead or the impure.

10

HUNTER

"SHOULD we bring the girl with us?" Illume whispered.

Trill glanced at the girl, then at the bodies, and nodded.

"Aye, I thank that's a good idea. Not very kind leaving her with bodies," Trill responded.

After snuffing out the hunters' torches, Illume, Trill and the girl made their way through the woods once again. The soft chirping of cicadas filled the dark air. It was a pleasant touch to an unpleasant situation. Illume fell in behind Trill with the little girl holding on to Illume's hand for guidance. Illume offered the little girl a friendly smile, and she giggled slightly.

It was strange, the longer Illume looked at her, the more she resembled his niece. Was this part of the immersion when they scanned him? Did they take images of friends and family and litter them into the game as NPCs? There was no time to dwell on that right now, as they had begun to move in on their next group of hunters.

Moving into a position ahead of their path, the hunters seemed to be looking for someone. Illume notched an arrow and drew his bow, holding the hilt of his sword in a reverse grip with his bow. Taking aim, he was about to release when one of the hunters called out that they'd found something. Illume moved closer as silently as he could.

Sneak Increased
Assassin now available for skill points.

As Illume got closer, he saw a little boy cowering against a dirt incline. His robes were tattered and filthy. Dirt streaks ran down his face, indicating he had been crying. Even though it was just a game, Illume felt a swell of anger fill his chest, especially when the hunters pointed their weapons at the boy. Almost as if Trill could read Illume's thoughts, he threw a rock right next to Illume, causing the hunters' heads to whip around in search of the sound.

He released his arrow and it found its mark inside one of the hunter's eyes with a soft *pop.* Illume's hands trembled with rage. He was worried he might miss, but with a six times multiplier on a sneak attack and critical hit, the hunter fell to the ground, lifeless. Trill leaped out first, hacking and slashing as he did before. This time, one of the hunters was able to stand against him.

Illume leaped out next, driving his sword into one of the hunters' foot, making his life bar drop by a quarter. Lunging upward, Illume slammed the grip of his bow into the hunter's face while pulling his blade free, knocking him out.

Illume hadn't been paying attention; the other two hunters managed to slam their swords into Illume's chest. Fortunately, his armor was thick and heavy as both swords bounced off. The impact still stung slightly and Illume's health dropped by a miniscule portion each time.

"Thank God for tanks." Illume laughed.

Bow in one hand, sword in the other, Illume parried and blocks each oncoming attack, getting a jab in here and a slap with his bow in there. Again, he was thankful for all the live action role-playing he did in high school and college; it was really paying off right about now.

All three combatants poked and prodded at each other, Illume knocking their life bars down bit by laborious bit. They got a few jabs in as well, causing minor damage, as the elven heavy armor was vastly superior to his leather armor.

Eventually, Illume noticed a pattern in their attacks. Making his move, Illume crossed his arms, deflecting one sword one way while hooking the other with his bow and drawing it into the other hunter's gut, impaling him. Just as the hunter dropped dead, Trill's opponent slammed into Illume's last remaining hunter, knocking him to the ground and rendering them both unconscious.

"You okay?" Illume asked, looking over at Trill, who had a small stream of blood running from his forehead.

"I'm fine. These poachers can't likely get the best of me!" he responded as he winked at the girl and she giggled once again.

"Okay, tie these two up, take their weapons, and put them aside. I don't want them to be able to move, and gag them so they can't warn their friends," Illume commanded before turning his attention to the boy.

Kneeling down, Illume offered the boy his hand, but the child cowered away. Illume was taken aback for a moment. He looked just like his nephew; in fact, both children were about the same age.

They had to have taken memories and put them in the game. After a moment, the little girl rushed in and threw her hands around the boy's neck and he hugged her back. This brought warmth to Illume's heart.

"All right, they're all tied up. I kindly don't think they'll be goin' anywhere," Trill exclaimed before putting the torches out.

Illume didn't have a chance to check the work before it went dark again. Trill had been a good cohort so far. There was no reason to doubt him. Illume accessed his quest's menu to see that two of the four hunting parties had been taken care of.

With their party growing by one, they were forced to move through the woods at a slower pace. The girl no longer clasped on to Illume, but rather, her brother. The children stayed within arm's length of either man while moving through the woods.

They paused momentarily as the children began to slow down. Trill pulled a bladder off his hip—must have stolen it from one of the hunters—and handed it to the little girl. Immediately, she opened it and drank before handing the water bladder to her brother.

"Why are these people hunting children?" Illume asked as he tried to catch his breath.

"They aren't after the children; they are after the children's parents," Trill responded. "I've seen these people before. They are known as the Hunters of the Order of Light…" Trill was cut off.

"That's ironic, because they seem to be into pretty dark deeds," Illume interrupted with a murmur.

"You have no idea," Trill responded as the children returned his water pouch.

Illume and Trill moved once again after taking a bit of a breather. Ahead, Illume saw four torches.

"Why would they only hunt in groups of four?" Illume asked.

"Four is their holy number. Everything is divisible by four. It makes their architecture… symmetrically infuriating," Trill growled, seeming more angry at the number than at their actions.

Trill's reaction struck Illume as odd, but he didn't have time to press the matter.

"Stay with the kids. I'm going to scout ahead, okay?" Illume whispered.

Moving forward through the forest, Illume had some trouble seeing. It might have been better for Trill to do the scouting, but this was Illume's quest and he'd be a monkey's uncle if he was going to let someone else do the heavy lifting.

Illume moved silently through the trees and undergrowth. As he moved forward, the distinct cries of a woman could be heard calling out through a gag of some sort.

Illume's heart raced as he felt his body temperature rise with righteous fury. One of his exes would have said he was being *soooo dramatic,* which was why he actually broke up with her, not appreciating the validity of his feelings. As he reached the edge of the small clearing, Illume's perceived anger catapulted into a rage.

Tied down on the ground with silver rope was a woman not much younger than Illume. The ropes held her arms and her legs outstretched as an intricate series of knots formed over her exposed chest, keeping her planted firmly to the ground. Judging by the way one of the hunters was fidgeting with his pants, Illume was glad he made the kids stay behind.

All strategy flew out the window as Illume's rage erupted. He lunged into the clearing, trembling in rage. His grip on his sword was so tight, the blood flow to his own fingers was cut off. Illume landed between the eager hunter and his prey.

Illume set off a concentrated blast of frost directly into the hunter's crotch, causing him to scream out in pain. When he delivered a powerful kick, the hunter's nether region shattered like glass, causing him to hit the ground. The hunter's life bar immediately dropped to half. The trophy notification dinged.

Trophy Earned.
Name: You Cold Psycho
Type: Silver
Requirements: Using frost magic to freeze then shatter an opponent's family jewels.
If you'd like, we can refer someone for you to talk to.

Spinning, Illume drove his sword into the mouth of a second hunter, prompting a "critical hit" and draining his entire life bar as blood erupted from his mouth down the front of his armor. Withdrawing his sword, Illume sliced the bonds of the woman, freeing her to roll to one side to remove the ropes.

A jolt ripped Illume's body to one side, causing his vision to blur. *Suffering from broken bones,* Illume was informed as his life bar dropped dangerously low. He grew lightheaded upon seeing a massive axe head protruding from his collarbone. The strike slipped past his armor, causing his blood to spurt, covering the armor, the woman, and the hunter before him.

A cold sensation of steel cut through his kidney as he was stabbed in the back and everything went dark, accompanied only by the screams of horror from the woman.

YOU HAVE DIED!

Cropped up in Illume's vision. Illume felt a violent jerk on whatever state he was currently in. Slamming into his own body, it jerked backward slightly. He was crouched with Trill and the two children. He felt for his sword, but it was gone, as was the purse of coin on his hip. Armed with only his bow and his little dagger, Illume offered his weapon to Trill.

That sucks, Illume thought to himself. *What are the rules again? If you die, you lose all your gear?*

"Take this, and whatever you do, don't let those children move past you," Illume growled.

His collarbone ached, as did his side from the trauma that brought about his death. Reaching up, Illume grabbed Trill's sword from his back and pulled it out of its sheath.

Pickpocket Leveled Up

Illume blinked twice, cutting off the information before it could continue. A pulse echoed through Illume like a lightning bolt as he took possession of the weapon.

Legendary Straight Sword: Toxic Light
Damage: +25
Weight: +0
Worth: 10 million polis
Toxic Light, the blade of the Dark King, ignores all armor ratings dealing +25 damage plus 200 poison damage.
Temporarily boosts all stats by 100 points. One scratch can prove

fatal and was once used by a single warrior to defeat an entire army. This should have stayed buried.

Illume immediately regretted stealing the sword, but his bow wouldn't cut it in this fight. Intending to return it to Trill as soon as he was finished saving the woman ahead, Illume charged forward. Knowing the exact setup of the field he was about to enter, Illume charged through the forest without tripping once. His stamina bar hardly moved.

Illume leaped into the clearing, firing a blast of ice in the same manner that he had before while cutting the woman free earlier. Illume felt his dexterity increase as he landed and was able to deliver the kick while freezing the axe head that killed him, sticking it to the ground. Shooting a frost blast at the hunter he'd stabbed in the mouth previously, he managed to freeze him solid as well before his mana pool was drained.

Glancing on the ground, Illume saw his coin purse and his sword where he had died last. Marching across the clearing, Illume retrieved his sword, using it to deflect the same dagger attack that had stabbed his side. Illume thrust Trill's blade into the hunter's neck, causing black tendrils of toxins to immediately course from the wound throughout his body. Typically, this sight would horrify him, but right now, it brought a twisted smile to his face.

Withdrawing the blade, Illume turned his attention to the last hunter, only to see the hunter's head ripped clean from his body, spinal column and all. Illume took a step back, in shock at the sheer violence as blood erupted from the hunter's neck like Old Faithful. Behind him stood the woman, her hands mutated into massive claws, and her eyes glowing a coppery gold.

"Where are my children!" she roared.

Illume immediately dropped both his weapons, upon which his stamina completely disappeared, as did his mana.

"Your children are safe, miss," Illume blurted in a way to say *please don't eat me!* "They are with my companion just out of sight." Illume stepped back from the weapons.

The woman slowly turned back to her humanoid self, her tattered rags falling to the ground. She walked to the side of the clearing. Illume hadn't noticed the chest that was tucked away behind a few ferns. Opening the chest, the woman grasped a cloak and threw it over her exposed body.

"I thank you, stranger," she whispered softly, gently rubbing her wrists. "Had you not come along, I fear what they would have done to me." Her accent seemed to be eastern European.

"I'm just happy I could help. My name is Illume. May I ask yours?" Illume asked.

"I am Kassandra," she responded as Trill emerged from the forest.

Immediately, the children charged their mother. She kneeled down and gave them enormous hugs as tears of joy filled their eyes. A swell of pride filled Illume's chest as he picked up Trill's weapon and offered it back.

"I'm sorry I stole it," Illume confessed.

"No need to apologize. Just don't do it again," Trill responded while returning Illume his bow.

"Thank you both. You have already done so much for us. Would it be too much to make one last request?" Kassandra pled.

Illume retrieved his sword and the coins, re-sheathing the weapon.

"We will happily help you find your husband," Illume responded before she could ask.

A massive smile formed on her lips, revealing slightly elongated canines. She sniffed the air, offering Trill a strange glance before approaching Illume.

"I bless you with the sight of Lycan," Kassandra whispered as she gave Illume a kiss on the cheek.

Blessing Received.
Name: Sight of Lycan

When in favor with the Lycan people and their god Lycan himself, a pack leader may bestow Sight of Lycan to a willing recipient allowing them to see as a Lycanthrope does for up to twelve hours, or sunrise.

As her lips left Illume's cheek, his vision burst into an array of colors, as if he was able to see into the ultra-violet spectrum of light. Illume staggered backward upon receiving the gift as his senses overloaded. Concentrating as hard as he could, Illume managed to gain a semblance of control over the sight.

Looking around, he could see more clearly in the dark than he could at mid-day. Notching an arrow, Illume almost growled.

"Let's go find their dad."

11

ALPHA

DODGING and weaving through the forest, Illume led his pack under fallen logs and over small streams. He found himself able to sprint full speed through the dangerous terrain without worry of running into or tripping over an unseen tree.

Stopping as his stamina fell dangerously low, Illume glanced ahead to see a large cave tucked into the side of a hill several hundred yards ahead. Eight torches illuminated the entrance to the cave, but Illume was unable to see if there were any guards outside.

"Trill, scout ahead. We need to know how many are outside that cave," Illume whispered.

"No need," Kassandra butted in. "There are only two outside. The rest are in that cave with my husband." She continued, tapping her nose after sniffing the air for several seconds.

Illume watched as Kassandra growled at her children and waved her hands at them as if shooing them away. Immediately, both children disappeared into the woods. Not willing to question the actions of a mother, Illume looked at his stamina. It was nearly full. He worked his way through the woods once again, followed closely behind by Kassandra and Trill.

Approaching the cave, Illume crouched and sneaked up on the

two men who were posted outside to guard the entrance, gripping the hilt of his blade tightly and preparing to charge. Kassandra placed her hand on his forearm, stopping him.

When he turned his attention to her, she held her finger to her lips before pointing to watch. Two high-pitched snarls rang out, accompanied with a blur of brown that streaked across Illume's field of view from left to right, then a second from right to left. Fountains of blood erupted from both hunters' throats as their lifeless corpses fell to the ground.

Illume's jaw dropped open at the sight of the children's lethality. Even fully armored and armed, Illume would have been no competition for them. In games like this, the developers made a habit of having side quests be morally ambiguous where players really didn't know if they were doing the right thing or not. At this very moment, Illume was certain he was.

Illume pushed forward. Patting down the guards, he retrieved their coin purses. Turning to Kassandra, he handed one to her before giving the other to Trill. Coming across a necklace, Illume pulled it from the bloody stump that was the hunter's neck. It had a soft, magical blue hue to it.

Silver Necklace of Purification
Weight: +0.5.
Worth: 300 polis.
This necklace staves off the effects of poisons, toxins, and venoms.
Decreases chances of contracting Lycanthropy by 60%.
Decreases chances of contracting Vampirism by 62%.
Prevents debuffs from affecting your magic and stamina.

This was a useful tool for Illume. Sliding the necklace around his neck, he felt a strange aura wash through him as if he'd stepped into a warm bath. Kassandra and Trill looked at the pouches of money before speaking in unison.

"Is this necessary?" Both had the same upward inflection to their tones.

"Trill, you're risking your life to help me. Kassandra, you and your family may need to make a break for it as soon as we save your husband. You'll need something to start over with, so yes, it's necessary," Illume responded, turning his attention to the cave.

Illume sheathed his sword before arming himself with his bow and notching an arrow. His sight pulsated through the cave. He could see faint colored outlines in the distance. It must have been the hunter's body heat. As they entered, Illume heard Kassandra give a dog-like huff. Her children extinguished the torches and remained at the mouth of the cave.

Sliding through the cave's mud, all three were careful not to make a sound. Illume's footing slipped once or twice, but neither Kassandra nor Trill ever missed a step. No matter how steep the decline or wet the ground, both walked through it as if they had spikes on their feet while Illume slid around like Bambi on ice. The hunters' voices echoed through the caverns as they closed in.

"I can't wait to skin this one and turn his pelt into my sheets!" one called.

"I call dibs on the wife… I have use for a woman like that. I mean, did you SEE what she's sportin'?" Illume felt his blood pressure rise at the Cockney accent.

Kassandra's hand landed softly on his shoulder, almost as if she could hear his blood pressure rising. Her contact grounded him once more to their quest as he calmed himself. They continued to move forward.

"What about the children? The girl is too young to be worked and the boy is too small for labor," a third voice questioned.

"The children are not ours, remember that. It is the Dark King who wishes to have the children and we dare not disappoint him." This voice was different; it was regal, noble even. As if the words were being spoken by a Scandinavian grizzled Karl Urban.

At the mention of this Dark King obtaining the children, a deep snarl rippled through the cavern. The sound reverberated through Illume like a roar of thunder with the monstrous resonance of what Illume imagined a dragon to sound like. Illume glanced over at Kassandra. She was not the source of the noise.

When he glanced back to Trill, he nodded as if able to read Illume's mind. Without a word spoken, all three charged through the tunnels. Screams filled the air, echoing off the walls like hundreds of men were dying, as opposed to probably six.

The path the tunnel took curves down at a dangerous angle. Leaping off rocks, Illume dropped nearly twice his own height more than once, each time damaging his health slightly. He had no time to worry about it, as these hunters had weapons that could kill a Lycanthrope.

Rounding the final corner, now nearly a quarter of a mile into the cave system, a massive beast reared on its hind legs. The creature was nothing like Illume had ever seen before. Dark, matted fur covered its body from head to toe. Its head reminded Illume of a Pomeranian, only larger than a grizzly and sporting far more ferocious teeth.

Each paw was large enough to rip a bear in half with a single swipe and only its victims knew exactly how sharp the six-inch claws were. Four men surrounded the beast, armed with long, silver pikes. At their feet were two of their compatriots cleaved in two, undoubtedly by the being they were hunting.

Noticing one of the hunters moving, Illume blind fired his bow at the beast's heart. The arrowheads were steel and would just piss the Lycanthrope off, unlike that pike, which would kill him.

Illume notched an arrow, zeroing in on the head of one of the pikes.

Sparks flew as a metal on metal TING filled the cave, knocking the pike's head off course just enough for the Lycanthrope to dodge the attack.

OH MY GOD PLEASE TELL ME SOMEONE SAW THAT! Illume screamed to himself as the remaining four hunters turned to look at them.

"Nice shot." Kassandra smirked as she transformed.

"Thank you," Illume responded, notching another arrow and firing.

This time, the arrow hit one of the hunters in the shoulder, causing his health to drop by a third. *I'm a ninja!* Illume called out in the privacy of his own mind as he dropped his bow and drew his sword. All three charged in on the hunters. One kept his pike aimed at the Lycanthrope's heart while the other three aimed their pikes at Illume and his little team.

As they closed in, Illume noticed that Kassandra was moving way too fast to outmaneuver the pike before her. With his left hand, Illume drew Bloodlust from his lower back and threw it at the hunter. Spinning through the air, the dagger hit the hunter square in the chest, handle first before falling to the ground.

Can't get lucky every time, Illume pointed out to himself. Fortunately, it distracted the hunter long enough to take his eyes off Kassandra for a split second. That was all the time she needed.

Using his sword, Illume struck a hunter's pike down and to the side, spinning in the process before bashing his opponent in the head with the pommel of his sword. The hunter's life bar dropped ever so slightly. More importantly, so did his pike. Out of the corner of his eye, Illume could swear he saw Trill pass straight through the pike with no harm brought on him, but he was too focused on his target to be sure.

A sharp pain echoed through Illume's leg. He ignored it, even though his life bar dropped by nearly a third. Illume bashed his opponent's face with the cross guard of his sword, each blow knocking his health lower and lower. A sharp pain erupted through Illume's leg again.

This time, his health dropped by a quarter and a notice popped up saying that he was bleeding. Finally, looking down, he noticed a dagger imbedded deep into his leg. The hunter had not only stabbed him, but was now twisting the weapon.

Illume slashed at the hunter, but the sword did no damage, only putting gashes in his armor. Illume's leg gave out and he dropped to a knee, sending off a roar in agony as pain howled through him like a banshee on the moors.

He looked at the hunter, whose face was caked in blood. The hunter drew his sword. He lifted it to strike at Illume, who tried to lift his sword but was unable. Just as the blade was about to drop onto Illume, a flash of silver then a spurt of blood stopped the attack.

The hunter's arm fell to the ground, still gripping his sword. He screamed in pain, but the white maw of Kassandra clamped down on the back of his head, splattering his blood, brains, and more than a few skull fragments against Illume. Flinching, Illume wiped his face as he briefly wondered how an "M" rating on this game was going to be high enough.

"STOP WHERE YOU ARE!" the Karl Urban lookalike shouted, pressing his pike a quarter of an inch into the Lycanthrope's chest, making him roar. "Take another step and this beast dies."

"That's not a beast," Illume groaned, hoping the bleeding would stop before his life bar dropped to zero and he had to replay this entire section again. "You are!"

Taking a deep breath, Illume ripped the dagger from his leg.

Using his right hand, Illume threw it at the final hunter, who was too distracted by Kassandra's snow white Lycanthropy form to notice until it was too late. The dagger found its mark, embedding itself into his shoulder. He flailed backward, giving his would-be prey just enough room to deliver a powerful swipe that sent his corpse splattering against the wall.

Just as Illume was about to pass out, a white light glowed, filling the cave. Illume noticed his health bar was beginning to fill. Illume turned his attention to Trill, who stood over him with both his arms stretched out and glowing white light flowing from his hands and into Illume. The pain in his leg dissipated; he was even able to stand with hardly any pain at all. As the light faded, Illume offered Trill a friendly smile.

"Thank you," Illume whispered.

"It's my honor," Trillian replied.

Illume turned his attention back to the beast, only now he was just a man with long, dark hair and stubble across his strong face. His body was well-formed with a nick that was bleeding in the center of his chest. Kassandra reverted back to her human form as both embraced.

They shared a kiss that hinted at the fact that they never thought they'd see each other again. After a moment of both Trill and Illume feeling awkward at their moment of voyeurism, the man looked at Illume dead in the eyes. A chill ran down Illume's spine.

"Who are you?" he demanded.

"I am Illume, this is my companion Trill. Your brother, William, told us that you were in trouble and asked us to help you," Illume responded honestly.

"And what's in it for you? A bounty, our pelts!" Victor lunged slightly, rage in his voice.

Illume now realized why William didn't come to save his family himself. Kassandra stepped between her husband and Illume, her hand on his chest. It seemed to calm him, or so Illume hoped.

"This man has gone to great lengths to save us. He rescued your daughter, saved your son, spared your wife…" Her voice trailed off. "…dishonor and took a knife for you."

"These beings will do whatever it takes to prove their loyalty, only to trade us in for the closest place to give them coin!" Victor protested.

"Victor!" Kassandra roared, trying to get it to sink in. "This Illume was able to receive the blessing of Lycan; is that not proof enough for you?" Kassandra asked.

This seemed to calm Victor quite a bit. Kassandra backed up as he pushed forward. He was an enormous man. Once again, Illume felt mildly inadequate in his presence. Victor looked both Illume and Trill up and down, judging them, sizing them up. Leaning in, Victor gave each man a quick sniff.

"Thank you for saving my family. We must go. It is no longer safe for us here," Victor said softly as he pushed past Illume.

"Wait!" Illume called out as an idea formed in his mind. "What if I told you there is a place where you and your children would be safe?" Illume asked.

Victor stopped in his tracks. Slowly, he turned to face Illume, raising an eyebrow.

"And where might this be, human?" he growled.

"The abandoned quarry. I am building a settlement. I can't guarantee it'll be an easy life… and you'll have to promise not to eat the livestock, but I can say that you will be safe from hunters," Illume continued, hoping his charisma was high enough to persuade him.

Victor hesitated for a moment. Kassandra leaned in and whispered in his ear.

"And what will this cost us?" Victor asked warily.

"Nothing in life is free. You would need to work, but I was thinking you would be perfectly suited for the night guard. You would be paid a fair wage and you would need to train more night guards as we get more volunteers. I counted twelve hunters. Trill gets one more coin purse for his part in helping rescue you, but your family will get the rest." Illume offered his hand. "Sound fair enough?"

Victor hesitated for a moment, goaded on by a stern look from Kassandra. Reaching out, he took Illume by the forearm, giving him a firm shake.

"We have a deal," he responded.

Illume returned his shake as his notification dinged once more.

Civilian: Victor
Occupation: Night Guard
Special Ability: Night Watch, being a Lycanthrope, Victor will be able to both see and smell danger coming from miles away. Being an alpha, any werewolf recruited will be instantly loyal to you.

+20% effectiveness of night guards.
+20% defense for each werewolf on the wall
+20% battle effectiveness of each werewolf on the wall.
Special Trait: Undying Loyalty
For saving his wife and children, Victor will be undyingly loyal to you.
Victor outranks you many times over. He could take over your city in moments but never will… most other players won't be so lucky.

Quest Complete: Save Victor's Family
Level Up Available:
1 Skill Point Available
5 Attribute Points Available.

"Now for the fun part," Illume huffed as Victor and Kassandra left his and Trill's company.

12

TRADE IN

ILLUME'S CURIOSITY tugged at the back of his mind as he and Trill got to work. If he had his fitness tracker on him, how many steps would he have taken tonight? Trill and Illume spent what felt like hours making a sled, collecting the bodies, or what is left of them, and piling them all on their little sliding cart.

Stripping the hunters of their armor, Illume and Trill divided their haul into three piles. Bodies in one, they went in the center of the cart since they were the heaviest; weapons, which sat to the left side since Trill kept boasting how strong he was; and the silvery cloth armor, which found its home on the right.

"You know, I should probably be the one that holds on to the gold and jewels," Trill explained as they loaded the last of their cargo.

"And why's that?" Illume asked.

Trill pointed to the hill crest a few hundred yards away.

"Because jast over that hill is our lattle pig farm. What are the chances William tald the guards to meet us there? Because I'm sayin' pretty high. They see you in the stolen armor, anything you have will probably be confiscated." Trill shrugged as he spoke.

Illume nodded. Trill's thought process made sense. Removing Bloodlust, the necklace he'd claimed from the fallen hunter, and his bow and arrows, Illume offered all of them to Trill to hold. After a moment of playful banter about maybe not giving the necklace back, Trill donned all of Illume's remaining supplies.

Both men each grabbed hold of one of the cart's handles and pushed with all their might. Trill's side moved first; clearly, he was far stronger than Illume. That just pushed Illume further in an effort to keep up. Eventually, both men made a decent pace, Illume's stamina bar dropping steadily, yet slowly, as they made their way back toward the pig farm.

Making it over the crest, Illume and Trill pulled on the cart so it did not slide away from them and down the hill. Like trying to rein in dozens of large dogs on a walk, Illume put all his weight backward and dug his feet into the dirt, just barely keeping control.

The sun began to rise. Illume look to see half a dozen men in glistening armor standing at the farm waiting for them. Their approach wasn't pretty, but eventually, they were able to bring their little makeshift sled to a stop. A familiar ping rang out:

Strength increased to +23, Stamina increased to 170
Weight Capacity increased to 550.

Trophy Earned.
Name: Sweat of Your Brow
Type: Bronze
Requirements: Conduct eight hours of continuous physical labor.
Automatically increases strength, stamina and carry capacity by one, ten, ten. One time deal.

Congratulations! You now know what it feels like to do a hard day's work, you lazy bum!

As the notification went away, Illume was happy to see he'd gotten just a little bit stronger. He was curious if the constant little jabs at him were necessary, though.

Stepping free from the handles of their sled, Illume let off a nervous laugh upon laying eyes on the seventh man. He stood with a black eye that contrasted starkly against his pale skin. Silken robes draped over his well-built body and his hand grasped the hilt of a nasty-looking sword attached to his side.

Illume immediately took off his helmet and placed it on the ground. Running back to the cart, he pulled the stolen pike off of it. The guards reacted by pointing their spears at Illume. Without a word, Illume put his hands out and moved slowly toward the guards, sticking the pike, sharp end first, into the ground.

Reaching up, Illume untied the bonds of the heavy armor and let the body plate slide free, catching it before it hit the ground, and placed it at the commander's feet before doing the same with the boots and finally gauntlets.

"You must be the rightful owner of this armor," Illume whispered with a nervous tone.

"I am," the commander growled, glaring at Illume so hard, he felt a bit of his soul die.

"I am very sorry for what happened last night. I swear I don't usually do this. And I assure you I would NEVER steal from a guard," Illume explained.

The commander hesitated for a moment, looking at the state of his armor then glaring back at Illume.

"You're lucky Senator William has paid your bounty. Otherwise, you would be in irons right now," the commander barked.

He looked Illume up and down. Illume was slightly embarrassed to be in mud- and blood-caked tattered rags. The commander then turned his attention to Trill.

"You, on the other hand, the one goading this one on to hit me. William did not pay your bounty…" *Crap, bet on the wrong horse!* Illume thought to himself as the commander continued. "… any stolen items will be confiscated by the law of Lapideous and you are to spend three weeks in our prisons." the commander barked as his subordinate handed him irons.

Without a moment's hesitation, Trill pulled one of the coin purses off his belt and held it out to the commander.

"I imagine my bounty is what, 500 polis thas time? I do profusely apologize about last night. I was just tryin' to make a new friend. I believe thas will be enough to cover what is owed." Trill's words slid off his tongue as if it were made of silver.

The commander stepped forward. Taking the pouch, he opened it and looked inside before giving a nod of approval.

"This will be enough. Senator William said you would have something else for us?" the commander asked.

Illume nodded, waving the commander and his men over to the back of the wooden sled held together by vines. A strange, satisfied smile tugged on the corners of the commander's lips. Illume turned his attention to the commander's men. Some were steadfast, others had a look of pure joy.

"I'm having trouble counting the bodies. How many Order of Light members am I looking at?" the commander asked.

"Twelve, sir. They were hunting a w—" Illume was cut off by Trill.

"Thay were huntin' Senator William's family. He hired us to rescue them. Their hunting grounds must be running low on prey," Trill added with a chuckle and a shrug.

"Twelve hunters, their bounty is 200 a head. That is 2400 polis. That being said, there is a ban on all Order of Light armor and weaponry. As a finder's fee, I will give you an additional 300 polis per piece of weaponry and 300 per piece of armor. Overall, I believe that is 9,600 polis," the commander said, waving for a small chest to be brought forward.

Two guards walked forward. Setting the chest at Illume's feet, they opened it, revealing a mound of polis large enough to make Illume's jaw drop. Kneeling down, Illume allowed the cold metal to dribble through his fingers before grabbing a rather large handful.

Regardless of whether or not his bounty had been paid, Illume still felt he owed this commander a debt. Approaching the commander, Illume held his hands outright, offering him a fistful of coin.

"I stole from you, I dirtied your armor, and I marked your face. For that, I owe you personal compensation as a way to apologize." Illume's voice was sincere as he spoke.

The commander hesitated for a moment before opening his own coin purse. Illume dropped the money inside.

"Thank you, Illume. You may be a scoundrel, but you are a man of honor." The commander nodded. Another ping chimed.

Trophy Earned.
Name: Right a Wrong
Type: Gold
Requirements: Make honest compensation to an NPC you have done wrong.
Congratulations! You have shown you are of rare character, well done, the guards under commander Stark will now listen to what you have to say.

Optional Quest Complete:
Turn in Bounty for Illegal Hunters

"I have heard of the town you are settling. Should you require, I might be able to help establish a trade route between our cities and help you grow. Should I find anyone willing to re-settle, I will refer them to you." Commander Stark spoke in a stern yet friendly tone, offering Illume a hand.

"Thank you, commander!" Illume replied as he grasped the commander by the forearm.

"Men of honor are hard to come by these days. It is always best to raise them up for when the time is most dire and honor is all a man has," the commander added.

Releasing Illume's arm, the commander turned and walked away. Two guards picked up his armor and followed suit.

Another two guards grabbed the cart and pushed it like it wasn't anything.

While the final two moved to the back of the column, Illume offered Trill a smile. He smiled back. Illume laughed as the stress of that night gave way to exhausted mania. Trill laughed as well, both men falling to their knees as the sun rose on a new and exhausting day.

Several minutes passed before Illume and Trill were able to regain their composure, Illume's sides splitting from the bout of uncontrollable laughter. He hadn't laughed that hard since he was a child. Looking at the chest, Illume gave it a nudge before glancing back at Trill.

"Half is yours, you know," Illume proclaimed.

Trill removed the necklace, bow, arrows, and dagger, placing them on the ground in front of Illume.

"You are far too much fun, Illume. I will not take your money so long as you lat me join you. I have a sneekin' feelin' that you'll be just a bunch of fun," Trill proclaimed. *9000 polis added.*

Illume hesitated for a moment. Trill had been indispensable in Victor's rescue; his weapon and skill with it were also unparalleled. Having such a weapon on his side would make the earlier levels, like now, far easier.

If he were betrayed, he'd just return to a previous save point and kill Trill before Trill had a chance to kill him. Closing the chest, Illume picked it up, nodding for Trill to follow.

"You've got yourself a deal. Now come on, we need to get back before everyone else wakes up," Illume stated.

Walking back to Lapideous with Trill in tow, Illume was nodded to in a friendly manner by the guards. He nodded back slightly. As they entered the city, it was still quiet, as its inhabitants hadn't yet awoken.

Illume and Trill continued to make their way toward Urtan's house, not saying a word. Passing an alleyway that seemed familiar, Illume got a brief flashback of the night before. Illume pickpocketed several polis from a passerby there.

"You do know one day you'll have to tell me everything that happened last night, right?" Illume more demanded than requested.

Trill gave off a hearty laugh, shaking his head.

"I most certainly don't! It's not my fault you can't hold your liquor," Trill retorted. "Plus, if I do that, then I won't have anything to dangle over your head and where's the fun in that?"

Illume couldn't help but laugh. In this moment, Trill truly reminded Illume of one of his oldest and dearest friends, someone he hadn't seen in years due to work schedules conflicting and with children in the mix.

Approaching Urtan's house, Illume and Trill entered to find a very angry Nari standing cross-armed inside the main quarters. Illume tried not to laugh as he swore he could see steam leaving her ears.

"Where the hell have you been? And who the hell is this?" she barked.

"It's okay, I had a job I needed to do," Illume replied.

"What kind of job, and why are you naked?" Her voice grew more shrill.

"All that matters is we have a new family moving into our little town to help with security. I managed to get on the good side with Commander Stark here. Also made 9000 polis last night. I figured most of it could go to infrastructure and paying the settlers. Also, this is Trillian. I call him Trill. He's the one who helped me earn this and he saved me more than once, so he'll be joining our merry little band." Illume splurged unintentionally. "And as for why I'm naked… well, I just didn't find any clothes after giving that dwarf my armor."

Nari hesitated for a moment. Illume could tell she wanted to retort, but was unable to argue with his results. Sighing, she nodded for Illume to follow her.

"Come on! We had a good day yesterday too. I managed to get a dwarf to move and help with forging. Five lumber masters will be joining us as well, two stonemasons and ten farmers. No one that works the market wanted to come. They said Urtan was bad news. I spent the evening talking to him. For the record, I like him," Nari informed Illume as she led him to the back of the house.

"We also made an additional 8000 polis, so I think that should be enough to get us moving. In the meantime..." Nari stopped as she came to a pool in the back of Urtan's house. A hole in the roof provided natural light to the sparsely decorated room. "... take a bath. You smell like pig filth."

With that final jab, Nari walked away.

Illume glanced back at Trill, shooting him an exhausted look. Trill shrugged and scampered off as well. Setting the chest down, Illume removed his tattered clothing, weapons, and necklace before climbing into the warm pool of water to clean himself from last night's shenanigans.

13

ARMORS AND LIVES

ILLUME WOKE UP, not realizing he had even dozed off. Looking around, he saw that the chest was still where he left it and dirt still caked his body. After getting himself cleaned, Illume pulled himself out of the makeshift tub.

When he looked around, he saw there was little to decorate the back room aside from cold stone walls. In the corner, a fluffy towel sat, folded and waiting for use. Picking it up, he dried himself off, all the while toying with the idea of leveling himself again.

Illume's axe and dagger wounds still throbbed with a dull persistence, even though the injuries had occurred several hours ago. Illume gently touched the wound, and like a bruise, it let off a sharp jab of pain. Looking down, he saw a scar wrap over his shoulder, reaching mid-way down his left pectoral muscle, while another was at rest on his lower right side.

It was beginning to look like death had more consequences than just dropping a few coin. Taking the towel to his hair, Illume finished drying himself before tossing the towel onto a small metal hook fastened to the wall.

Turning, Illume approached the chest, but noticed something

shiny from the corner of his eye. Following the gleam, Illume saw a set of silver-ish armor sitting in the corner.

The sun shined off of it. The metal had a light bronze hue. Running his fingers through his hair, slicking it back, Illume approached the armor set. A piece of folded paper was placed before this beautifully crafted piece of artwork. He retrieved the paper, which read:

You are proving yourself to be not an incompetent leader. This is what your sacrifice has bought, a little something from our new smith, the armor, and a little something from me. I hope you enjoy your new sword and protection.

-Your indebted

Nari

It almost seemed like she was being nice to him. Setting the note down, Illume grabbed a set of soft undergarments that were folded and set atop the armor. Sliding the pants onto himself, he heard a soft voice come from the bathroom's entrance.

"You need to be more careful," the voice advised. Illume recognized it.

A smirk formed on his lips as he kept his back to Nari.

"Are you enjoying the view?" he asked.

Another painfully awkward moment; at least she giggled softly this time.

"Not what I was referring to," Nari responded.

Illume turned to face her and stopped dead in his tracks. His heart skipped a beat upon laying eyes on her. A tight corset pushed her bosom up and a white frilly shirt threaded across the front kept her chest hidden.

A deep tan leather jacket complemented the corset perfectly, given the actual body of the jacket ended halfway down her back.

Bracers peeked out from under the jacket, looping between her pointer finger and thumb.

Soft leather pants hugged the curvature of her strong legs, adorned with numerous daggers slid into built-in sheaths. Her boots were solid yet stylish, lifting her body just enough to show off the muscles of her lower body.

"Are you enjoying the view?" Nari teased.

Illume swallowed hard; his mouth had gone cotton once again.

"Um… yeah, Imeanno… I mean…" He stopped talking as his cheeks heated up.

Nari approached Illume, exuding confidence, which was a turn-on for him. Grabbing his undershirt, she fluffed it out to help him don his new armor. She paused and gently touched the scar on his chest. Goosebumps cascaded over his body as an icy grip, colder than his own, took hold of his, causing every muscle in his body to tighten.

"You died last night," she whispered. Was that concern he heard?

"It's not a big deal," Illume reasoned, shrugging off the event.

"It is," Nari protested. "You don't have infinite lives, Illume. Two more and it's game over," she whispered.

Game over? What the hell did that mean? Illume accessed his menu and attempted to exit out of the game. It was still greyed out. He panicked slightly as he frantically "clicked" on the button.

"What do you mean game over?" Illume asked as he closed out his menus.

"I mean you will only come back twice; the third time you die is permanent," she whispered once again before sliding his undershirt onto him. "Will you promise me you'll be more careful in the future?" she asked almost pleadingly.

"I will," Illume promised, stunned and panicking internally. He really needed to hold on to his level ups now!

Nari went to the armor. Picking up the main piece, she approached Illume, who put his hands up. Nari gently slid the thick metal onto him, activating a notification:

Superior Dwarven Armor: Hybrid
Armor: +40
Weight: +35
Worth: 500 polis
Hybrid nature enhances armor attributes by 25% when worn as a full set. Able to be improved.

Nari gently cinched his armor closed around him. It fit perfectly. Her fingers moved nimbly over the leather straps, pulling them tighter before tying them off.

"I helped our dwarf friend make this. She used a smithing technique she developed and I used an old enchanting trick I learned to help make it stronger than normal dwarven armor," Nari informed Illume while placing his gauntlets onto his forearms.

Superior Dwarven Gauntlets: Hybrid
Armor: +15
Weight: +4
Worth: 200 polis
Hybrid nature enhances armor attributes by 25% when worn as a full set. Able to be improved.

"We wish we could have made it better. We just don't quite have the know-how yet. There are legendary smithies in a city north of here that may be able to help train us further," she added while retrieving his leg/boot armor.

Superior Dwarven Boots: Hybrid
Armor: +13
Weight: +5
Worth: 200 polis
Hybrid nature enhances armor attributes by 25% when worn as a full set. Able to be improved.

"Well then, it looks like that will have to be our next stop," Illume responded as she continued to armor him before retrieving his helmet.

Superior Dwarven Helmet: Hybrid
Armor: +20
Weight: +8
Worth: 300 polis
Hybrid nature enhances armors attributes by 25% when worn as a full set. Able to be improved.
Overall Armor Rating: +88 (+25%)

One hundred and ten armor rating this early in the game? Not bad! he thought to himself.

Nari turned around one final time, retrieving a bastard sword, the kind that could be wielded with either one or two hands.

"Obtaining this sword was… tricky to say the least, but I think it will serve you well for the foreseeable future." Nari gave Illume a bright smile.

As she held his weapon out to him, Illume accepted her gift.

Mystery Sword: Bastard
Damage: +15
Weight: +10
Worth: 400 polis
This beautiful bastard ignores 10% of enemies armor rating.
Enhances both single and double handed combat simultaneously.
+20 damage to imps.

Illume let off a stunned scoff at the beauty of this sword. Not looking dwarven in the slightest, it appeared more elven in origin, reminding him of Narsil.

"I cannot begin to thank you enough," Illume confessed in awe.

Taking a step back, he gave the weapon several practice

swings. To his amazement, the weapon moved like an extension of his own arm. It was perfectly balanced and flowed like water.

"There is no need to thank me, Illume. I am your indebted." Nari's voice seemed a bit colder this time.

Sheathing his new blade, Illume turned his full attention to Nari.

"There is that word again. What is an indebted?" Illume asked.

Moving to his bow, dagger, and necklace, Illume finished gearing himself up.

"An indebted is someone whose life was saved by another. I am yours completely," she murmured.

Illume's brow knitted together; there was no way she could be saying what he thought she was saying. Illume walked over to Nari, his new armor hardly making a sound as he walked. Lifting her chin with a bent forefinger, he made eye contact with Nari.

"In my town, everyone is free to live as they choose. There will be laws in place, but there will be no form of slavery." Illume's words were earnest.

Nari was one of the most beautiful women he ever laid eyes on, and all he'd managed to do was trip over himself and bumble his way through conversations. He thanked his past self for putting points into charisma because this conversation could have gotten really weird really fast. If she was being kind to him and staying around him because she was indebted to him, Illume found that unacceptable. He would rather have had her company of her own accord.

"You are not my indebted, you are my friend… my blacksmith, and I am hoping a companion for my adventures." Illume spoke truthfully, wanting her to join him on his quest to beat this game.

Nari nodded in agreement all the while letting off a soft laugh.

"I would be happy to be one of your companions!" she exclaimed. Her excitement then turned to a question. "You have room for one more. Any idea on who to bring?"

Illume hadn't put much thought into who would be a good

fourth member for his party. Nari was clearly skilled with throwing knives and twin swords. Trillian was skilled at combat and also had healing abilities, and he himself was a powerful mage who happened to be a decent fighter as well. Deciding to leave the fourth spot blank, Illume shook his head.

"I've got no one in mind right now, but we'll come across someone, I'm sure," Illume responded.

Nari gave Illume a playful push as she moved past him. Bending over, she grabbed Illume's chest of polis before looking back at him as she stood.

"How much of this do you plan on keeping?" Nari asked, cracking the lid slightly.

Illume walked over to her, grabbing several handfuls and placing them into his coin purse. *1000 polis added to personal coin purse.*

"I figured a thousand will be good for investing and item purchasing with the rest going back to our little camp," Illume replied.

"I was thinking the same thing. I used about a thousand to get two horses to help pull the carts. Our farmer friends have some cattle and their own supplies they are going to be bringing too, which will drastically save on costs."

Illume couldn't help but grin like an idiot. She had brains as well, another thing Illume found very attractive about her.

'She's just an NPC! Cool down, man!' he screamed to himself as he took the chest from her.

"Well then, perhaps we should head back and see how well the settlers are settling in!" Illume emphasized his pun.

Nari rolled her eyes and scoffed at his failed attempt to make her laugh. Brushing past him, she exited the bathroom and re-entered the main house. Illume followed, the weight of his money chest slowing him down slightly.

Reaching the main house, Illume was surprised to see over a dozen people eating their breakfast and packing their things.

Urtan approached Illume, a massive bag slung over his shoulder and an even larger dual-headed axe sitting on his back.

"Is Illume ready to leave with Urtan?" he asked.

Illume gave the orc a nod.

"Yes, I am, big guy," he responded. "Listen up!" Illume said, loud enough to get everyone's attention. "We have a vulnerable caravan, so this is what I want. Whoever is slowest, you take point. That way, you can keep the pace. Urtan, you stay with the leading cart because if we get ambushed, I'll need you to protect them. Can you do that for me?"

"Urtan smash!" he exclaimed with enthusiasm.

"Good, then what I want is the animals in the center of our column with their farmers surrounding them. Those with weapons who can fight will be spaced evenly throughout. I will take the rear in case there is any trouble. That way, I can move forward quickly. At night, we circle in, using carts and anything we can as a barrier between us and the rest of the world," Illume instructed. "We'll sleep in shifts. Our new town is a three-day hike from here, and since we will have been gone for almost ten days, there should be lodging ready for you to rest. Do you have any questions?"

Illume laughed at himself, feeling a bit like his kindergarten teacher while going on a field trip. Fortunately, nobody raised their hand, which was a relief because he didn't have much else planned other than his little spiel. Clapping his hands together, he nodded in approval.

"Okay, good! What do you say we go home?!" Illume projected loudly enough for everyone to hear.

In one big roar, the nearly two dozen people cheered before moving toward the door.

"That was quite motivational!" Trill's voice was steeped in sarcasm.

"Bite me, Trilly." Illume responded with a laugh before making his way out to the streets.

14

RETURNING HOME

THREE DAYS OF TRAVEL PASSED. They were uneventful, but it allowed Illume to meet all of his new townsfolk. Some had interesting stories, others were just filler NPCs, but the level of detail on every single person was amazing, down to the little scar above Sombria's eye that he got dueling with his brother when he was four.

Everything was planned down to the tiniest detail and regardless of whether or not they were real, Illume enjoyed getting to know them and genuinely started caring for them.

On the third day, Illume could see the quarry ahead. His jaw nearly dropped, as there was already a small house built, along with a larger tavern nearly completed and a sign that read Cryo's Quarry. The sign had a sigil on it that reminded Illume of a simplistic snowflake.

Illume moved to the front of his group as Abe and Balathor approached. Making a fist, Abe pressed it to his chest, bowing slightly. Assuming it was some sort of salute, Illume did the same.

"Illume, it is good to have you back!" Abe declared.

"That it is," Balathor added.

"It's good to be back. How have things been going?" Illume

questioned, turning his attention to Balathor after saluting Abe back.

"Things are moving along smoothly. We have a rudimentary barracks for people to sleep in and I expect that the tavern will be finished by nightfall," Balathor informed Illume.

Illume's brow raised.

"Why do we need a tavern? We have no brewers yet. What about a farmhouse or stables? Or even more housing? A tavern is a luxury. Right now, we can't waste resources on luxuries," Illume pointed out, trying to hide the frustration in his voice but failing.

Balathor turned his nose up to Illume before turning and walking off.

"I will have them focus their energies elsewhere then!" he called out as he walked away.

Illume and Abe made their way to the land bridge, allowing Illume to get a closer look at that symbol. He had to admit he was impressed and was curious as to who made it.

"While clearing the forest, Andreas found a river. He has been working for the past four days setting up irrigation in the flats behind Cryo's Quarry. He's even started sowing crops," Abe informed Illume as Balathor barked orders to people here and there.

"How has Balathor been?" Illume asked. Something about the man didn't quite sit right.

"He's been a leader, sir," Abe responded.

Illume rolled his eyes. He could tell a "diplomatic" response when he saw one.

"No need to censor yourself, Abe. How has he been, really?" Illume pushed once more.

"He's behaving as if he still runs the place. He wants what he wants and has threatened exile to the people who don't listen," Abe said with a huff. "I don't know if he is a bad man. He's just—well, I just don't know if he's a leader."

Illume nodded, dwelling on Abe's words as he tried to think about how to deal with Balathor. Reaching the flat of Cryo's

Quarry, Illume looked around; there were several tents pitched for those who didn't have room to sleep in the finished structure.

Passing the building, Illume peeked in. There was a single bed tucked away in the center, on the far end of the building. Something told Illume that was Balathor's.

"Urtan!" Illume called the orc to him.

"Yes, Illume?" he responded as he jogged over, each step shaking the ground.

"You are in charge of the markets right now. While we are small, our market will need to be here. As we expand and are able to get some walls built, I would like to allocate an entire section of the city to our markets. Find a spot to set up shop, make a list of things that you will need, then bring it to me, okay?" Illume questioned.

"Urtan is grateful! Urtan will do his best!" he roared with a nod before moving around the slightly elevated camp.

Civilian Job Assignment
Civilian: Urtan
Occupation: Merchant
Special Abilities: Boost of Gold;
Urtan is an excellent merchant, knowing the ins and outs of the business. Urtan will be able to cultivate your market given the opportunity.
+10% polis per trade deal
+10% ability to draw patrons.

"Nari!" Illume called as he glanced back at the bed.

"How may I be of assistance, my governor?" she asked.

Such an NPC response, Illume thought to himself. He thought they could program better.

"You and the dwarf set up a forge. It doesn't have to be anything fancy, but we will need rivets, nails, and hinges along with God knows what else." Illume glanced around as he spoke.

A hint of shame tugged at him for not knowing the dwarf's

name, but in sprawling RPGs like this, with hundreds of NPCs, Illume didn't have time to get to know everyone.

"We can do that. I already have a nice little spot picked out," she declared.

Making her way back to the small caravan, Nari grabbed a bag from one of the carts. She tapped the bearded lady's shoulder, and they loaded up on their blacksmith gear and headed across camp. Illume continued to look around.

He didn't see the people he was looking for. After several moments, Halfdan crossed Illume's path. Illume put his hand on Halfdan's massive shoulder to stop him.

"Several days ago, I sent a family here: a husband, wife, and two children. Where are they?" Illume asked.

Halfdan fidgeted for a moment, looking around as if expecting to be watched.

"They are Lycanthropes, sir," he whispered.

Illume nodded in agreement with him.

"I know. I saved them from hunters of the Order of Light, and as a thank you, Victor offered his loyalty to me. I accepted that loyalty, which means he's under my protection. Now where is Victor and his family?" Illume's voice dropped, worry invading his thoughts.

Halfdan hesitates for several moments. He glances at Balathor, who is shooing people this way and that.

"Balathor banished them to the base of the quarry," Halfdan whispered.

Illume's stomach turned upon hearing the news. A fire burned in his gut while Halfdan's breath turned visible. Halfdan took a step away from Illume as he seriously contemplated just killing Balathor. He still needed a steward, however, and there was no telling if another was able to be appointed.

"Balathor!" Illume roared, getting everyone's attention.

Illume turned his attention to the old man. He took several steps back and smiled nervously, waving at Illume.

"Y-yes, my lord?" he stammered.

Illume hardly noticed his mana falling as the air around him grew colder.

"Where are Victor, Kassandra, and their children?" His question was rhetorical, and had he been a dragon, it would have been laced in fire.

"They offered to stay at the base of the quarry, f-for our safety." Balathor almost sounded like he was trying to convince himself.

It took every fiber in Illume's being not to draw his sword and cut Balathor in half. Instead, he reached out, grabbing Balathor by the back of the neck just as his mana bottomed out.

"Then let's go pay them a visit!" Illume snarled, almost as beastly as Victor would.

Shoving Balathor, Illume made him walk back toward the land bridge. Passing the caravan, Illume noticed Andreas had touched base with the other farmers and had been discussing plans for the agriculture of Cryo's Quarry.

Passing everyone, Illume gave Balathor another shove as he slowed down, not due to his age. He was still spry and not so old that Illume felt bad for roughing him up a little.

"Hey, boss, do you want me to come wath you?" Trill called out as they passed the humorous "Irishman."

"No thanks, Trillian. I'm going to handle this myself." Illume shoved Balathor one more time. "Thanks for the offer, though," he called back.

Balathor tried to plead with Illume as he escorted the former governor to the base of the quarry. Hugging the stone wall, they made their way around the quarry's edge. After about twenty minutes of walking, Illume saw Victor, Kassandra, and their two children sitting around a fire with two small makeshift tents.

Balathor stopped, and Illume shoved him once again to get him moving. Upon seeing Illume approaching, Victor stood to his feet, his expression violent.

"You told us we would be safe here!" Victor called.

Illume drew near then, grabbing Balathor by the shoulder and pushing him to his knees.

"And I meant it," Illume responded.

Noticing his mana had returned, Illume channeled just enough frost through his hand to hurt. Balathor let out a grunt of pain.

"This… THING has something he'd like to say to you," Illume commanded.

"I-I-I'm so sorry I kicked you out," Balathor whimpered.

"I'm not convinced," Victor snarled.

Illume shrugged.

"Me either. What was that?" Illume asked, this time actually inducing frost onto Balathor.

"I'm sorry! I thought you would be a threat to our people! I was just looking out for their best interests!" Balathor sniveled.

"Victor, you and your family pack your things. You're not sleeping down here one more night," Illume commanded with a soft tone.

Immediately, Victor's children grabbed their toys and clothes. Kassandra did the same as Victor glared at Balathor with a deep-seated animosity.

"I beg your forgiveness to my lord! I didn't mean to go against your wishes," Balathor continued to whine.

Illume wasn't going to lie; he enjoyed the whole "my lord" bit. It would be more convincing if Balathor didn't seem so skeevy.

"Balathor, this is your camp now. You may have what Victor's family leaves behind. I don't want to see you inside Cryo's Quarry unless the sun is high in the sky." Illume's voice dropped as he handed down his sentence.

Illume continuously reminded himself that Balathor was responsible for the burning of Tanner's Folly and the deaths of nearly 90 percent of his people. That he had most likely raided his city's own coffers, which was why the vaults were empty. And that he had clearly made women and children sleep outside while he hogged a building that was big enough for thirty people.

Victor and his family packed almost everything save a few

scraps of food and a sheet that wouldn't warm a rabbit in the desert. As they moved past Illume, Balathor dropped to his knees and began to plead.

"My lord, my lord, this is all some kind of misunderstanding," Balathor said, looking around at what was to be his new home. "I was just telling our new friends to stay out here and enjoy the fresh air for a bit. They can come inside the city, of course they can. Just please don't leave me out here. I'm not built for these kinds of things. My skin is too soft to sleep on the ground; it's a condition."

His pleas fell on deaf ears. Illume turned and caught up with Victor and his family.

"I apologize greatly for your treatment at the hands of Balathor. As a sign of good faith, I would like to offer the structure that they have completed to you as compensation for his assholery." The bite in Illume's voice was softened now.

"We accept your apology, but we will not take charge of that home until all of your people have a place to live," Victor replied.

Illume couldn't help but smile, placing a hand on Victor's shoulder.

"OUR people... all of our people, Victor. You're one of us," Illume asserted.

As they returned to the rapidly developing town, all eyes fell on Illume as he climbed onto one of the carts.

"Ladies and gentlemen of Cryo's Quarry! This is Victor and Kassandra. Their family is part of ours now. Victor agreed to be part of the night guard. I know most of you are hesitant about having a family of Lycanthropes in this city. Mark my words, they will not be the last." Illume announced, "Cryo's Quarry is a haven for those destitute, homeless, and outcasts. So long as you live in peace, you will be welcome here. If that is too much of a problem for you, you may join Balathor," Illume declared loud enough for everyone to hear. "He's taken to the camping life outside of the city."

Illume looked around. Finding Trill, he pointed at his new friend.

"Should Balathor try to steal any supplies, do me a favor and remove his hands." Illume's tone dropped a little lower so not everyone could hear.

"It'll be my great pleasure," Trill purred.

"Now, the sun will be setting soon. I want the farmers to help Andres finish preliminary irrigation. Those of you who are part of the market, find Urtan and ask him what he needs you to do. He's in charge of our markets. Those strong enough can gather lumber, I want you to retrieve as many trees as you can before it grows dark and everyone else… move beds into the completed structure. I want as few of you sleeping outside as possible," Illume instructed. "And if anyone has experience caring for a small city, please come to me. Cryo's Quarry is in need of a new steward."

As Illume finished speaking, everyone scattered to follow his commands. Jumping off of the cart, he turned his attention to Victor.

"Victor, get your family settled in and get some rest. You and I will be taking first watch tonight and I want you well alert." Illume offered Victor a smile as he spoke.

Victor nodded.

"Yes, my lord," he responded, bowing slightly, then turned to lead his children to their new home.

Illume was taken aback by the "my lord" from Victor. That was truly a strange thing to hear an alpha say.

"Thank you for keeping your word," Kassandra whispered. "You know, being the wife of an alpha, I do have experience running a town. Given it is slightly different, as ours was more of a pack, but I would like to offer myself in consideration for the role." She seemed almost pleading as she spoke.

Illume pondered for a moment, wondering if she would make a good steward, if he could even grant her stewardship. Giving in, he nodded in agreement.

"We will try it out. If things get to be too much, please don't hesitate to speak with me," Illume offered with a grin.

A flash of light shot to the sky from over the edge of the quarry's cliff. That same flash of light dropped onto Kassandra as she walked away. No one else aside from Illume seemed to notice, just like no one noticed the trumpets, coins, and dings that constantly happened around him. Speaking of which:

Civilian Job Assignment
Civilian: Balathor
Occupation: Stripped of Title, Balathor had NPC exclusive quests that are now locked to you.
On the other hand, new quests will be available now that Balathor is gone.
Great job ruling your city with an iron fist, buddy!

Great, more sarcasm. Illume hoped that nothing too useful was now closed off to him.

Civilian Job Assignment
Civilian: Kassandra
Occupation: Steward
Hunters now gain +33% chance of running into wild game while hunting.
City's defenses +10 Lycans are always good to keep around.

15

GEARING UP

WITH THE ADDED bodies to help out, Illume was able to finish a makeshift gate to block off the land bridge. It wasn't pretty, but it would stop any bandits from trying to get in.

The first people to take beds in the safety of Victor's new home were the children. It was nice to see that Khal had kids his own age to play with, unlike Illume, who only had his siblings to play with. It wasn't their fault that his father spent most nights with a beer in hand, which made it impossible to go to other kids' houses or have other kids come over. Illume always assumed it was a coping mechanism for their mother's death.

Next were the women, starting with the mothers, before working their way back to the more combat-ready women. After that, a handful of men were able to fit into the structure, leaving ten men, Illume included, and Nari to sleep in tents. Illume took the first watch at the gate, standing with his hand on the grip of his weapon while keeping his eyes trained on the receding tree line.

With the moon full, its light was illuminating enough for Illume to be able to see deer grazing before bounding off and wolves lurking in the plains below, all of whom gave Cryo's Quarry a wide berth.

"You know the blessing of Lycan would be vary useful right about now." Trill's voice was hushed.

Illume's heart leaped into his throat. He didn't see or hear Trillian approach. He wasn't listening for anything that could be sneaking up.

"Dear Lord, Trill! You can't just sneak up on people like that," Illume whisper-yelled at him.

"Sorry, didn't mean to startle you. Why not have Victor or Kassandra bless you again?" Trill replied in a similarly hushed tone.

"I'm not here to exploit people, Trill. We will have Lycanthrope eyes watching at night, but while I'm here, I will take first watch," Illume responded with a hint of compassion in his voice.

"You're a good man, Illume, far better than most men I've met. I have noticed you have a bit of trouble with the ladyfolk. I'm a bet of a ladies' man myself…" Trill bragged.

"You sure? Because so far, the only person you've managed to wake up next to is me," Illume interrupted jokingly.

Trill stifled a laugh and nodded in agreement while leaning against the gate.

"That may be true, but I'd like to help build your confidence. I see the way you look at Nari, the way she looks at you. And I've heard the absolute cart wreck of things you've said when trying to interact. Let me help you build that confidence, and maybe, next time you go to market, you'll actually be able to sell something worth anything." Trill offered Illume the grin of a used car salesman.

Letting off a laugh, Illume nodded in agreement.

"Okay, fine, tomorrow while we work, you and I will be paired together and you can teach me what you know," Illume relented.

"Good! Now there is a soft bed over there for me. I'm going to get a bit of rest. See you at next watch!" Trill proclaimed.

Patting Illume on the shoulder, Trill made his way to a nearby tent and climbed in. Illume kept his eyes peeled on their surroundings, deciding his people needed far more rest than he did.

Illume stayed up all night, not waking anyone to relieve him as he drank in the beauty of the glistening stars overhead.

The horizon changed from black to blue. Stars vanished as daylight broke. The sky turned to a fiery pink, reflecting off once darkened clouds. A soft smile formed on Illume's face as he watched the sun rise.

It was peaceful, allowing Illume to harken back to his days at boarding school. He would sneak out of his boarding house before sunrise and go to the shore of Lake Mälaren to watch the fiery sunrise over the shimmering waters and green hills.

"Have you been up all night?" a voice asked.

Illume turned to see Nari approaching him with a cup in her hands. He nodded as she offered him the cup.

"Would you like a drink?" she asked.

"Pleasady please please…" Illume said before screaming at himself, *'SHUT UUUPPPP!!!'*

Nari let out a laugh as Illume took the warm cup from her.

"Sorry." Illume groaned at his own embarrassment.

"No need, some people just don't know how to talk to the opposite sex. I used to be the same way." Nari responded, resting her hand on a hammer that sat on her hip.

Illume smelled the drink. It had a smoky scent to it, almost as if dried leaves were burning.

"What is this?" Illume asked.

"I call it black mana. It's a little something I discovered a few years ago," she replied.

Illume took a sip, the smoky flavor dancing across his tongue with a hint of bitterness to it. A familiarity strikes him as he realized what it was he's drinking.

"Where I'm from, we call this coffee," Illume added before starting to walk toward the livestock, huddled together in a makeshift pen. "I can drink this stuff by the gallon. I want to show you a little something that makes it better," he continued. "I'm a city man now, but my upbringing was a little country. We had our own livestock on the farm. One of my chores was to care for the cows."

Nari followed close behind him as Illume made his way into the pen. Kneeling down, he squeezed one of the cow's teats, causing some milk to squirt out. Placing his cup under the cow, Illume caught the milk in his coffee, changing it to a caramel color. Standing, Illume held the cup back out to Nari.

"Give it a try," Illume encouraged.

After a moment of hesitation, Nari took the coffee and sipped it. Her eyes bugged out.

"By the gods, this is amazing!" she exclaimed loud enough to wake up half the camp. "Why have I not thought of this before? Of course this would work, but it never crossed my mind."

Illume reached out and stole the cup from her.

"None of that now. You brought it for me, remember!" His words were laced with laughter.

"Right, I'm sorry. I'll just make some myself," she quipped back.

Cryo's Quarry began to stir. People climbed out of their tents and funneled out of the house as the sun crested over the horizon. Most looked groggy, but several were ready to get to work.

Illume finished his coffee as his people grabbed breakfasts of bread and cheese. Nari returned to work on her forge and Illume couldn't take his eyes off her. She seemed so real, even compared to the impressive NPCs he'd come across.

Illume strolled through camp, sizing up each new addition as he thought of tasks that needed to be done throughout the day. Mentally allocating chores for each person as he passed them, Illume stopped at the gate where Abe and Victor stood discussing defenses. Both men stopped before Illume could hear any specifics and salute him. Illume saluted back.

"What do you have planned for today?" Abe asked.

Illume pointed to the forest.

"I want five strong men bringing in trees. We'll need two

hunters. I don't want everyone living off of bread and cheese alone. We'll have two chefs—the bandit we captured will be one. Get someone to watch him closely who has an affinity for food to help," Illume instructed. "Five of our best farmers will help Andreas prep the fields and sow crops. Anyone else that is strong enough will be helping with construction. If they can't help build, they will sew clothes, make sheets, and work with teaching the children." Illume pointed here and there as he spoke to both men.

"Any questions?" he added.

Abe and Victor shook their heads.

"Not at all. We'll get to work," they said, almost in unison before moving through the camp assigning tasks.

Illume pulled the bolts of the gate to their unlocked position before pulling on the heavy structure, allowing it to swing inward. Illume let the gate rest on the ground before turning his attention to the land bridge. Jumping slightly, his hand instinctively went to his sword as Balathor stood at the gate, dark circles under his eyes.

"May I enter your city, sire?" Balathor asked, his reverent tone steeped in sarcasm. He looked as bad as Illume could ever remember seeing him.

Illume released his grip on his sword.

"Balathor, if you are going to come in, you are going to help with construction. For your labor, you will be fed and we will provide you with a tent for tonight, and if we catch you stealing anything, you will be banished from Cryo's Quarry and all the land she rests on. Do I make myself clear?" Illume spoke with a distinctive authority.

"Of course, my lord," Balathor responded with a bow. "You are as gracious as any."

Balathor pushed past Illume and walked into Cryo's Quarry. Illume soon followed, coming across the stonemasons huddled over a piece of paper. Illume leaned in, getting a glimpse of their sketch. An involuntary gasp left his lips. It was a beautiful stone city with high walls and battlements that would have put even Lapideous to shame.

"Are these your plans?" Illume asked as he picks up the sketch as if picking up a baby.

"That they are," one of the masons replied.

"This is beautiful," Illume marveled. "What do you need to turn Cryo's Quarry into this?" Illume asked, glancing to both men over the paper.

"We'd need men," one said.

"Lots of men," the other replied.

"We'd need money and access to heaps of stone, and time. That will take time," added the first.

"I can allow you to hire on ten men of your choice to help you right now. Our defenses and our cities infrastructure is a top priority, I would like to have fifty men under each of you at some point. Speak with Kassandra; she will be able to let you know what we can spare to get you started." Illume set the paper down as he spoke.

The masons' faces lit up with massive smiles before one of them stood and ran off. The others gathered their things together before starting to work on a list. Illume left the masons to their work and approached a group that had gathered near the would-be tavern.

Taking his sword off, Illume leaned it against a tree that had grown up on the quarry's peak. Taking his armor off as well, he placed it into an orderly pile.

"Today's goal, finish this and turn it into an inn. That way, we have a small source of revenue coming in AND not everyone has to sleep in the same room," Illume called out, loud enough for everyone to hear.

Illume's suggestion was met with a roar of approval. The men who were armored or armed, stripped down like Illume and set up ladders, leaning them against the nearly finished structure.

"What would you like me to do?" Khal's voice was unmistakable at this point.

Illume turned to the boy, offering him a friendly smile before kneeling down.

"I want you to learn as much as you can today. Urtan, the orc, may have some wares that you will find useful in your potions," Illume suggested as he reached into his coin purse and placed several polis into Khal's hand. "Why don't you practice on those? Any city worth its salt needs a good alchemist."

Khal thanked Illume before taking off in the other direction, screaming for Urtan.

"You know, for someone who's never done thas before, you're a natural leader," Trill taunted as he dropped his armor next to Illume's.

"What can I say, I was born for this," Illume declared. He had to admit that he was starting to look more and more forward to working his way through the game.

16

HELPING HANDS

ILLUME HAMMERED the last strut into place, sweat pouring from his body, soaking his clothes. He attempted to wipe some off of his eyes. The salty liquid caused them to sting. Illume let out a soft chuckle as he descended the ladder, amazed at how realistic this simulation is. Reaching the ground, Illume took a deep breath, only to realize that he was feeling thirst for the first time since arriving.

A barrel sat under the tree, filled with water. He didn't know who put it there, but he was glad someone thought of it. Moving to the barrel, Illume took a scoop with the ladle that hung inside and drank from it.

The cold water immediately quenched his thirst, as its satisfying consistency almost instantly rehydrated him. Wiping the dripping water off his chin, Illume nodded to Kassandra as she approached him, a book in hand.

"How are we doing, Kassandra?" Illume asked.

"Well, by day's end, Andreas says they will have enough crops sown to sustain a population of three hundred or more. Also, Halfdan reports that their lumber will be enough to build several more structures. He suggests one of them be a lumber mill… he found a river tucked away in the woods." Kassandra turned her book over, handing it to Illume as she spoke.

Wiping sweat from his brow, Illume turned the pages of her ledger, noticing detailed reports and note-taking. He couldn't help but laugh to himself and the luck he fell on by his decision-making of appointing Kassandra as the steward. Illume noticed that they were already halfway through their polis count with only 8000 polis left.

Illume noticed a note stating that the masons had left to recruit and had brought several items that had been forged and enchanted to sell. They had been allotted a thousand polis themselves, which seemed steep at the moment, but that was none of Illume's concern, as he was the one who put Kassandra in charge of those affairs.

"Might I suggest we send a handful of people back to Tanner's Folly to scavenge for more items that can be sold?" Kassandra suggested as Illume returned her book.

"That's a good idea. Why don't you send Victor to lead the party. That way, if there are any issues, he can take care of them, no problem. Then the day after tomorrow, we will send a small group back to Lapideous to sell what was scavenged," Illume added.

Kassandra nodded in agreement with Illume before leaving to put together a scavenging party with her husband at the head. Everyone seemed to realize it was time for a break at the same time Illume did, making their way around the chef bandit's tent.

The former bandit ladled out bowls of soup to everyone with a ripped piece of bread at the side to dip. As Illume made it to the front of the line, the chef offered him a smile.

"Thank you for allowing me to do what I am passionate about, Illume. I know I have a long way to go to earn your trust, but I promise until then I will make the best dishes I can come up with to keep you and your people's hunger satisfied." The chef seemed genuinely happy as he spoke.

Illume took a bite of the soup. His knees went weak at the

sheer perfection of the hot broth-y meal. Pointing at the soup with his spoon, Illume let out an audible MMMM at the many flavors that were intricately layered into the meal.

"Keep this up and you will be head chef in no time!" Illume proclaimed.

Civilian Job Assignment
Civilian: Tantor
Occupation: Chef
Special Ability: Iron Chef
When Tantor says he's the greatest cook alive, he isn't lying.
+40% success rate for diplomatic missions when Tantor's cooking is involved.

Sitting down, Illume spent about an hour eating and letting the food digest. Hardly anyone spoke to one another as they were so enthralled with their meals that the last thing they wanted to do was let it grow cold.

Several of the children, including Kassandra and Victor's children, moved through the camp taking dirty dishes and bringing them to a makeshift sink to clean them. They laughed and giggled as they make a game out of their work.

Illume pulled himself to his feet and walked around the largely empty budding town as most of its inhabitants were still eating. He was impressed with how quickly they worked.

Two more foundations had already been dug and were almost ready to be laid.. Illume took a deep breath, holding down a swell of pride that attempted to grow in his chest before returning to his people as they got up to return to their projects.

"What do you want to work on now?" Trill asked as he approached Illume while wiping his chin on his sleeve.

"Well, there is a river not far from here; the farmers have already tapped it for irrigation. Why not dig a moat a ways out to offer a little more protection?" Illume suggested.

"That sounds good to me. I'll gat the shovels and meet you out there," Trill exclaimed before leaving to retrieve their needed gear.

Illume walked over to the forge where Nari and their dwarf friend hammered away making nails and equipment for farming.

"How are things going over here?" Illume asked.

"Well, we're starting to run low on iron and steel for tools and building materials. I'd say we have enough supplies to last us a day or two at the most, then we'll have to shut down the forge until we can get some more materials." Nari responded, wiping sweat off her brow, replacing it with soot.

Illume nodded; they were starting to run low on supplies AND money. He needed to come up with a plan and fast to prevent Cryo's Quarry from collapsing in on itself.

"Victor is returning to Tanner's Folly. Tell him what you need so he can keep an eye out for supplies," Illume suggested.

"Better yet, I'll go with him," Nari interjected as she put her hammer down. The dwarf nodded in agreement. "I'll be able to decide what is better to bring back and leave behind," she continued before leaving her station.

Trill approached Illume, holding out a shovel, which he took. Movement of six other men behind Trill caught Illume's attention. They all had shovels and pickaxes and began to move toward the exit.

Leaning against Victor's home, behind the men who would assist in the trench dig, was Balathor, fast asleep. Illume wanted to wake him up, but the pain in the butt probably didn't sleep a wink last night, and Illume wasn't heartless.

Illume and Trill fell in behind the other six men, their shovels resting on their shoulders. Passing Kassandra on their way out, Illume informed her that she was in charge and he was going to dig a trench.

Making their way out of Cryo's Quarry and nearly a hundred yards away from the land bridge, Illume began digging. He instructed his men to keep any stones that turn up and place them on the inside of the trench that was ultimately going to be ten feet deep and ten feet wide.

Illume and his crew dug, making shallow ruts as guidelines before actually starting the digging process. When asked why they were so far out and making the moat such a far distance from the main town, Illume pointed out that they weren't just building a town, they were building a city. He went on to explain that, yes, the moat might be impractical now, but as the city grew, they would not have to dig a second moat later.

While digging, the sun began to set and Trillian coached Illume about how to not only speak with women, but how to feel confident enough not to sound like an idiot around them.

"Af you think you might start stuttering like an oaf, then take a moment to pause and gather your thoughts," Trill said, resting his shovel in the ground for a moment. He leaned on the handle. "It's better to seem quiet than trip over your words like a moron."

"Great, thanks, I think," Illume said with a smirk. "Is all the name-calling necessary?"

"Oh yeah, it helps with the lessons I'm teaching ya." Trill grinned.

The initial ditch for the moat was only about ten inches deep and five feet wide, but all the men seemed to move at an impressive rate. As the sun began to set and the hunters returned with two deer and several birds, Illume and his team of diggers had finished one long ditch that reached the entire length of Cryo's Quarry.

After complimenting them on their work for the day, Illume informed his men that over the next few days, they would be finishing the other three sides as a template so that others could cycle through moat duty.

His hands burning, Illume looked down at them; they were blistered and dirty with countless splinters. Trill placed his hand over Illume's, letting off the same white light, and the pain in Illume's hands dissipated. As Trill stopped casting his healing spell, Illume was pleased to see his hands return to normal.

"You have to teach me that spell!" Illume exclaimed, astonished at its effectiveness.

"I can't. It can only be learned from a healing tome and those are very rare," Trill responded.

Illume gave a grunt of disapproval. At least Trill would be in his party and able to help with healing. Climbing the land bridge back into Cryo's Quarry, Illume spotted Victor handing a toy doll to his daughter. He hadn't seen them return but clearly their job was a success.

Illume approached Victor as he stood up and wiped his hands on his clothing. Offering Victor a friendly smile, Illume nodded to Victor's daughter.

"I assume things went well at Tanner's Folly?" Illume asked.

"Better than expected. We found a hidden vault that was full of gold, jewels, and thousands of polis pieces. It confirmed that Balathor was stealing from his town. Nari salvaged several buckets of nails and scrap metal she said she'd be able to use. Overall, it was a good trip," Victor informed.

Victor nodded over to a new cart they had found, as well as several fresh horses and a bull and cow they didn't have before.

"Great work, Victor. Any valuables that can be sold, make sure they are given to our merchants before they leave the day after tomorrow, okay?" Illume said.

"Yes, sir, and thank you for taking first watch last night. I'll take it tonight," Victor offered.

Exhaustion set in as Illume offered Victor a thumbs-up and made his way to the nearest tent, wanting nothing more than to let the weariness from his hard day's work take over. In the tent, Illume found his armor set aside with his sword and a nicely made bed waiting for him. Not knowing, and at the moment not caring, who was responsible for the kind gesture, Illume collapsed onto the soft bed as the notifications began to ring in.

Attribute Increased.

Charisma: +22, drops to +14 when in the presence of women.

Congratulations! Your interactions of leadership and working with Trill have increased your lowered Charisma attribute by two.

Trophy Earned.
Name: Lead by Example
Type: Gold
Requirements: While building your base, don't just delegate. Take part in its formation. A leader who works with his people is the foundation of success. Well done!

Illume soon passed out and fell into a deep, dreamless slumber. The next day, Illume was awakened by Trill kicking the bottom of his foot.

"Wakey, wakey, fearless leader," Trill said with a mischievous smile. "The early sea serpent gets the bird, am I right?"

"Ugh," Illume said, yawning as he tried desperately to grasp on to memories of the delightful dream he was ripped from. "I was in the middle of the most wonderful dream."

"Yeah, I can guess who it was about, but lat's keep things like that on a need-to-know basis and I don't need to know." Trill screwed up his face. "I have no desire to know about your fantasies."

"It wasn't like that," Illume protested, wiping the drool from the corner of his mouth.

"Right, that's what they all say," Trill said, jerking his head outside the tent. "Come on, then."

Grabbing some breakfast, Illume then headed out with Trill and his six-man team, working all day on the next portion of the ditch. They made better time than before, and by the day's end, they had two and a half sides partially dug in.

The town got its first guests to stay in the inn that night, a businessman and his wife who were traveling to Lapideous from the unknown lands to the east. They paid handsomely as Illume played host to them after cleaning himself up from a long day's work.

The businessman offered to help them establish trade with Lapideous in regard to lumber, which Illume accepted. After dinner, everyone returned to bed. This time, a third building had been erected, set up as a bakery/kitchen for Tantor and the other chefs to sleep.

Now Illume, Trill, and just a handful of others were left sleeping in tents, but by week's end, they would all be in beds of their own. Assigning a new group of men to the gate allowed both Illume and Victor to sleep through the night in peace.

The next morning, Illume woke up to the sound of men yelling instructions to one another.

"This was your new home! Welcome to the city of Cryo!" one of the masons yelled.

"It's not much to look at yet, but we're building every day and making progress. You'll all be part of this soon enough," the other mason shouted. "It's good honest work you can be proud to partake in."

Illume pulled himself from his bed to see the two stonemasons returning on horses larger than a Clydesdale, each pulling a cart with five new men inside.

Illume grabbed his sword, fastening it to his waist as he approached his masons. He gave the gigantic horses a pat on the nose. Their fur was short and soft with a shine in it to rival most mirrors. Illume stopped at the saddle of one of the horses and looked up at the mason.

"Looks like your trip was a success?" Illume asked. The mason nodded.

"We were able to use the funds we earned through selling items to pay these men, and all of them wish to help build up the city," the mason proclaimed, looking back at the workers.

"Good, there is a ditch that we've started digging. I want it to be a ten foot by ten foot moat. You and your men are going to be in charge of finishing the moat and using what stones you find inside to start construction on a wall," Illume explained. "You can use one of these horses, but the other is going back to Lapideous today with the merchants. They have some wares they would like to sell."

The mason nodded in agreement, dismounting the horse. Andreas approached them, giving the horses water and food. Illume turned his attention to the merchants, who had already begun to gather. The businessman and his wife were with them.

"Travel safe. In three days' time, I want you to return. You will need some rest." Illume pushed on, only for Halfdan to step in his path.

"Illume, I found the perfect spot for a mill—but—we need you. There's—well, you should see it for yourself." His tone was solemn as he spoke, causing a knot to form in Illume's gut.

17

CAVES

ILLUME AND TRILL accompanied Halfdan to the woods where Halfdan and his people had been clearing out the trees. Having donned his full set of armor, Illume examined their clearing. On the far side of a small river sat a cave, mostly hidden by hanging moss, but something about the cave just seemed evil.

Opening his map, Illume noticed that most of the "fog of war" in the area had cleared in a circle that stretched several miles in all directions around Cryo's Quarry. That being said, it was all in black and white, save the paths that Illume had taken since arriving. Tanner's Folly was named, as was Cryo's Quarry and Lapideous. As Illume observed the map, a symbol faded in resembling a cave mouth. Its name faded in above the symbol. *Life Stealer Cavern.*

"I'm thinking there is another reason why Lapideous abandoned this quarry," Illume whispered softly, his heart racing as he closed his map. "This is called Life Stealer Cavern."

"I've hard of this place! It is said there is a lich inside that can drain life using magic. It is said in life thas lich was the creator of the first vampire." Trill had a hint of nervousness hidden in his voice.

"Well, we can't leave something like THAT this close to our

town. Halfdan, go back and assemble any volunteers that are willing to help us clear this cave. See if Nari has any silver she can fashion into crude weapons and get back here as soon as you can," Illume commanded.

Halfdan jogged back toward Cryo's Quarry.

"And, Halfdan, leave Victor and his family out of this!" Illume added with a shout. "They've been through enough."

In most lore, vampires and werewolves have similar origins, usually going back to the same source. If this lich was able to create vampires, he might have had a hand in werewolves that would make him Victor's alpha and someone he would be forced to obey. Illume armed himself with his bow and notched an arrow.

"You got any tricks that could light up a cave?" Illume asked Trill with a sly grin. "I don't know, can your butt glow like a firefly or something?"

"Not really. I've got a healing spell that gives off some light, but that won't be near enough to guide us safely through," Trill responded with a raised eyebrow, ignoring Illume's joke.

Illume nodded, wanting to get a peek inside the cave, mainly to test out map dynamics. Approaching the hanging moss, Illume drew his bow and aimed it into the mostly blocked darkness. Trill drew his sword and cut the moss down.

A blur overtook Illume's sight. He instinctively released his arrow and stepped to the side. Hitting the ground where he was standing, a massive spider, larger than an average St. Bernard, writhed and twitched with Illume's arrow burrowed deep into its maw.

Its life bar drained rapidly as black ooze poured from its wound. Eventually, the spider flopped over to its back and its legs curled up into themselves. Illume swallowed his stomach; it had leaped into his throat upon seeing the monstrous creature. The fact that its legs stuck up higher than Illume stood tall sent a chill down his spine.

Its fangs were nearly a foot long and appeared to be able to pierce any hardened armor. Its exoskeleton was so thick that had Illume not hit the arachnid in its open mouth, chances were he'd have experienced death number two.

"I thank I just broke a containment spell!" Trill cried out in concern.

Illume notched another arrow and looked back into the darkness, drawing once again.

"What do you mean?" Illume asked as he moved toward the cave's entrance. A cool breeze flowed out of the cave, racing across his skin and forcing goosebumps to rise over him.

"There are no spiders like that out here and our people haven't said anything about seeing evidence of tham. Chances are that moss was enchanted to keep things from getting out," Trill explained. "And now we just opened Pandora's box."

Illume pushed forward. Trill hesitated. He stammered in protest before cursing under his breath and following Illume in, igniting his healing spell to cast a pale light into the cave.

"Keep those eyes peeled. If you see anything, let me know," Illume whispered.

Moving several more feet into the cave, Illume fully intended to turn back in another fifteen feet. A soft glint of light caught Illume's eye from the darkness. Turning, Illume fired his arrow at the light source, which echoed through the cave with a resounding THUD. Illume slowly approached where his arrow struck, only to realize it was a chest.

Illume's heart rate dropped upon his realization. Pulling his arrow from the wooden box, Illume reached for the lid and opened it. A loud creaking noise echoed through the damp mold-scented tunnel until Illume managed to get the chest all the way open.

Peering inside, Illume found a dilapidated quiver filled with ancient-looking arrows. Next to the quiver was a journal that was tied shut with blackened leather.

A small coin purse sat in the chest's corner, as did a deep red leather-bound book that had a symbol on the cover that seemed related to fire. Gathering the contents of the box, save for the arrows, Illume exited the cave with Trill. *20 polis added.* Illume handed Trill his bow, followed by four arrows.

"Keep an eye out. I am going to give these a quick read," Illume demanded.

Illume opened the thin journal, only to find all but the last entry covered in old crusty blood.

Praetorian Alkon Horthorn of the King's Blood guard,

After a week of hunting the lich inside the cave system, I understand it was a fool's errand to try and hunt him in his own home.

Even equipped with the most advanced armor and weapons from the gnome wizards themselves, we are no match for him. I say 'him,' although I'm not sure that is accurate. It is a monster.

It has picked off my warriors one at a time. I will not allow it to kill more. Whoever is reading this book means you have dismantled the protective spell at the mouth cave.

It is up to you to defeat this nightmare. Use fire. That is its weakness. If there is any hope for you at all, it is in the flames of the righteous fire.

Kill it without mercy. The lich has had none on us.

Illume sighed. They would have been safe had he not decided to move in with Trill. Now they would have to clear the cave. Setting the journal down, Illume held the book with a flame on it. When he opened it, a burst of orange and red light erupted from the spell book. An intense heat enveloped Illume as he staggered back, instinctively dropping the book.

As he released the book and it fell to the ground, the light faded and it turned to ash, raining into a small pile before him. Illume felt a fever overtake him almost instantly as his body began to cook from the inside out.

Is this what a hotpocket feels like? Illume wondered as his knees buckled and he collapsed.

Ancient Spell learned.
Name: Flames
Ancient flames deal 5 points of damage and cost 3 mana per second.
Destruction skills increase damage output by 25% for each point allotted.
Knowledge of ancient flames allows a 20% resistance to fire runes.
Watch your step or you might lose a leg!

Illume's vision cleared, his fever dissipated, and a smirk formed on his lips as he made eye contact with a concerned Trill. Pulling himself to his feet, Illume opened his hand, and a flame burst from it, hovering in place. Walking to the cave entrance, Illume extended his arm and opened his hand.

Focusing just as he did while using ice, Illume sent a pillar of fire deep into the cave, filling it with light and even setting some tree roots ablaze. Involuntarily, Illume laughed at the power he was able to wield. After about half of the time it took for frost to eat through his mana, flames completely consumed his bar.

Illume dropped his hand as he grew curious as to why fire drained so much more mana than frost. Was it because it was an ancient spell? Was it because he learned frost from a "God of" book? Or was pyromancy just not a natural attribute of his? He wanted to find out. His thought process was interrupted by Nari.

"Did you think you all could go on a little adventure and not bring me along?" she yelled from several dozen yards away.

Behind her, Halfdan and three other men approached Illume and Trill, stopping momentarily to look upon the spider in horror. Moving along, they approached Illume.

"What is that?" Halfdan demanded.

"A giant spider. Apparently, they live in this cave, which was sealed, and we unsealed it... Now we have to go in and kill literally everything, otherwise we're all up a creek without a paddle," Illume informed everyone. "According to a journal we found, the lich that is in here believed to have an aversion to fire, so whatever you have that can burn, use it."

Illume turned his attention to Trill, who still had the bow drawn and aimed into the cave. The flames were almost out, save those clinging to the tree roots, offering just enough light that a torch wasn't necessary but still would have been nice. Illume grabbed a torch from Nari and used the burning roots to light hers. Returning it, she used her torch to light the others.

"I'll take point. The rest of you fall in behind me and keep an eye out in all directions. Trill, you are second in line and will be my archer. Anything jumps at me, shoot it," Illume instructed. Trill nodded in agreement.

Illume drew his sword with his right hand, allowing the flame spell to move into its passive state. He held his left hand in front of him, illuminating the path as he entered the cave once more.

Illume took the lead, with Trill and Nari side by side behind him, then each of the other six men in rows of two. They passed the chest that held the spell.

As they pushed deeper into the cave, a soft dripping filled the relative silence, with only dull echoes of their footsteps adding to the damp atmosphere. Illume kept a slow pace moving forward.

His eyes darted from one portion of the slick ground to another, seeking any traps that might be hidden. Throwing his hand into the air, Illume came to a dead stop as a tripwire caught his attention.

Following the tripwire, he noticed that it held a stick that kept several large, round rocks from falling onto anyone who broke the wire. Illume waved for everyone to step back.

Illume placed his sword against the wire, prepared to cut it, when a scuttling noise from the darkness stopped him. Raising his head, Illume heard more and more scuttling like little bony fingers on damp ground.

"Illume, we've got company," Trill whispered.

Illume sent a quick blast of fire forward. The pillar of flame illuminated the tunnel ahead, where dozens of large spiders resided, all of which immediately charged Illume. Illume staggered back, his heart jumping into his chest. Acting on instinct, he blasted the walls and ceiling with a wave of flames, leaving only the ground for the massive spiders to charge.

Trill released his drawn arrow, which found its mark in one of the spiders' faces. His projectile didn't stop there and continued to pierce three more spiders before stopping.

"HOLD!" Illume yelled to his team. He could feel their tension building behind him.

Had his concentration not been wholly focused on their impending attack, Illume would have been impressed with his archery level. The spiders closed in, tripping the wire and causing nearly a dozen massive rocks to fall from the cave's ceiling. The falling rocks squished several spiders before rolling down the decline, killing even more.

"NOW!" Illume yelled.

Illume led the charge, sending blasts of flames in two- to three-second spurts while traversing over the slick gore of their crushed foes. Trill fired as many arrows as he could, killing any spiders that attempted to flee, clicking to one another as they did. After several moments, all of Illume's mana bar, and Trill's arrows, their path was finally cleared.

Moving through the tunnel toward a lower and more open room, Trill retrieved as many arrows as he could while the remainder of Illume's team executed any screeching spiders that were injured yet still alive. A ding informed Illume he leveled up a skill:

Magic Increased:
Spike Magic now available for skill points.
Flames/Shock/Ice turn into sharpened projectiles dealing 15 magic damage +10 physical damage, costs 20 mana per cast.

Level Up Available:
Level 5 Reached
6 Attribute points available
2 Skill point available

Town now available to hold 200 people
Increasing by leaps and bounds!

Every level milestone reached you get a little extra points to use.
Don't spend it all in one place!

Illume pumped his fist slightly in excitement. He was getting better and the side notifications were getting nicer. Reaching the base of the decline, Illume noticed the tunnel opened into a vast cavern.

What little light they emitted was enough to reveal pustulating egg sacs and spiderwebs everywhere. No spiders seemed to be visible within their little area of light.

Taking advantage of the moment, Illume opened the map, only to see a zoomed-in version showing the inside of their cave. Most of it was greyed out, not allowing Illume to get a good look as to what lay ahead.

Sighing, Illume closed the map and pressed forward. Illume hit the egg sacs that appeared closest to hatching with a quick blast of fire. Immediately, they were incinerated, killing the babies inside.

Sneak Level Increase
Silence now available for purchase.
For three skill points, armor will no longer make noise while sneaking.

Oh snap! Illume thought to himself.

"Oh snap!" Trill whispered.

Illume glanced back to see Trill looking up, aiming his bow at the ceiling.

"Mind giving me a light?" he whispered to Illume.

Immediately, Illume lit the tip of Trill's arrow on fire. He released it, the flame illuminating spiderwebs that caked the cavern walls. Finding its mark, Illume's heart stopped, thanking God he was not an arachnophobe as the arrow pierced the thorax of a spider the size of a tank.

A deafening screech ripped over Illume and his team, causing his ears to ring before the beast dropped from its perch.

18

ARACHNOPHOBIA

"NOPE, I'M OUT!" Trill screamed.

The spider landed several yards in front of them and let off a bone-chilling rattle. Illume unleashed a blast of fire. It did next to no damage on the spider's health, only illuminating the beast enough for him to see its two-foot-long fangs and a stinger the size of a katana.

"Fan out!" Illume yelled.

Following his orders, everyone scattered while Trill vanished completely into the darkness with a girly squeal. The spider seemed to have all six of its remaining eyes trained on Illume as it scuttled toward him.

Illume beat his sword against his breastplate in an attempt to pump himself up. If he died, he would get two more respawns; if one of his people died, they were probably gone for good.

"Bring it on, Shelob!" Illume roared as he charged the prickly spider.

Even with the reference, this spider was many times larger than Tolkien depicted. Closing the distance between himself and the monster, Illume dive-rolled under its front mandible as it swiped at him. Aiming for a diagonal dive, his strategy proved sound.

The spider slammed its stinger into the ground, where Illume would have been had his leap been straight. Throwing his left hand back, Illume froze the stinger into the ground so completely that when the spider tried to turn, its stinger snapped off.

A sliver of the spider's health dropped, having lost a total of one-eighth of its health. Shrieking in pain, it slammed one of its center legs into Illume's chest; the blow felt like a sledgehammer before a sense of weightlessness gripped him. After a second or two, Illume crashed into a wall so hard, he lost half his health upon impact.

With the air being forced from his lungs and his ears ringing from the blow, Illume raised his head. He saw his people charging in, attacking the spider with everything they had. The only two people doing any real damage were Nari and Halfdan. Everyone else was just a distraction. Illume forced himself to his feet as he caught his breath, his lungs burning.

"I really need to start bringing potions with me!" he growled to himself.

Charging back into the fight, Illume noticed one of his men had been knocked to his knees. The spider stomped down at him, trying to crush him under its enormous foot. Illume slid between the spider and his soldier, throwing a torrent of ice at the foot before hitting it with a blast of flames.

The one-two punch of spell casting completely depleted Illume of his mana, but something he'd learned about in physics and chemistry turned out to be true. The rapid change of temperature from frozen to overheated fractured the spider's leg, causing a fountain of its black blood to splash onto the guard as Illume slid out of the way.

His spell knocked the spider down to nearly half health and caused it to stagger back. Illume felt a tinge of remorse about having to kill the creature, but something this size could easily overrun Cryo's Quarry.

Two streaks of light slammed into the spider's thorax. Illume looked to see Nari pulling her daggers free from their sheaths and sending them flying with surgical precision into the monster.

Each dagger caused its health to drop more and more until it had only a quarter of its health left. Illume helped his spider-blood-soaked man back to his feet as the rest of his team formed an offensive line to finish the beast. Out of the shadows above the spider, Trill fell into the flickering light of the flames that still illuminated this spider's lair. With a single stab into one of its eyes, the spider reared up with one final scream as its health bar dropped to zero.

Falling to the ground, Trill was thrown from the spider's back as its body twitched and surged, rolling over to its back before dying. Trill shook his entire body in disgust as he retrieved his sword before putting it back in its sheath.

"I'm all for taking down an eval lich! But fook the spiders! I'd rather face a bear as naked as the day I was born than these infernal things!" Trill exclaimed.

Illume couldn't help but laugh, glancing over to the soldier that was covered in spider guts.

"At least you're clean," Illume replied. He turned to the soldier who had nearly been pulverized by the spider's massive foot. "You've done enough. Scavenge what you can and return to the creek. Get yourself cleaned up, soldier."

The soldier nodded, grabbing his torch before heading back toward the exit.

"You ready to move on or are you going to whine some more?" Nari taunted Trill.

"Not funny!" he growled, shooting her a dirty look.

"Halfdan, you and your men okay?" Illume checked in. Halfdan raised a thumb in the air.

"We're a little banged up, but all intact," he responded.

"Good, we rest for a few minutes, then we're pressing forward. Trill, have you seen any more spiders?" Illume asked as his mana restored itself fully, as did his health.

"No, they are either dead or fled. There is a tunnel ahead that goes deeper into the caves, though. Something is wrong with the air that direction. It smells toxic," Trill shared with slight concern in his voice.

Illume walked to where Trill had dropped his bow. Retrieving it, Illume slung it on his back. Making his way to the spider whose exoskeleton seemed like it would make for fantastic armor, Illume retrieved his arrows, turning his attention to Nari.

"You think you could forge armor out of this stuff?" Illume asked.

Nari took a close look, shaking her head.

"I don't have the skill for organic material like this. I could use it to make arrowheads swords, and other weapons, though," she responded with a hint of confidence.

"Okay then, after we clear this place, we are going to harvest the spiders. Maybe they'll provide something we can sell, or give us a leg up on anyone who might try an attack," Illume declared. His team, aside from Trill, all seemed ready to go.

"Who's ready to take down a lich?" Illume asked with a laugh in his voice. Nari was the only one that raises her hand. "Let's go. Trill, would you kindly lead the way?"

"I hate you," he mumbled before taking point.

19

WHERE OTHERS FAILED

PRESSING FORWARD, Illume and his team dispatched several more spiders with ease as the death of their apparent "queen" left them more cowardly than aggressive. Illume burned any egg sacs they come across in an attempt to prevent a resurgence of the spiders at a later date.

Illume checked his map occasionally as they moved forward. The air grew more and more stale the deeper they delved into the cave. Everything appeared to be linear as any branch-offs of the main corridor were dead ends after about fifteen feet.

Nobody made any unnecessary noise, not wanting to attract any more attention than they needed to or even alerted the lich that apparently lived deep within these halls.

The corridor they descended through gradually to opened up. Illume noticed that parts of the wall seemed to be blasted away. Time had done its best to cover the destruction, but its abnormally jagged edges gave away the damage. Illume gave a quick blast of fire, brightening their immediate surroundings.

Illume's stomach turned at the sight, Nari gave an audible gasp, and even the hardened Halfdan and his men let out a form of a mumble. Surrounding them was a veritable ocean of skeletons, armor, and weapons. They appeared to be of all different ages and of different qualities. Clearly many civilizations that had risen and fallen had attempted to take down this lich.

Illume's heart beat so hard, he could hear it in his own ears. Adjusting his grip on his sword, Illume could feel his knuckles whiten as his mouth went dry. Every tiny noise caused Illume's head to whip one way, then another, expecting a flash of light followed by a painful respawn.

"Push forward," Illume whispered, doing his best to keep his voice from shaking.

Moving forward in silence, Illume's curiosity overtook him as he wondered how large this cavern was. They'd been walking for nearly five minutes and skeletons still littered the ground around them.

Illume brought up his map once more to see that they were in a final chamber. The far edge was visible and a wheel popped up, making the "saving" symbol in the corner of his vision.

"Stock up, everyone!" Trill whispered.

Illume closed the map to see Trill holding several potions of varying colors and sizes. He passed them out like water bottles at a marathon. Illume's eyes darted from side to side as he held out his hand. A cold sensation made him close his fingers.

Potion Added to Inventory
Name: Potion of Perfection
Attributes: Fully restores health, stamina and mana.
Increases regeneration of all three by 200% for 300 seconds.

A Gandalf meme Illume saw once appears in his mind as he whispered to everyone around him.

"Big open room, no enemies… This is a boss room. Brace yourselves." Illume flipped his sword to a reverse grip as he spoke.

Taking his bow off his back, Illume notched an arrow before continuing to move slowly forward. A cold blue light started to thrum on the far end of the room. Softly at first, but then it grew brighter. A pulse of energy bursts through the room, igniting torches that line the walls with the same cold blue flame.

"Drop your torches! Get a shield!" Illume yelled.

A mass of tattered robes attached to a skeleton holding a staff and wearing a strange mask rose out of a sarcophagus, completely encompassed in light. Its movements were jittery as it turned to face Illume. Two black holes where eyes used to be glared directly at Illume as if seeing into his very soul. Fighting the urge to void his bowels, Illume drew his arrow just as blue flames ignited in the lich's eye sockets.

Illume released his arrow and it found its mark directly in the lich's eye, knocking the beast's head back. The blow caused his health bar to appear, showing his attack literally did nothing. Illume kicked himself.

He had clearly just wandered into a dungeon that was meant for much later in the game. Illume grabbed two more arrows, firing them both. One struck the lich in the head, the other in his chest; still no damage.

Lifting its staff, a ball of blue light formed overhead, growing brighter and brighter with each passing second. Illume exhausted his arrows as Nari exhausted her throwing daggers. His health only dropped by a sliver.

The lich cast its spell. The force of it being cast was so powerful, it knocked everyone onto their backs, which was the only reason anyone survived.

The ball of blue magical light tore over their heads, narrowly missing them before smashing into the back wall, making it explode from the magical force. Illume clambered to his feet, grabbing a shield. He held it up just as a torrent of blue flame shot at him. The shield protected him, but it started to heat up rapidly and turn red.

"Flank that thing!" Illume roared.

His men got to their feet, grabbing shields as well before moving to the sides of the cave and charging forward. Illume cast a frost spell to slow the shields heating so it wouldn't melt onto him.

It worked, but only for a few moments before the metal failed. Illume dove to the side as the tail end of the lich's spell blasted past him, setting the bones on fire.

The lich caught his people's movements, turning its attention to them. It charged to another massive attack, leaving its side open. Illume rushed in, blasting it with as much ice as he could muster. The frost distracted the lich, interrupting its spell and slowing it down physically. On the other hand, his magic only seemed to heal the tiny bit of damage they had done.

Illume leaped into the air and drove his sword into the lich's chest, pinning it to the wall behind it. A critical hit notification flashed in the corner of Illume's vision. His heart sank upon seeing that just another sliver of the lich's health vanished. Illume's attack did manage to stun the lich, allowing his people to close in, all jamming their weapons into the masked monster's body.

All of their attacks, Trill's included, made his life bar drop less than ten percent. Trill, being the man of flourish that he was, slid his sword into the side of the lich's head. As Trill withdrew his sword, their opponent's mask fell off, revealing a skull with sharpened and elongated canine teeth. Its jaw dropped open and it let out an unearthly screech that made Illume, and almost everyone else, save Trill, drop their swords and stagger backward.

The lich moved toward Illume, and one of his guards charged in, attempting to strike it down, only for the lich to grab the guard, wrench his dagger from him, and bite his neck in an explosion of blood and screams. After it finished biting the guard, it flung him halfway across the room. Halfdan retreated to check on his man as Illume put both his hands up, one fire, the other ice, and blasted his opponent with a massive burst of mana. It did nothing.

"We aren't hurting it!" Nari screamed.

"Tell me something I don't know!" Illume responded as he

backpedaled. "Everyone, fall back!" Illume ordered as he tripped over a body, dropping his potion.

The bottle shattered on the floor in a glow of red, blue, and green plasma. The loss of his potion was hardly felt as the lich charged Illume and grabbed him by the throat. Illume felt his feet lifting off the ground as the lich grabbed him by the neck.

Hovering over the potion, Illume noticed that the lich's health dropped significantly. Gritting his teeth, Illume grabbed his dagger and sliced the lich's hand, allowing him to be dropped. Coughing as the lich snarled, Illume pointed to the potion on the ground while calling out to Trill.

"Use healing hands on it! Everyone else hold it in place!" Illume rasped.

Immediately, the remainder of Illume's forces charged in, picking up pikes and swords from the corpses around them before driving them into the lich's body. Once again, all their attacks did nothing, until Trill stepped in.

Grabbing the lich by the back of its head, Trill used healing hands on it. A white light flowed from Trill into the lich, causing it to scream and writhe. It attempted to strike Trill, but Illume managed to close the gap and grab its wrists, preventing its thrashing from doing any real damage.

Illume watched with joy as its life bar dropped rapidly. It only took about ten seconds of Trill doing his thing before the blue light of the lich exploded outward and its skeleton fell to the ground, just as lifeless as all the others.

Strangely enough, the blue torches remained lit. Illume let off a laugh as he staggered backward.

"How the hell did you know that would work?" Trill demanded.

"Lich, it's undead. Healing brings life. What happens when you bring life to something already dead?" Illume asked.

Grabbing a potion from one of his guards, Illume walked over to his injured man and gave him the healing liquid. As he drank it, his bite wounds closed.

"They cease to exist," Nari answered Illume's question.

"That's what I was hoping for!" he responded with a laugh.

"Wait, you dadn't know for sure that'd work?" Trill roared.

Illume shook his head as he approached the lich's resting place.

"It was an educated guess," Illume replied as he grabbed the lich's mask and staff.

Staff Obtained.
Name: Legendary Staff of Unyielding Magic.
Damage: +1000 to the living.
Weight: +18
Worth: 100,000 polis
Legendary Staff of Unyielding Magic was thought to be myth. It is said to have been responsible for the creation of all creatures that are considered unnatural.
Warning: Should the living wield this staff, the consequences will be dire.

Mask Obtained.
Mask: Lich of the Undead
Defense: +28
Weight: +9
Worth: 10,000 polis
Lich of the Undead is a mask that grants its wearer unending life. Most should consider its cost.

Destruction Magic Level Up
Dual Casting now available for point allocation.
Able to cast the same spell on both hands for an extra 5 points of damage, costs 2 skill points.

Heavy Armor Level Up
Deflector now available for point allocation. 15% chance to

deflect melee and ranged attacks back at their caster, costs 1 skill point.

The leveling up would usually bring a smile to Illume's face, but not this time. The data on these objects was terrifying and in anyone's hands would be like giving a toddler a nuke. Illume turned to face his people, holding up the lich's items.

"No one touch anything until we can comb this cave for any more magical items. No one is to know of these items, and when we return to Cryo's Quarry, any of the lich's magic we come across will be locked away in a safe inside a safe. Do I make myself clear?" Illume nearly stammered over his own words, but his team seemed to appreciate the gravity of his tone as they nodded in agreement.

Illume looked around, finding a cape that used to belong to a soldier. He pulled it free from the corpse's armor. Setting it on the ground, Illume placed the lich's items in it. Loot like this tended to corrupt characters that came in contact with it. Out of the corner of his eye, Illume noticed Trill giving him an odd stare.

"What's wrong, Trill?" Illume asked as he tied the cloak around his terrifying loot.

"I've heard about the worth of those items. My father showed me in an ancient text what they are capable of. With those, you could rule this world in a matter of days." Trill's voice was tense with trepidation.

"I could!" Illume responded, nodding in agreement. "But at what cost? Thousands, millions of innocent lives lost just so I can flex some magic muscle? The loss of who I am so I can blow a hole in a wall like it's made of glass? There are certain things in this world that are never to be messed with and these items are just that!"

"You're a rare man, Illume. I'm not sure I could have your strength," Trill whispered before walking back to the group. "You might just be exactly what this world needs."

Over the next few hours, Illume and his team scavenged every last inch of the lich's "home," only to find a dagger of undead that was said to resurrect those who were slain with it to fight alongside the knife's wielder. Not wanting a zombie situation on his hands, Illume opted to add it to the pile.

"Nari, why don't you return to Cryo's Quarry and start working on something that can contain this stuff," Illume suggested while indicating the staff.

"You sure?" she responded, clearly still wanting to help.

"Yes!" Illume re-enforced.

With that, Nari gathered a few items here and there, things she could use at the forge, before leaving the cave. A cloak was found as well that was said to enhance the power of any item their wielder was holding one hundred times. It also found its way into the pile.

After a thorough search to the point where Illume was satisfied with what they'd found, Illume and his team exited the cave. Trill and Halfdan collected spider eggs and certain mosses as they exited, as well as parts of the dead spiders. By the time everyone left the cave, the sun hung low in the sky and each member of Illume's team, himself included, were unable to move very quickly.

Unable to move swiftly while over-encumbered appeared in Illume's field of view. It did not go away. Feeling as if he were walking through knee deep mud, Illume looked around to see the others moving just as slowly.

"Now that the cave is clear, it looks like we can build that saw mill," Halfdan hinted behind labored grunts.

"Yes, you can build the saw mill," Illume replied like a parent having been asked for a toy by their child for hours before relenting. "And you'll get five whole people to help you put it together too."

"Wow, that dan't sound sarcastic at all," Trill marveled in a patronizing tone.

"Shut up!" Illume responded with a laugh.

It took nearly an hour for the over-encumbered group to return, grunting every step of the way.

By the time everyone returned back to Cryo's Quarry, the sun was nearly completely set. Illume placed the lich's items in his tent and sat down inside while watching Victor escort Balathor from the city.

20

A REQUEST OF FRIENDS

QUEST COMPLETE.

Name: Save Your City
Investigate the mysterious undead that is a curse on your city and deal with it.

Trophy Earned
Name: Jumping the Gun
Type: Bronze
Requirements: Complete a story mission meant for ten or more levels down the road.
Look at you! You're just such an overachiever!

THE NOTIFICATIONS PULLED Illume from his slumber, interrupting a dream he'd been having from his younger years when he was watching cartoons. His dad returned from work. He went straight into the kitchen and made Illume a ham sandwich before grabbing a beer, changing the channel to sports and sitting in his recliner. Illume would then boot up his Game Boy to help keep him company while his siblings worked part time jobs.

Illume groaned as he sat up. A dull throbbing reverberated through his chest and back from the spider's attack. He was happy for Nari's advanced skill in smithing, which was certainly what prevented his bones from turning to mush. Moving his attention to his loot, Illume was relieved to see that it was still firmly in hand.

Rubbing his eyes, Illume exited his tent. The sun appeared to have already been up for several hours and his little town had come to life. People went this way and that, doing chores, building structures. In the distance, an entire team worked on digging the moat. Stones were being harvested and shaped at the same time, forming the beginning semblance of a wall

Leaving his tent, lich loot in hand, Illume made his way to Nari's forge. He passed Kassandra, who sat at a table by herself handing out coins to a line of people waiting for their weekly wage. She offered him a wave, and Illume reciprocated the gesture.

Illume approached the forge where an exhausted Nari hammered away at a piece of molten metal. Illume's brow furrowed as he leaned against the little building that had been constructed for her. Holding his hand over the furnace, Illume felt the heat singe his skin, not enough to cause any damage but enough to satisfy his curiosity. Even the fire reacted realistically, causing a satisfied chuckle to exit his lips.

"Are you just going to stand there?" Nari asked, her tone sharp, probably due to exhaustion.

Illume turned his attention to her, shaking his head.

"No, but you look like crap. You okay?" he asked, kicking himself as the words leave his lips.

Nari offered Illume a look so cold that it made his frost spell seem like an inferno.

"Sorry, that came out wrong," Illume mumbled.

"You think?!" Nari's tone was still as sharp as her daggers. "I've been up all night working on a safe for you, so I don't want to hear it!" she growled.

As she pointed her hammer at Illume's face, he couldn't help but feel like it was meant to be a threat.

"How'd it turn out?" Illume asked.

He noticed her current project appeared to be more closely related to a plow. Nari shouted something in a language Illume didn't understand, probably the language of the dwarves. Moments later, Nari's forging partner emerged from their little storeroom with a chest in hand.

Thick straps of steel encompassed the wood core connected by thick rivets, the likes of which Illume had never before seen. A massive, intricate lock sat closed on the safe's front, left dangling open.

"Your order, my lord." The dwarf's voice was gruff, so much so had he not known she was a she, he wouldn't be able to tell.

Illume approached the chest, sliding his hand over its strong frame. He gave the rounded top a gentle push, and it opened without a squeak, allowing Illume to place his loot inside. Intricate concentric circles were carved within the box. They were mesmerizing and beautiful.

"What are these?" Illume wondered, running his fingers over the carvings. They flared a soft blue upon contact.

"They are forging spells I learned as a child," the dwarf responded with pride in her voice. "They reinforce the item that is forged, amplifying the skill of the forger. This box will not yield, not for the ocean, not for a mountain, nor for dragon fire. This box will hold strong."

"Thank you, both of you, for this. Your craftsmanship is unparalleled. Might I ask your name, my forger?" Illume asked, having no issue speaking to the dwarf.

"I am Buthrandir of Balacor. You may call me Buthy for short," Buthrandir introduced herself.

"It is an honor to meet you, Buthy. If ever you need anything, please reach out to me." Illume spoke softly, bowing slightly as he retrieved the chest.

"Actually, my lord, I do have a request." Her voice was tense with trepidation.

Illume set the chest down, sitting on it so he was eye level with the dwarf.

"What is it?" he asked.

"I have received news that my people have been taken captive. I don't know by whom, but they are across the great plains being forced to work in a mine. They are slaves, my lord. Dwarves are not meant to be slaves." Her voice trembled as she pled with him.

Illume glanced up at Nari for confirmation. She nodded. Illume sighed; he couldn't just let something like slavery go unpunished, even in a video game. Illume opened up his quest log to see that he had nothing pending. Closing the log out, Illume drew his sword and placed it, point first, into the ground before kneeling in front of Buthy.

"I swear to you I will find your family and return them home," Illume responded in a solemn tone.

Quest Accepted
Name: Rescue Buthrandir's Family.
Optional: Bring the slavers to justice.
Potential Perks: Dwarves are extraordinary craftsmen, having a few extra around will increase your town's overall defense and building quality.

The quest information was unique. No other quests had presented with potential perks before. Illume was curious exactly HOW important this quest would end up being. He would undertake it anyway, but how could anyone turn down something with such a foreboding potential perk?

"Thank you, my lord," she replied as tears of joy filled her eyes.

Buthy turned and ran into their storeroom.

"You know, you're not supposed to do that with a sword. Putting it tip down is a great way to blunt the instrument. How do you expect to be effective with a blunted instrument?" Nari taunted Illume.

Standing, Illume sheathed his weapon, offering Nari a sarcastic smile.

"That's what she said," he retorted, hoping it came out as cool as it sounded in his own head. It didn't.

Buthy returned with a piece of paper in her hand, holding it up to Illume, who graciously took it. He opened it up; the paper had a map drawn on it heading west. Almost instantly, the ink disappeared, only for the words *Addition to world map available* to scroll across his screen.

Immediately, Illume re-entered his menu, selecting the map icon. This time, a grey line was painted across his screen. The line moved west, across plains of crops and grass, skimming the southern tip of a forest before finally ending on the symbol for a city at the base of a mountain. Illume sighed internally. If Lapideous was a three days' journey, he was guessing that, moving very quickly, it would take nearly two weeks to go one way.

Why can't there be fast travel! Illume yelled at himself.

True, he'd still have to travel that one direction, but at least it cut his travel time in half. He was curious how much progress they'd make in a whole month, though. Illume dropped the map and offered a grin to Nari, who sighed as she set down her hammer.

"I'll go pack," she grumbled.

Illume laughed and shook his head.

"We leave at first light. You need sleep, so take the rest of the day off," Illume suggested.

Nari hesitated for several seconds before complying and wandering to her bed. Illume picked up his trunk and made his way across camp. It was starting to come together and actually look like a town now. Stopping by Kassandra, he set down the trunk and used it as his seat.

"Kassandra, I am going to be leaving again. Nari and Trill will be joining me and we will be gone for a month. Invest where you feel necessary, and if we start running low on funds, there is a cave near where Halfdan wants to build the mill. Inside that cave are countless sets of armor and weapons from years past," Illume whispered, not wanting to draw attention to the cave.

"I thought I smelled a change in the air. Was that earthquake because of you?" Kassandra whispered back. Illume laughed and nodded.

"Yes, it was. I trust only you, Halfdan, Abe, Victor, and the six men that joined me yesterday to clear that cave. Keep what could be useful, be it an enchanted item or armor suits. If Buthrandir needs metal, give her all she can handle. Sell everything else and use it to build up the infrastructure," Illume instructed. Kassandra nodded in agreement.

"Of course. Shall I take care of your trunk as well?" she asked as she glanced down at Illume's seat.

Illume hesitated for a moment. The contents were dangerous and that might be too much to ask of her, but she was the steward and an alpha's wife. He nodded.

"Please, don't, under any circumstances allow it to be opened, though. The contents are not to be disturbed." Illume's voice took a hushed seriousness as he spoke of the chest's contents.

"You can count on me, my lord," she responded with a playful wink.

Illume spent the rest of his day gathering the supplies they would need for the trip: bags of food, pouches of water and enough polis to get them there and back with plenty to spare. Trill was nowhere to be found, but Illume did not hunt for the man very hard. He deserved some rest.

"Illume, a word?" Victor said, rounding a corner to his left. "It won't take long."

"What's going on?" Illume asked, reading his friend's demeanor. He didn't seem angry for once. That was a good sign.

"Handar is requesting to be placed on the night watch," Victor said with a hard stare. "Since he was bitten by the lich, he says he can't sleep."

No way, Illume thought to himself.

"Do you trust him?" Illume asked out loud. "I mean, if he was bitten by the lich, are there side effects we should be worried about?"

"Side effects?" Victor asked.

"You know, can't see himself in a mirror, can't enter a house without being invited in, allergic to garlic?" Illume fished for an answer.

"I think you're thinking of vampires. Handar was bitten by a lich." Victor shook his head like a wet dog after a bath. "He just can't sleep for now."

"Well, I trust you, and if you're okay with it, then it works for me," Illume said with a nod. "Just keep an eye on him."

"As you wish," Victor said with a bow before departing.

Moving on, Illume swung by Urtan, who was constructing booths with the assistance of other merchants. Upon seeing Illume, Urtan finished tying off one of the covers and approached him.

"How are things going over here?" Illume asked, his eyes scanning several well-constructed booths.

"Things with Urtan go well. Merchants from Lapideous show interest in Urtan's new wares. Three even relocate for growth potential." Urtan spoke as a point of pride.

"That is incredible. Thank you, Urtan," Illume praised before asking, "These booths aren't permanent, are they? I want something a little more solid for our market, something more permanent."

"This is temporary. Urtan plans on having masons build shops into rock wall, create store fronts. Urtan feels structures bring higher paying clients, we can charge more," Urtan explained, pointing to the quarry's walls.

"That's a good idea. Defense first, then the shops can be made," Illume replied.

Urtan nodded in agreement, reaching into a little pouch on his side. Urtan pulled out a little glass flower that was blue. He held it out for Illume to see, its detail so fine, so intricate that the glass seemed to almost be alive.

"Urtan's new sculptures," he exclaimed with pride.

"That is beautiful, Urtan! How much?" Illume asked.

"Fifty polis," Urtan replied.

Without another word, Illume removed fifty polis from his coin purse. Placing it in Urtan's hands, he retrieved the flower for himself with the intent of giving it to Nari.

After obtaining everything he would need for the trip times three, Illume prepared bags for each of his party members. Illume placed the little glass flower at the top of Nari's bag, its twisted blue petals reaching for the sun like a real flower would. Had he not known it was glass, Illume would have believed the piece of work to be of nature.

"Going somewhere again, fearless leader?" the slimy voice of Balathor sounded from behind Illume.

He was surprised at how quickly Balathor seemed to change. Part of it could be thanks to his decision-making and how he treated Balathor, or it could be just part of his programming; either way, something about him sat wrong with Illume. Illume closed Nari's bag, cinching it tight before tying it off.

"I am, Balathor. One of our people's family has been taken captive and I am going to bring them back," Illume responded, not looking at the older man while tying Trill's bag shut.

"I would like to offer my services once more to you. I see now that you are a gracious lord, allowing me to stay close by in the quarry's natural shelter. I would offer my services to you however you would see fit." His words were like venom. They dripped from his lips in such a toxic manner that anyone who would be foolish enough to listen to them would certainly pay dearly.

"Kassandra, Victor, and Halfdan are in charge while I'm gone. If you want work inside the city, ask Kassandra. If you want a patrol, ask Victor. If you want manual labor ask Halfdan. You are not allowed to stay inside Cryo's Quarry at night. You must return to your camp. If any of them tell you to do something, you do it without hesitation." Illume's words were stern. He might be an idiot to let Balathor get close, but what could the repercussions be for alienating a man like him? "I will warn you, should you try anything that makes their hair stand on end, they all have permission to exile you. Am I clear?"

A slimy smile warped onto Balathor's twisted face as he bowed to Illume, albeit sarcastically.

"You are a gracious lord. I hope to prove myself in your absence," he almost hissed as he slithered away.

Illume caught a guard as he passed, informing him that Balathor needed to have a pair of eyes on him at all times, and that if he tried anything, an execution was permitted.

21

ON ANOTHER QUEST

THE MORNING CAME to leave for the west. With Cryo's Quarry requiring all their available horses, Illume toyed with the idea of traveling by cow, but dismissing the idea, as cows were not natural beasts of burden. The trip would not be fair for the slow-moving creatures. Lifting up his pack, Illume moved toward the main gate, waiting for Nari and Trill to arrive. Illume stood fully armored, bow on his back.

When he looked out over the plains as the sun rose, the merchants could be seen traveling back toward him. From Illume's point of view, the cart appeared to be full of assorted supplies. On either side were three guards in their Lapideous uniformed armor. Illume opened the gate as they grew closer.

Upon entering the city, Illume greeted the merchants, who pointed out that they had a successful trip, even managing to convince several other wealthier citizens to commence trade with Cryo's Quarry. One of the guards approached Illume, placing a hand to his chest, saluting him.

"I am Sergeant Caldwell, under the orders of Commander Stark. We six have been sent to help bolster your garrison." His tone was point of fact.

"Sergeant Caldwell, thank you for making sure my people

returned safely. And be sure to send my thanks to Commander Stark for offering us your services." Illume's voice brimmed with gratitude before continuing. "I will give you and your men the same offer I give everyone else. A place to live, in time a firm roof over your head, and an opportunity for those of you who have families to join us. But it must be voluntary. I do not want anyone that does not wish to be here."

Sergeant Caldwell turned to his men. Approaching them, he murmured to them in whispered tones. Illume got the distinct impression that they were taking a vote. After several minutes of deliberation, Sergeant Caldwell returned to Illume.

"We will stay. Two of my men will be bringing their families along," Caldwell reported.

"Welcome, then, to all of you! After you get settled in, report to Halfdan, he is hard to miss. He will give you your assignments and work out a training regimen with you to help make our defensive forces better," Illume replied. "Should you have any questions about the city, please touch base with Kassandra." Illume pointed her out as she passed several yards away. "She is my steward."

"With pleasure," Caldwell replied.

The sergeant led his men away. Once again, it was nice seeing elves not portrayed as racist or with a superiority complex.

"Stop chattin' with the locals. We got a long way to go," Trill taunted as he passed Illume, picking up a rucksack as he went.

"You're the one that's late!" Illume retorted.

"Waiting on you now!" Nari continued Trill's jest as she passed Illume, grabbing her bag as well.

Illume slung his pack over his shoulder, charging after them to catch up. Glancing back, Illume noticed Balathor was waiting at the gate like he did every other day. Curiosity tugged at him as to why this could be.

"Illume, wait!" a soft voice echoed over the quarry.

Illume stopped, turning back to see Khal running after them with a crate in his hands. Catching up to them, Khal huffed and puffed, holding the crate up. Inside were various potions and poisons.

"I made these. You might need them for this trip," Khal exclaimed.

"Thank you, Khal. I greatly appreciate this," Illume responded as he took the crate with +10 weight.

"Is there anything you'd like me to do while you're gone?" Khal asked as his eyes widened.

Illume paused for a moment, handing the crate to Trill before crouching so he was eye to eye with the boy.

"I want you to keep practicing your alchemy. You seem to have a gift and that should be nurtured. If we find anything that you can use, we'll bring it back with us, okay?" Illume promised while ruffling Khal's hair.

"Right away!" he yelled.

Turning around, Khal ran back to his little corner of the camp, disappearing behind some of the few remaining tents. Illume laughed before turning and continuing to move forward with Nari and Trill on either side of him.

"He's a cute kid," Illume remarked.

"The most kind-hearted boy you'd ever meet," Nari added.

"Well then, if he's so beautiful and parfect, why don't you two adopt him?" Trill tauntingly suggested.

Illume noticed that Nari fell eerily silent at Trill's suggestion. She glanced away, clenching her jaw. Illume recognized that expression; it's the exact same look his brother had when they found out he was sterile before exploring adoption. After several moments of tense silence, Illume finally decided to break the tension.

"We are adventurers. The road is no place for a child... Perhaps if one of us takes an arrow to the knee, we can return home and adopt the little alchemist," Illume suggested.

The remainder of day one continued much the same, in silence. There was an occasional comment here and there, but the overall vibe Nari was giving off clearly indicated she didn't want to talk.

Illume and Trill glanced at each other, having a mental conversation back and forth about how Trill's comment was a stupid one and how Trill had no idea about Nari's sensitivity to children.

As night fell, they set up camp. Nari volunteered for first watch as Illume used his pyromancy to start a campfire. Trill lay down, using his pack as a pillow before falling off to sleep and starting to snore immediately. Illume was astounded with how well the game could project sorrow and the awkward and intangible pain that often came with it.

Although he attempted to sleep, Illume was unable to as the soft sniffling and crying of Nari filled the silent night air. Rolling onto his back, Illume looked at the stunning forger sitting on a fallen tree. Her shoulders heaved in an unmistakable attempt at hiding a silent sob.

Illume sat up, making his way over to Nari, grabbing a blanket as he did. The night was cold and Nari's breath was visible. With her distance from the flames, there was no way she was staying warm.

Illume gently wrapped the blanket over her shoulders before sitting next to her. Illume said nothing; he just put a comforting arm around her. Both sat in silence for what felt like hours before Illume glanced back at Trill, who was snoring. An ornery grin formed on his lips as he nodded to the accented man.

"You want to help me shave parts of his head?" Illume asked.

Nari finally looked at him, her eyes bloodshot with a soft red tinge to her skin where the tears had rolled down. This was one time where Illume was happy that his awkwardness manifested in a humorous way.

"What do you mean?" Nari asked as she let off a sniff.

Illume drew the dagger that he kept on his lower back.

"I mean like shave a bald spot at the top of Trill's head so when we make it to Lapideous, everyone but him sees the spot and laughs," Illume explained.

"That sounds like a good idea, but we shouldn't," Nari responded with an attempted held-back laugh.

Illume sheathed his dagger and shrugged.

"Well then, I guess we'll just have to wait until we get near a water source," Illume led, baiting Nari into conversation.

"And why is that?" she responded, taking the bait.

"Well, when someone is asleep and you put their fingertips in warm water… how to put this politely?" Illume paused as he searched for the words. After several seconds of being unable to find them, he decided to be blunt. "They pee themselves."

The comment made Nari laugh some more, nodding as she covered her mouth with her hand. Illume liked the way she smiled, her pearly white teeth, the glint in her eye, the shyness in her shoulders.

For an NPC, she felt… real. Nari ran her fingers through her hair, pinning it back behind her ear. This was the first time he saw them since he'd been in this world. To his surprise, they came to a point at the top.

"You're an elf?" Illume asked. She'd just become even more attractive to him.

"I'm half elf. I don't know who my father was, but people joke he was a dwarf because of my skill at the forge," she replied.

"Eh… I don't think he was a dwarf. I mean, no offense, but if Buthy is anything to go off of, you'd at least have a five o'clock shadow," Illume replied as he rubbed his fingers over his own growing scruff.

"And how do you know that I don't?" Nari retorted, her playful eyes dancing in the shadows cast by the firelight.

Is she flirting with me? Illume thought to himself.

"Well, if you do, you HAVE to tell me your secret because that is the absolute closest shave I have ever seen." Illume played along, gently rubbing her soft, warm cheek with the back of his finger.

Illume didn't even realize what he was doing until Nari's blink slowed as if she were savoring his touch. His heart slammed against his ribcage like a war hammer and his mouth instantly went dry.

He could feel himself about to say something idiotic and had to abort before this beautiful moment turned into a train wreck.

As Nari's eyes opened, she gazed into Illume's; it was a look he'd only really seen once before and it wasn't even for him! Illume tried to swallow hard but was unable to thanks to his dry mouth. He dropped his hand from her cheek as it trembled with nerves.

"Why don't you get some rest? I'll take second watch," Illume managed to squeeze out.

Nari's eyes changed from kind and warm, almost inviting, to cold and frustrated. With a *'fine,'* she got up and moved to a spot around the fire, lying down before giving an audible huff. Illume breathed a sigh of relief. He might have shot himself in the foot just now, but at least he didn't quote a movie, say something cheesy, or completely kill whatever THAT just was.

Standing from the log, Illume paced to the edge of their little clearing to the waist-high grass. He ran his hand over the blades, and they tickled his palm as he sighed, glancing back at Nari. Illume shook his head. He wanted to kiss her full, soft lips, but he froze, *AS PER-FREAKIN' USUAL!*

"Illume,
You suck!
-Sincerely,
Illume,"
he whispered to himself before a soft ding rang in his ears.

Charisma in the presence of women +1. Overall score +13.
Practice makes perfect. Keep up the good work, Romeo.
You're getting there!

Illume scoffed at the information. At least something was moving.

22

TO LAPIDEOUS AND BEYOND!

AS DAY BROKE, Illume put out the fire with a blast of ice, freezing the flame itself into a solid statue of the tongues that were licking the air all night. Illume gave Trill a kick to the bottom of his boot, waking him up before holding a finger to his lips, indicating for him to be quiet. Both men silently packed the camp, preparing to move forward.

"Thanks for latting me sleep all night," Trill whispered as he examined the frozen fire.

"I was awake anyway, figured you could use a full night's rest," Illume responded while gathering the packs and potions together.

"Ooooo gettin' a little late-night exercise?" Trill jested.

"It's not like that. Although I did manage not to make myself out to be a total idiot," Illume replied with a scoff.

"So what happened then?" Trill persisted.

"We talked for a little bit and it was lovely! Then she gave me this look. My heart started pounding so hard, I thought she could hear it. My mouth dried up more than a desert and my hands went clammy," Illume explained.

"Sounds about right!" Trill jabbed.

"Bite me!" Illume retorted. "Anyway, I could feel myself just about to say something stupid like 'okie silly dilly okie do,' so I just suggested she get some rest and I'd take over," Illume continued.

"That was probably the better of the two." Trill couldn't help but laugh in his response.

"Well, I do have you to thank. Had it not been for your coaching, I probably would have gone default idiot. But will you do me a favor and not bring this up with Nari? My pulling the ripcord seemed to agitate her a little bit." Trill gave a confused look at the "ripcord " reference but nodded. "Also don't talk about children either. I don't know why and I wasn't going to ask, but that is what seemed to really upset her."

Trill gave a nod and a thumbs-up as he finished gathering his things. Illume made his way over to Nari. Kneeling, he gently placed his hand on her shoulder, whispering her name. She stirred.

Her long-lashed eyelids fluttered open and she made eye contact with Illume. The coldness of last night seems to have gone. There was a little warmth left but mostly indifference. Illume nodded toward the city.

"We're gearing up to head out," Illume said softly.

Not wanting her first experience of the day to be abrupt, Nari sat up and threw the blanket off of her. Pulling herself to her feet, she folded the piece of cloth and held it out to Illume, who took it.

"Thanks." Nari's words had a venom to them that would have made a copperhead jealous.

Nari grabbed her pack and walked toward Lapideous. Illume threw the blanket into his pack, slinging it over his shoulder before tossing Trill a glance. Seeming to be able to read his mind, Trill picked up the potions and both men followed Nari, who was now a good distance ahead of them.

"You did well, boy," Trill jested with a sarcastic tone.

Illume rolled his eyes as both men attempted to keep up with Nari. At points, they felt like they were jogging, and any time they got close, she increased her speed. Illume was astonished that by just walking, she was able to keep so far ahead of them.

She maintained this pace for hours. Even as Trill and Illume grew hungry and thirsty, retrieving food from their packs, Nari didn't stop, she didn't slow down, and like a machine, she didn't eat.

Illume did give her credit, though, because of her determination to keep distance between them. As the sun fell, Lapideous could be seen in the distance. A trip that usually took three days on foot, she managed to finish in two. As they approached Lapideous' gates, the guards stepped aside, saluting Illume as they did. Illume saluted back, drenched in sweat and struggling to breathe. His stamina bar was beyond zero. Entering the gates, Illume handed Trill his pack.

"She's probably going to Urtan's place. Could you bring this there for me? If I go, it'll just make things tense and awkward. I'll try and find supplies before everything closes," Illume begged between pants.

Trill took the bag, nodding before attempting to follow Nari, who was already out of sight. Illume continued to try and catch his breath but was still unable to. After several minutes of waiting for his stamina to recharge and it didn't, Illume turned his attention skyward, activating his leveling screen.

Level Up Available
Two levels available, 1 skill point and 5 attribute points per level.

Illume sighed as he scanned through his points, only going to use one level this time just so he could breathe and regain his stamina. Never before had an RPG made it possible to backlog stamina usage. It was a nice change.

Illume placed one point in wisdom, wanting to get his mana to an even 200, one point in strength in an attempt to get both his stamina and weight capacity to even numbers. His speed needed to increase as well, especially now that he was set with heavy armor, placing one in dexterity.

He debated putting his last two attributes in intelligence but decided not to, as intelligence and wisdom were typically intertwined and if one was leveled high enough, the other wasn't needed. Illume decided on his last two points to be put into constitution and charisma, not wanting a repeat of last night.

Moving on to the skill tree, Illume knew exactly what he was going to put his skill point into. Flipping through the trees, Illume let out a frustrated sigh. Why was it that he always seemed to specialize in the one skill that was on the far side of a skill tree list, making him have to spend over a minute flipping through skills before finally getting to the one he wanted. Illume stopped on destruction magic. The skill would cost both his skill points to unlock, but there was no way in hell he was going to miss this opportunity. Illume activated dual cast in destruction magic.

Closing his level up screen, Illume watched as his stamina regenerated completely. A sigh of relief escaped his lips as a "ding" indicated he was about to be updated with his new stats.

New Attributes

Health: 160 regenerates 1% of max health a second while not in battle.

Mana: 200 regenerates 3% of max mana a second while not in battle.

Stamina: 180 regenerates 5% of max stamina a second while not in battle.

Weight Capacity: 40/560, +10 per skill point added to stamina.

Survival: Unique skill, player has 70% resistance to cold attacks.

Charisma: +23, drops to +14 when in the presence of women.

Strength: +24 average for male humans.

Dexterity: +22 average for a human.

Intelligence: +20 average for a human.

Constitution: +23 without armor rating, average for a human

Wisdom: +33 +10 mana

His lower levels of charisma were starting to reach an acceptable number. Pretty soon, he'd be able to actually have a full conversation without wanting to put his foot in his mouth. Looking over all of his new stats, Illume nodded in approval. As the page disappeared, both his hands frosted over, then ignited into flames before fizzling out.

"None of that inside the walls!" a familiar voice rang out.

Illume turned to see Commander Stark with a group of guards at his back. Approaching Illume with his arms outstretched, the commander gave him a strong, almost brotherly embrace. Returning the commander's greeting, Illume then pulled away.

"Thank you for your guards, commander. They are greatly appreciated. I told them that their families are more than welcome to settle with them," Illume informed Stark.

"Good man. I don't want to break any families up!" Stark replied.

Illume noticed his armor was slightly different. It was shiny like all the others, but the scuffs and nicks that were sustained while Illume was wearing it were gone. Probably a new set, which he didn't blame the commander for.

"What brings you back to Lapideous?" Commander Stark asked.

"One of my forgers, Buthrandir. Her family was taken by slavers to work in what looks like an abandoned city several weeks journey east of here. She's one of mine, which means her family is one of mine too. Myself, Nari, and Trill are going to free them. It will take some time to get there and back, so if you have any need of Cryo's Quarry or any questions for my people, look to my steward Kassandra," Illume informed Stark as they walked through the not-so-busy streets.

"Man of honor," Stark declared with a smile.

Stark led Illume up a spiral walkway that hugged the outside of the city's levels, passing through several heavily guarded gates.

"Thank you, commander. I appreciate any help I can get. Is there a place we can purchase horses before we leave? It will cut our travel time by two-thirds," Illume asked as they passed sprawling white stone homes that were pure as the driven snow.

"The stables are closed for the night. They open again at first light. You should be able to purchase your horses then," Stark informed Illume.

Commander Stark brought Illume to a house with crimson banners flowing down either side of the door. The banners had black accents to them, which, if he tilted his head just right, appeared to be fangs.

Illume grew nervous. Was all this friendliness a ploy? Illume rested his hand on the pommel of his sword, ready to use it at a moment's notice.

"Senator William wishes to speak with you. We would ask that you hear what he has to say." Commander Stark's voice was a little more solemn than before.

Illume nodded, and without saying a word, approached the house. If the worst should happen, he still had one more level up and dual casting available to scorch or freeze whatever was on the other side.

Stark opened Senator William's door. It was very dark inside, illuminated by only the dimmest of candlelight. Illume hesitated before entering.

As he entered, the door shut with a "BANG," making Illume grip the handle of his sword. Not yet drawing the weapon in case this isn't a trap, Illume looked around at the gothic architecture, very reminiscent of Notre Dame in Paris. A soft *whoosh* filled the room. Illume focused with all his might to keep his heart rate even.

"Thank you for saving my brother," William's voice echoed from the darkness.

Illume hesitated as the thanks seemed to have a sinister feel to it.

"You're welcome?" Illume replied to the shadows.

The light from the candles danced, desperately trying to illuminate the darker corners of this house but to no avail.

"When disposing of those hunters and their gear, I came across something that is very disturbing." William's voice echoed once again.

"And what is that?" Illume asked.

His eyes darted from side to side, desperately trying to pierce the darkness and see where the source of the voice was coming from. A gust of wind blew behind Illume. He could feel William's presence towering over him. Clenching his jaw, Illume prepared to blast this potential threat with both hands on fire.

A piece of paper was held out before him. The hand that held it was pale and its nails long and sharp like five stiletto daggers attached on each bony end.

"This was found amongst the bodies," William informed.

Illume hesitated for a moment and grabbed the heavy sheet of paper and opened it. Inside was a note written in what looked like blood. Illume gulped hard as he read the scrawled handwriting that just seemed to scream evil.

Order of Light,

Accompanied with this letter is a sizable chest of funds. For this, you are to venture into the other three kingdoms and retrieve those that are deemed unnatural. Griffins, vampires, werewolves, druids, and barnogs, should you find a dragon or a dragon egg, I will compensate you tenfold. Bring all of them to me starting with alphas. The first one you can find resides in the forest near Lapideous. Know that if you take this contract and break it, I will bring you into my throng. You have seen what that entails.

-Ierret

Not knowing how to receive the letter, Illume returned it to William and took a step away from the man shrouded in darkness. He swallowed hard and pursed his lips, searching for what to say. After several moments of not saying anything, William broke the silence.

"Ierret is one of the many names of a being known as the Dark King. He has been around far longer than I have and he comes to power every few centuries. He'll amass an army and march across this world, burning it to ash and leaving nothing standing in his wake. I have tried to fight him at a great personal cost. Alas, I am not strong enough. Perhaps you can be. The Dark King is rising to power. We need the cryomancer to stop him." William's words were soft, almost as if he was scared to speak of the Dark King.

New Quest Added: Defeat the Dark King
An old power is resurging in the north.
Should he reach his full strength, no one will be spared. Seek out and defeat the Dark King.

As the quest popped up, he thought that finally, the big boss was revealed. All he needed to do was hunt down and kill this being, then maybe he could go home. Illume nodded to William as he accepted the quest.

"I will need to get significantly stronger, but I will hunt down and remove this threat from your world." Illume's voice was rife with new purpose.

"Thank you. Return to me before you begin your final march and I will supply you for your journey. Speak to no one of this. The Dark King has many spies," William warned.

With a wave of his hand, William's front door creaked open. Illume exited William's house to find no guards or even Commander Stark waiting for him. Time seemed to move differently as the moon was now high in the sky. Illume made his way back down to the main level of Lapideous. He noticed that the streets were vacant, even for night time.

Taverns were empty, inns had no horses tied up outside, even the guard patrols were lessened. It seemed as if a dark shadow was being cast over Lapideous and everyone knew it except him.

Illume heard something shuffling around him. Pursing his lips, he only used his eyes to search for the sound, not wanting to alert its source.

Illume continued his descent. The shuffling grew louder and louder. Placing his hand on his sword, Illume came to a stop at an intersection of the spiraled streets. The shuffling stopped. In the blink of an eye, Illume drew his sword, turned, and dashed at the being that was behind him, pinning it against a wall while placing his sword at the cloaked figure's neck.

"Whoa whoa! Not necessary, buddy. I've just been lookin' for you for several hours," Trill's voice echoed from a robe that shrouded his face from moonlight.

Illume sheathed his sword, releasing his pin on Trill.

"You shouldn't sneak up on people," Illume instructed.

"I wasn't sneaking. I was tryin' to figure out if you were actually you or a guard. There's a curfew in effect and I don't feel like goin' to the stocks for searching for you," he added.

"I've only been gone ten minutes. Why all the cloak and dagger?" Illume asked.

Trill's brows knitted together. He shook his head.

"You've been gone for near four hours. Nari sent me to find you. She's mighty concerned," Trill responded.

Remembering what William had said, Illume glanced around. Just because he couldn't see anyone didn't mean they weren't being watched.

"I'm sorry. I must have lost track of time. Let's get back," Illume whispered.

Illume wrapped his arm around Trill's shoulders, and both men headed back toward Urtan's house. Slipping in unnoticed, Illume realized it was because Nari was fast asleep already.

Sitting in a chair, facing the front door, she was clearly waiting for them to return. Illume grabbed a blanket and covered her yet again before moving to the soft feather bed of his own and letting sleep take him.

23

HORSEBACK

ILLUME AWOKE JUST as the sun crested over the horizon. He'd always been a morning person. Since his bedtime was 6:30 pm as a child, his body had been used to waking up before the sun. After running his fingers through his hair, Illume grabbed his coin purse as he heard movement outside.

Poking his head out, Illume saw a group of guards pass by as well as several merchants. The city was beginning to stir. Illume left the confines of Urtan's house and made his way to the stables, which were not yet open.

Illume took a seat on a bench outside, watching people as they walked from here to there. Their faces were darker than they had been previously, with not as many smiles or greetings to one another.

"Can I help you?" a voice called.

Illume looked toward the voice's source to see a man in light cloth garb approaching the stables. His long dark hair was pinned back above unpointed ears. Clearly this man was completely human. Illume stood, grabbing his coin purse and nodding.

"Yes, sir. Are you the owner of the stables?" Illume asked.

"I am. Do you need horses?" he replied.

"I do. Friends and I are going on…" Illume explained.

"I don't need to know your story. I have two horses I can sell at six hundred polis apiece. The third is for my work, it's not for sale," the man interrupted.

Illume opened his coin purse. He loved video game mechanics, as his coin purse could fit in the palm of his hand no problem, but as he opened it, there were thousands of polis pieces within, as if it were bigger on the inside. The Doctor would be proud. Illume reaches in, removing the subsequent 1200 polis and handing it over.

The horses cost him nearly half of his coin, but they would be well worth the investment. The stable master took his polis and opened the stables. Inside were three painted horses. They were not quite as large as Clydesdales, but they were close.

"Have your pick," the stable master said while moving to the back of the structure.

Illume approached the first horse, holding his hand out. The horse nuzzled it. Illume saddled the beast and put reins on him then moved to the second horse. It reared up and tried to kick Illume, so he moved on.

The last horse was quiet, reserved, but after making eye contact with her, Illume could see that she was thinking things through, that she was a smart one. Illume saddled her as well before leading them both back to Urtan's house.

Upon arriving, he found that Nari and Trill had already woken up and packed, ready for the road ahead. Trill worked on breakfast as Nari drank her "black mana." Illume held the reins.

"I got us a ride. Trill, meet your steed Neighthan Fillyan! Nari, this was yours. Meet Horson Wells," Illume proclaimed.

Nari let out a laughing scoff at the names. Horse puns were a gaming trope of Illume. Being able to make them here and have someone enjoy them brought warmth to his heart.

"What about you, don't you get a horse?" Nari asked as she approached Horson and gave him a gentle pet.

"They only had two available to sell, so we're going to have to share," Illume explained.

"NOT IT!" Trill shouted. His words were so loud that several people on the street stopped and looked at him with a hint of concern.

Nari laughed again. Grabbing her bag, she tossed it on the back of Horson's saddle before looking at Illume.

"You can ride with me," she teased.

Illume's brow furrowed at the comment, but he dismissed it. Helping prep the beautiful beasts for the trip only took about ten minutes. Wanting to be on the road as quickly as possible, they all climbed onto their steeds. Illume wrapped his arms around Nari's narrow yet strong waist as they exited the city.

Following the main road out and around Lapideous, Illume was surprised at how long it took to actually pass the city, nearly forty-five minutes at a decent riding pace. Having never ridden a horse before, Illume gripped Horson as tightly as he could with his knees, apologizing mentally the entire time because it had to hurt the big guy.

Illume held Nari tightly out of fear of falling off. He certainly did enjoy being able to hold her. He just wished it weren't in such a violently bouncing scenario. Her hair whipped into his face; he honestly didn't mind as the scent of roses filled his nostrils. There were several moments where Illume could have sworn she was nuzzling into him.

After nearly two hours of hard riding, both horses instinctively slowed down to a quick trot. Neighthan Fillyan was ahead a decent distance, but he only had one rider. Illume was thankful for the tiny bit of privacy, even though he had zero personal space.

"Are you okay?" Nari asked. Her voice had a hint of concern to it.

"Yes, why?" Illume responded.

"You're rocking strangely," she responded.

Illume was mortified as he realized that his heart was pounding so hard that his body had begun to move with each sternum-rattling beat. Riding had nothing to do with it either; it was his nerves from being so close to Nari for so long, they were finally beginning to fray.

"Yeah, just haven't ridden a horse in a while. A little nervous to fall off," Illume lied.

"Just hold on to me, you'll be fine!" Nari responded.

'SCORE!' Illume called out to himself; she had bought it. Now it was time for the hard part.

"Listen, Nari, about the other night…" Illume started.

"Don't worry about it," she replied with a shake of her head.

"But I will. I'm really sorry. You've witnessed it first hand, you know how I am with women…" Illume paused to try and find his words.

"Woefully incapable of talking to a beautiful woman without embarrassing yourself so badly that you kind of want to ride off and die somewhere?" Nari finished his thought with brutal precision.

"Harsh… but yes, that exactly," Illume responded with a laugh.

"I understand, sometimes nerves get the best of you. So to protect yourself from doing something embarrassing or stupid, you pull the ripcord, destroying both a beautiful moment and making the other person feel awkward that they were opening up." Nari's voice had a playful "ball busting" tone to it.

"My God, woman, you are brutal," Illume said with a laugh.

"That's why you love me," she jested back.

Illume fought all his urges, holding back his desire to agree with her wholeheartedly. They rode for several hours at a slow trot in silence, Illume enjoying the breeze in his face, the sun's beams kissing his skin, and the soft rustle of the plain's grass. The peacefulness of this serene ride was interrupted by the shriek of a woman.

Illume immediately searched for the source while Nari and Trill stood in the saddles looking around. Illume let his hands frost over as he released Nari's hips, her shapely posterior now in his face. Had there not been a life or death situation, he would enjoy the view. But right now, there was no time.

Mounted Battle Commenced
While on a mount, you may ride into battle. Depending on your speed, your physical damage is increased by between two and ten times.
A word of caution, your mounts can be slain and they are unable to respawn.

A warning scrolled across Illume's vision as a small farmhouse appeared in the background from behind lazily dancing grain. As the words disappeared, Illume saw three raiders pulling a woman by her foot away from her house as they tied down her husband.

Trill and Nari gave the horses a kick, making them charge the bandits. As they got closer and drew the attention of the bandits, Illume yelled out, "DISMOUNT!" not wanting to risk the horses this early in their journey.

Both Nari and Trill leaped off their respective horses with style, drawing their weapons and landing like superheroes. Illume slid off the back of his horse and tried to move directly into a charge. Never having ridden a horse pseudo bareback before, Illume wasn't ready for his legs turning to jelly the moment his feet touched the ground.

Illume's battle cry was quickly undone by an "*oof*" and thud as his legs give out and he face-plants into the dirt right next to Nari. Coughing from the fall and subsequent inhalation of dust, Illume strongly considered letting the now laughing bandits kill him just so he could respawn before his fall. Illume looked to see the bandits moving toward them. Trill and Nari offered a confused look to Illume.

"Sorry, my bad, my bad!" Illume grumbled in a winded tone.

Pushing off the ground, Illume dusted himself off, throwing his hands out to either side, making them frost over instantly. The bandits drew their weapons; one had a war axe, another a claymore, and the third two maces. A gleam of sunlight erupted from their armor, indicating it was metal. They had to be higher levels than the ones he'd previously faced.

Illume put the base of his hands together, leaning to his right as he brought both hands to his hips, mimicking one of his favorite childhood cartoons. Illume dumped all of his mana into his dual frost cast, allowing it to build as the bandits moved closer while he mentally screamed. *Kaaameeeehhhaaaameeeeeha!!!!*

Throwing both his hands forward, a massive spike burst from his hands and slammed into the bandit with the war axe. As the spell struck the bandit, his health dropped by just over half as it glanced off his breastplate denting it, before embedding itself into his shoulder. His axe dropped to the ground. Illume drew his sword.

"Dibs on Windu," Illume called.

"Who?" Trill asked with a look of confusion.

Illume stopped, pointing his sword at the bandit with two maces.

"The mace guy, I got the mace guy!" Illume explained in frustration as Nari let off a laugh at his attempt at humor.

Nari threw daggers at the bandit with the great sword, and he deflected them with ease. Charging in, Illume engaged the mace-wielding bandit, eager for a new challenge. Keeping his stance fluid and his gait squared, Illume was able to deflect most of the blows delivered by his opponent. Illume was unable to strike at him due to the sheer speed and ferocity of the bandit's attack, but he didn't need to. Illume was waiting for his mana to recharge. He was curious to try out his new abilities.

A guttural scream followed by the sputtering of blood rang in Illume's ears. Glancing back for a split second, he saw Trill withdrawing his sword from the first bandit's throat. A fountain of blood spurted out to the side as his life bar hit zero. Nari danced around her opponent with both her swords; his health was nearly halfway gone as he tried to block her. Had his armor been anything less than plate, he would have been dead right now.

A shudder rumbled through Illume as his life bar dropped by a quarter. He'd let his guard down and now was struck by a mace. Doing a quick glance at his stamina, he saw it was almost empty. His mana, on the other hand, was almost completely filled back up. Illume deflected the second incoming attack before throwing his free hand out and unleashing a torrent of frost as a third blow was incoming.

Illume's frost slowed the attack enough so when it finally reached his palm, Illume was able to grasp the mace in his hand, freezing it solid. With a powerful swing of his sword, Illume shattered the mace like glass before headbutting the bandit in his unprotected face, making him stagger. Kicking his opponent in the chest sent him on his back, causing his destroyed mace to fall from his hand. Illume's forehead throbbed from the headbutt as he stood over the bandit and held his sword to the bandit's throat.

"Why were you raiding this home?" Illume demanded.

The bandit threw both his hands up, effectively surrendering.

"W-we are under orders!" he stammered.

Illume pressed the tip of his sword down, drawing a thin line of blood.

"Whose orders!" he roared.

"Our commander! One day he just started sending us out on daily raids with orders to bring people back! That's all I know, I swear!" The bandit spilled his guts.

Illume withdrew his sword. Pulling his map out, he offered it to the bandit.

"Where are you being sent from?" he demanded.

Illume noticed that his eyes danced all over the map as if he could see it in its entirety. He wondered if he was the only one that got the fog of war. After several moments, the bandit put his finger on Strang.

Grabbing the bandit by his breastplate , Illume pulled him to his feet.

"Remove your armor!" Illume barked.

The bandit initially hesitated. Illume didn't and slammed his fist into the bandit's face. The blow caused him to stagger backward. That seemed to make him compliant as he immediately untied his breastplate, letting both sections fall to the ground.

"Return to Strang, tell your chief that the Cryomancer is coming for him. Tell him what you saw here today and know that it is only a taste of my power. He's to disband and release those he's taken or I will freeze his chest and rip his heart out while he watches," Illume snarled.

The bandit staggered backward before running away, tripping and falling several times before actually managing to sprint away from them. Illume got a notification. *'Speech increased, intimidation now an active effect.'*

"That was a bit excessive, don't you think?" Nari asked.

Illume shook his head.

"My plan is that he'll be able to get at least some of his people to scatter with what he's seen here. That way, there is less to fight later," Illume responded.

"Not bad, boy," Trill called out as he removed a coin purse from his bandit.

Illume retrieved one from the pile of armor left behind by his bandit and pulled one off of Nari's opponent. Approaching the farmer, Illume cut him free before handing him two coin purses.

"Are you okay?" he asked.

The farmer nodded, stunned from what he'd just witnessed.

"Good. It won't be safe for you and your family here for several weeks. Go to Lapideous, use these to pay for your stay. Take the armor and weapons and sell them. We won't need them," Illume suggests.

"What about my crops?" the farmer asked.

"You can always plant new ones. If these bandits return, we won't be here to protect you," Nari replied as she comforted the farmer's wife. "Your life is more important. Think about your wife and family."

It didn't take any more convincing than that. Illume, Trill, and Nari helped the farmer and his wife load a cart and their horse to pull it before sending them on their way to Lapideous. As they left and finally dropped out of sight, Illume glanced at their house, then at the setting sun. A smirk formed on his lips.

"How much of bad form do you think it would be for us to stay the night here?" Illume asked with an ornery tone.

"Very bad form," Trill responded.

"The worst," Nari added.

24

PRESSING ON

THE HOUSE MIGHT HAVE BEEN quaint, but Illume wouldn't lie. The farmer's bed was so comfortable, it rivaled most beds in the real world. He might have also enjoyed it so much because Nari snuggled in with him in the middle of the night when the temperature dropped.

Packing and leaving the house just the way they'd found it, Illume and his team were back on the road before the sun completely rose. Ahead in the very farthest distance were tufts of green that appeared to be bushes. Everything beyond their location and those tufts were fields of boundless plains.

"About three days on the plains, then it'll be near a week in the forest. After that, foothills before finally reachin' Strang," Trill informed.

Watering the horses and replenishing their supplies from what they could scavenge, Illume, Trill, and Nari were off once again. As they rode and the sun grew high in the sky, a low rumbling filled the air.

Nari pulled the horse to a stop, as did Trill. All three looked around in search of the source of the sound. Illume removed his bow from his back and notched an arrow, drawing his weapon to half draw length.

"By the gods!" Nari whispered in shock. Illume followed her gaze.

In the distance, a herd of at least fifty beasts charged across the plains diagonally to them. As they grew closer, Illume noticed that the sun shined off of metallic objects in the creatures' possessions. After several moments, they stampeded across the road before Illume and his team.

The beasts were massive, their hoofs the size of a man's head. Each of their four legs were as thick as a tree trunk and their backs, even though in horse form, were higher than the upright heads of their own mounts. One of the beasts stopped before Illume, Trill, and Nari and looked directly at them. His helmet covered so much of his face that Illume couldn't see his eyes. A row of spikes ran from the forehead all the way to the back of his helmet accompanied by two massive horns that bowed several feet into the air and back even further.

Antler-type growths protruded from his back and a pelt of some kind was draped over his shoulders. With a body that would make Dwayne "The Rock" Johnson jealous and tattoo-like markings to boot. Illume's head was hardly mid-chest to the being.

Its grip tightened around an axe so large, it could have cleaved both horses in two with a single swipe. Nobody moved, not wanting to agitate it. After the herd passed, the beast gave off a deep huff before riding off after them.

"What the h—" Illume started.

"Centaurs!" Nari whispered in awe, cutting him off. "I never thought I'd see one!"

Illume's palms were so sweaty, if he tried to summon fire, it would have immediately been extinguished. Never before had he seen centaurs portrayed in such a way; the raw strength and size of the beings was so intimidating that had they attacked, he would have been wanting to wear brown pants.

"It's a good thang we weren't closer, otherwise, that big beast would have come after us!" Trill proclaimed.

"How would you fight those things?" Illume wondered, having no intention to ever provoke a beast that size while on a horse roughly the size of a Clydesdale.

"You don't. Hell, I wouldn't, not in a thousand years," Trill replied.

"Just run and hope you're fast enough to get away," Nari added.

Illume nodded with a strained scoff.

"Okay then, what do you say we keep going and get as much distance between us and those things as possible?" Illume suggested.

"Agreed," Trill seconded.

Nari gave Horson a kick, sending him down the road once again. Illume glanced back every once in a while to see the location of the herd. For several hours, he could still see them moving in the distance, and even when they disappeared, the cloud of dust gave away their position.

It was a bit of a signal letting bandits and potentially the Dark King know where they were. Given the size of their weapons, however, Illume figured no one would be dumb enough to actually attack the centaurs.

With the sun setting, Illume, Trill, and Nari stopped and set up camp with Illume taking first watch. Illume kept his eyes peeled in the light of nearly a full moon, deciding it would be best to not start a campfire for at least tonight. A strange noise filled the air, like the sound of a broken recorder, the kind you'd play in fourth grade.

Illume glanced behind him to see Nari and Illume out cold with the horses standing over them asleep as well. The recorder whistle kept filling the otherwise silent air. After several hours, Illume decided to investigate, taking a health potion with him. *Potion of Ultimate Healing: Fully restores health, worth 200 polis.* Moving into the long grass with his bow at the ready, Illume followed the source of whatever that annoying noise was.

With each silent step, the noise grew louder and louder. Illume found his way to a clearing. Someone had matted down the grass into a large circle. At the center was a centaur about the size of his horses; it must have been a baby. Deer fur covered the human parts of her body and a mask was clasped tightly over her face, a mask that looked all too familiar.

The centaur baby saw Illume and pulled away from him, only to be tripped by a massive bear trap that was clamped tightly around her hoof. Illume put his hands in a non-threatening manner as he approached.

She pulled even harder, causing the trap to dig into her leg even further. Illume stopped in his tracks so the baby centaur would stop pulling. Illume's heart broke for the little lady, unable to speak or cry out for her mother.

Illume attempted to take a slow step forward. His foot caught on something and he fell flat on his face, which made the centaur jump some. Letting out a groan at his face-plant, Illume slowly turned over to his back and looked at the source of his clumsiness. He backed away rapidly upon seeing a pale, emaciated face with lifeless eyes staring back at him. Illume stopped for a moment. The face was familiar.

Getting up, Illume approached the corpse; it was the bandit he'd freed the day before. Illume gave the body a push, rolling it over with his foot. The bandit looked like those photos of a holocaust victim he was shown in history class, a stark difference to the strong man he had been yesterday. Illume noticed a dagger in his hand. Bending down, Illume pried it out of his cold, dead, and rather stiff fingers.

Supreme Dagger
Name: Dagger of Bestial Slaughter
Damage: +13 to humanoids an additional +20 to non-humanoid beasts
Weight: +3 Value: 10 polis

This dagger has been used in horrific acts of hunting and killing innocents. This is so well known no one will wish to buy it.

NOT WANTING to keep the dagger but knowing it would go to better use in his hands than in one of these bandits, Illume took the sheath from the bandit's corpse. Tying it around his waist, he slid the dagger in before giving the bandit corpse a kick. He had shown mercy, only for it to nearly cost this child her life. How many times would that happen? How many people had he or would he show mercy to only for something dark to come from it?

Illume turned his attention to the centaur. Clearly she was not responsible for the bandit's death, otherwise, he'd probably be dead right now too. Taking his time, Illume approached the baby.

"Hey, it's okay," Illume said, opening both arms in a non-threatening way. "I'm going to help you. Will you let me help you?"

The young centaur didn't respond. She look frightened.

As Illume got closer, two glowing red eyes became visible among the grass blades. They might have been her mother's or another centaur's.

"I'm not going to hurt her!" Illume called. "I just want to free her, then she can go with you, okay?"

A chill ran down his spine. Something about those eyes seemed wrong. They might have been glowing, but they appeared to be both dead and vengeful at the same time. With each step Illume took, the eyes seemed to grow even more angry. Finally at the centaur's leg, Illume held his hand out, not knowing if she would want to sniff him or not. To his surprise, she did.

Leaning in, her hot breath erupting from the sides of her mask, Illume forced himself to keep calm, his peripheral vision locked in on those pair of glowing eyes. The moment he felt the silver of the mask touch his hand, Illume leaped into action. With only a few flicks of his fingers, the mask fell free from her face, allowing her to let out a call that was somewhere between a woman's scream and an elk's.

To his relief, the eyes did not move forward. They did, however, continue to watch him from the darkness. Illume drew his sword, only for a growl that wasn't of this world, to reverberate through him. Strange, he couldn't hear the growl, but he could feel it. Illume put one hand out toward the angry eyes as the baby continued to call for its mother.

Illume kneeled next to the trap and slid his blade between the trap's teeth. As he did, the growling stopped, allowing Illume to feel the ferocity at which his heart was beating. Illume attempted to use leverage with his sword to open the steel jaws; nothing. After several minutes, he was unable to open them. Dropping his sword, Illume pulled on the trap with both hands, only for a ding to fill his ears.

Trophy Earned.
Name: Weakling.
Type: Bronze.
Requirements: Use all your physical strength in a task, only fail miserably. Well done; you're going to be centaur paste once mommy shows up.

Typically, Illume would grumble at the trophy passive-aggressively insulting him, but not this time. An idea formed as the words "physical strength" stuck in his mind.

Illume pulled Bloodlust from his lower back. Walking over to the bandit, he sliced off a thick piece of the dead man's clothing. Sheathing the weapon, Illume approached the trap once again.

Wrapping the cloth around the metal next to the baby's hoof for insulation, Illume grasped the black metal with both hands. His right hand glowed as he summoned his fire magic, heating the trap. With his left, Illume summoned his frost magic to cool it.

Both spells canceled each other out as to not freeze or burn the centaur. Right in the center, that sweet spot where both spells met, Illume noticed a stress fracture form in the trap.

A deep, familiar huff sounded from behind Illume. His heart

stopped as he looked over his shoulder, making sure to keep both hands on the trap. A nervous smile made its way to his lips as he saw Mommy Centaur towering over him with a battle axe whose head was larger than him.

Illume glanced to the side to see the red eyes still watching closely, less angry now. He still had two lives left. If she were to strike, at least it would break the trap and free her daughter.

Illume noticed her hand grip her weapon tighter. Another unearthly growl erupted from the glowing eyes. Immediately, the mother loosened her grip on the weapon and took a step back while huffing something that sounded like "Acheri" at the glowing eyes as if addressing the unseen being.

Illume turned his attention back to the trap, continuing to dump his magic into the metal. As his mana ran out and his spells wore off, Illume picked up his sword and slammed the pommel of his weapon into the trap, shattering it.

The baby centaur staggered away from the trap. Her hoof was bent under her like a dog that hurt his leg. She limped over to her mother, who took her hoof and examined it before giving her daughter a loving hug. Illume sheathed his sword before grabbing his potion and holding it out to the centaurs.

"Wait, maybe I can help," Illume called.

The centaur looked at Illume, seeming to recognize the bottle. She waved him over. Illume walked toward the baby. Reaching out, he gently took her lacerated hoof in his hand, biting the cork out of the potion and pouring the liquid onto her wounds. The baby centaur let out a whimper and her mother embraced her, holding her daughter close to her chest.

Illume moved with the baby's erratic jerks and tugs while she tried to get away from the healing potion. As Illume emptied the vial, the baby's leg was fully healed and good as new. Releasing her leg, Illume took several steps back. The baby hesitated and put her hoof down, which was able to bear weight with no pain. Illume smiled as the mother looked at him as if sizing him up before offering her massive hand, palm side down, to Illume.

Stepping forward, Illume reached out toward the mother, only for her to touch his forearm and drag her rough fingers down, past his hand. A soft light shined before fading, leaving what looked like the letter "C" with an arrow piercing its center on his forearm. Illume ran his fingers over the mark, curious as to what it might mean.

"We are in your debt," a deep woman's voice asserted.

Illume looked in shock. She was speaking to him. Her helmeted face hidden from the moonlight, she dropped to her front knees and bowed slightly before Illume.

"I am Sagis of the centaur. You have saved my daughter. No human has shown our kind such graciousness. For that, I bless you. What is your name, human?" she asked as she stood back upright.

"I am Illume of Cryo's Quarry and I was just doing what is right," Illume responded as he bowed back to show respect.

"Illume shall now be a name of honor among my people. I hope our paths will cross again. Come, Illuma," Sagis called to the little girl. Both trotted off side by side.

Blessing Received.

Name: Elatus.

Some blessings are permanent, this is one of them. The blessing of Elatus grants the receiver the ability to understand centaurs and those of the centaur family.

If invoked, any member of the centaur family must aid the bearer of Elatus without question. Blessing only able to be bestowed by the centaur monarch.

Watching mother and daughter move off into the darkness, Illume could still feel the eyes of whatever had been watching him still on him. Gathering his supplies, Illume slowly retreated back toward his camp, not turning his back to whatever was in that clearing the entire time.

Back at camp, the mark on Illume's arm flared before disappearing, leaving only the slightest discoloration to his skin in the shape of Elatus.

Now bored out of his mind, Illume activated the game's waiting mechanic. Selecting a four-hour wait time, Illume accepted, causing the time lapse to take over. After several moments, the sun rose. Trill got up, soon followed by Nari. Illume canceled the waiting. If he knew what was in store for them, he wouldn't have been so eager to prod Father Time.

25

THROUGH THE NIGHT

ILLUME HELPED LOAD THE HORSES, eating breakfast while small talk overtook the conversation. After a little over half an hour, they were ready to continue on their journey, mounting the horses. Illume wrapped his arms around Nari once again before asking when he would be able to take the reins.

She just laughed at him. Looking off in the distance, Illume could see part of the flattened circle from this height. Massive swaths around the clearing were flattened, obviously made by some creature.

"Guys, I don't want to stop riding until we hit the forest. I know it'll mean riding all night, but it's not safe camping in the open anymore," Illume spoke softly as his eyes were locked on the patches of flattened grass, those red eyes burned into his memory.

"It'll be perfectly safe. We don't need to wear out the horses or ourselves trying to make up a little extra time," Nari interjected with a laugh.

"She's right, we can take on anything that is in these fields," Trill proclaimed confidently.

"And what about an Acheri?" Illume asked.

Nari let out a non-believing laugh while Trill's face turned white as a ghost.

"What did you just say?" he asked through what could only be described as dry mouth.

"An Acheri, glowing red eyes, a roar with no sound but that shakes you to your very soul," Illume described.

"Acheri are just a myth to scare kids," Nari rebutted.

"How do you know about the roar?" Trill continued, ignoring Nari.

Illume pointed to the masses of leveled grass that were no more than ten yards away from where they'd been sleeping.

"Because last night, one was watching me," Illume explained.

Upon seeing Illume's evidence, Nari stopped laughing and kicked Horson to make him take off in a full sprint. Trill wasn't far behind them and Illume gripped Nari's waist tightly, not wanting to fall off.

"By the gods, you see something like that, you wake us up!" Nari yelled back to Illume.

"What is it?" Illume asked as the sensation of terror coming from both was genuine.

"It's a spirit of vengeance, only instead of seeking justice, it just kills everything. It's said should you die by Acheri, your soul will be incapable of entering any of the afterlives," Nari yelled over the sounds of rushing winds and trampling hoof prints.

Side Quest added: Find out more about the Acheri, confront one face to face.

Illume scoffed at the new quest; no way in hell would he actually seek out this creature if it was as monstrous as it sounded. They continued to ride through the day, passing travelers going in both directions. They slowed only long enough to warn about the Acheri and tended to the horses. They didn't stop. Even as night fell, they continued on their path straight for the forest.

Illume glanced back into the darkness of the night. Every so often, he'd see a set of glowing red eyes appear then vanish just as quickly. He was unable to tell if they were real or a figment of his imagination as the very real fear of his teammates bled over to him.

Illume resigned himself to it as fighting that particular fear made him see those red eyes in greater numbers peering through the grass as if to battle his own denial. Only after accepting it did the glowing red orbs vanish.

The sun rose once again just as they reached the woods. Bringing their horses to a stop, everyone dismounted. Illume glanced back to the vast plains that stretched out behind them and sighed. Nari led the horses to the grass, letting them graze for a little while as Illume grumbled.

"We're not going to be able to bring everyone back this way, are we?" he asked, looking over at Trill.

"It'll be too dangerous. We'll have to go the long way. Either south along the coast and the borders, but those have their own risks. Or north through the foothills and to Mobrebalku," Trill suggested.

Illume opened the map. A trail of color illuminated their path thus far, and as Trill spoke of Mobrebalku, it filled in grey, as did the entire southern border and coastal area of this section of his map. It had begun to fill out; he'd say about 65 percent was now at least visible.

Closing his map, Illume toyed with both path ideas. Going north would allow whoever was rescued to have the safety of a city while they got their feet on the ground, also offering a chance to recruit more people for his town.

"It's settled then, we're going north after we were finished at Strang," Illume stated decisively.

"That's great. Then can we get moving now that your little two-thirds vote has been completed?!" Nari yelled with a sarcastic tone.

Nari led the horses into the forest, followed closely behind by Illume and Trill, moving carefully as the topography changed drastically the further they delved. Gnarled roots twisted from the ground with boulders protruding out from under them. At points,

Illume could have sworn it looked like the forest was consuming part of the mountains that lay on the other side.

Illume caught up to Nari, resting his hand on the pommel of his sword as they weaved between the trees. Letting his eyes wander, Illume noticed that the tree's bark was darkened almost as if it had a rot to it. Illume's gut dropped out from under him, as he couldn't tell if some of the trees were actually twisting and contorting to "look" at him or if it was just his imagination.

"What is this place?" Illume whispered as a worry of eaves-droppers listening in creeped into the back of his mind.

"This was once the great white wood," Nari replied softly. "A safe haven for all to enjoy should they need to."

Illume glanced back at Trill, who nodded.

"She's not wrong. Hundreds of years ago, a darkness started to overtake the forest. A tree here and a bush there, nothing too great. But that darkness was not carved out, and as a result, it spread, encompassing it all until not a white tree was left standin'," Trill continued.

"Like a cancer, it had to be cut out at the source, but no one could ever find what that source was," Nari added.

"Do you know what the source was?" Illume asked.

Nari shook her head. Illume looked back at Trill, who seemed to instinctively brush his hand over the breastplate of his armor.

"It was the Dark King. The only thang able to corrupt some-thin' so pure. If the forest is to turn back to its former glory, then he must die." Trill's tone was that of a whisper.

"Well then, we'll get powerful enough and find this Dark King and put him down once and for all," Illume spoke as confidence in his abilities and his friends grew within him.

Nari and Trill both lost it, Trill leaning against a tree for support while Nari laughed so potently that no noise came from her rapidly reddening face. Illume glared at both of them in their side-splitting mirth and snarled a bit.

"Why is that so funny?" he demanded.

"That lich that we took out was probably created by the Dark

King and it nearly tore us all apart!" Nari managed to squeal between bouts of laughter.

"Yeah, but we killed it, didn't we?" Illume retorted.

"That we did, but that lich would be like Nari cuttin' the very tip of her pinky fingernail off and unleashing it on the world. That lich was an insignificant speck compared to the Dark King's power," Trill replied with a laugh as well.

"Then what would a real taste of his power be like?" Illume's tone grew sharp.

Just as Illume finished speaking, a deep, unsettling roar tore through the forest, instantly killing Nari's and Trill's fits of laughter. Illume quickly retrieved his bow, notching an arrow. He glanced over at Nari, who had both her swords drawn while crouching behind a boulder.

"What was that?" Illume whispered.

Trill walked calmly over to the horses, his sword still on his back before grabbing both animals' reins. Trill led them into the trunk of a massive tree that had mostly been hollowed out by termites and rot. As he turned to face Illume, the roar rippled through the woods once more.

Such power resonated behind the sound that even the trees' leaves rustle in its presence. Illume's hands trembled no matter how hard he fought to maintain control of himself. When he glanced at Nari, she held a finger to her lips, her eyes wide in terror as well. Trill was the only one who remained calm as he provided an answer.

"It was a real taste of the Dark King's power," Trill spoke at a normal volume.

Trill nodded to a small embankment overtaken by knotted and twisted tree roots. Illume followed his friend's nod to see the horrible truth. Illume's stomach dropped, and his hands went numb as terror gripped him. His bow fell to the ground. His knees wobbled.

"By God, that can't be," Illume whispered, his throat tightened as if he'd breathed in a balloon full of helium.

26

CORRUPTION

ATOP THE HILL'S CREST, a mountain of a being that could only be described as an orc was looking down at them. A war axe larger than Urtan's was held tightly in one hand, accompanied by thick metal bracers on each forearm, far too thick for any of their weapons to breach. Rippling muscles were held back by skin as black as pitch that was so tight, Illume could count each individual muscle fiber.

Two pieces of wood arched over his shoulders, providing protection to both his joints and his head from lateral attacks. They appeared to be made of the roots of trees. Crimson tusks protruded from his lower jaw, be they dyed or just soaked from a kill, Illume couldn't tell. The orc stared directly at Illume, not with eyes—there were no eyes—but rather deep recesses that seemed to have no end.

Illume's breathing grew erratic, his heart palpitated as he felt his blood rush to his extremities, trying to get him to flee. What filled Illume with terror wasn't so much the snarling orc, but what he was sitting on. A massive beast with the head of a lion, the likes of which could have swallowed one of their horses whole, let off a trembling roar while digging its front claws into the dirt.

Horns, like that of a goat, protruded from the beast's mane. From the angle Illume was standing, it looked like its body transitioned to that of a goat as the hindquarters of the mount became apparent. Illume's mind raced, trying to take him anywhere else but here.

Opening the menu, Illume desperately attempted to quit the game, to no avail. A ball of fire tore through the air, narrowly missing Illume, causing him to close his menu. A blue streak of light slammed into the beast's upper left shoulder. It was one of Nari's throwing knives. The attack caused the beast to let out another roar as a serpentine tail weaved its way into the air over its rider.

"You just going to stand there?!" Nari screamed.

Illume found his courage. Leaving was not an option.

You can do this, he coached himself. *You can do this. Be the hero you've always wanted to be in the real world.*

Illume leaped into action, picking up his bow. He fired an arrow at the orc, hoping to kill the rider and neutralize the mount. The orc held his axe, blocking that arrow. Illume let out a groan of frustration while following Nari's lead and running up the opposite ends of the embankment.

Nari threw daggers, striking the beast and causing it to rear up. Its serpentine tail struck at Nari with such force that when it missed and hit a tree, the tree exploded into tiny splinters.

Illume noticed the lion's mouth began to smolder as its eyes locked on Nari. Drawing an arrow, Illume fired. His arrow found its mark in the chimera's jaw. The arrow's impact caused its head to jerk sideways just as a ball of fire erupted from its gaping maw, causing its projectile to narrowly miss Nari. Its health bar became visible to Illume, indicating that a mere sliver of its health was taken away.

Nari threw several more daggers, both trying to keep their distance as Illume rapid fired arrows at the beast. Each blow drew the chimera's attention to a different location.

The serpent would look one way while the lion would look another, both attempting to attack but cancelling each other out, keeping the beast relatively motionless. That was until Nari ran out of knives, allowing both heads to focus on Illume.

All four eyes were locked on to him, the fiery red of the lion and the icy blue of the snake. They growled and hissed at Illume as they moved toward him, each step revealing the three-foot-long claws that protruded from the four-finger-like appendage. The chimera geared up to fire another ball of heat at Illume, who prepared to dodge-roll out of the way, only to be met with a plume of black smoke.

"It's out of mana!" Illume roared.

Grabbing his last two arrows, he notched them and drew them back while aiming at the beast. Illume heard the deep huff of the orc on its back, granting it permission to strike. With the dexterity of a cat, the beast was in the air, soaring at Illume, covering the near hundred-foot gap in the blink of an eye. With no time to aim, Illume blind-fired at where he thought the beast was going to be as he dove out of the way.

Archery Level Up x2
Focus now available
Reinforced Shot now available
'Critical Hit x3 damage opponent induced with blindness.'

Appeared at the top left of Illume's screen. Hitting the ground and rolling, Illume turned to face his foe, only to be greeted by a hoof the size of a smart car directly into his face. Everything flashed black for a moment as Illume was gripped by a weightlessness he wished would be peaceful.

It wasn't. Illume slammed into a tree so hard, his helmet rang like a bell. With three-fourths of his health gone, Illume staggered to his feet, looking down at his bow. It had been shattered into four pieces.

"Catch!" Trill yelled.

Illume tried to orient himself just as a potion hit him in the face. His heath dropped by a sliver. Putting his hands out, Illume caught the potion as the chimera roared in the background. The very earth under his feet shook from the beast's rampage. Pulling the cork out, Illume drank the potion, which restored his health back to 100 percent.

As Illume's vision focused, he saw Nari charging in under the beast, slashing at its ankles. Her sword did nothing but bounce off its skin. Illume drew his blade and rushed in as well, noticing the lion's head had an arrow protruding from each eye. The snake head whipped around, trying to orient the creature before locking on to Nari.

Illume's stamina drained rapidly as he pushed himself as hard as he could. The snake weaved in toward Nari's flank. Diving under the beast's belly, Illume tackled Nari to the ground just as the snake struck, narrowly missing them both. Their swords were of no use against such a monster; perhaps magic would be.

Illume engulfed both his hands in frost, firing ice spike after ice spike at the mount. Each projectile hit the chimera, causing minuscule damage with each attack. He would run out of mana before his opponent would die, leaving both him and Nari utterly defenseless.

Grabbing Nari, Illume dashed to the nearest tree, pressing himself against it. With one hand on her hips and the other against the tree, Illume watched both the chimera approach and his mana bar deplete.

"What are you doing?" Nari growled as she struggled against Illume.

"Trust me!" Illume barked in a whisper, holding her in place.

The chimera slid closer to Illume and Nari, sniffing the air as the serpent flicked its tongue out before looking directly at Illume and Nari. The chimera and the orc made their way toward Illume as if taunting his prey. Nari attempted to break free once again. Illume held her tight.

"Wait," he whispered.

The snake slid forward, now mere inches from Illume. Had it not been for Nari giving him the strength to fight, he would have caved by now. It was for her safety he was forcing himself to act. The serpent's tongue flicked against Nari's cheek before drawing back, preparing to strike. Like the world's worst game of chicken, Illume watched for any hint of movement. It might only be a split second, but the moment felt like hours.

As the snake struck forward, Illume shoved Nari out of the way to his right while diving to his left. The serpent's face slammed into a frozen tree trunk, causing it to shatter into thousands of tiny pieces. Illume held his breath, praying to any of the gods that might or might not exist for his plan to work. A deep groan rippled through the forest as the snake turned its attention to Illume.

The orc dismounted, holding his axe tightly in one hand as he approached Illume as well. His stomach sank, hoping to kill two birds with one stone. The tree began to fall and with the orc and the snake's eyes on him, neither realized until it was too late. *'THUD!'* The massive tree landed on the chimera, its health dropped down to zero, and a ding filled Illume's ears.

Trophy Earned.
Name: Environmental Kill
Type: Gold
Requirements: Cause an enemy to damage the environment in such a way that results in its death. You might want to duck!

Illume obeyed the prompt, which vanished just as the orc's axe whizzed over Illume's head. The weapon was massive, definitely a one-hit kill. Illume realized he was way too weak to deflect, let alone block.

The orc attacked. Illume threw his sword away and drew his two daggers. Leaping from one side of the field to another and using the forest's roots for cover, Illume was able to keep one step ahead of his opponent, even though his stamina was starting to run out.

A warrior's scream filled the air. Illume looked to see Nari leaping from the fallen tree, both her swords aimed downward. Each slammed into the gap of the orc's armor next to his neck; his health dropped to half from the attack.

Spinning, the orc sent Nari flying off with her swords and his own shoulder armor. The orc growled as the hollow places within his eyes grew red with an orc berserker rage.

If this had anything in common with other RPGs, then once the orc entered berserker, nothing they had would be able to get through its hide. Illume fired two ice spikes at the orc, only for them to shatter, confirming Illume's fear. The ice shattered against his skin, doing no damage and only bringing Illume to the center of its attention.

The orc's roar rivaled the chimera's as he charged at Illume. A flash of a memory from when he was a kid overtook Illume's mind, giving him an idea. Charging toward the body of the chimera, Illume headed directly for the snake. Illume could feel the orc getting closer, hearing his heavy breaths, the earth shaking with each monstrous footstep.

Come on, COME ON! Illume screamed in his mind as he got even closer to the snake. A sharp inhale from the orc indicated he had drawn back for an attack. Illume dove forward just as the serpent twitched to life and instinctively struck at Illume.

The snake narrowly missed him but sank its fangs into the orc, who let off a whimper. His eyes stopped glowing as his body relaxed, and his health bar dropped to zero as he fell to the ground dead.

Illume climbed to his feet, standing over both fallen monsters, adrenaline surging through his veins. He was unable to hold back a primal roar in victory over his fallen foes. His body trembled with exhilaration, relief, joy, and rage all at once. His lungs burned as the last vestiges of air left them, causing his roar to die out naturally while still echoing through the woods. Falling silent, Illume continued to breathe heavily as his mana, stamina, and health fully recharged.

Level Up Available x 2.

27

LEGENDARY

"WHAT THE HELL!" Nari roared.

Her voice echoed from the small ravine they hid the horses in. The scream brought Illume out of his trance-like state his adrenaline had him in. Turning his sight to Nari's voice, Illume looked just in time to see Nari punch Trill so hard, he hit the ground. He attempted to get up, but she stepped on his chest, putting her sword to his throat.

"Where were you for that?" she continued to yell.

Illume sheathed his daggers and ran towards his team members. Illume reached their side just as Trill threw his hands up, surrendering.

"I couldn't leave the horses; they would have escaped!" Trill blurted loudly.

Illume gently placed his hand on Nari's. This seemed to calm her as she lowered her sword. Her foot was still firmly planted on Trill's chest.

"First you run from the spiders, now you shy from a chimera. You're a coward!" Nari growled.

"Everyone calm down!" Illume interjected in a gentle tone.

"No one in the history of calming down has ever calmed down when told to CALM DOWN!" Nari's frustration boiled over.

Nari sheathed her swords and stepped off of Trill. Turning her back to him, she ran her hands through her hair. Illume gave Trill a hand up.

"You're not off the hook with me. She has a point; you could have been a real help," Illume added.

"I was just…" Trill tried to defend himself.

"Protecting the horses, I know. You forget, I've seen what that sword did to someone's stats. There was no way you obtained a weapon like that without having some major mojo. You could have put up a barrier." Illume's tone was softer as he spoke to Trill.

"I'm sorry," Trill whispered, hanging his head.

Illume put a hand on his shoulder.

"You will be." Illume's voice had a hint of playfulness to it. "You get to harvest that chimera. That hide, bone, venom; all that has to be forgeable." Illume nodded for Trill to get to work.

Trill sighed, nodding as he remarked that the punishment fit the crime before making his way up the hill. Illume walked over to Nari, who was trembling, probably with rage, but also with adrenaline.

Walking over to their packs, Illume opened Nari's. Urtan's flower still sat on top. Grabbing the glass flower, he walked over to Nari, placing an arm around her shoulder. He held the ornament out to her.

Upon seeing the flower, Nari's shaking lessened. A smile formed widely on her face as she reached out and gently took his gift. Clearly the stress of the battle was having a similar effect on her as it did on him.

Nari lunged at Illume, who barely had enough time to brace himself. She threw her arms around him, and to his surprise, pressed her lips against his.

Illume's heart skipped a beat, and his hand found its way to her cheek as he returned her tender yet passionate kiss. The taste of strawberries teased his tongue as it brushed against her lips as her floral scent filled his lungs.

It was so real, so visceral, that Illume could feel his body naturally reacting to her touch. Not wanting to, but for the sake of what little dignity he had left, Illume gently broke the kiss.

"This doesn't make me want to not kill him any less, you know," she whispered.

Illume nodded to the chimera corpse that Trill was harvesting.

"True, but if you kill him, then we have to do that," Illume replied.

Nari paused. An all-too-familiar look filled her eye, one of regret. She took a step back.

"I'm… I'm sorry. I shouldn't have done that," she murmured.

Clutching her flower, Nari turned her back to Illume and walked toward the horses. Illume tried to protest, but she ignored him. With a disappointed huff, Illume decided to check out the orc. Approaching the beast, Illume was surprised to see that the once invincibly strong orc was now a pile of rotten flesh. Its stench had already begun to fill the air and Illume covered his nose.

"That's what the Dark King's corruption did. Upon death, the corrupted immediately rot away," Trill called out as he hacked at the chimera's horn.

"Is there any way to purge a corruption?" Illume asked.

Leaning down, Illume felt around a squishy satchel that was on the once strong orc's hip. The stench mixed with his physical contact made Illume's stomach violently turn. His gut spasmed, but he managed to keep it down and actual food from coming up.

"I wouldn't imagine so," Trill responded.

Illume pulled three books out from the satchel; two were spell books and one was titled *The Lusty Barnog*. Illume opened the book about halfway through and read. He only got about three sentences in before he let it fall from his hands. *Fantasy fifty shades of grey… that's fun,* Illume remarked to himself as he opened another of the books.

Just like before, a flash of light overtook him. This time, Illume felt a bolt of electricity surge throughout his body, burning his insides as it did. Letting out a roar, Illume dropped to his knees as his vision blurred. After several seconds, his vision cleared once again and the flashing lights around him subsided.

Spell learned: Shock.

Illume took several seconds to recover. Neither Trill nor Nari seemed to have noticed the light show. Grabbing the last book, Illume opened it. His vision blurred red, his heart beat so loudly, it sounded like a battle drum. Rage filled Illume like coffee fills a mug before subsiding instantly.

Special Skill Learned
Name: Berserk
Attributes: Once a day you may activate Berserk. All stats increase tenfold and your skin becomes as hard as dragon's scales. Be wary as using berserk prevents you from differentiating friend from foe.
Illume angry, you wouldn't like me when I'm angry!

After the book turned to dust, Illume used flame on the orc's stash of literary naughty tales before searching the rest of him for any trace of valuable items only to find a ring covered in the orc's putrescence.

Illume used what pieces of the orc's armor were clean to get the ring as non-disgusting as possible. Giving it a spit polish, Illume finally felt comfortable enough to slide it onto his hand.

Legendary Ring Found
Ring: Ring of Clarity
Defense: +1
Weight: +1
Worth: 1000 polis
Clarity offers greater dispersal of the fog of war on players map. Mana regenerates 20% faster.

Ring allows wearer a one percent chance to keep in control of the Berserk form.

"Illume not angry!" He smirked to himself.

Illume tried to pick up the axe. Wrapping both hands tightly around its handle, Illume lifted with all his might. He was unable to lift the orc's weapon more than a few inches off the ground. Not wanting anyone else to stumble across this weapon and use it against him, Illume began the painstaking task of sliding it down to their horse.

The rest of the day was spent harvesting from the chimera. Extreme poison from the snake's fangs, then the snake's fangs. Trill pointed out that the eyes, ears, and tongues were potent alchemy items, so Illume helped harvest those as well.

What parts of the hide and scales that could be salvaged were, as well as the beast's meat. By the day's end, the only thing left of the chimera was a bloody skeleton, tendons, and the bits of meat they were unable to safely clean off.

Illume harvested the pyro glands in hopes that they could be used to help increase his pyromancy to the same level as his cryomancy. Perhaps bits and pieces of legendary beasts could help him reach legendary statuses as well. Returning to the horses, Illume noticed that Nari had set up camp and had already begun to roast the chimera's flesh.

"Shouldn't we move away from the scent of a fresh kill?" Illume asked.

He was no expert, but what he remembered from the Discovery Channel was that dangerous scavengers would be swarming that carcass any moment.

"We are actually safer here than anywhere else in the woods," Nari said softly as she turned the meat over. "The scent of a dead chimera will scare everything that could be a threat to us. Including other chimera." Her tone was significantly less entertained as the last time they had spoken.

"Hm, like sharks," Illume whispered to himself as he took a seat.

Illume glanced back to the gory corpse. He'd hunted before. This wasn't so different, only much MUCH larger.

"How'd you know the tail would strike?" Trill asked, leaning toward Illume.

Glancing back at the skinned serpentine tail, Illume smirked. "When my brother and I were kids, we were helping my mom in our garden. She had a green thumb like no other. I tell you, she could run a farm in a desert. One day, a snake struck at my brother, but my mom cut its head off with a shovel before he got bitten. I remember sitting there, watching as its head continued to strike while the body kept lunging, looking for something to attack," Illume explained in a hushed tone as the memory danced back like the breeze on a field.

Memories like this brought back vivid picture of his childhood. His mother, who'd worked herself into an early grave. A father who was never in the scene, at least not sober. His brother and sister doing what they could at such a young age to shield him from his father's alcoholism.

His father wasn't a violent man when he drank, but sometimes Illume wished he had been anything but the self-medicated ghost he knew. Once he got home from work, it was straight to the fridge without so much as a hello.

Illume's father would drink for the rest of the evening until he was drunk, usually falling asleep in his rocking chair. Most of the time, a line of drool would fall down his face. A few times, he'd piss himself in the seat.

Looking back, Illume didn't have a single memory with his father that didn't revolve around him being drunk or in the process of getting drunk.

His father never taught him how to ride a bike, never took them on any kind of family vacation, never taught him how to talk to girls.

Early on, Illume promised himself he'd never be like his father.

If he chose to be a father at all. Part of him was terrified he'd end up like his own.

"Even in death, snakes are looking to sink their fangs into the nearest living thing. I just helped it find something to bite," Illume said, tearing his mind from these thoughts and placing a plastic smile on his lips.

"Well, it's a good thang you remembered that. I'm thinkin' we find someone to forge this stuff, we'd be able to get legendary items from it," Trill proclaimed.

"Yes, we!" Nari responded, pointing to Illume and herself. "We killed it, we get the loot," she adds.

Illume looked at her, and she turned away.

28

A WALK IN THE WOODS

ILLUME PUT Trill on guard duty that night as punishment for his lack of assistance in the battle with the chimera and orc. Drawing from a survival show he'd seen a few weeks prior, Illume gathered leaves and moss from the ground and fashioned two beds from them. Illume lay on his, and Nari lay on the ground, leaving the second bed unused.

The next morning, Illume woke up early and began to pack up the camp.

"There were several wolves sniffin' round the camp last night. Soon as they sniffed that chimera, they tucked tail and ran," Trillian informed as he assisted in the packing.

After packing the camp up, Illume revisited the corpse of the chimera. Grabbing the fangs, Illume yanked both of them out after some force being applied. Placing them in his coin purse, Illume returned back to camp.

Trill had woken Nari up in his absence, and upon seeing Illume, she grabbed Horson and led the horse out of their camp and toward Strang. Illume took his spot next to Trill and Neighthan as they followed relatively closely behind her.

"What'd you do to merit my lovely company?" Trill asked with a chuckle.

"I was the one that broke the kiss," Illume mumbled.

His tone was hushed. He only wished that Trill's were just as quiet. It wasn't. Trill smacked Illume with the back of his hand, a wide smile on his lips and a twinkle in his eye.

"So you CAN talk to women now?! Good for you!" Trill declared quite loudly.

Illume shot Trill a "would you quiet down" glare, which shut him up.

"I've had more and more success since I have been dumping most of my attribute points into charisma, but that's not the issue," Illume growled in a hushed tone.

Nari led them to a river and waded across it, her horse leaning down and taking a drink as it walked across. Illume and Trill followed, stepping into the frigid water that was only about knee deep.

Crossing the river, Illume looked both up and down. There were no animals drinking. Being near a water source, however, Illume put his guard up. His hand rested on his sword and his eyes scanned every tree for a potential threat.

"That's good! Why did you break off first?" Trill asked.

Illume huffed, not wanting to talk about it but knowing that Trill was "that friend" who would press the issue until he spilled his guts.

"Because it was the adrenaline from battle, the real thought that we were going to die that pushed her to kiss me. It wasn't out of her own desire. Not to mention she's an NPC! When I log out of the game, I am going to disappear. She will probably re-set for the next player, where she will be a romance option for them," Illume explained.

Illume bent down, picking up a rock before throwing it at a tree, hitting it straight in the center.

"It wouldn't be fair to either of us for me to pursue anything with her," Illume continued, tossing another rock.

"That's a very noble way of lookin' at it," Trill responded in a hushed tone. "Illume the Chaste has a good ring to it."

Illume shot Trill a "shut up" glance before making his way to Neighthan and climbing on his back.

"I've got some work to do. Bring me back if we get attacked. Hopefully, I'll just be a minute," Illume explained while he activated his leveling screen.

Illume saw that he had reached level seven and had sixteen attribute points he could spend. Harkening back to the last few mini-boss fights he'd had, there was the painful reminder that his health was ridiculously low for being this far along in a game.

So far, he'd relied on his tank armor skills to save him. If the set-up of this RPG was like any other he knew, he was about to have all his equipment taken and he'd have to rely on his base stats to escape.

Illume cycled through, selecting *Constitution.* Illume placed four attribute points into it, bringing his *Constitution* rating up to +27 and increasing his health to an even 200. Needing his stamina higher, Illume placed two points in *Strength,* bringing its rating to +26 and having his *Stamina* round out to an even 200 as well. Everything at an even 200, it did good things for his OCD.

Illume looked at his leftover *Attribute Points,* to which there were ten. Cycling through, he couldn't decide where he wanted to place them. Illume talked out the process in his head.

I could put six into Charisma. It'll bring my lower stats down to a normal level, could help out later in the game. I could dump eight into Dexterity, get me to above average. Speed and Agility would be good to have without my armor, or hell, even with my armor, Illume thought to himself.

Illume spent what he would assume was the next half hour trying to talk himself into dozens, if not hundreds of different combinations. He played out dozens of different scenarios as to the inevitable battle to come versus his ability to make things right with Nari. After getting both bored and frustrated with himself, he decided an even split would just have to do, putting five and five, figuring that both would be so close to above average that he would be able to get both just over that hump with no problem. Illume placed five points in

Charisma, bringing it up to +28 and the lower stat up to +19. He then put the last five in *Dexterity,* bringing its overall rating to +27.

Illume transitioned over to his skill tree, cycling through and knowing precisely where to put his skills. Illume then opened his sneak skill and placed both his perks in that tree. One went into *Sneak* and the other into the sub-perk *Assassin.*

Would you like to lock in these perks?

Yes | *No*

Like always, Illume selected YES, only to be greeted by his page of new stats.

New Attributes:
Health: 200 regenerates 1% of max health a second while not in battle.
Mana: 200 regenerates 3% of max mana a second while not in battle.
Stamina: 200 regenerates 5% of max stamina a second while not in battle.
Weight Capacity: 40/580, +10 per skill point added to stamina.
Survival: Unique skill, player has 70% resistance to cold attacks.
Charisma: +28, drops to +19 when in the presence of women.
Strength: +26 average for male humans.
Dexterity: +27 average for a human.
Intelligence: +20 average for a human.
Constitution: +27 without armor rating, average for a human
Wisdom: +33 +10 mana

New Skills:
Sneak: Player is now 20% harder to detect while sneaking
Assassin: Sneak attacks do 5x more damage with both blades and bows

ILLUME CLOSED HIS MENU SCREEN. Glancing around, he noticed that the trees had grown denser, their bark darker, and their leaves smaller, allowing streams of light to pour through. Illume rubbed his eyes as they attempted to acclimate to the brighter surroundings compared to his leveling menu.

"Nice to have you back," Trill said with a smirk as he bit into an apple.

"How long have I been out?" Illume asked.

Trill shrugged, handing the rest of his apple to Neighthan.

"I'd say about four hours, maybe more," Trill replied.

Illume's jaw dropped. Four hours, really? That was a serious gap in time. He'd only felt he'd been gone for maybe thirty minutes. Illume dismounted, Neighthan not slowing down in the slightest. The forest floor was no longer knotted with roots, blackened decayed moss crunches under Illume's feet.

Illume jogged to Nari, the dried-out moss crunching under each footstep. Moving right by her side, Illume offered her a quick, albeit awkward smile.

"Can we talk?" Illume asked.

Nari gave him a shrug reminiscent of his sister-in-law when she was mad at his brother.

"I'm sorry about yesterday. I didn't pull away because I'm not attracted to you… I very much am. To me, this is just a video game, a form of entertainment. For me to get involved with you for my own entertainment… it's not fair to you. For me to get emotionally attached to you, that's not fair to me. Once I've beaten this game, I will be able to return to the world I came from…" Illume attempted to explain.

"How do you know?" Nari interrupted. "I've seen that look before. That look you sometimes get when you go into your menu. It's one that says you're stuck here, that you can't get out of this 'game.' So what if you are stuck here, then will you pursue me because it will no longer be 'unfair to you?'" Nari's tone had a bite to it with a hint of sadness.

Her words hit Illume in the chest harder than the chimera ever could have. Slowing down, he briefly considered the fact that he might not be able to escape. A lot of good those charisma points did. Illume started to move forward once again as Trill moved to his side.

"How'd that go?" he asked.

"I think I just made it worse." Illume sighed.

His dismay caused Trill to laugh. The next several days of hiking through the forest seemed to go on forever. Nari kept pace, staying separated from them both. Illume and Trill did their best to keep up, picking berries and harvesting water when they could. More than once, Illume saw a bird staring at them.

The animal appeared to be the exact same one over the course of several days and the way it stared puts Illume on edge. Assuming it was one of those spies he'd heard about, Illume managed to hit it with a rock, killing it. No one seemed to care. The farther they got into the woods, the larger the animals they came across. Sheep at first, then horses, then wolves.

All of which were mutated in some strange, dark form and all of whom seemed to take several steps back, if not flat out run away. Illume instinctively touched the chimera hide at each incident. He was glad that they had taken down such a beast; it made this trip significantly easier and allowed Illume to level up twice.

Illume opened his map. They had to be getting close by now. Stopping where he was so he didn't trip, Illume noticed they were approaching the forest edge and that hopefully by the next morning, they would be at the gates of Strang.

Illume heard Trill calling for him. The sound was muffled and did not seem urgent, so he kept his eyes locked on his map, the ring allowing Illume to have "seen" twice as much, leading to almost all of this section of the forest being explored.

Trill's muffled voice called out again, this time with slightly more urgency. Illume chalked it up to Trill just being impatient, until Nari screamed at him. Illume dropped the map to see Trill and Nari about forty yards ahead and pointing behind Illume.

Turning to look behind him, Illume was greeted by the largest wolf he'd ever seen bearing down on him, maw gaping with razor sharp teeth glistening in the sunlight. Illume forewent his sword and threw out his hands. The explosion of thunder erupted from Illume as torrents of lightning flew from his hands and into the wolf.

Its health bar immediately became visible and started to drain as it fell to the ground, sliding lifelessly to Illume's feet. Illume didn't stop, not wanting to risk the corruption resurrecting the wolf. He continued to unload his new shock magic into the beast.

"UNLIMITED POWER!!!!" Illume roared, unable to help but quote *Star Wars*.

Illume's mana pool depleted, causing the lightning to dissipate. The stench of charred flesh filled his nostrils as smoke rose from the smoldering corpse. Illume coughed, attempting to fan the flesh-scented smoke away from his face.

"Sorry, couldn't resist!" Illume called.

It was the first time in several days Illume saw Nari smile, let alone hear her chuckle. Trill rolled his eyes and waved for Illume to catch up. Opting to leave the corpse behind, Illume ran toward his team, catching them in no time.

"You think that was a bit over the top?" Trill asked.

There was a hint of frustration in his voice, almost like Illume had just murdered someone. Illume nodded. He didn't have to keep scorching the beast after it had died.

"Maybe a little. I was just sidetracked because this ring doubles how much I can see on my map," Illume explained.

Trill sighed and rubbed his forehead.

"I'm sorry, this darkness is starting to get to me," he explained, motioning to the forest.

"We're almost out," Nari announced, pointing ahead.

Illume could see the very edge of the woods, which ignited a glimmer of excitement in him. The constant overcast nature of a darkened wood certainly would get to anyone, and had they stayed much longer, Illume would have likely started feeling its effects too.

Illume charged toward the forest's edge. Nari took off closely behind him. After several minutes of running and his stamina bar depleting, Illume came to a stop, taking his last few steps within the woods and onto a foothill facing Strang. Illume's knees went weak at the sheer beauty before him.

"By the gods," Nari whispered.

Before he had a chance to drink in the image before him, everything went black as words scrolled across the dark screen.

You've been stunned.

29

ALWAYS PLAN AHEAD

MOLD, that was the first thing Illume's senses detected. That and a throbbing in the back of his head. Illume opened his eyes. The world around him was dark and blurry. Holding the back of his head, Illume noticed his health bar was at 75 percent with the first quarter greyed out.

You have been concussed. Don't fall asleep.

Scrolled across his field of blurry vision. Illume fell back, holding the back of his head and groaning. Feeling a crusty build-up in his hair, Illume could only assume that the blow had split his skin and he'd been out for some time. After several more moments of blinking, Illume saw a dwarf standing before him, leaning in closely as he investigated Illume.

"Have yet to see humans here," the dwarf declared.

Illume felt it poke him in the forehead, almost as if testing to see if he actually existed. Illume grunted and swiped at the dwarf's hand before pushing off the ground and standing. Reaching for his sword, Illume grabbed nothing but air, soon realizing he was in only his rags. Smirking to himself, Illume gave himself a pat on the back for predicting this.

"Where am I?" Illume asked.

His vision finally focused to see a stocky dwarf standing before him. The dwarf wore only pants and cloth on his feet, indicating that the dwarf was a male by his lack of feminine features. Heavy shackles bound both Illume's and the dwarf's wrists together and heavy bars surrounded two sides of the room while the other two were solid rock walls.

"You're in Strang. Abandoned keep of the dwarves," Illume's prison companion pointed out.

Illume nodded. At least he got inside. He pulled on his chains; he might be disarmed but he wasn't defenseless.

"There was a woman and a man with me, were they brought in as well? Where would they have taken her?" Illume pleaded.

"I heard nothing of two men being brought in, only you and a woman. Is she pretty?" the dwarf asked after a moment of thinking.

"The most beautiful woman I've ever seen," Illume admitted.

The dwarf hung his head, shaking it. A knot formed in Illume's stomach and a lump overtook his throat.

"I'm sorry, boy, anyone of beauty is brought to the commander and what he does to them is a fate worse than death." The dwarf's tone was somber as he spoke.

Illume kneeled before the dwarf, offering the man his hand.

"I am Illume, Lord of Cryo's Quarry," Illume introduced himself.

The dwarf grabbed Illume's hand, giving it a shake.

"I am Uthrandir Lord of Balacor." The dwarf's voice was full of pride.

"Uthrandir of Balacor, what a coincidence. I was sent by my forger Buthrandir of Balacor to rescue her people," Illume informs Uthrandir.

"My niece. Great smith, better woman. It looks like you've done a mighty fine job so far," Uthrandir jabbed.

Illume stood and walked to the bars. Placing his hands on them, Illume attempted to heat them up. A soft purple glow and glyphs appeared, but nothing happened. Illume attempted to use ice. The same purple light, the same strange glyphs, and the same result of nothing.

"The creators of these cells ensured that no magic could damage them. You won't be able to break your way out," Uthrandir informed him.

Illume turned his attention to the dwarf. Having seen plenty of prison breakout films, Illume was already almost finished with a plan.

"When do the guards make their rounds?" Illume asked.

"Every hour, why?" Uthrandir informed Illume.

Illume smirked and took several steps back, glancing back out into the dark abyssal cavern they were in. Torches lit cells on the far side of the cave, and a pit separated Illume from the far side.

Opening his map, Illume was thankful for the ring, as it had completely filled in the entire city of Strang.

It looked like at the very bottom was the commander's quarters with mine shafts on all sides of the hole that stretched down several hundred yards. There was evidence of the city stretching out farther in all directions, but if he were reading the map right, they were cut off by cave-ins. Illume dropped his map and nodded toward the guards.

"How many are stationed here?" Illume asked.

"Several dozen, why?"

"I'll need to know how many I need to take care of. Go, lie down against the back wall, and no matter what happens, don't move," Illume instructed.

Uthrandir stood firm, ignoring Illume's instructions.

"Uthrandir, this isn't just a mine… I know of places like this. They will corrupt you and you will end up serving the Dark King, or they will kill you. Your only chance at survival is to listen to me," Illume pressed.

After hesitating, Uthrandir lay down against the back wall. Illume positioned himself away from the cell door and pressed his face against the cool metal, listening intently for any guards that could have been nearby.

For several minutes, Illume only heard the crying of the prisoners and the cracks of whips. Eventually, the sound of voices filled the damp air.

"Help! Somebody help me! My cellmate just collapsed!" Illume yelled.

Two guards came running out of the darkness, a torch in hand. Illume was shocked at their sight. Their armor was the same as the guards at Lapideous, only it was dark and cracked, contaminated just like the trees. The elves inside had unnaturally grey skin and almost glowing yellow eyes.

"What happened?!" one of the guards demanded.

"I-I don't know, he just collapsed in the back of the cell!" Illume delivered his best "fake prisoner" line.

"Crap, we can't let the lord die. We need him to keep the other dwarves in line," the other guard murmured.

Both guards moved to the door and fumbled with their keys. Illume charged his hand, dumping nearly all of his mana into his right hand.

Once he heard the squeak of his cell door open, one of the guards stopped and looked at Illume. A smirk formed on Illume's face, knowing that his hand was sparking with thunder magic.

"Shocking, I know," Illume said with a laugh.

When he unleashed his entire bar of mana into the cell bars, Illume's magic surged through them. Heat and ice might not have been able to affect the structure of the bars, but they were still metal and a conductor of electricity. Both guards seized, their bodies thrashing and dropping their weapons as their health dropped to zero.

Trophy Earned.
Name: Conductor
Type: Bronze
Requirements: Use a magical spell on something that naturally

conducts the element used resulting in instant kills on lower level opponents.

Bill Nye would be proud!

Illume released the bars, causing the guards' bodies to collapse. Uthrandir immediately popped up and ran over to the bodies, feeling their necks. Grabbing one of them, Uthrandir dragged the corpse into their cell's darker recesses. Illume quickly followed suit, dragging the other guard in as well. Illume moved to take their weapons.

"Don't!" Uthrandir stopped him. "Their weapons and armor are corrupted. If you take possession of them, they can corrupt you too." The dwarf's tone was deadly serious.

"Thank you for the heads up!" Illume replied.

Using his foot, Illume slid the weapons next to their bodies before retrieving their dropped key ring. Illume tried both keys on his shackles but to no avail, attempting the same on Uthrandir's shackles, only for them not to open either.

Illume tried to melt his bindings. They glowed, but the glowing runes prevented them from melting. Trying ice, Illume exhausted his mana in an attempt to freeze and shatter them, again to no avail. Giving up on getting free from his cuffs, Illume locked the cell door behind them and kept the keys on his person.

Prison Keys Added.

Weight: +2

Worth: 3 polis

Prison keys are only capable of unlocking cells.

Only commanders have access to the cuff keys.

Staying low, Illume and Uthrandir kept close to the cave walls where it was darkest, figuring the best way to get Nari back was to delve deeper into the cave. Uthrandir grabbed Illume by the elbow, turning him around with a grip far more powerful than Illume would have expected.

"What are you doing?" Uthrandir whispered.

"One, we will need a commander's key to get out of these cuffs. Two, there are more people imprisoned below us, and three, Nari is still here. According to my map, the man in charge is at the very bottom of the mine. Chances are that is where we will find both the keys and Nari," Illume murmured.

Uthrandir nodded. Illume could tell he understood what he was trying to say. The dwarf waved for Illume to continue. Turning forward, Illume and Uthrandir continued to make their way through the darkness.

They used the faint torch light to determine where sheer drop offs were. Several dozen yards ahead, Illume could see two guards speaking to one another with a single torch shared between them.

A smirk formed on Illume's lips. Keeping low, he continued to sneak forward. Illume was surprised at how quiet Uthrandir was capable of being, as dwarves were typically depicted as hammers, something you'd hear coming a mile off. Illume and Uthrandir closed the gap after several minutes of stop/go sneaking.

Sneak Level Up.
Shadows now available.
Sneak maxed out!

Trophy Earned.
Name: Master of One
Type: Silver
Requirements: Fully level up a skill.

Illume was glad his sneak was all the way leveled, even more so that he put points into the skill. Crouching behind both guards, Uthrandir was the first to move, punching the guard in his leg, shattering it, and denting his metal armor. As the guard fell to his knees, Uthrandir grabbed the guard's helmet and snapped his neck with a CRACK as if it were nothing.

Illume jumped into action as well, kicking the guard in the back of his knee to make him fall back. Illume wrapped his chain around the guard's neck and pulled backward, attempting to choke him. The guard thrashed, making noise.

Not wanting to alarm the others, Illume froze his cuffs. After several seconds, the guard stopped struggling as a softer "crack" filled the air and Illume fell back with the guard's frozen head in his hands.

"I thought I was the brutal one," Uthrandir whispered with a smirk. "Glad you're on our side."

Illume dropped the head before moving to the bodies. Observing the bodies, Illume noticed they were of Lapideous as well, and corrupted. Illume's worry for Cryo's Quarry grew. If Lapideous was compromised, then his town was in grave danger. Illume found both men's keys; neither was what they were looking for.

"The more we kill, the faster we're going to have to move," Uthrandir offered quietly while extinguishing the torch.

"Then let's get moving!" Illume whispered back.

Both men continued to make their way through the mine, transitioning to the lower levels that were littered with pickaxes and shovels. With each step they made, a pungent and rotten smell grew more and more pronounced.

Illume ignited his hand with a soft burn to illuminate their darkened path. Looking around, Illume's stomach instantly dropped as he regretted bringing light to this portion of the mine.

30

NEVER ANGER A DWARF

BODIES WERE STREWN EVERYWHERE. Some were fresh, others were decaying, and even a handful were just skeletons. There were dwarves, elves, and orc corpses piled high on either side of the tunnel before them. Illume's hands formed a fist so tight that his nails sliced into his palms.

The anger growing within him, however, was nothing compared to what was growing within Uthrandir as his breathing became heavy. A deep snarl, more intimidating than any beast's, emanated from his throat. Illume grabbed a pickaxe and a shovel, offering them to the dwarf.

"Hold on to that anger, Uthrandir. We will need it," Illume whispered.

Uthrandir accepted the weapons, his fingers gripping their handles so tightly, Illume was worried they might break. Illume grabbed a shovel that was broken into several jagged pieces with only one bladelike piece still holding true to the handle.

Shovel Added.
Name: Rusty Mine Shovel
Damage: +5 against armor +10 against flesh
Weight: +8

Worth: 1 polis

Sneak, sneak, stab, stab, someone's getting tetanus.

Bet yo momma! Illume thought to himself as they moved on.

"We will give them a proper burial when the time is right," Illume replied.

Illume seriously considered using his Elatus blessing, but beasts of such size had no reason to be in such a confined space. Ultimately, they would be ineffective. Ahead, several more voices could be heard, guards joking about the torture and pleading of those who were trapped down there. Illume fought every urge to activate berserker just to see what would happen.

Wearing only cloth on their feet gave Illume and Uthrandir an advantage; they were far more quiet than had they been wearing boots. Sneaking behind one guard, Illume slid the shovel shard under the guard's armor. With a swift jerk to one side, Illume severed his spinal cord.

Insta-kill, Illume was informed in the corner.

Uthrandir wasn't so quiet this time. The guard next to Illume jolted and a hot sticky liquid spattered all over Illume's face. Wiping it away, Illume watched in horror as Uthrandir yanked his pickaxe out of the guard's head, using the shovel to decapitate his victim. Illume wasn't even sure that was possible until now, but apparently, it was.

The decapitation wasn't quiet, alerting the other fifteen guards in the area. Illume let out a frustrated sigh. The guard nearest to Illume turned to see what was happening. Illume managed to get the shovel into the slit of the guard's helmet, triggering another insta-kill notification. More blood spurted onto Illume as he yanked the shard from his latest victim.

Illume grabbed the guard's pike. He felt a slick oil permeate into his hands and travel up his arms. It seemed alive and it was aggressive. This must have been the corruption he'd heard about. As quickly as he could, Illume threw the pike, piercing another guard in the neck, causing him to fall lifeless to the ground, all the while being informed that each attack was considered a sneak attack.

Illume was happy that they were in the darkness. It helped with Illume getting the upper hand. Retrieving his shovel prison shank, Illume slid around the boulders that protruded from the ground, moving as silently as he could. He wondered if the guards even knew he was there, as all of them seemed to be drawn toward Uthrandir. Not that he blamed them; the dwarf was making enough noise to wake the dead.

Illume noticed an archer taking aim at Uthrandir, who was tearing through the guards like they were nothing in a truly brutal fashion. Illume threw the shovel, striking the bow and causing it to shatter.

Charging at the corrupted guard, Illume leaped into the air and drop-kicked him off his perch. The kick did a little damage; the fall did more. As Illume hit the ground, his life bar dropped somewhat, still having a max of three-fourths health.

Illume got back to his feet. As he looked down, a dagger flew past his head. The guard was about ten feet below him, now disarmed and putting his fists up. Illume slid down the slick rock, dropping to be on an even level with the guard. Illume held his right hand in a fist with his left hand slightly outstretched and open. Sparks flared from his right hand.

The guard jabbed at Illume, who batted the punch away with his left hand. The guard punched once again. Illume batted the fist away once again, this time pairing it with a jab to the face.

Sparks flew from Illume's fist into the helmet, dropping the guard's health. The guard threw a slightly more reckless punch. Illume sidestepped the attack. This time, he was able to land two punches to the guard's breast plate with two electrified fists.

While his punches weren't doing any real damage, the magic he was imbuing within them was. Never actually activating the spells, Illume noticed that his mana wasn't dropping, only his stamina with each dodge and jab. The boxing exchange went on for several more moments before Illume actually channeled electricity into his punch, finishing off the guard for good.

With his opponent defeated, Illume made his way back to the roaring battle that raged just out of sight. Rounding a boulder, Illume stopped to see Uthrandir standing in the middle of six guards, all with their pikes aimed at him. Uthrandir looked like Carrie, drenched head to toe in blood with his hands still gripping his now breaking pickaxes. No one saw Illume yet, save Uthrandir, who nodded to the water they were all standing in.

"I can take it!" he roared, the guards thinking he was talking to them.

Illume's hand sparked. He didn't want to hurt his new friend but knew he wasn't fast enough to kill them all before Uthrandir died.

"Okie dokie!" Illume called back.

The guards all turned and look at Illume, who waved at them with one hand while the other fired an arc of electricity into the water. The bolt immediately refracted, splitting into dozens of arms and traveling into each of the guards. Uthrandir let out a primal roar as the electricity got to him. His health bar hardly moved.

"He wasn't joking!" Illume whispered to himself.

Illume charged in toward the pool as the electricity dissipated. Grabbing one of the stunned guards with electrified hands, Illume snapped his neck. Sliding across the water, he kicked the legs out from under another guard before tackling Uthrandir out of the rapidly de-electrifying water and onto solid ground.

Illume still had half his mana left. The guards moved once again.

"You will find that my mana is quite operational," Illume snarled.

He intentionally made his voice froggy as he threw his hands out. Torrents of electricity surged from Illume and into the water once again. All the guards stiffened and fell into the net of electrified water that surrounded them. Even after Illume's mana dissipated and he stopped casting the shock spell, its effects still cycled back into itself within the water for several more seconds, killing the other guards.

Level Up Available
One-Handed Level Up 2 x
Arm Wrestle now available
Endurance now available

Scrolled across Illume's screen. He had just snuck for several hours successfully and managed to kill thirteen guards as well. Illume glanced at Uthrandir, who was clenching his jaw and swinging his arms as if trying to loosen them.

"You okay?" Illume asked softly.

"I'm fine. I told you I could take it," he grunted.

"Undoubtedly. I've never seen anything resist a shock to that level before," Illume said softly as he leaned against a boulder.

"Dwarves are intertwined with the magics of the earth and ground. That gives us an extreme resistance to any form of spark," he explained as he wiped blood from his face.

Uthrandir pointed to several brightly burning torches in the distance. They had already made it to the bottom of the cave, which was surprising to Illume.

"The commander will be in there, as will your girl. Are you ready to face a fully armored foe with nothing but your hands?" Uthrandir asked.

"We just took out nearly two dozen men with pretty much our hands. I think we'll be fine so long as we're quiet," Illume said with a nod. "But I've been wrong before."

31

JUSTICE

ILLUME IGNITED his hand once more. The act of killing the guards caused their torches to be extinguished. Staying low and keeping his hand as low to the ground as he could just in case there was an archer in the darkness, Illume came to a stop after several minutes of weaving through boulders as the ground dropped out from in front of them.

Illume threw his hand out, stopping Uthrandir from falling into the crevice before him. Leaning over, Illume picked up a rock and tossed it into the hole. After staying silent for nearly a full minute, Illume heard it hit the bottom.

"Well, that puts a damper on things," Illume whispered.

"Not quite," Uthrandir replied, pointing to Illume's left.

Raising his hand, Illume saw a thin bridge that crossed the gap a few yards away. Moving to the cliff's edge, they hugged the wall, with about six inches for their feet. Illume and Uthrandir held on to the wall as tightly as they could. Without so much as a word, they scooted to the bridge to cross it.

Illume extinguished his hand, using the torchlight from the building before him to keep an eye on the path ahead.

Praying with each step that an archer didn't decide to use them as target practice, Illume finally made it to the far end, stepping on solid ground once more. Turning, he helped the dwarf get to safety as well.

Looking back, Illume could see almost all the way up the massive shaft. There were dozens of prison cells packed full of slaves weeping for their freedom.

"Why did no one shoot at us?" Uthrandir asked.

"I could not tell you," Illume whispered back.

Moving in complete silence, they finally got to the carved-out structure's heavy wood door. On the other side, Illume heard a man's muffled voice followed by the cries of a woman. It had to be Nari. Knowing it was a longshot, Illume held up both the keys in his possession.

Neither would fit into the lock. Illume then placed his hand on the door knob and gently turned it, pushing on the door. Nothing but a soft "clunk" left the heavy door. It was bolted from the inside.

The noise, however, seemed to work to Illume's advantage as he heard the footsteps of the commander making their way to the door. Illume backed up, pressing himself against the wall next to the door, Uthrandir doing the same. A muffled "clunk" emanated from the door, followed by a soft creaking sound.

"I told you I was to be left alone!" the commander's voice called.

Illume and Uthrandir stayed silent. The door creaked some more, opening ever so slightly.

"Who is out there!" he barks. "I will have your hides for insubordination!"

Illume snickered to himself. It was almost too easy to get inside of this supposedly super-secure structure. Whipping around the corner, Illume slammed full force into the door, causing it to jar open and the commander to stagger back.

Stepping into the commander's quarters, Illume noticed that he was wearing a different kind of armor than most of the other guards they had come across. It was light armor that had tints of silver to it, almost like Order of Light handiwork.

Illume turned to see Nari strung up in the far corner of the room, her wrists gouged deeply with wire that kept her suspended. Bruises decorated her delicate face and gashes covered her body nearly head to toe.

She had been put into what could only be described as leather straps, one binding her breasts so tightly that it hurt Illume. The other appeared to be bottoms but seemed to be designed to cut off circulation from the wearer's legs.

Illume felt a fire ignite within him. Shooting a blast of ice at the wire caused it to shatter with ease, as it was thin and brittle. Illume slid under her with his cuffed arms out, catching her before she hit the ground.

Illume moved the hair from her face, feeling her tender, long neck as he held his breath. Two soft thumps pressed against his fingers. Illume breathed again; she was alive. Illume felt his blood boil. Looking at Uthrandir, who had followed him in, Illume broke the frosted wire around her wrists, freeing them and handing her to the dwarf.

"Get her out of here and across the bridge. If I don't come out, or I come out charging at you, take out the bridge. Do you understand?" Illume's words were commanding.

Uthrandir attempted to argue, but with a single look from Illume, he did what he was ordered. As Uthrandir exited the structure, Illume turned his attention to the now standing commander, fully armed. Illume's rage boiled over. He felt his body turn feverish, as all he wanted to do was rip this commander's head off.

Illume was surrounded by weapons, but he didn't notice them. His heart pounded so hard that it rocked his body. Even his vision attained a slightly red tint. Illume walked toward the commander with enraged purpose. The commander hesitated for a brief moment as Illume snapped his bonds as if they were nothing, accompanied by a soft purple flash of light.

The commander stepped forward, grabbing a pike that leaned against the wall, and jabbed Illume, hitting him square in the chest. The pike head shattered against his skin. Deep down, Illume wanted to question the commander, but his body seemed to act of its own accord, leaving him to just be an observing passenger. After what he saw with Nari, Illume was more than okay with not being able to question this commander, should he not survive their encounter.

The commander then grabbed a mace and swung it at Illume, who threw out his hand and caught it. Throwing his head forward, Illume headbutted the commander so hard, it slammed the man into the floor. As he attempted to stomp on him, Illume's opponent rolled out of the way just as his foot hit the ground with so much force, it cracked the floor.

Illume's prey drew his sword. Spinning, he sliced at Illume's Achilles tendons, causing his sword to spark and fracture. Illume managed to get a kick into the commander's chest. With the singular blow, his breastplate dented as if it were made of tin, sending him flying across the room into his rack of torture tools. His health dropped by a quarter.

Illume tried to ask him where the keys were, but his body did not comply to his brain's demands. Instead, Illume marched toward his target with a cold ruthlessness that would freeze even Elsa's heart. Arrows shattered against his skin, and had he been in control of his body, it would have been pretty cool. Being a loose cannon, however, didn't bring him peace.

Several more arrows skimmed him before Illume grabbed the bow and snapped it like a twig, tossing the limbs away but keeping the bow string. Illume grabbed the commander's wrists, tying them together with the bow string before stringing him up in the same manner he'd strung up Nari and who knows how many other women. They were muffled, but Illume could hear the commander's cries as everything faded to black.

As Illume came to, he looked at his hands; they were drenched to his elbows in the hot, slick blood of the commander. Turning his attention forward, his stomach churned, causing him to lean to one side and vomit involuntarily.

Before him were the arms of the commander dangling from the ceiling and not much else. Blood, gore, bone, and sinew were strewn all over the room. It looked like he stepped on a land mine or was struck with some kind of explosive.

Illume ripped his clothes off, using them to wipe as much of the commander's blood off of himself as he could. His hands trembling and his heart racing, Illume tried to keep his mind focused, to keep it clear.

It was hard to cut through the fog of panic as he overturned tables and threw trunk lids open, actions that would typically need a delicate touch. He was unable to help but behave like a hammer.

In one of the trunks, Illume found all of his and Nari's possessions along with what could be referred to as a "crap ton" of polis and precious stones. Grabbing his armor and weaponry, Illume donned them before piling several more precious items into the trunk. Illume slid it near the door before rummaging through what was left of the commander, finding his key ring. Illume placed it on his belt.

Doing one more quick sweep, Illume grabbed several weapons that would be suitable for a dwarf. Lifting the trunk, he exited the structure to see Uthrandir halfway across the bridge. A look of concern filling his face, he stopped upon seeing Illume.

"What happened in there?" he questioned, no longer bothering to be silent.

"You really don't want to know," Illume replied, still in shock at seeing what he'd done with his bare hands.

"Well, I hope you have good news because everybody else is on their way down here right now! Did you have to make the fight so loud?" Uthrandir barked.

Illume didn't respond. His face was somber and even, not knowing what kind of pain he put the man through before killing him. Illume crossed the bridge with Uthrandir in the lead. Uthrandir led Illume to a small alcove of rocks where Nari was lying. She was barely conscious and whimpering in pain.

"I can't... I can't feel my legs," she said softly, drifting in and out of consciousness.

Illume opened the trunk. Finding the garments for her lower half, Illume drew his dagger, forcing a finger under the leather strap at her hip to make a gap so he wouldn't accidentally cut her. Illume made a quick slice, the pressure under the extremely tight leather causing it to rip all the way up.

Illume did the same thing to the other side before sliding her own pants up her legs, sitting them snugly around her waist.

Illume was working mostly off of feel, as it was completely dark. The guards all charged past their little hiding spot. Illume gently placed a hand over Nari's mouth so her groaning wouldn't catch their attention. It didn't.

After a few brief moments, all the guards were across the bridge, allowing Illume to unlock Uthrandir's cuffs after several seconds of fidgeting.

"Take the trunk and run. I'll unlock the cages as we go," Illume whispered.

Without a second thought, Uthrandir grabbed the trunk, tossed it onto his shoulder, as if it weighed nothing, and booked it the way they'd come. Illume gently picked Nari up, cradling her close to his chest before following Uthrandir.

Passing the first cage, on their way up, Illume unlocked it, giving the key ring to the dwarves inside. They broke the ring like it was made of playdough, allowing two dwarves to have keys. The rest followed Illume and Uthrandir.

Passing cage by cage, some full of dwarves, others with elves, men, and even orcs, all of whom were freed as the army of escapees behind Illume grew exponentially.

Illume glanced down to see the torches of the guards working their way up. They were still a good ways behind them, but they were gaining.

"They are catching up! We need to hurry!" Illume yells.

After fifteen minutes of sprinting and unlocking, several hundred prisoners were free and all heading toward the exit.

Reaching it, the last of the prisoners all piled onto a massive plateau at the entrance of a heavy gate.

"Earth Breakers at the ready!" Uthrandir roared.

Illume turned to see nearly two dozen dwarves, armed with pickaxes, standing on the edge of their plateau. Uthrandir lifted his arms.

"NOW!" he yelled.

Every dwarf swung in unison, their strike trembling the very foundations of the mountain range in which they dwelled. A huge chunk of stone slid away. Illume walked to the edge, looking down. A smirk curled on his lips as a massive rock slide flattened every cell, every path, and every guard on its way down.

"Good work, Uthrandir," Illume said softly before looking at the massive door before them. "Any idea on how to open that?" he asked.

"I might have an idea," Uthrandir said quietly.

Approaching the gate, the dwarf placed his hand on it and spoke in a tongue Illume couldn't understand. After several moments, a deep rumble filled the mountain as the massive doors gradually slid open. A beam of sunlight burst through like a flame, causing everyone to squint and shield their eyes.

As the doors opened, Illume recognized a figure standing at the door, blade in hand and drenched in blood. It was Trill. Surrounding him were the bodies of dozens if not hundreds of corrupted and the opening of the doors caused him to bolt around, lifting his sword to strike before relaxing as Illume pushed his way to the front with Nari in hand.

"You okay?" Illume asked.

"I've been tryin' to get in for the past three days!" Trill exclaimed, indicating the bodies. "They haven't been makin' it easy," he added with a laugh.

His smile quickly vanished, however, as he saw the state Nari was in.

32

FREEDOM

SLOWLY APPROACHING NARI, Trill placed a hand on her forehead. The soft light of his healing hands flooded her body, closing her wounds and healing her bruises. Illume glanced down to see the color returning to her toes; they twitched slightly. Nari let out a groan, still unconscious. Illume held her tightly as Trill finished healing her.

Finding a clean place, Illume laid Nari down and covered her with a blanket. Sitting on a nearby stump, Illume waved over the former prisoners and unshackled them one at a time.

It would take several hours, but freeing them was his top priority. Trill scavenged the corpses of his victims, taking anything of value while piling the rest up and setting it on fire.

"We owe you our lives," Uthrandir exclaimed as he pushed through the crowd to Illume.

"You owe me nothing. Slavery and wrongful imprisonment isn't right. I couldn't stand by and let it happen. I'm glad you're free, but we are far from safe. My team and I will escort you to Mobrebalku... I'm just going to call it Mobre for short because that's a mouthful. Any money, weapons, and armor that you can scavenge that won't corrupt you is yours. Everything else burns," Illume replied. He didn't stop unlocking shackles as he spoke.

"Why don't we just go to Lapideous? It is far closer and the terrain is easier to traverse," one of the men asked.

"You can't. Acheri infest the plains between us and Lapideous. Anyone that takes that route will be a sitting duck. Also, the forest is corrupted, so we will be moving at the base of the mountains until we can cross above the forest," Illume explained.

Several people grumbled, but a single stern look from Uthrandir shut them up really quickly. Uthrandir disappeared for a few minutes before returning with Illume's trunk. He set it next to Illume as Illume finished the last few shackles.

"I believe this belongs to you," Uthrandir said softly as he took a seat next to Illume.

"Only what I need; the rest will be yours. You and all these people will need a fresh start. That is something you can't do without coin," Illume said softly.

He opened the trunk and retrieved all of Nari's weapons and the rest of her clothing, leaving most of the money and gems within. Illume placed Nari's equipment in a neat pile next to her.

"Most of their homes were burned to the ground. Some are the last of their villages. We don't have much of a home to return to," Uthrandir explained.

"Well then, Cryo's Quarry is open to any who wish to settle a new home," Illume said softly. "They will have to work, but they will be well compensated for their labor."

Uthrandir looked down at all the enchanted shackles and shrugs. Trill approached Illume with both horses attached to carts. One of the carts was nearly completely full of usable materials while the other was mostly empty, save some food.

"Load up the shackles. I believe Buthrandir could use a lesson in how to forge metal infused with magic," Uthrandir proclaimed softly before standing.

"Are your people strong enough to move?" Illume asked.

Fastening the keys back to his belt, Illume moved to Nari, picking her up. He laid her down gently in the open cart. Returning to her equipment, he retrieved that as well. Uthrandir climbed atop the cart's driver seat and scanned the prisoners. He grunted and nodded.

"They look strong enough to hike," he replied.

"Good," Illume said. Standing, he looked out over the group of former prisoners. "Men and women, orcs and elves... my faithful dwarves. It is far too dangerous for us to stay here for the night. Any who are strong enough to walk will walk, those who cannot may cycle in and out of this cart. I will need volunteers for hunting and security." Illume noticed several men step forward as well as a handful of women.

"We have a long road ahead of us and this will not be easy, but I would appreciate unity in this travel. Once we reach our destination, you may go your own way. I know this isn't an ideal path we are taking, but know that there are monsters in the woods and worse beyond that. I have only your best interest and safety at heart. We leave in fifteen minutes!" Illume concluded before stepping down.

The ones who stepped forward were approached by Trill, who armed them and briefed them on what they would be doing. Several old individuals and young pregnant women with a few children made their way to the cart carrying Nari and climbed on.

One of the children asked if she was dead. Illume shook his head and told the child she was only sleeping.

A group this size was typically a logistical nightmare to move, but in ten minutes, they were already starting. Illume chalked their uniformity up to a mix of being terrified of Uthrandir and just happy to be out of a cage. Several people wept uncontrollably as they hiked and the gravity of their freedom hit them for the first time. Others couldn't help but let out a primal roar.

Most, however, remained quiet, reflecting on the beauty of the snowcapped mountains to their left, the crystal blue sky above them, and the rolling hills before them. Illume walked in the center of the group with Nari's cart. He didn't wish to leave her side unless necessary. The mass of people traveled all day, and as the sun set, everyone piled into a low point of the rolling foothills.

Some people set up tents, others made campfires and several just lay out under the gradually emerging stars. Trill took the first watch of men and stood on the hill's crest, keeping a close eye on their surroundings.

As the night carried on in relative silence, Illume sat looking at his ring. He had unwittingly entered the berserker mode and it scared him. Illume had done some stomach-turning dark things. He was glad no one had been there to witness them.

Illume gently ran his finger over the ring, curious as to what it would have been like to be able to control that state. Never wanting to use it again, Illume gripped the ring tightly against his finger and let out a labored sigh. The unmistakable footsteps of Uthrandir caught Illume's attention.

"What happened in there?" Uthrandir asked.

Illume knew he was referring to the berserker.

"I killed a corrupted orc. He had a book with the spell on it, and when I opened it, berserk was given to me, like it was uploaded into my brain. I didn't intentionally trigger it. Hell, I don't even remember about ninety percent of what I did," Illume replied.

"Most don't. But I have to warn you, as a human, tapping into that power means you are far stronger than you think. The last human who was able to use berserk ended up taking over the world, several times," Uthrandir whispered, hinting at the Dark King.

"Which would make me a target for bounty hunters and slavers," Illume replied softly.

"Not just them, the scientists too, and the mages. Everybody will want a literal piece of you to find out how they can achieve that power. So please, be careful," Uthrandir pled.

Illume nodded, giving the dwarf a pat on the shoulder. Uthrandir was called away. He got up and made his way to a group of dwarfs and began talking to them. Illume turned his attention to Nari. He sighed softly and shook his head, gently placing his hand on her forehead. She wasn't warm, which was a good thing, no infection. But he was worried about how long she would be unconscious.

Illume stayed up as late as he could, monitoring Nari for any changes. Nothing. He held her hand and spoke to her, hoping she'd be able to hear him and come back. Eventually, after everyone else had fallen asleep, Illume passed out. He had a dreamless sleep that night as exhaustion from his escape finally took hold.

A heavy '"THUD" woke Illume. Bolting straight up, Illume drew his dagger, only to see Trill standing above him with the grin of an idiot. An uncorrupted deer carcass lay before him as the scent of venison filled the camp.

"So you're the one who kills Bambi's mom," Illume said, softly rubbing his head.

"I don't know who Bambi is, but at least you get meat," Trill replied.

"He's exhausted, Trill. Let him have his black mana first." A familiar voice caused Illume's heart to jump.

Dropping his blade, Illume looked to see Nari standing before him with a mug of steaming coffee. She offered it to him. He took the cup and looked inside. It was the perfect caramel color.

"I found a goat. Figured you'd want that milk in there," she added with a soft smile.

Illume set down the coffee before bolting to his feet and slamming his body into hers, wrapping his arms around her. Illume hugged her so tightly, he heard her exhale involuntarily. After a brief moment, Illume felt her arms around him.

"Thank God you're okay," Illume whispered.

"Thank you for rescuing me," she replied in just as soft a tone.

Illume held Nari tight. The sight of her strung up like a piece of meat had shaken him to his very core. Seeing her standing before him caused relief to wash over him like a tidal wave.

"What do you remember?" Illume asked as he pulled away.

Nari's brow knitted together for a moment and her full lips pursed.

"Not much. My feet went numb. When I couldn't stand anymore, I was strung up and my hands fell asleep. Most everything else is just a blur. Why?" she asked with slight concern.

"No need to worry about it. The important thing is you are safe," Trill jumped in.

"And that we are all free," Illume added before releasing Nari and returning to his coffee. "Where do you keep finding these beans?" Illume asked.

Nari shrugged as she adjusted her clothing, which seemed to not quite fit her right.

"Those plants are all over the place; they are like weeds here. Most people just pull and burn them," she replied.

Illume gathered his pack together, sipping from the crisp light-flavored beverage as he did.

"Well, that's good, because where I come from, those trees take five years before they bear fruit and thus beans," Illume informed Nari while tossing his pack onto one of the carts.

"We ready to move out?" Nari asked Trill.

"I do believe so; just have to get a few things situated and we'll all be good to go," he answered.

"Awesome, let's get moving then. I'll take point. Nari, why don't you ride in the cart for today. You were pretty beat up and I don't want you collapsing on the hike." Illume's words were insistent.

Nari moved to argue but upon seeing the concern for her on Illume's face, she nodded.

"Okay, but only for today. I'm not taking some child's seat because I might faint," she relented.

"Thank you," Illume replied before moving to the head of the group.

Within ten minutes, the entire group was on their way, moving as a single unit toward the city of Mobre. As they hiked, Illume opened his map periodically to see if there were any hidden structures that his ring could reveal to him. There weren't; only caves, mountains, and trees.

Day two went off without any incident either as the sun set behind the mountains. Illume, Uthrandir, and Trill all helped set up camp while Nari played with the children and talked about forging with several other dwarves.

Like a well-oiled machine, everyone ate, got cleaned up, and settled in for the night by the time the stars decided to freckle the night sky with their glittering beauty.

33

MOBREBALKU

OVER THE NEXT FOUR DAYS, moving camp continued to go smoothly. Corrupted forest animals sniffed out the camp but kept their distance as if being commanded to. Illume and Nari grew closer as they had breakfast every day together, even though their duties kept them separated for the remainder of the day.

Illume found himself traveling next to Trillian most of the time. Uthrandir had taken a liking to Trillian, as both men were warriors at heart.

"You are far too young to remember this, but I fought in the Great Gnome War," Uthrandir informed Trill.

"I remember that, actually. I was to the east, so I could not participate... wait, you're not THE Uthrandir, are you?" Trill exclaimed.

"The gnome slayer," he replied.

This piqued Illume's interest. He tilted his head, listening in a little more carefully.

"You're the one responsible for their extinction!" Trill was completely fanboying at this point.

"Not exactly. I just killed their king. With the war claiming all his heirs, they just died out," Uthrandir replied before asking, "How about you, any great battles I may have heard of?"

"I fought in the battle of Yggdrasil against Hastir the Yellow," Trill replied.

"How is that possible? That was nearly a hundred years before my time!" Uthrandir proclaimed.

"I am much older than I look," Trill responded. "When the battle ended, the only two left were myself and Hastir. On that day, he promised not to bring desolation should I remain free from his lands."

"Then what happened?" Illume blurted, his curiosity boiling over.

"I don't know," Trill replied with a shrug. "I haven't seen him since."

As noon broke on the sixth day, a glint of light struck Illume's face, making him flinch and throw his hand up. He came to a stop. As a result, the rest of caravan did as well. The light continued to shine on them like a spotlight, making Illume growl in annoyance.

"What is that?" Illume whined.

"Mobrebalku," Trill responded, approaching Illume's side.

"The city of the forge, said to be founded by Domacius, god of the forge. Its metal walls were built from his very bones. It is said to be completely impenetrable in battle," Uthrandir marveled.

"Good, then let's pick up the pace," Illume said softly before turning to face the freed slaves. "WE'RE ALMOST THERE!" he yelled.

This bit of information boosted the moral of the exhausted group, causing their pace to nearly double. Focused on moving forward, no one really spoke. They did, however, retrieve their goods, money, and items of usefulness, greatly reducing the strain on Horson and Neighthan.

Before the sun set, Illume and his people approached the gates, only to be greeted by a full battalion of guards. Their armor was unique yet familiar; he'd seen it on the commander in Strang.

The guards drew their weapons and aimed them at Illume and his party. Illume threw his hand up, making the caravan stop.

Unbuckling his sword and daggers, Illume handed his weapons to Trill, who stood beside him. Placing his hands on his head, Illume gradually approached the guards, stopping about twenty yards away from them.

Illume raised his eyes to see dozens of archers aiming at him from behind the dark yet shiny metallic walls. If they wanted him dead, he would be dead.

"What is your business in Mobrebalku?" a voice shouted from the battlements.

"My business is to return these freed slaves to safety. I am Illume of Cryo's Quarry. I could not return these people to Lapideous because our path was blocked by Acheri and this was the only safe path to civilization," Illume called back.

"The Acheri are a myth!" one soldier yelled.

"Silence!" a familiar voice bellowed from in front of the gates. "What he speaks is the truth!" the voice rang out once more.

Every soldier stood down and stepped to the side, creating a path straight to the main gates. Standing at those gates was Commander Stark with two of his guards. A sigh of relief left Illume's chest. He marched toward his friend and both men grabbed each other's forearms and gave them a firm shake.

"It is good to see you again, Stark," Illume proclaimed.

"Likewise. I do wish it were under better circumstances," he replied.

Stark looked and made a circular motion with his hand. As he did, a deep rumble belted from the gate before them as it gradually swung open. Stark led Illume into the city. Illume's eyes wandered from metal structure to metal structure. It was like a crude version of New York City while still enthralling nonetheless.

"Unfortunately, numerous notable guards have been going missing, not just from here but from Lapideous as well. I was sent to investigate when the city was locked down," Stark explained.

"Well, I can tell you where those guards went. A few dozen at least were in the abandoned city of Strang, using this lot to mine for materials. I'm assuming for the Dark King," Illume informed his friend as everyone made their way to the center of the city.

"Can you tell me where they are now?" Stark persisted.

"Yeah... dead," Illume replied coldly.

Approaching the city's royal home, Illume glanced around to see hundreds of guards surrounding him and his people. Nari, Trill, and Uthrandir all made it to the front of the group, standing only several yards from Illume and Stark.

"Was there any way to save them?" Stark asked

"They were corrupted by whatever is affecting the forest. I don't know how we can fix it nor does anyone else I've come across so far. Now if you don't mind, I need to find these people a place to sleep before returning to Cryo's Quarry," Illume added, wanting to get home as quickly as he could.

"Not so fast!" a regal voice echoed from the lavishly adorned metallic structure before him.

From the edifice, a man wearing deep purple robes with green trim descended the steps. Not a single strand of his raven hair was out of place. He approached Illume, looking him up and down before offering a friendly smile.

"I am Morbre, king of Mobrebalku. Unfortunately, no one is allowed to leave. Someone has murdered my Vizier and everyone is a suspect. No one is leaving the city until I get to the bottom of this. As an outsider, I would like to hire you to investigate for me." Morbre's voice was that of a stuck-up rich kid.

New Side Quest.
Name: A killer among us.
Investigate and uncover who murdered the Vizier.
Bonus: Take them alive.

Illume sighed; he needed to return and gear up. The plight of the Dark King was spreading rapidly and it was only a matter of time before it overtook his town. Illume nodded in agreement with the king's request.

"Okay, fine. I will investigate under three conditions. One, your best forger works with Nari and Uthrandir on crafting better weapons and armor. Two, all these people have a safe place to stay for free until the week's end. And three, when I solve this case, I want enough horses for every individual who wishes to come with me to have one." Illume's voice was strong.

Illume had bargained several times in his life: to get the cost of his car down, to negotiate the price of his furniture. He'd even gone to flea markets to master the art of haggling just for fun. Apparently, all that practice worked and the king offered a hand to Illume.

"You have yourself a deal," he proclaimed.

Illume nodded as both men shook hands. Nari and Uthrandir left with a single guard and the cart full of forging supplies. Before leaving, Nari managed to talk Illume out of his armor and sword, saying she'd upgrade them for him while he investigated. Illume was then draped in a purple cloth, which was unsettling for him.

"I have heard much about your honor," the king stated, his near black eyes scanning Illume up and down. "And a man of such honor deserves the robes of a king."

Illume let out a sigh. In other games he played, these types of things were as easy as just following the trail of blood. They were so easy, a baby could often do it. He was curious if anything had changed from that trope.

"Please, lead the way, King Morbre. The sooner I start, the swifter justice can be served," Illume relented.

The king and his royal guards led Illume into the palace, whose metal was polished like marble. Stark kept a close step behind Illume as they entered a great hall. On the far side was a small corridor, which they entered.

The corridor led to another large room stacked high with books, floor to ceiling. Illume instinctively took a step back and looked at the library in awe. *In your face, Belle. This library is ten times better than Beast's!* Illume thought to himself before continuing on.

Walking to the back of the library, Illume saw a body slumped over with a book in hand and blood spattered all over the place. As Illume approached, everyone else dropped back, including the king himself. Illume paused. Observing the scene from a distance, he glanced back at the king.

"Has anything been moved?" Illume asked.

"Absolutely not," Morbre responded.

Illume stepped a little closer, channeling his inner Gil Grissom. Crouching, Illume looked for any signs of spatter being blocked, but there was nothing immediately noticeable. Illume moved closer to get a look at the body. The corpse was pale and cold to the touch. Illume assumed he'd been dead a little over a day.

Reaching down to the Vizier's collar, Illume lifted his cloak, noticing a broad stab wound at the base of his neck, just above the collarbone. The wound had dark tendrils stretching out from it in a similar grey to the skin of the orc he'd faced a week prior.

"Did the victim have any enemies?" Illume asked as he drew on the knowledge he'd picked up from watching crime scene investigation shows.

"He was the Vizier; he had as many enemies as I do!" the king replied.

Illume nodded as he gathered evidence, mentally logging spatter positions against the height of the Vizier and the angle of incidence of the blade.

"And why has he been left here for nearly a day without any formal investigation starting?" Illume asked.

"He was murdered inside of a locked down city in the depths of my home on a quiet night with no evidence of breaking in or out," the king replied. "Frankly, everyone is a suspect and I wanted someone who was not in the city at the time to investigate. Our messenger birds left the moment his body was found, asking for assistance."

Illume nodded. There was logic to his reasoning. Illume pried the book from the Vizier's cold, stiff hand. Turning it over, he read the cover: *Tome of Souls.* Just by holding the book, Illume could feel power coming off of it like the Elephant Foot in Chernobyl.

"Has anyone left the city since this discovery?" Illume asked, opening the book.

"Of course not," the king replied.

Illume flipped through the pages, coming across spells about how to make a grimoire card, a magical bomb of sorts. A half-demon, half-giant hybrid named Cambion and how he'd foretold to become a god among men. And even a serpent queen who could turn people to stone with her gaze.

There were binding spells in several pages of the books, including those talking about Cambion and this Medusa-like woman. A bloody thumbprint caused Illume to stop on a page near the back.

Having no earthly idea what he was looking at, Illume eventually came to the conclusion that this page in particular was about how to rip souls from bodies and use them as a fuel source.

Illume investigated the page closer. Soft grey lines were etched into the edge of the page. Illume turned to face the king, holding the book out as evidence. Approaching Morbre, Illume offered the page to him.

"What is this?" Illume asked.

"It's a spell that is supposed to be unknowable," the king replied. "Why do you ask?"

Illume closed the book. Clearly, Morbre had no idea what he was looking at.

"This is the reason your Vizier was killed. I am going to need every person who knows magic in the city brought together. I am going to want their weapons brought with them as well," Illume commanded.

Walking over to a fireplace, Illume threw the book inside before blasting it with a torrent of flames. Watching as the *Tome of Souls* burned, Illume huffed. He could have learned a lot from that book, but it was far too dangerous to be left in existence while the Dark King was rising to power and was clearly involved.

Illume didn't move until every page of the book was burned to ash. He turned to the king, who looked at Illume, petrified at his actions as every other guard aside from Stark left the room.

"Whoever killed your Vizier wanted a very particular page in that book. A page that could bring an end to your city, and every other city within days. I am going to need to see the Vizier's room," Illume demanded.

The king nodded, and without hesitation, led Illume to a small private stairwell attached to the library. After climbing a circular staircase several stories, Illume was introduced to the Vizier's chambers. Illume scoffed; his singular room was nicer than the combined fanciness of Illume's home.

34

TO CATCH A KILLER

ILLUME SPENT an hour snooping through the Vizier's room. Most of what he found was inconsequential just notes from council meetings or letters both to and from family. Investigative notes on the Order of Light even popped up from time to time, but nothing that indicated he was about to be killed. In his own personal library, there were no gaps where a book was missing, and even the false bottoms of his desk held nothing of importance.

Pacing back and forth for a few moments, Illume worked out how the murder could have potentially taken place. He paused as he realized that this was one of the wisdom/intelligence quests. Laughing to himself, Illume returned to Morbre and Stark just as the captain of the guard appeared at the top of the stairs.

"We have gathered all the mages, sir. They are in the main hall awaiting questioning," the commander declared before returning down the steps.

"Are you sure this is wise? These are some of the most powerful beings in my city; should they decide to turn on us, it is unlikely my forces will be able to withstand them all," the king advised.

"Don't worry. Those who are innocent will want the guilty party caught, probably more than we do so that their names will be cleared. If any of them try something, the others will jump in to assist us," Illume commented before descending the stairs.

Passing back through the library, Illume took one final look at the corpse. Lifting a hand, Illume noticed that there was blood under the fingernails—not much, but just enough for a noticeable scratch.

Leaving the man to rest in peace, Illume entered Morbre's main hall. Inside, there were roughly two dozen mages who stood in a horseshoe shape. Behind them were guards with pikes pointed at them from several feet away.

Illume entered the center of the horseshoe. Tables were set before the mages with their weapons displayed before them. Illume walked slowly around the inside of the tables, looking closely at each ornate weapon.

Some were normal yet highly decorated, others were bland with a unique magical shine to them. Illume grunted several times as he ruled out the shorter daggers or the full-length swords, leaving about half of the mages with weapons that matched the wound on the Vizier.

Next, Illume looked over the mages themselves. It was entirely possible more than one person was involved. Illume ruled out several as the actual killer as they were walking humanoid cats with fur, none of which he saw at either scene. Others were reptilian, who were eliminated for a similar reason to the cats. There were several dark-skinned beings that Illume ruled out as well since the skin under the Vizier's nails was just as pale as his own.

Illume narrowed it down to five mages. Pointing each out, he positioned them at the end of the horseshoe, instructing the other mages to line up behind the prime suspects. It was likely none of them knew why they were here, which meant throwing an accusation out would not do much good if there were a patsy involved. Illume decided to show part of his hand.

"There was a murder last night. The king's Vizier was slain in the other room while attempting to protect a book. Now, with this particular kind of book, only a certain kind of individual would be able to read it. One adept at magic. While I am not accusing all of you for this murder, there is a decent chance one of you has committed it. Should any of you have information about this, please step forward. You will be handsomely rewarded," Illume spoke plainly.

Keeping his eyes focused on several mages, Illume marked three who had no reaction to Illume's accusation. Approaching the final suspects and their weapons, Illume nodded to the first one.

"Since you don't wish to come forward, would you kindly draw your weapon and place a cut on your hand?" Illume insisted.

The first mage hesitated; this caused the guards to step forward, lifting their pikes toward him. That was all the goading he needed. The mage drew his short sword and placed a small slice onto the meat of his hand. Nothing but blood oozed from his hand.

"Thank you, sir. You may leave your weapon and step aside," Illume said softly.

The first mage left the table, moving behind the line of guards as he cast a healing spell on his hand. Illume moved to the second, a short woman who was about six inches too short to have actually committed the murder, but her sword fit the wound, and with magic, she could have elevated herself.

"Now, ma'am, would you kindly slice your hand with your sword?" Illume insisted once again. "Just a small cut will do."

"Hell no!" she barked and took a step back.

"Ma'am, I must insist. This is to prove your innocence," Illume persisted. "Please, it's for your own good. Alternate means will be less pleasant."

The woman hesitated. Stepping back to the table, she pulled her sword and held it to her hand, glancing at Illume, then she glanced at the guards. Illume could tell she was about to run. Reacting before the mage did, Illume fired a blast of frost at her just as she moved to throw her sword at Illume. His magic froze her sword to her hand. The guards charged in and grabbed her.

Illume approached the woman, looking at her weapon then over her form. She seemed rage-filled, not scared. Illume shook his head.

"You didn't kill the Vizier, did you?" he asked.

"No!" she growled back.

"Okay, I didn't think so. Do you mind telling me then why you just tried to kill me?" Illume asked, gently tapping her frozen hand, making her groan in pain.

"Because my sword has an illegal enchantment on it!" she blurted in agony.

Illume placed a flaming hand over her frozen one, gradually bringing it back to a normal temperature. The mage's fingers were blue as she released her sword. She held her hand close to her chest. Illume picked up her sword, observing it closely. It appeared rather unremarkable.

Short Sword
Name: The Blunder
Damage: +10
Weight: +5
Worth: 0 polis
This sword is illegally enchanted with a torturing truth spell. Anyone cut by this will immediately be engulfed in fiery agony until they give up all their secrets or die from the pain.

"That's interesting," Illume whispered wryly. "Ladies and gentlemen, what we have here is a sword of agonizing truth. Now we can continue my little experiment or I can give each and every one of you a little poke with this guy until we find what we want," Illume threatened.

Having no real intent to induce that much pain on so many innocents to catch one murderer, Illume wanted to see who would volunteer first. Hoping that Stark would not object, Illume toyed with the weapon's sharp edge. In the middle of the remaining suspects, a young mage, no older than twenty-two, pulled up her sleeve and thrust her arm out to Illume.

"I volunteer first!" she cried out, her voice trembling.

Illume walked over to the woman. Setting the sword down in front of her, he leaned on the table. She was so fresh-faced, so innocent, and so desperate to prove her innocence, she was willing to die for it. A perfect patsy. Illume lifted the sword and placed it gently against her soft flesh.

"You do know what you are about to go through, correct?" Illume asked, not looking at the mage but those behind her.

"Yes, sir!" she whimpered, trying so hard to stay strong.

Illume turned the blade and pressed it against her skin, not yet slicing but getting just a tap of pressure away. The girl closed her eyes and let off a soft squeal of fear and that was when he got what he was looking for. In the back, one of the hooded mages smirked. All the others were sweating bullets and trembling in fear save this one mage.

Illume dropped the sword behind him with a clatter, causing the girl to exhale and nearly collapse. Illume stood before her, observing her for a few moments until the color returned to her face. He offered her a friendly smile before reaching down and grabbing her weapon.

"You did wonderfully, darling. I'm sorry that I scared you." Illume's tone softened. "You can take your place back in line."

Weapon in hand, Illume approached the only mage that smirked and held out the weapon. Illume did not speak initially, thinking that his actions would speak for themselves. The mage didn't move. It grew so silent, Illume could hear a pin drop. Reaching up, Illume yanked the hood off the mage.

"Would you kindly cut your hand," Illume commanded, his tone deeper, more menacing now.

"That isn't my blade," the mage replied.

Illume pushed the weapon closer.

"I'm not asking if it's your blade. I'm telling you to cut your hand," Illume pressed. "Do it, now."

There were several seconds where both men engaged in a stare-off against one another in a tense battle of wills. After several seconds, the mage threw his hands together, only for a purple light to slam into him, holding him in place.

Illume looked back at the girl he'd just interrogated; her hand was outstretched and a ball of purple energy glowed within her palm while holding the sword out to a guard.

"Guards, this is the man you're looking for. He will have fresh scratches on the back of his neck, and in his home, you will find a letter from a man named Ierret. Destroy the sword. It is contaminated. And make sure this young mage is well compensated for her troubles." Illume spoke softly as the guards rushed the mage and locked him in cuffs.

Illume approached the girl, who was holding her would-be framer in place, anger filling her face. Eventually, she dropped the spell once the mage was completely restrained, letting out a frustrated sigh.

"I do apologize for what I put you through. I want you to know I would never have cut you. I just needed to see the one person who was not scared for you. They would have been the one responsible and you would have been their scapegoat." Illume's tone was apologetic. "There is a dwarf here named Uthrandir. He has access to magical metals. Tell him Illume says to forge you a new weapon with those, okay?"

She was trembling, but offered Illume a large smile and nod. She was adorable, like a fluffy little puppy that was scared of everything, yet something deep within her could rip everyone apart should it be let out. Illume could tell from her demeanor that she was a good person. Guilt tugged at his gut for what he did to her.

35

EXPLANATION

ILLUME WALKED BACK over to the would-be assassin. Reaching up his sleeve, Illume pulled out the copied page of the *Tome of Souls,* unfurling it for the king to see. Once the king nodded, Illume incinerated it to prevent the spell from falling into anyone's hands. Illume approached Morbre and Stark, escorting all the mages from the building.

"How did you know?" Morbre asked in awe.

Illume chuckled, moving back into the library. He waved for both men to follow, and they did. Walking over to the Vizier, Illume pulled back his collar, showing the toxic lines stemming from the wound.

"This is a typical short sword injury, meaning anyone who had any weapon other than a short sword would be above suspicion. Next, the black veins coming out of the wound indicate the weapon was contaminated by the Dark King." Illume paused for a moment.

"So that's why you had them slice their hands!" Stark jumped in. Illume pointed at the captain.

"Exactly. If the person who did it knew the blade was corrupted, then they would find an excuse not to cut themselves. Next is the angle of the entry wound and the way the blood spatters against the books. It shows whoever did this was behind the Vizier and just a few inches taller than he was."

"But magic could have been involved!" the king added, his voice enthralled with the deductions.

"Exactly. That is why I did not discriminate against height, but skin tone, on the other hand." Illume laughed at his own pun. He didn't even mean to make it as he lifted the Vizier's hand. "If you look under his nails, he scratched whoever killed him, and as you can see, the skin is as pasty as an Irishman in the winter."

"So the illegal weapon?" Stark asked.

"That was a fluke, a fortunate accident; it just helped me sell my strategy a little more," Illume replied with a laugh.

"Did you even suspect that smaller group?" Morbre asked as Illume left the library, the king and Stark following once again.

"Partially, but with no evidence in the Vizier's room indicating he was about to be killed, I figured the more likely scenario is someone would be framed. I just looked for the one person who didn't show concern for the safety of their fellow mages," Illume concluded as he turned around to face the king.

"Looks like that magician lost his sleight of hand." Illume did his best Horatio Caine impression before turning and walking out of the king's house while shouting at the top of his lungs. "OOOHHHH!!!"

Speech Level Up
Attraction now available
Persuasion now available

Side Quest Complete:
A Killer Among Us
Bonus Objective: Capture Alive
Successful.

Exiting into the darkness, Illume wondered how long he'd been at the investigation game. It was an easy quest, one that a lot of RPGs did, and he would have wished it could have been longer so he could channel more of his inner Hercule Poirot.

Illume wandered around in the dark for nearly an hour, kicking himself for wanting to make such a flashy exit, he'd forgotten to ask for directions. No way he could return now as he'd look like an idiot. Not like pulling the "oh" made him look like any less of a moron.

"Hey!" Nari's soft voice caught Illume by surprise.

Illume turned to see her standing against one of the metal buildings, clearly hiding something behind her back.

"I've been looking for you," she added with a teasing tone.

"You have?" Illume played back.

"Where'd you go?" Nari asked.

She pushed off the building and slowly approached Illume. Each step seemed to be an intentional tease to him as she moved closer with each step.

"I was just solving a murder," Illume said, trying not to sound like he enjoyed the hunt. "No big deal."

"Did you get your guy?" she asked, arching an eyebrow.

She stepped closer, now only several feet away. Illume's heart raced. He didn't seem to have to fight as hard not to say something stupid.

"I always get my guy," he teased back.

"Well then, I guess you have earned this as a congratulations." Nari's voice was sultry as she spoke, sending chills down Illume's spine.

Nari pulled out from behind her back a longbow, nearly as tall as Illume, crafted from the horns of the chimera. There was a shimmer to it as the moon's light fell on the weapon. Nari held it out to Illume for him to accept. He hesitated for a moment.

"I heard how you wouldn't leave my side when you found me back at Strang. Apparently, without you, I would be dead or worse. I just wanted to say thank you in some small way." Nari's tone changed to something a little more sincere.

Illume reached out and coiled his fingers around the soft

leather grip of his new bow. It was heavier than the last one, but it had a durability to it. Illume grabbed the string and drew it back. It took some strength to fully pull the string back, but it would undoubtedly be able to pierce armor at close range.

Flawless Legendary Bow
Name: Chimera's Bane of Confinement
Damage: +25
Weight: +19
Worth: N/A
This one of a kind bow automatically infuses any arrow shot by it with the venom of a chimera. Confinement enchantment prevents magical spells from being cast, has a 10% chance of the spell backfiring, further damaging your opponent.
Sometimes it's better to fight than run.

Illume couldn't help but let a smile crack on his lips as he read the true potency of his new weapon. He looked at Nari with thankful and longing eyes before giving her a tight hug.

"Thank you so much!" His voice muffled into her hair.

Illume felt her hands gently find their way onto his unarmored back. Her touch made his hair stand on end. His heart pounded in his chest and his adrenaline surged. If she were real, he would commit himself wholly to her today.

They embraced for what seemed like hours, and yet mere moments. Enthralled by Nari, Illume eventually reluctantly let her go. She released him in the same reluctant manner. Illume slung the bow over his shoulder before turning his attention back to the city.

"So where the hell are we?" Illume asked in confusion.

His question made Nari laugh.

"We were put up in a storehouse not far from here. Most of the people no longer have homes and want to join Cryo's Quarry. There are several who are going to accompany us, but they will be leaving after a few days. You really inspired them, Illume. You gave them hope," Nari said softly while gently rubbing Illume's upper back almost instinctively. "They need someone like you. This world needs someone like you."

Illume offered Nari a smile, not wanting her to stop but needing to get some rest. He nodded for her to lead the way. Lowering her hand, she made her way down a slight incline. Illume followed closely behind. Illume wanted to stay and explore the city longer, but if there were trouble at his town, it would be better to make the trip to deal with it, then come back later.

Rounding a corner, Illume could hear music and singing coming from a large structure ahead of them. It was a celebration, one that brought a smile to his face. Out front, a forge was burning brightly with several forgemasters working with Uthrandir, shaping weapons. Illume recognized one of the figures leaving the forge. It was the mage he'd accused. She managed to get her weapon replaced.

Approaching the structure, Illume offered Uthrandir a nod. The dwarf responded in kind while pounding a sigil-laced hammer into magical metals, shaping them to his will. He had been busy and clearly had some help as several swords, sets of armor, and shields pile to the side, all with a similar shine to them.

"Learning a lot. Thanks for bringing us here!" Uthrandir called out over the clanging of his hammer. Illume just waved.

Illume fell back behind Nari, handing Uthrandir the chimera fangs, whispering a request for them to be turned into daggers. Uthrandir nodded with a smile as if he was never happier than when swinging his hammer. Entering, Illume was taken aback by the sheer joy that stood, or more like danced, before him.

Awe filled Illume as he saw dwarves dancing with elves, orcs dancing with humans, and a massive makeshift band playing whatever they could get their hands on. A fire pit was in the center of their structure, and above the long corridor of flames, sat the remaining food that they had not yet cooked from their trip.

Illume walked around greeting everyone he came across, talking to some, dancing with others, albeit clumsily. Illume glanced over at Nari, who was pulled into an orcish folk dance that was surprisingly graceful for such a lumbering species.

It was nice to see, even with her dance partner a mountain compared to her. Wandering even deeper, Illume scanned around, looking for familiar faces or for someone to get to know.

"I'm buying!" Illume heard ring out over the crowd.

Instantly, Illume whipped around to see Trillian sitting next to some poor elf sucker with a mug of ale in front of him. Illume wanted to go over and warn the elf, but at the same time, he was curious to see history repeat itself. Perhaps he'd get a sneak peek into whatever happened to him the night Trill and Illume met.

Illume grabbed a flagon of ale as a human barmaid walked by with a tray full. Illume offered her a smile and several polis for the delivery. She curtsied to him, he bowed slightly to her, and she was on her way once again. Illume took a swig of the sweet, crisp ale. It had a slight taste of apples, his favorite fruit.

Feeling a bit like a creeper but not really caring, Illume continued to watch as Trill drank the elf under the table like it was nothing. He managed to talk the elf into doing a little jig, but he ended up falling over and passing out before he got three steps into the dance.

A green-skinned orc female apparently was watching too and found Trill's ability to put back ale an attractive trait. The orc pulled a seat next to Trill and handed him a drink before ordering one herself. Trill took the drink and they slammed glasses together. She drank, as did he.

Illume noticed he tried to stop but was unable to since the orc hadn't stopped either. It would be rude for him to stop drinking first, and with a woman the size of a barn, the last thing Trill would want to do was insult her.

In no time at all, Trill was in another drink-off, only this time, he seemed to have met his match as she put away two drinks to his every one. Desperately wanting to join the party, Illume was unable to pull himself away from the train wreck that was before him. He sat there and laughed as their mugs piled up until Trill collapsed into the orc's lap. She picked him up and tossed him over her shoulder.

"What's so funny?" Nari yelled as she finally found Illume again.

"Trill got himself a girlfriend!" Illume replied, pointing out the nearly unconscious soldier slung over the orc's back.

collapsed into Biddie's lap. She picked her up and threw her over her shoulder.

"What's [illegible]?" Nan yelled as she finally [illegible] again.

"Tell you [illegible]!" Hattie replied, pointing out the nearly unconscious [illegible] over the girl's back.

36

RACING HOME

ILLUME, much like everyone else, he suspected, woke up the next morning with something a little larger than a minor headache, and a slight aversion to light and sounds that made the elephants' march in the Jungle Book seem quiet.

Letting out a soft groan, Illume held his head as he pushed himself off the floor; his mouth was so dry, his lips felt locked together and a constant urge to vomit tugged at his stomach.

"By the gods, kill me now," Nari whimpered from the floor.

Illume looked down to see her resting the back of her hand over her eyes swearing she'll never drink again. Illume staggered over to her and offered her a hand up, and just like two wet noodles, their dance to standing was a wobbly and painful one.

"Have you seen Trillian?" Illume asked in a whisper.

"I think he may have died," Nari replied with a groan.

Illume took Nari's hand, partially for stability and partially so she wouldn't step on any of the sleeping people they had their lovely little party with. Making it to the structure's door, Illume leaned against it and squinted in the light of day.

On the forge lay Trill, out cold with his orc companion on the ground next to him. With feet feeling like they'd been locked solidly into concrete, Illume and Nari struggled to make it to Trill who, just as they approached him, sat up screaming.

His yells sent sharp pains through Illume's head as he cowered back holding his ears, with Nari doing the same. After several seconds, Trill calmed himself down and let out a painful groan. Reaching out, he instinctively used healing hands on Illume and Nari.

Illume's health bar completely opened, no longer greyed out from his concussion. The hangover didn't go away completely, but they were healed enough that every little sound didn't threaten to kill them.

"Would you like to buy a healing spell?" a gravelly voice called from behind Illume.

Turning, Illume saw a goblin with a cart full of books, most of which were healing spells. Nodding in desperation, Illume found two books titled *Healing Hands* and *Kind Hearted.*

Pulling off his purse, Illume dumped out nearly two thousand polis for the goblin just to make him go away. Illume opened both books, absorbing each spell in a desperate hope that it would get rid of his hangover. No dice.

Spells Learned:
Kind Hearted: Able to heal others for 5 points of health for 3 mana per second
Healing Hands: Able to heal one's self for 5 points of health for 3 mana per second
Dual Casting carries over increasing healing to 20 points of health for 6 mana per second.

Remembering he had a level up available, Illume toyed with the idea of using it but decided not to in case a situation arose where he'd need it. Reaching out, Illume used his Kind Hearted healing ability on Nari, helping her recover. Walking over to the horses, Illume grabbed a mana potion out of its sack before heading back into the building.

Illume walked into the building with all the passed-out people in it. Holding his hand out, he cast his healing spell to rid everyone else of their hangovers too. As his mana started to drop, Illume chugged the potion, allowing him to make one round through the building and heal everyone just a little bit.

Restoration Leveled Up
Dual Casting already learned.

Illume looked around and saw Uthrandir standing at one of the small side doors waving for Illume to come to him. Illume followed his friend's suggestion and exited the side of their "housing." Uthrandir held out two beautifully carved arched daggers that were as sharp as a razor. Illume's eyes began to well.

"These are beautiful!" Illume whispered.

"Careful, they are highly toxic. One stab and the victim will be down before you can even blink," Uthrandir warned while handing Illume their sheaths. Illume placed the weapons in them as Uthrandir continued, "I also took the liberty of using the chimera hide to enhance your armor." The dwarf revealed his armor, which now had a matted finish to it.

Illume leaned down, grabbing the armor. He placed it on his body, where he got his new armor notifications.

Flawless Legendary Dwarven Armor: Hybrid
Armor: +80
Weight: +30
Worth: N/A
With chimera hide added, this now top of the line armor is one of the best on the market.
Armor attributes enhance by 25% when worn as a full set.

Flawless Legendary Dwarven Gauntlets: Hybrid
Armor: +25
Weight: +4

Worth: N/A
With chimera hide added, this now top of the line armor is one of the best on the market.
Armor attributes enhanced by 25% when worn as a full set.

Flawless Legendary Dwarven Boots: Hybrid
Armor: +25
Weight: +4
Worth: N/A
Eh… you get the point.

Flawless Legendary Dwarven Helmet: Hybrid
Armor: +30
Weight: +5
Worth: N/A
Overall Armor Rating (including bonus): +200

Illume dropped down to his knees ever so slowly. Uthrandir grew uncomfortable asking what he was doing. Leaning in, Illume gave Uthrandir a massive hug, to which the dwarf reacted similarly to the way a cat would, backing up until he wiggled free of Illume's embrace.

"I enhanced your weapons as well; they should be twice as good as before. Now where is that lady friend of yours?" Uthrandir asked. "I have something for her as well. Just don't, just don't hug me again. It's weird."

Illume gathered his weapons and his chimera bone arrows, which had a +20 base damage with an additional +10 poison if struck on non-armored areas. Nodding for Uthrandir to follow, Illume found Nari by herself fiddling with the forge. She offered Illume a warm smile when she saw his new armor.

"You look good!" she exclaimed.

"I'm not the only one who got a new wardrobe," Illume replied while nodding to Uthrandir.

The dwarf approached Nari and held up an outfit made of the

chimera's snakeskin. Nari was hesitant to accept the gift. Eventually giving in, she took the clothes and disappeared around a log pile. Illume heard her struggling to change with several "oofs" and "ahs."

After several more minutes, she emerged from behind the wood pile. Illume's jaw dropped. The outfit was similar to her previous one only much tighter, leaving almost nothing to the imagination. Nari moved and twisted in it. She had a pleased look on her face until she looked down.

"Does it have to be so form-fitting?" she asked. "This is kind of sexist."

"Unfortunately, the serpent parts of chimera aren't stretchable, but I assure you that is just as tough as Illume's armor. Nothing short of anything legendary is getting through that armor," Uthrandir explained. "There was only so much snakeskin to go around."

"Oh, these are supposed to go with your suit as well," Illume added while handing Nari her new daggers.

Nari unsheathed them, looking at them closely before mouthing a thank you to Illume. The lovely and quiet moment was interrupted by Commander Stark and his men approaching on horses with Trill close behind on foot.

"Illume," Stark's voice was strained as he talked, "we just received word from Victor. Cryo's Quarry is under attack."

37

WAR

"WHAT? BY WHO?" Illume asked, confused.

"We don't know. Our messenger bird just returned. Victor said an army is marching on Cryo's Quarry and it is unlike anything he's seen before," Stark responded as Morbre rode up with two dozen unmanned horses behind him.

"Cryo's Quarry has got to be three days ride from here!" Nari exclaimed as she moved to untie Neighthan Fillyan and climbed on.

"Three days' hard ride!" Stark retorted.

"We don't have the defenses to withstand a battle for that long!" Trill snarled, mounting one of the free horses.

Illume mounted Horson Wells. Reaching down, he grabbed the mark of Elatus. It glowed, then turned black on his forearm. He had to admit it looked like a cool tattoo. He focused on Cryo's Quarry as he summoned them for aid.

"I have some friends who will buy us time. Wake whoever you can. We ride now!" Illume roared, giving his horse a quick kick.

Like a shot, Illume took off down the streets of the city and out the front gates. Nari and Trillian were close behind, followed by Stark and a large contingent of Morbre's mounted forces for aid.

Staggering behind were two dozen of the rescued slaves who had pledged themselves to Illume, be it in public or private.

The downside of not having a horse to match him was that all the horses had to stop and rest, eat, and drink. Otherwise, they would die. Illume figured they'd be able to make it to Cryo's Quarry in less than two days if they didn't have to make camp and let the beasts rest.

He was thankful for the downtime, however, as he used it to formulate a plan of attack for whatever forces were descending on Cryo's Quarry.

Illume didn't just make one or two—no, Illume made dozens, hundreds of different battle plans. He went over them and over them, briefing Nari, Stark, Trill, and Uthrandir on every possible scenario. As they rode, Illume had his "commanders" recite the plans to him over and over again, giving each a special designation.

Alpha was a head-on assault, should the forces be between them and Cryo's Quarry, just turn into a wedge and ride through them. Gamma was if they were already inside the walls and a sneak attack was required and so on and so forth.

At noon on the third day, Illume saw billows of smoke rising on the horizon; it had to have been Cryo's Quarry. Just beyond, Illume noticed a familiar dirt cloud that seemed to be growing larger with each passing moment.

As they crested a hill, Illume's heart sank. Massive white walls were stained with soot as the ground around them burned. The moat had been dammed off, allowing for siege ladders to be more easily raised up the sides of the city.

Illume could see a small contingent of Lapideous guards within the walls assisting the fight while a small pack of Lycans were in their beast form knocking the siege ladders off. A massive force had moved to the front of their land bridge, and from the looks of it, had started trying to break down the main gate.

Buildings were burning and screams can be heard echoing over the plains. A knot formed in Illume's stomach. He fought the urge to release the berserker and only drew his bow and notched an arrow.

"No matter what happens, no enemy will set foot in our city," Illume growled as his hands instinctively frosted over. "When the centaurs come, don't get in their way. Just focus on finding and killing whatever leads that army."

Illume could feel Trill wanted to make a centaur joke but refrained. Illume turned back to the small band that had ridden with him for the past three days.

"I will ask none of you to ride with me, but Cryo's Quarry is my home! The Dark King is laying siege to it because it is a threat to what he stands for and I for one will NOT stand idly by and let him bring ruin to this world any longer!" Illume roared. "Will you!?"

Although the band was small, the roar they released was mighty, trembling the very ground and sailing over the plains with such force that the Dark King's forces turned to see what the source was.

"Charge!"

Illume stood in his stirrups, rocking back and forth to maintain his balance as he charged across the field. Notching an arrow, Illume drew and took aim at the horde that had begun to turn towards him. These corrupted looked different from others, like an art piece that was rushed. Their skin was grey but pustules formed all over their bodies with black goo oozing from them.

The same ooze poured from their mouths as if wanting to corrupt everything they came in contact with. An unearthly roar filled the air in a blend reminiscent of a Nazgul and the Hulk combined. Illume released his arrow. In the blink of an eye, his projectile crossed the field of battle, missing his intended target but still slamming into another soldier. The soldier fell to the ground, lifeless, as did three others behind him. The chimera arrow pierced through all their bodies before hitting the ground.

Illume notches another arrow and fires, this time into the stampeding army toward them. As the gap closed, Illume continued to shoot his bow as quickly as he could, hitting his target about half the time but killing at least one corrupted soldier with each shot. Now less than fifty yards away from one another, the enemy's commanders emerged, two berserker orcs riding chimera.

Illume had two arrows left. Nocking both, he drew back, aiming for the chimera's lion head. They both let out roars; even better. As he released the arrows, both chimera immediately fell dead as the toxic arrows found their targets, sliding down their throats and piercing their internal organs. Illume pointed his bow at the chimera.

"Stay clear of the tails!" he yelled loud enough for everyone around him to hear.

The spear-wielding riders lowered their weapons, aiming them forward as the chimera tails both struck their orc riders, followed by snapping at everything around them without bias. Illume slung his bow over his back before drawing his sword, lining up his trajectory to pass between the chimera, just out of either tail's reach.

As he passed through, both struck at him but narrowly missed as he swung his sword into the chest of one of the soldiers near him. The strike took down over two-thirds of his health while an arrow finished him off.

The pikemen ripped through the first wave of soldiers as if they were nothing, as metal clashed with metal and ripped into flesh. Roars and screams echoed from all around Illume as he hacked and slashed his way through the corrupted army. Illume pushed farther forward than the rest of his forces, intentionally getting himself surrounded and putting distance between him and his forces.

Glancing back as the corrupted close in, Illume saw Nari, on foot—dodging, slashing, stabbing, and throwing her daggers with the grace of a ballerina and the ferocity of an angry bull.

Illume threw his sword into the ground as he brought his horse to a stop. Horson reared on his hind legs, and with a primal roar, Illume unleashed a torrent of electricity out of both of his hands.

The metal armor of the corrupted acting as a conduit prevented Illume's spell from dissipating as rapidly. Bolts of electricity branched out in all directions, surrounding Illume in flickering lights, the scent of charring flesh, and the agonizing screams of corrupted soldiers. Feeling a bit like Raiden, Illume used all of his mana to clear a thirty-foot circle around him.

Dismounting Horson, Illume pulled his sword from the ground while grabbing a mana potion from his steed's saddle bag. When he guzzled the potion, Illume's mana regenerated completely. An arrow struck Illume in the shoulder, causing his health to drop by one-eighth. Illume growled as the pain from the attack howled through his body like a banshee on the moors.

When he ripped the arrow out, Illume was informed he was bleeding. Dropping the projectile, Illume summoned his healing spell, holding it to his shoulder as he marched toward his enemies. As his health regenerated, Illume deflected the next arrow fired at him.

Dodging sideways, Illume watched as the health bar of another attacker dropped by a third. Deflecting the corrupted's sword, Illume drew Bloodlust and stabbed it under the soldier's armor, invoking bleeding damage that would finish off the remnants of his life bar.

Illume could hear his people hacking and slashing behind him as they reached about a third of the way through the corrupted forces. Out of the corner of Illume's eye, he caught an axe dropping down for him.

Opening his palm, he flash-froze the weapon, not having the clearance to dodge properly. He tanked the axe blow on his shoulder armor and it shattered while causing his life bar to drop hardly at all.

Turning, Illume ran his sword through the corrupted orc that had attempted to axe him, dropping his life by half. Illume placed his fist against the orc's chest and pushed him backward as hard as he can, all the while using frost on him.

The orc's life bar dropped to roughly a quarter when Illume pulled his sword from its gut, causing a fountain of black blood to erupt from the wound, and slammed the pommel of his sword into its chest, shattering its heart and killing it.

Illume went back toward the land bridge and was struck in the chest by another arrow. It bounced off his armor, doing no damage at all. He was glad Uthrandir upgraded it. Retrieving the arrow, Illume unslung his own bow and returned fire. The corrupted that shot at him fell back as he was pierced by his own arrow, making his health drop to almost half.

Illume's forces managed to carve their way up to him just as a deafening roar rippled through the battlefield. In all the commotion, Illume didn't notice the trolls, mountainous beasts nearly twice the size of an orc.

They carried enormous columns of granite on their shoulder, which was chained to them. Three charged through the corrupted, stomping their own people down without a care.

"You're going to want this!" Nari yells.

She ran beside Illume, chimera arrow in hand. He took his arrow back; at least he'd get to kill one. Drawing, Illume aimed directly for the beast's heart, releasing his arrow. It found its mark. The troll didn't slow down; his health only dropped an eighth and the attack only made him roar in rage.

The howls of wolves rang out as Victor and his pack leaped from the battlements, ripping through the corrupted before leaping onto one of the trolls. Eight Lycans and its health dropped slowly. At this rate, the battle would be over by the time the first troll died. Illume threw his sword down and began to hyperventilate; not out of fear, out of intention.

"Nari, get out of here!" Illume snarled. She immediately obeyed.

Slamming his fist into his chest, Illume forced his heart rate to rise and his adrenaline to start pumping. A shadow cast by the troll's stone weapon fell on Illume as he felt a deep-seated rage activate within him. Throwing his hands up, Illume stopped the pillar with his bare hands, throwing it to the side and imbedding the troll's weapon into the ground.

Trophy Earned.
Name: Control
Type: Gold
Requirements: Control the Berserker Rage for the first time.
Not even the gods can save your enemies.

Illume hopped onto the stone pillar and ran up it while unleashing a volcano of flames at its face. The magic didn't do much damage, but it did blind the troll as it swung at Illume and missed, shattering its weapon into pieces. Drawing his daggers, Illume dug them into the troll's arm as he approached its head.

The troll attempted to shake Illume off but only succeeded in throwing Illume towards its head. Illume dug his dagger into the troll's shoulder, holding tight. The momentum slung him onto the troll's back. He reached around its head, grabbing one of its orc-like tusks, and punched the troll in its temple with his other hand. Each blow did more damage than his arrow.

Illume saw the third troll meet his forces, and with a single swipe, nearly ten men fell. Illume had to end this quick before his berserker state wore off. Illume slammed his fist a few more times into the troll's skull before grabbing the back of its head.

With all his strength, Illume jerked the troll's head to one side so hard that he felt the bones of the troll's neck crumble. The subsequent snapping sound was one of the loudest things he'd ever heard.

Illume rode the troll's back as its lifeless body fell to the ground, landing right next to his sword. Illume grabbed his blade, charging across the battlefield. Enemy weapons bounced off his skin like bullets against Superman, and with a single punch,

Illume took a life. Controlling the berserker certainly was a good thing.

The third troll managed to get several more blows in before Illume was able to get between them and catch the troll's pillar as well. Illume slammed it into the ground, holding it still. He could feel the berserker starting to wear off. Not having time to snap its neck, Illume looked around at his men.

"NOW GIVE IT EVERYTHING YOU'VE GOT!" he roared.

Spears, axes, arrows, and even swords all flew at the troll's face. Most bounced off its tough skin, the ones that didn't causing hardly any damage to it. Illume felt the berserker rage completely fade.

With a flick of its wrist, the troll caused its pillar to buck so violently, Illume was sent on his back. The troll raised the pillar above its head, its eyes locked on Illume.

"This re-spawn is going to suck," Illume grumbles.

Just as it was about to bring down the pillar on Illume, a massive battle axe, larger than anything Illume's seen, sliced clean through the troll's arms like a hot knife through butter. The axe slammed into the battlefield several dozens of yards away like an artillery shell. Dirt flew everywhere. Dozens of corrupted were blasted to bits and the earth itself shook.

Another axe skimmed the back of the troll's legs, now spurting fountains of its black blood. The troll roared in pain. A blur passed the beast, accompanied by ground-shaking thumps, and its head fell off, hitting the ground before Illume. Illume pulled himself to his feet as the centaurs finally arrived.

The beautiful giants rode through the battlefield, mowing the corrupted down like the grass in Illume's backyard when it got too long. Massive axes and swords took out droves of corrupted. Those who didn't die by metal were trampled into paste.

Illume sheathed his sword, enjoying the view of the centaurs riding straight through the opposing army without slowing down. Within three minutes, the battle was over with no corrupted still standing outside the gates.

Nari and Trill made their way to Illume's side as the "show" unfolded before them. Trill had a look of concern spread across his face while Nari couldn't help but smile as she cleaned her daggers. The matriarch circled around as her people trotted to the far side of Cryo's Quarry and fell into formation. Illume approached her, bowing to her slightly as she did the same.

"Thank you, you saved my people," Illume called.

"Our people," she replied softly. "You are marked as one of us, your tribe is our tribe."

"Then Cryo's Quarry's doors are always open to you. They may be a little small, but we will help you in any way we can," Illume replied.

"Until next time, cryomancer." She bowed once again before turning and trotting off with her people.

"Where the hell did they come from?" Nari asked.

"You remember when I told you I saw an Acheri? That was because I heard her daughter caught in a bandit trap. I managed to free her daughter, and as a thank you, she gave me this," Illume replied holding up his arm, showing off the mark. "Pretty cool, right?"

"You're a centaur, then!" Trill exclaimed with a hint of worry.

"ILLUME!" Victor roared as he and his pack tore across the battlefield.

Illume approached Victor as he took human form, panting and exhausted from battle. Several deep gashes decorated his body. Reaching out, Illume healed his friend to the best of his abilities.

"What is it, Victor?" Illume asked as his mana dropped to zero. "What's wrong?"

"It's Balathor; he's the cause of all of this! And he has my family," Victor pleaded. "I need your help once more."

38

SOMETIMES DEAD WAS BETTER

ILLUME ORDERED Trill to stay behind and tend to the wounded after Nari asked where he was the entire battle. Uthrandir and Stark managed to catch up to Victor and Illume as they walked toward the land bridge.

Illume instructed Stark to have his men find any and all healing potions tucked away in Cryo's Quarry while Uthrandir was to gather non-corrupted metals and burn the corpses and equipment of the corrupted. Stark whistled and several of his men ran, catching up with them as well.

"How was Balathor able to overtake you, Halfdan, and Abe?" Illume asked.

Nari walked next to Illume, harvesting any arrows they came across that were still usable.

"He got his hands on some hidden magical items that outclassed anything we had," Victor replied. "He was a snake all along."

Illume gave Nari a concerned look. She returned the same gaze.

"Where is Buthrandir?" Illume asked.

"She went to Lapideous almost two weeks ago for supplies. Why?" Victor had a hint of confusion in his voice.

"You don't think she would have?" Illume turned to Nari.

"Never, she loves Cryo's Quarry," Nari retorted.

Illume nodded. Nari's word was all he needed. Ascending the land bridge, Illume gazed at the massive wooden gate that was reinforced by metal. Illume was happy to have left Buthrandir in charge of metal work. Anything less than perfection and the gate would have given way.

With a loud creaking, the gate slid open. Illume looked around at the now nearly fully developed Cryo's Quarry. The inn had stables now, there were several houses, and even the blacksmith's shop was completely built.

On the far side was a massive structure that wasn't there before. It appeared almost like a palace made of sliced logs. Halfdan must have gotten his mill.

"He's in there," Victor said softly, nodding in front of them.

"Do you know where?" Illume asked.

"I don't, but I overheard someone say my family is in the dungeon," Victor continued.

"Okay, Victor, Nari and I will take on Balathor. I need you to find the mason and see if he made a hidden passageway out of the dungeon that you both can use to get in unnoticed and free your family," Illume thought out loud.

Victor nodded in agreement, knowing that Illume wouldn't let him enter anyway. As Nari and Illume approached the building, a guard ran toward them.

"Handar reporting for duty, sir!" It was the guard that had been injured while clearing the cave.

"I don't want to put you in any more danger than you've already been in, soldier," Illume replied.

"I am the only one still alive or of use who's seen this kind of magic in use, sir. You are going to need me," Handar retorted.

Indicating that Halfdan and Abe were likely dead, Illume sighed and nodded, relenting.

"If things go south, I want you, both of you, to get out, okay?" Illume commanded. "I will come back, you won't."

Nari offered Illume a pleading gaze but said nothing as both nodded. Illume notched an arrow and approached the massive wooden doors of the new building. Putting his shoulder against them and pushing, Illume caused the door to give way as all three moved into the building.

Pillars holding the roof up were symmetrically divided around the room. As soon as they entered, all three darted behind one of the dozen or so pillars.

"Anyone see him?" Illume whispered.

Nari and Handar both shook their heads. Nari drew her chimera daggers as Handar drew his sword, holding his shield close to his chest. Illume glanced around his pillar. The room was reminiscent of a wooden version of a king's house from *Game of Thrones*. On the far side, a fireplace crackled, illuminating the room. A soft purple glint of light caught Illume's eye in one of the dark corners.

After he fired, Illume's arrow was interrupted by a sphere of deep purple light that rippled out into a bubble. Illume could see Balathor within the shield, staff in hand and mask on. *How the hell did he get inside that chest?* Illume thought to himself.

"He's got a shield. I'll wear it down, you two flank," Illume whispered.

Notching another arrow, Illume drew slightly. Glancing back to Balathor's location, he immediately yanked his head back as a blast of purple energy was sent hurtling toward his face.

"You never should have cast me out, Illume!" Balathor taunted. "You didn't know who you were messing with, you fool, but now you will. Now you will see me more powerful than ever before."

Illume took several deep breaths as he tightened his leg muscles. Diving out from cover, Illume fired another arrow. A blast of magic narrowly missed him as his arrow bounced off the shield once again.

"You're right, I should have executed you when I had the chance!" Illume taunted. "Better late than never, I guess."

This brought Balathor to his feet. He floated just into the light cast by the flickering flames. He faced Illume, allowing Nari and Handar to skirt from cover to cover around the perimeter. Notching another arrow, Illume fired it into a far wall, in the opposite direction of Nari and Handar.

A blast of magic hit his arrow, allowing Illume to step out from behind cover and fire a gust of frozen air at Balathor. Above Balathor, a grey bar emerged. It was depleting slowly but depleting nonetheless. Illume dodged back behind a pillar just as Balathor fired another magical blast at him.

Come on! Start monologuing! Illume pled, recalling a scene from a movie *The Incredibles*. Notching two arrows, Illume fired them both just as Balathor charged a magical blast. As the arrows made contact, Illume's bow flared blue, causing the spell Balathor was charging to backfire. Detonating, it took out the remainder of his shield.

Illume chuckled to himself. He'd forgotten about that attribute of his bow. He took cover as the resulting explosion sent a blast of energy through the building, making it rattle and creak. Illume notched his last two arrows and fired once again. One arrow hit the mast, the other whizzed right by his staff and into the wall behind Balathor, the strike doing no damage.

Balathor didn't immediately return the attack. Illume glanced to Nari and Handar; they both shrugged. Illume slung his bow onto his back before unleashing all of his frosty potential. Illume's mana gradually dropped, as did the temperature in the room. Frost built up on nearly every surface. Even the fire turned to a cold blue.

Illume's mana was eventually exhausted once he got within grabbing distance of Balathor. Illume delivered a powerful punch to him, knocking him to one side while grabbing the staff and attempting to pull it away. That was when his stomach dropped. Balathor's health bar, now at half, started regenerating as Balathor turned back toward Illume from the punch.

A flash of purple light encompassed Illume, followed closely by an electric burning sensation overtaking his body. Illume's muscles spasmed and his body seized as it was lifted off the ground. Illume watched in horror as his life, mana, and stamina bars all began to be depleted.

"GET THE MASK!" Illume managed to say between cries of agony.

Nari and Handar leaped into action. Nari jabbed both of her daggers into Balathor's throat as Handar pulled on the mask so hard, Balathor's head nearly turned all the way around. In a flash of light, both were thrown from Balathor, slamming into a wall before falling to the ground.

"Only what was made can destroy the maker," Balathor hissed. "You are actually an idiot, aren't you?"

Increasing his magical torment of Illume, he noticed that his life bar was near empty. Looking, Illume activated his leveling screen, placing three of his points into *Dexterity* and the last two into *Strength.* Quickly shifting to skills, he placed both his attributes into *Arm Wrestle,* increasing his one-handed weapon damage by 40 percent.

Level 9 Reached

New Attributes:
Health: 200 regenerates 1% of max health a second while not in battle.
Mana: 200 regenerates 3% of max mana a second while not in battle.
Stamina: 210 regenerates 5% of max stamina a second while not in battle.
Weight Capacity: 40/590, +10 per skill point added to stamina.
Survival: Unique skill, player has 70% resistance to cold attacks.
Charisma: +28, drops to +19 when in the presence of women.
Strength: +28 average for male humans.
Dexterity: +30 average for a human.
Intelligence: +20 average for a human.

Constitution: +27 without armor rating, average for a human
Wisdom: +33 +10 mana

As the menu closed, Illume fell to the ground, his leveling breaking Balathor's spell. Drawing his sword, Illume knocked Balathor's staff away before slicing off his hands. His life bar dropped momentarily before completely regenerating.

Illume staggered. His swords blew with healing magic as he drove Balathor against a pillar. The healing magic only brought his health back faster as Balathor was still alive, unlike the lich.

Illume ran Balathor through the heart and pinned him to a pillar. His health dropped to almost nothing and his head hung. Illume staggered back, his stamina completely gone as he heaved heavily, catching his breath. A deep, maniacal laugh emanated from the mask. Balathor's health regenerated once again.

"Son of a Seabiscuit!" Illume screamed.

"You can't kill me," Balathor taunted.

"You're right. But I can!" Handar yelled.

Illume turned his attention to the guard as he took his helmet off. His skin was sickly pale, his eyes an icy, inhuman blue. Opening his mouth, he revealed two massive fangs and an unhinged jaw as an unearthly screech left his mouth. Faster than Illume's eye can pick up, Handar was on top of Balathor, his fangs buried deep into Balathor's throat.

Balathor attempted to struggle against Handar but was unable to fight off the vampiric guard as his life ebbed away. Once it hit zero, Handar remove his fangs and took several steps back, wiping the blood from his chin.

Handar nodded toward Balathor, whose life bar rose once again, and he took in a labored deep breath.

"Heal him now," Handar suggested.

39

GEARING UP

NOT BEING one to argue with a vampire, Illume held his hands up, summoning his healing spells as he approached Balathor. He twitched and seized. His life bar depleted once again. This time, once it hit zero, Balathor's body turned to dust, allowing for his clothes, items, and mask to fall to the ground.

Illume turned his attention to the very pale Handar beside him with his brow raised in confusion. Handar let out a scoffing laugh, returning to his helmet before helping Nari to her feet. Handar placed his helmet onto his head, hiding his face once again.

"When I was bitten, the cave magic turned me into this. I figured my bite would turn him into a lich," he explained.

"Who else knows?" Illume asked, not sure if he should be wary of Handar, as vampires were known for losing control if they didn't feed.

"Victor and Tantor. I help Victor with the night guard," Handar responded.

"And the whole blood-drinking thing?" Nari asked as she retrieved her daggers.

"Animals work perfectly fine. I hunt them, drain them, and bring them back for Tantor to clean and prepare for everyone. My bites aren't toxic unless I want them to be and I swear I'd never harm a soul here," Handar defended himself.

Illume could tell Handar was worried that he would react poorly to the news. Illume pulled his sword from the pillar and sheathed it before crouching at Balathor's remains.

"So long as you don't feed on people, we won't have a problem," Illume replied softly.

Illume lifted part of Balathor's robes, and a note fluttered out. Illume picked up the paper. It had a wax seal with an 'I' on it. Illume got a hunch as to how the chest was opened in the first place. When he flipped the note open, it read:

Balathor,

I know of you. The outcast of Cryo's Quarry. A lich I had placed near there has fallen. If what I know about Illume is true, he will lock my lich's objects away. Use this skeleton key to find where they are hidden. Take them for yourself and draw my corrupted to burn Cryo's Quarry to the ground. Succeed and you will have a place of honor at my side.

-Ierret

A metallic clank caught Illume's attention. A piece of metal the size of a key fell from Balathor's robes. Illume retrieved the black piece of metal. As he did, it shifted into dozens of different key types over the course of a few seconds before returning to its piece of metal form.

Item Found.
Name: Key of Unlocking
Weight: +.01
Worth: 5 million polis
This key is unbreakable, unable to be replicated and said to be made of the flesh of the Dark King himself.

Takes the form of whatever key goes to the lock before you.

Illume places the key into his coin purse before grabbing the mask and staff.

"Well, at least we know what opened the chest. These should be sent far from here. Handar, are you able to stay in daylight without burning?" Illume asked.

"So long as I'm in my armor, yes," he replied.

"Okay, south of here is a herd of centaurs. They will be more than capable of protecting these. Take it to them," Illume commands.

Handar grabbed the staff and mask, disappearing before Illume could even blink. Illume turned his attention to Nari. His hands glowed with healing magic. She stopped him.

"I'm fine, but that is a problem," she said, nodding to the letter.

"We don't have much of a choice. We are going to have to take the fight to the Dark King if we want anyone to be safe," Illume replied.

Illume sighed. His people would need him now more than ever, but if he stayed, then his opponent would grow even stronger. Illume nodded after deliberating with himself for several moments.

"Help the injured in any way that you can. Get our absolute best weapons, equipment, and spells and ask around to see if anyone knows how to find this Dark King. We leave at first light," Illume replied, his tone heavy.

Nari nodded. She reached out and gave Illume's hand a gentle squeeze as if to tell him everything would be okay. Illume offered her a forced smile before she left, not saying a word.

The flames gradually changed back from blue to their orange tint as Illume gathered Balathor's robes and tossed them inside.

Restoration Magic Level Up
Anti-Dead now available

Destruction Magic Level Up
Impale now available
Like a Hammer now available

Heavy Armor Level Up
Feather now available
Rocky now available
Deflector now available

Two Handed Level Up
One Two Strike now available
Stance and Gait now available
Sweep now available
Grievous Wound now available

One-Handed Level Up
Sharper now available
Squishy Flesh now available
Savage Strike now available

Archery Level Up
Bullseye now available

Level Up x3
Active Skill Points: 7
Active Attribute Points: 17
Pending Level(s): 10 (extra skill and attribute points), 11 and 12

War is a hell of a thing!

"Ain't it just," Illume whispered to himself.

Next to the fireplace was an ajar door. Illume walked over to it, pushing it open to reveal several treasure chests stocked full of money, jewels, and precious metals. Several books sat on top.

Illume reached down and picked one up. *'Healing Hands.'* Illume winced a bit, grabbing another. The cover read *'Kind Hearted.'*

"Come on! I spent over a thousand polis for you!" Illume grumbled. He could have had them for free!

Illume lifted the third book, flipping it over. He couldn't help but scoff. *The Lusty Barnog Volumes 2-4* read the title. Illume immediately stepped back into the previous room and threw it into the fire.

"Dirty bird," Illume grumbled.

With nothing of use in the treasure trove, Illume exited the way he came in, only to be greeted by Victor standing with his family and a mason. Illume nodded to Victor as he approached.

"I am sorry once again your family was put into this situation. Balathor is dead, so he will no longer be a threat to you. But it looks like the Dark King is behind your attempted abductions. I am leaving at first light to hunt him down and kill him," Illume said soft enough where the children couldn't hear.

"Then I'm coming with you," Victor replied.

"You can't. The Dark Lord wants you. If you come with us, you will be handing yourself over to him. Your safest place is here with your family and an army surrounding you," Illume attempted to persuade him.

Victor seemed like one of those characters who would have been good to bring into the final battle, only for them to be killed. Not wanting that on his conscience, Illume wouldn't allow the alpha to join.

"As you wish. What can I do instead?" he asked, looking around at the scores of injured.

"Find Khal. His potions are top-of-the-line. Use his stock to heal the injured, cure the poisoned, and restore the mages' mana for healing spells. Kassandra, you, and your children… get some rest, you have been through more than enough," Illume suggested.

Kassandra and her children followed Victor to the trauma tents to lend a hand. Illume made his way to a tent nearby where

Abe and Halfdan lay, both injured and both unconscious. Their health bars were dangerously low and depleting. Their wounds must have been infected.

Illume held out his hands. Using his healing spell, he brought both men back from the brink and far enough along that they would be able to operate on their own without assistance.

Over the next several hours, Illume moved from tent to tent healing the wounded, focusing on the alchemists and people with healing magic first. With the ranks of healers growing as each were brought back, they were able to spread out and save significantly more people as a result. It took most of the day, but as night fell, the injured were healed, the dead were buried, and the contaminated were burned.

Handar returned without the mask and staff while Illume finished healing a guard from Lapideous. As his healing light faded, Illume turned to Handar as weariness set in.

"I found the centaurs. They gladly took the staff and mask," Handar informed Illume. "They wanted me to pass along the message that they will hold on to them until the Dark King is dead. Apparently, once he dies, the magic that fuels those artifacts will dispel and will no longer be a threat."

"Good. Thank you, Handar. You did great work," Illume responded as Handar disappeared to help with reconstruction.

"I know where the Dark King is," Trill called out from behind Illume.

Turning, Illume smiled at his friend, who was caked in the blood of those he'd helped.

"And how is that?" Illume asked.

Trill drew his sword.

"Have you forgotten? I stole thas from his keep. I will lead you, but I will only take you and Nari into his keep. Any more and we risk lettin' him know we're comin'," Trill explained.

"Sounds like a plan. How long of a ride is it?" Illume asked as he activated his map.

"I'll highlight it fur you," he replied.

A valley appeared on Illume's map almost directly west of Mobrebalku in the center of a mountain range that bordered the top of this land. It would be about three days' hard ride given nothing got in their way. Illume dropped his map, nodding that he'd seen it.

"That looks good. I have Nari gathering every little thing that would give us an edge. You know the area. I want you to do the same, then get some rest. We have a big ride and the more energy we have the better," Illume replied.

Sending Trill off, Illume decided it would be best to get acquainted with his city. As the sun set and most everyone who was capable had found their way to beds, Illume strolled down the main street. Buildings had been constructed to a very high standard all around. Moving to the lower section, Illume found the markets and grain stores.

Illume located Urtan's booth before tracking down Horson Wells and leading the horse to his stand. Removing the massive axe that belonged to the corrupted orc, Illume lets it drop behind the booth. No need to cover it, as no one was strong enough to wield the weapon, save for Urtan.

Illume let Horson walk around on his own for a little while. He grazed on grain then drank some water before returning to the upper portion of the city. The masons did a wonderful job constructing the walls.

They were high and thick, probably the only reason Cryo's Quarry was still standing. Battlements were evenly spaced all around the city. It was truly a testament to their skill as even real life medieval walls weren't built so fine.

After nearly an hour, Illume found himself outside of the walls next to the dam put in place by the corrupted. Illume outstretched his hands and torched the top logs. His mana depleted. Pausing and letting it recharge, Illume did this again. Eventually, the dam sprouted a leak. Illume did this again and again until the top log finally gave way.

The pent-up water poured over the first log and back into their moat. After several minutes, the second log was dislodged, causing more water to come through. Another few minutes later, another log. Illume watched as the dam broke apart piece by piece, allowing the moat to be filled back up without any sort of violent reaction.

Illume walked back to the city. Piles of bodies were being burned downwind as to not stink up Cryo's Quarry. As he approached the land bridge, Commander Stark stood there waiting for him.

"You did well today," Illume said softly.

"As did you," Stark replied, handing Illume a quiver filled with his chimera arrows. "Uthrandir says he can make more weapons with the chimera hides, even something from the trolls too. It looks like your city guard will be protected by the hide of monsters. Can't say that's a bad thing," Stark remarked with a scoff.

"I'd hoped he'd stick around and help. Glad to hear he will. How did your men fare?" Illume asked.

"Lost ten. Could have been worse; hell, would have been had you not helped out. How did you do that?" Stark's voice was rife with curiosity. "You moved like a god out there."

"Something just overtook me; can't really explain it," Illume replied, avoiding the berserker explanation like the plague.

"I sent word to Lapideous, told them about what happened here. Senator William is going to send a battalion to help reinforce your city until you are able to get it back on its feet," Stark informed Illume as both men approached the main gate. "This won't happen again. We won't let it."

"That is more than generous. As a show of good faith, ten percent of anything we find on our next mission will be given to Lapideous as a gift," Illume offered. "It's the very least I can do."

"Illume, my boy, this is the beginning of a beautiful friendship," Stark remarked, making Illume laugh.

"That it is," Illume agreed.

40

TRAVERSAL

ILLUME DIDN'T SLEEP a wink that night. He guessed Nari and Trill didn't either. He spent all night double- and triple-checking everything, ensuring to add rope to everyone's packs.

He made sure the horses were well stocked, that not only was his quiver full of chimera arrows, but that he had a backup as well. Illume even found his way into the potion storeroom and spent over an hour picking up and putting vials down just so he could see the stats.

Illume finally selected the most potent poisons and several potions that fully restored health, mana, and stamina, distributing them all evenly among the three. Illume stood on the wall for the remainder of the night keeping watch, occasionally checking his stats tree, only to realize he hadn't touched anything in theft and alchemy.

Alchemy would be useful; able to make potions and poisons himself would save a lot of money, and potentially several lives if he ran out of mana. As the sun crested, Illume made his way off the stone wall, stopping at a tablet that was set over the gate. Illume ran his fingers over it, curious as to why a flat tablet was just sitting there. Gradually, words etched themselves into the stone.

Cryo's Quarry
Residents: 300
Capacity: 350

People decided they wanted to stay, and with three hundred people, the town's infrastructure would erupt in the best of ways. Illume continued his route down to be met by Nari and Trill, each with their own horses all geared up. A soft smile greeted Illume from Nari while Trill gave a nervous sigh.

"Well, we're all goin' to die sometime, may as well be in a fit of glory. Am I right?" Trill jested.

Illume grabbed Horson, walking him over to Nari and Trill before mounting the beast.

"The only one who dies is the Dark King. We've worked together and had each other's back this far. Just a little further and we can end this." Illume said in a stern tone, not adding that he would then be able to go home. At least he hoped that was the case.

"I agree. We run into any spiders, are you going to be okay?" Nari teased Trill.

"There are no spiders where we're goin' and I'd appreciate it if you didn't mock me about that," Trill added before giving his horse a kick and taking off down the land bridge. "I'm more sensitive than I show."

"What's his problem?" Nari asked. "I was just teasing him."

"He knows what we're about to face. He's probably worried," Illume replied, noting his odd change in behavior. "Maybe we should all be."

Nari and Illume took off behind Trill, doing their best to keep up, but his horse was just a little bit faster. He stayed ahead of them by several yards almost all day as they backtracked the way they'd come, making it just over a third of the way to Mobrebalku before setting up camp for the night.

Trill took watch the first night, waking Nari and Illume as dawn broke before feeding and watering the horses. After Illume and Nari grabbed some breakfast to keep up their strength, they packed up camp and loaded the animals. The entire process was done in silence; with tensions very high all three were stuck deep in their own heads. Illume was more concerned with the safety of Nari and Trill than for himself.

The topography changed as they entered midday of day two. They entered a sparsely treed forest. Illume dodged several branches here and there and even leaped over a few fallen trees and small streams. A telltale glint caught Illume's eye in the distance to his right as the sun set.

Bringing the horses to a stop, Illume dismounted and set up camp. As the sun continued to set, Mobrebalku continued to taunt them on the horizon with glints of light. Nari wandered off while Trill and Illume started a fire and set out the bed rolls. After a long bit of silence, Trill finally spoke.

"We will be within striking distance tomorrow," he whispered, his eyes locked on the task he was doing.

"We will set up camp out of the keep's view and leave while it is still dark out," Illume replied.

"That's smart, the castle is surrounded by sentries, who knows how many eyes," Trill added before laying his head down on the mat.

Illume could tell that this castle haunted Trillian; it probably did every day of his life, only now that he was going back was the toll starting to be taken. Illume kneeled next to the fire, poking it with a stick a few times. He had to admit, he missed s'mores .

"Everything is going to be fine," Illume whispered softly.

"Just promise me one thing, Illume." Trill hoisted himself onto his elbow. His voice carried a hint of sadness. "No matter what happens when we make it there, you will not think less of me."

"You're my best friend, probably the only real friend I've ever had. I will always hold you in the highest esteem," Illume replied as concern clawed at the back of his mind. "I'm going to go find Nari. She shouldn't be in the woods alone. If you see anything, holler."

Standing, Illume moved into the forest the same way Nari had gone. Illume used his flaming hand to light his path, following her footprints as he went. A soft babbling of a river overtook Illume's hearing. Illume continued to follow Nari's footsteps, his hand alight, until the angelic voice of a woman floated through the air.

Illume immediately extinguished his hand and reached for his sword. There were singing entities who lived in the water that liked to feed on men. Illume cautiously moved forward as the song became louder and more beautiful.

Illume was stopped in his tracks by the sight before him. His hand fell limply to his side as the source of that beautiful music became clear. It was Nari. The full moonlight illuminated her as she stood waist deep in the river completely disrobed. Something about her back caught Illume's attention.

On her upper right shoulder blade, there was a strange birthmark, a single crimson line about six inches long. Across her back was a scar that crossed over her spine. Whatever made that wound had to have been agonizing. She lifted her arm, causing her body to turn slightly. On her side was an exit wound from what looked like a spear.

Illume's heart sank as he saw such tragedy that befell Nari. Whatever it was that caused her injuries, she must have repressed, as he'd never know had he not seen her in the moonlight. Illume wanted to walk over to her and embrace her, not because she was naked but because his heart broke for her.

"I know you're there," Nari said softly as she washed her hair, still turned around.

"I'm sorry," Illume stammered, embarrassed that it seemed like he was more of a pervert than he was.

"Don't be. You don't seem like the kind of guy who'll spy on a girl for fun. Let me guess, worried about my safety?" she teased as Illume turned his back to her.

"We ARE going after a being who is able to touch just about everyone we've come across," Illume counter-argued.

"I appreciate that," Nari replied with a coo.

Illume heard the sloshing of water as if she's getting out of the river. After several moments, she appeared next to Illume wrapped in one of their blankets. She ran her hand over her long dark hair, squeezing the excess liquid out like a small waterfall.

"You're a good man, Illume, one of the few that I've met in my life," Nari said softly. Gently, she placed her hand on his shoulder. "Most men I've adventured with have sought me out while I was bathing in order to sneak a peek. I appreciate you turning your back," she added before giving him a kiss on the cheek and disappearing behind him.

"How many adventures have you been on?" Illume asked with a tinge of jealousy. He had no idea why.

"Four or five," Nari replied as she shuffled to get back into her armor.

"Why did you stop?" Illume pressed.

The sound of Nari struggling to get into her clothes halted. After what felt like an eternity of silence, she finally decided to answer.

"I know you saw why, Illume." Her tone softened. "I was in a few battles and almost died. After the second time, I decided that it would be best for me to stay in a city and be a forger."

"Then why join me?" Illume asked with confusion.

Nari struggled with her armor once again. After a few hops and grunts ending with a "there," she finally stopped moving long enough to reply.

"I already told you, you are different. You don't horde precious metals and money, you take only what you need and give the rest to your people. Your town is open to everyone, not just beautiful women who will sleep with you. You want to pour yourself into this place to make it better, not the other way around, and for that, I am willing to follow you," Nari explained.

She approached Illume while rubbing her hair with the bed sheet before wiggling her pinky finger in her ear to get some water out. Her words resonated with Illume. He didn't think there was anything special about him; he just treated others the way he'd like to be treated.

Illume wished he couldn't fathom people like that, but chances were, he wasn't the first person to be in this game and the others were BranCo employees that she's talking about. Illume was curious if any were still able to log in, or if due to this unable-to-log-out glitch, he was the only player in game right now.

"I promise not to let any harm come to you," Illume said softly. "You're my tribe and I protect my tribe with all that I am."

Nari offered Illume a sympathetic smile as Illume caught up to her. She reached out and took his hand, giving it a gentle squeeze. Stopping where she was, she paused for a moment or two.

"Illume, two lives left; any more and that's game over. I don't want you to game over for me," she replied.

Her voice was slightly more broken, reminiscent of Trill's earlier. She gave Illume's hand another gentle squeeze before walking back into the clearing of the camp and lying down. Illume followed a few moments later, arming his bow and notching an arrow.

"Go to sleep," Trillian said softly with his eyes closed.

"We need someone to stay watch," Illume protested.

"No we don't. Nothing is going to be bothering us here. Now go to sleep!" He yelled this time like a grumpy teenager.

Illume laughed and shook his head. Keeping the arrow notched and placing one of his daggers under his makeshift pillow, Illume lay down on his little mat. He tried to adjust himself several times to get comfortable but was unable to do so. This was the first time he'd been unable to get into a comfortable position for sleeping.

With a huff, Illume eventually just closed his eyes, giving up on a good night's rest and settling for just a night's rest. Illume took to counting sheep in a desperate attempt to get some shuteye.

41

KING'S CASTLE

A KICK to the bottom of his shoe jerked Illume awake. Drawing his daggers, Illume jolted, his senses sharp as he searched for an impending attack. Trill laughed as he walks away from Illume, having been the one to wake him, before placing his sleeping roll on the back of his horse. Illume relaxed, sheathing his weapons as he climbed to his feet and packed up his bedding.

"How long have you been awake?" Illume asked while rolling his mat.

"Hours," Nari replied.

"I didn't sleep," Trill seconded.

Illume packed his horse before going to Trill, who had spent the last several minutes just petting his horse. Standing on the other side of the beast's neck, Illume gave the horse a gentle pet as well.

"Are you going to be okay, Trillian?" Illume's voice was rife with concern. "If going back there is going to cause you to lock up and get you killed, you are perfectly fine to stay outside the castle. Nari and I can take down the Dark King ourselves. There will be no hard feelings."

Trill nodded, scratching the back of his head.

"That castle messes with you, true enough, but I'm not going to doom my friends to face its traps and monsters alone. I am with you, Illume, to the end," Trill replied before mounting his steed.

Illume and Nari climbed onto their horses after Illume used his frost magic to put the fire out. Once again, Trill took the lead. Within an hour, they were out of the forest and riding over the vast plains and foothills that surround the very same mountain range that Strang sat under.

The mountains that lay before them were massive, larger than almost any others he'd seen and reminiscent of the Swiss Alps. Snow caps off the awe-inspiring monoliths and weaved between rocks and trees about halfway down their sides. Their peaks pierced the few clouds that passed around them, standing unhindered and free.

The golden grass they rode through was significantly shorter than that around Lapideous, allowing visibility of grey stones that protruded from the ground as if they were the very roots of the mountains themselves. Soaring high above them, a flock of birds flew toward the south, but that wasn't what held Illume's attention.

To the far west, above the peaks of other mountains attached to this range, Illume could swear he saw a lion's body attached to an eagle's head with wings that had to stretch greater than those of small plane.

Illume scoffed as a sense of wonder pulled him deeper into this game. The second he got a chance, Illume would be returning just to further explore the winged beasts that called the far side of those mountains their home.

As the day went on, they grew closer and closer to the foot of the mountains. Illume scanned every inch of them in desperate search for the Dark King's castle but to no avail.

There were no unnatural structures bound on the mountain's side and he didn't note any paths that could lead to something within the mountains themselves.

Trill slowed to a trot, causing Nari and Illume to do the same. Illume rode up beside his friend with the foot of the mountain now only several dozen yards away. Illume glanced at Trill, who seemed to be staring straight ahead at something at the mountain's base. Illume followed his line of sight but saw nothing.

"What are you looking at?" Illume asked.

"That." Trill pointed to a rock that was standing on its end.

"A rock?" Nari asked in confusion.

"When I left, I marked the path in a way that only I would recognize it. That is how we get to the castle. Once inside, we leave the horses."

Illume's brow arched as he glanced at Nari while mouthing "inside?"

She shook her head, replying with a mimed "I don't know."

Illume looked for a cave entrance but saw nothing. Getting closer and closer to the rock, Illume and Nari were side by side with Trill.

Illume and Nari both leaned forward in anticipation for their horses to climb, only for a sensation of compression to overtake Illume, like sitting at the bottom of a deep pool, as his horse continued on straight. Illume fell back in his saddle as Horson came to a stop. His eyes widened and his mouth fell open as he was not believing what he was seeing.

A valley straight out of Jurassic Park sat before him. The sky was overcast with dark, angry clouds that flashed with lightning strikes every so often. Strangely enough, no thunder ever sounded. Illume followed Trillian's lead and dismounted his horse, tying it to a nearby tree that was something out of a Tim Burton movie.

"What is this place?" Illume whispered in awe.

"It's the Dark King's hidden valley. Everything here is long since dead or cursed," Trill replied in just as hushed a tone. "From here on out, we need to be as silent as we can."

Illume gathered his back-up quiver, holding his sword close and taking his portion of the potions. An eerie fog settled along the bases of countless dead trees that decorated the hidden valley's floor.

Trill took point, drawing his sword as he crouched, almost completely vanishing into the fog. Illume switched to his bow, notching an arrow. He and Nari stepped in line right behind Trill .

The air was both damp and stale, as if the illusion spell trapped the decomposing ecosystem from any natural effects of the outside world. Illume stopped the moment he saw Trill's closed fist shoot into the air. Out of the tangle of branches, a swarm of bat-like creatures whirled above Illume's head.

Illume got a quick glance at one; its eyes were blood red and with teeth like a piranha. Illume wasn't sure he'd be able to blast them all before someone died. Discretion being the better part of valor, Illume kept quiet.

After the swarm passed, Trill waved them forward. Illume moved as silently as he could, making almost no noise with each step. He was glad he leveled his sneak as much as he had.

On one of the corpse-like trees, Illume noticed an animal that was once a lizard sticking to it. Bony spines protruded from its grey skin as if its own skeleton had mutated to the point its flesh could no longer contain it.

Illume shuddered at the sight, not wanting to know what actual beasts could be dwelling here. All three slid forward through the murky fog in relative silence until Trillian raised his fist once more. Turning, he held his fingers to his lips before waving Illume and Nari to him.

Illume creeped ahead, coming to a stop as a small campsite was set up before them. Sitting around the fire were a number of grey-skinned creatures, the likes of which Illume had never seen.

Illume attempted to get a better look, when Trill grabbed his shoulder, forcing him to crouch. Trill gripped his shoulder so tightly, he could actually feel it through his armor. Looking over, Illume saw he had his hand on Nari's shoulder as well.

A soft huff brought Illume's attention back in front of him. His heart skipped a beat and he inhaled sharply to stop from making a noise as less than two feet in front of him was one of these creatures.

Grey skin with black lowlights painted its body. It wore no clothes and showed no sign of gender. It had teeth protruding from its square, almost pug-like jaws. Two slits formed just above its mouth that flexed as the beast sniffed the air.

It had yellow glowing eyes that felt as if they were looking straight through Illume while two large bat-like ears emerged straight from its skull and arched backward. The ears hardened into reinforced horns.

The beast opened its mouth, letting out a series of hisses and snarls, the breath turning Illume's stomach as it smelled like rotting corpses. It held a two-handed rusty battle axe in one of its three-fingered hands. Illume got a look at the claws; they were onyx black and so sharp, their edges almost glistened.

With a wave of its axe, the creature ran off into the fog, followed by several others with only the frills that ran down their spines visible as they moved. Trill released Illume, facing him as he mouthed the word "imps." Illume returned his bow back to its resting place on his back and gripped his sword, recalling it did extra damage to these beasts.

Illume, Nari, and Trill all stayed put for several hours until it turned to night and most of the imps went to sleep. Four stayed awake and stood at the clearing's edge looking into the forest. Illume wondered why they would be on guard. Nothing could find this place and had Trill not been with them, chances were anyone who did would be killed before they even got this far.

Trill grabbed Illume's bow and an arrow. He made a few hand motions to Nari, who drew her daggers and disappeared into the fog. Trill turned to Illume, bringing his mouth to Illume's ear. He whispered so silently that not even Illume was sure he heard Trill.

"Wait for my signal then move quickly and silently. If even one of them gets away, we are all dead." Trill gave Illume a thumbs-up before disappearing into the fog as well.

Illume drew his sword. He positioned himself next to one of the sentries but just out of sight and reach. The night was still and its accompanying silence was deafening. Illume heard soft noises all around him, unsure if it was actually movement or if it was just his mind desperately attempting to fill the silence. He didn't move.

An unmistakable soft whistle rippled through the air. One of the imps fell to the ground. The death of their comrade caught the other imps' attention as they turned to investigate.

Nari and Trill emerged from the forest at the same time. Illume swiped his sword diagonally. *Sneak attack against imp, 10x damage* scrolled across his screen.

A silent splatter of glowing yellow blood erupted from the corpse as its upper half slid off of the lower half, causing the body to fall into two pieces on the ground. Illume looked to see Nari slitting its throat and Trill running his sword through the heart of his imp. Moving in silently to the camp where the remaining six lay, Illume stood between two that were sleeping.

Raising his sword, he looked at Nari, who nodded, both her daggers at the ready, then at Trill, who nodded, taking a page out of Illume's book as he had two arrows nocked. All at once, Trill fired his arrows.

Nari slammed her daggers into the imps' skulls and Illume let his sword swing in a circle, decapitating, lobotomizing, and piercing hearts. All six died at the same time without making a noise.

Trill stepped toward the fire and kicked dirt over it to put it out. Illume walked over, opening his hand to fire a blast of ice at it. Trill grabbed his wrist like a vise grip. Eyes wide, he shook his head.

"Any magic cast here will amplify its sound, actin' as an alarm. We camp here tonight. Imps are secluded creatures, so another patrol won't be coming by here," he whispered as he sat down.

Illume and Nari sat next to him, Nari gently placing her hand on Illume's and giving it a gentle squeeze. Illume turned his attention to her, and for the first time, he saw a hint of concern tucked away behind her brave facade . Illume gave her a reassuring nod before turning to Trill.

"How far out are we?" Illume whispered.

"Thirty yards north to the bridge, another ten to the castle gates. We just have to find a way around the minotaur," Trill responded, pointing to the north.

"How do you know for sure?" Illume asked. He understood Trill had been here before, but there was no way his memory could be that precise after all these years.

"I have a way to see in bad lighting, remember. That includes fog. To me, it's not even really here. Now get some rest. Tomorrow is going to be one hell of a day," Trill commanded.

No rest would find anyone that night. Nari sat sharpening her swords and daggers while Trill piled the imps together, crossing their hands over their chests in almost a ritualistic way.

It spiked Illume's curiosity, but he decided not to ask. Illume retrieved his arrows and bow and played numerous scenarios of the fight to come over and over again in his head in an attempt to prepare the best he can.

42

BRIDGES

TIME OF DAY was irrelevant in a place as dark as this. The ambient light went from nearly pitch black to heavily overcast with a darker shade of grey. Trill climbed to his feet, the first time he'd moved in hours, and waved to Illume. Rising as well, Illume made his way to his friend.

"We move now," Trill whispered, unsheathing his sword.

Illume followed suit and Nari wasn't far behind. The silence of this place started to get to Illume, who swore he heard things moving in the fog, only to look around and see nothing. Illume looked at Trill for cues that he saw anything; nothing as well. The noises finally stopped as Trill led Illume to the woods' edge.

Peering through the fog, Illume's head dropped back, unsure if what he was seeing was a hallucination or reality. A massive tower, as black as night, rose from the fog nearly ten stories high. The tower's base hinted at more than just a staircase behind its walls. At the top, a bulbous room came to a point as if it were in defiance of the sky.

At its base, the tower was surrounded by walls in a sharp star pattern with battlements that protruded outward and up. This gave the tower a feeling of a battle mace shoved head first into the ground. A rusted portcullis stood open before rotten doors with the drawbridge in nearly as bad of shape.

A trembling of the ground drew Illume's attention off the menacing black citadel before them. Crossing through the fog a mere twenty feet away, two minotaur strode through the mist. The fogs cover only raised about mid-thigh high, making them just as massive as the centaurs.

"How are we going to get past that?" Nari whispered.

"There was only one here last time. I don't know," Trill replied.

"Have you seen him yet?" a deep voice echoed through the air.

"No one has, not for centuries," another voice huffed.

Illume raised his eyes. The minotaur were speaking with one another. They crossed each other's paths once again as they were on patrol. Illume observed them closely; they didn't appear to be corrupted and seemed to be guarding the castle of their own free will.

"Then how do you know he's still alive?" one minotaur asked the other.

"His magic still holds this place in shrouds. His moat has begun contaminating the kingdoms once again. If he were dead, that would not be the case," the larger of the two explained.

"Why are you loyal to him?" the smaller one asked with a huff.

"My family has protected him for generations, since his first rise to power," the larger replied.

Illume didn't realize it, but he'd been drawn to their conversation and snuck out of the cover of the forest. His still form remained unnoticed by the minotaur while they continued to talk.

"How did he fall previously?" the smaller one asked. Illume figured he was a child.

"He's never been defeated. He just grows bored after conquests and lets the world rebuild so he can do it again," the larger one replied, "like a wildfire that goes through the land, only to have the rain water replenish the soil."

"Is it true he does that in an attempt to find someone strong enough to kill him?" the smaller one asked yet again. "I've heard rumors."

The larger minotaur held his hand up. Sniffing the air, he turned and scanned the area. It was only then that Illume realized how exposed he was. Stopping in his tracks, he prayed that his lack of movement would keep him concealed.

He was wrong. The larger minotaur pointed his massive battle axe at Illume. It was large enough that the centaurs would have been jealous.

"I mean you no harm!" Illume called out, raising his hands. He tried desperately to activate his charisma. "I am only here for the Dark King. You said he's looking for someone to end him? I am that someone."

The larger minotaur lowered his axe, tilting his bull-like face to one side as confusion washed across his fur.

"You can understand us?" he asked.

Illume glanced at his forearm; he noticed the blessing that had been given to him was glowing softly. Illume rubbed his hand over, giving both minotaur a nod.

"I can, and as bearer of the blessing of Elatus, I command you both to step aside and let my team and me pass," Illume spoke in a forceful tone.

Instantly, as if being controlled by something else, both minotaur stepped to the side. They placed their weapons at ease and slammed their human hands against their hybrid chests. Illume let out a soft laugh. He had no idea the mark worked on minotaur too. Lucky it did! Nari and Trill emerged from the fog, looking at both beings in shock and wonder as they passed between them.

"Should anything try to enter this castle while we are inside, you are to kill it. Our mission is of the utmost important and I don't want any of the monsters that live in these woods getting in our way," Illume continued to command.

"We will protect your flank!" they both said in unison.

Illume followed Trill and Nari, who had already made it to the bridge. The minotaur then stepped together and face the woods, both so massive, they block nearly the entire entrance.

"How did you understand them?" Nari asked.

"Better yet, how did you control them?" a hint of power lust trickled from Trill's lips.

"They must have been some sort of family member to the centaurs. The blessing of Elatus must hold sway over them too," Illume replied, just as surprised as the other two.

Illume took one look at the bridge and nearly turned back. Most of it was collapsed and what wasn't was full of holes or covered in rot. Below, the moat was full of a black tar-like substance that reeked of dead flesh. Illume covered his nose and let out a guttural moan at the visceral nature of the smell. It was so potent that even his eyes involuntarily watered.

"It's rotted away a bit since I was last here, but I think we can go across safely. Step where I step," Trill whispered.

Trill stepped forward, investigating the bridge closely. He probed the rotten wood with his foot; it creaked but didn't give way. Ever so gingerly, Trill stepped onto the bridge. He took each step deliberately, carefully choosing where to let his feet land. Every time Trill brought his weight to bear, the bridge sagged just a little more.

Thankful he'd thought to pack rope, Illume grabbed some from his pack. Finding a rock that protruded from a piece of the mountain, Illume tied a knot to one end and jammed it down securely between both the rock and hard place. Illume tied the rope to the end of one of his arrows and approached the bridge once more.

"I'm across. Nari, you're next!" Trill whispered just loud enough for them to hear.

Nari stepped out onto the bridge. Illume grabbed her shoulder and pulled her back. He shook his head and held up the bow.

"Give me one second. Trill, lie down. You've got incoming!" Illume called.

The fog was so thick, he could hardly see Trill's outline, but Trill did manage to lay down. Illume drew his bow, aiming as far away from Trill as he could without making the arrow inaccessible to him. Illume fired. A soft thud rang out. *No screaming, that's a good sign,* Illume thought to himself.

"Tie the rope off to something," Illume instructed.

Several moments passed as the rope bobbed up and down, going slack then tightening. After about five minutes, Illume stepped forward and was about to ask if Trill was okay.

"Okay, got it tied off. You're good now!" Trill beat Illume to the punch.

"Hold on to this, and no matter what, don't let go," Illume pleaded with Nari.

She offered Illume a sweet smile before grabbing the rope and making her way across as well. Several creaking noises came from the bridge while the minotaur's heavy breathing rang out as well. Illume's rope moaned softly under its use, but aside from those minor sounds, everything else was dead silent.

"I'm good!" Nari called back.

Illume took a deep breath. He never liked rope courses and now he had to go on one over a boiling lake of nasty. Grabbing on to the coarse rope as tightly as he could, Illume inched his way across the few sturdy boards that still existed in this bridge.

"Don't look down, don't look down, don't look down..." Illume whispered over and over again to himself.

Illume felt the bridge give way slightly. He fell about three inches. His heart rate skyrocketed and he breathed rapidly. He could hear Nari and Trill urging him to hurry across before the rest of it fell. Illume froze for several seconds, taking short, shallow breaths. His hands trembled and his vision blurred as a cold sweat encompassed his body.

Illume locked up. He wasn't quite sure for how long, as time seemed to smear, but it had to have been at least a few minutes. Nari's voice broke through the mental fog that had overtaken him. Illume finally managed to get control of his body once again. Turning his attention to Nari and Trill, he took one more step.

A loud CRACK echoed through the valley as the bridge collapsed under Illume. Gripping tightly to the rope, Illume bounced to a stop mere feet from the corrupting ooze. The bridge melted upon impact and Illume bobbed for several moments, taking in a sharp breath to prevent him from shouting.

"Illume!" Nari instinctively yelled. The second half was muffled, presumably by Trill covering her mouth.

"I'm lookin' down, Shrek, I'm lookin' down!" Illume whispered to himself in an attempt to use humor to mask his pants-wetting terror.

Taking several deep breaths, Illume flung his legs against the rope, locking his ankles. He began to shimmy. Moving inch by fastidious inch, Illume got closer and closer to the far side. He felt the rope give slightly. Looking back at the boulder he tied the rope to, he noticed it shift.

"Guys, grab the rope!" Illume whispered in a minor panic.

"What?" Trill asked, his voice laced with confusion.

"Grab the rope and be prepared to pull! My anchor is about to give way!" he called out once more.

Illume dropped several more inches as the boulder fell even more forward. Illume shimmied as fast as he could, but it wasn't fast enough. The boulder gave way, causing Illume to fall toward the corrupting moat. He felt the rope pull up as Nari and Trill ran backward.

Illume braced his shoulder as he slammed into the side of the moat, his feet mere inches from the goo. As the rope fell in, it completely disintegrated as well. Illume attempted to climb, which was never his strong suit.

"Keep pulling!" Illume called as he felt his grip slip and saw his stamina bar falling fast.

A powerful tug drew Illume up to the moat's ledge, where Nari grabbed Illume's forearms. Thankful for their haste as he struggled to get up, Illume rolled onto the ledge's safety as Nari fell on her butt and released him.

"There are times when heavy armor doesn't have its perks!" Illume remarked in a hushed tone.

Illume laughed once the stress of the situation started to dissipate.

43

INTO THE CASTLE

IT TOOK several minutes for Illume to compose himself. Eventually, he was able to. Pulling himself to his feet with the assistance of Nari, Illume retrieved his arrow and placed it in his quiver. Turning to Trill, he raised an eyebrow

"So where to now?" Illume asked.

"The Dark King's throne room is at the top of the tower. I suggest we go there last. The lower levels of his castle are filled with items. Some may be useful. I say we hit there first," Trill said.

"Yeah, I'm sure the fact that you'd like to get yourself a little rich off this has nothing to do with it," Nari jested with a laugh.

Trill fired her a cold look, which took Nari and Illume both by surprise, fully expecting for him to make a jab back. He didn't this time, only drawing his sword and shaking his head.

"There is no time for riches," he murmured.

Trill turned and walked into the castle. Illume shrugged to Nari before notching an arrow and following suit. The air changed as they entered. It was cold and crisp. Illume would go so far as to even say fresh. A stark difference to just outside.

Illume gazed at the surprisingly small main hall that greeted them. Black marble stretched before them, forming spiked pillars that held black flames. The flames illuminated the hall, though not by much, revealing that it was roughly the size of an average church. Illume was expecting corrupted knights in full plate armor waiting to slaughter them, but there was nothing.

Tapestries were hardly visible on the walls. Illume squinted to see them. They were filled with life and acts of kindness, not at all what Illume had been expecting.

"Come on! Lower levels were this way," Trill whispered.

Trill hugged the darkened wall, his armor allowing him to blend in almost perfectly. They approached a spiraling staircase that led them under the main hall. Reaching the bottom of the stairs, Illume looked at three separate paths to take.

"Illume, you go right to see what is tucked away back there. Nari, you go left. I'll take the center," Trill suggested.

"Shouldn't we stay together?" Illume asked. "I know you haven't seen a horror movie, but splitting up is like the worst idea ever. Nothing good ever comes of it."

"We could be down here for hours, if not days, with a small army of people moving in one group. We need to do this quick before our presence is made known. Half hour is all I'm thinking, then we meet back here!" Trill added.

Illume looked at Nari for her input. She shrugged as if to say "why not."

"Fine, but the first sign of trouble, I want everyone to come back here," Illume stipulated.

"Of course," Trill agreed.

"Will do, boss man," Nari added.

Illume turned his attention forward. The walls automatically ignited with black fire torches as if to welcome him into the bowels of the castle. Illume raised his bow, drawing back to half-length as he creeped down the corridor. Each step offered a soft echo back to him, his eyes bolting from one side to the other of the thin corridor.

A door became visible on Illume's right. Moving against the opposite wall, he aimed his bow at the door while lining himself directly up with it. Illume noticed a soft light on the far side as the door was cracked ever so slightly. Pressing himself against the wall next to the door, he gently pushed it open.

The old wooden door let off a soft creak as it gave way to him. Illume kept his weapon aimed into the room as he swept with the opening of the door. Once it swung fully open, Illume dashed in and turned, covering the final corner. Nothing; the room was clear.

Closing the door behind him, Illume relaxed his grip on his bow before turning his attention to the contents of the room. Illume scoffed; the room was full of scrolls and magical tomes. There was more than one staff that adorned the walls; some were pretty macabre-looking. Worse than the one he entrusted to the centaurs.

Illume retrieved a tome that read *Burden of Knowledge.* Illume opened the book, causing flashes of fire, ice, and electricity to engulf his field of view. Hundreds, if not thousands of images flashed in Illume's mind of magic being fashioned into a spear and wielded. The light eventually faded and the book fell to ash.

Impale Learned

Trophy Earned.
Name: Skip a Grade
Type: Bronze
Requirements: Use a book to activate a skill on your skill tree without having to use skill points.
You big ol' cheater!

Illume laughed at being called a cheater before letting his attention fall to the source of light in the room. A thick book sat on a pedestal, elevated above all the others and letting off a soft blue light. Illume approached the book and blew a thick layer of dust off of it.

God of Ice: Volume 2. was what the cover read. Illume nearly jumped for joy, as the first volume made him formidable with ice.

He couldn't wait to see what this one will do. Grabbing the book, Illume opened it. Instantly, all his weapons were covered in a thick sheet of ice before the book shattered.

Cryo-god Imbue Learned

Scrolled across Illume's screen. Drawing his sword caused the ice that encased it to shatter and fall away. Holding his sword before him, Illume focused on fire. Nothing happened, save his sword's hilt glowing slightly with heat.

Changing to electricity caused his weapon to spark as any metal conducting electricity would. As he focused on his ice abilities, Illume's sword was instantly encased in a thick layer of jagged ice, extending his weapon's reach.

Cryo-Blade
Increases all stats by 35%

Illume let out an impressed laugh, giving his sword a few swings, each one letting off a soft rumble that resembled ice cracking. Illume withdrew the ice and sheathed his sword before drawing his bow. Imbuing it with ice, Illume got the same message.

Cryo-Bow
Increases all stats by 35%

Illume grew excited at the prospect of finding the other volumes of the God of Ice books. Illume notched an arrow, which caused ice to dance up from the notch and feathered end, stretching out all the way to the arrow's head. Illume turned back. He could spend all day in this room, but he needed to press on.

Exiting back into the hallway, Illume continued down the corridor, coming to another room, this time on his left. Illume proceeded with caution, as he did with the first room.

His eyes darted back and forth, only for him to stop dead in his tracks. A scuttling creature floated through the air with a soft hum. Hardly able to believe his eyes, Illume took a deep breath and held it.

Aiming carefully, Illume took the creature in his sight. With the appearance of an imp wearing beetle armor and with the wings of an insect, Illume didn't need to see its tools of torture to know that this thing was one of the Dark King's monsters. As he released his arrow, a deep pop rippled out of his bow like ice itself shifting.

The sound drew the creature's attention, but it was far too late. Illume's arrow found its mark, passing through its helmet as if it were made of tissue paper. Ice formed rapidly over the imp's body as it fell to the ground, shattering into thousands of little pieces while Illume was informed his attack was an "insta-kill." The greatest thing about his frost attacks, they didn't take up mana.

Illume notched another arrow and entered the room. A quick scan proved that there were no more threats, but Illume wasn't alone. In the center of the room was a young woman with long blond hair that was matted with dirt. Deep cuts were gouged all over her body and her hands were tied above her head by a wire.

Illume noticed that her toes were hardly on the ground, meaning her entire weight was being pulled on her wrists, the wires, and her shoulders. Illume threw his bow on his back, firing a quick blast of frost at the wire, just as he did for Nari. The wire snapped as it grew brittle, and the woman fell. Illume managed to catch her before freeing her hands from the wire.

Illume immediately summoned his healing magic on the woman. Her wounds healed, but she remained caked in dirt and blood. Her toned form had a blue tint to it, as the same leather outfit that Nari had worn was on her. Her eyes fluttered open; they were a bright frosty blue as her lips parted, gasping for air.

"My name is Illume. I am here to help you," Illume said in a friendly tone.

"I ca-I can't feel my legs," she huffed in a panic, unable to take any deep breaths from the constriction of her chest.

"You have been captured by the Dark King," Illume explained. Her eyes widened in terror once she heard his name. "You have been put in leather that cuts the circulation off to your legs so you can't run away and constricts your chest so you can't get as much oxygen as you need. I am going to need to cut this off."

The woman, still gasping for air, nodded as she grabbed Illume's arms tightly.

"Do it," she was hardly able to whisper.

Illume drew his daggers, and carefully, with three slices, freed this woman from the bonds that constricted her body. Illume left her covered and laid her on the ground as he turned to search the blood-caked room for something she could wear. Coming across a trunk, Illume opened it to see a set of women's armor inside.

"I believe I found your supplies," Illume said.

"Can you bring them to me? My extremities are still a little tingly," she managed to get out.

Illume lifted the chest and set it next to the woman; putting out his hands, he used his healing spells once again. Looking at her feet, Illume saw the color return to them, as it did to her fingertips. The woman sat up, holding the strap that was constricting her chest over herself. Illume turned around to give her privacy.

"Who were you?" she asked in a whisper. Illume heard her rifle through her belongings.

"I'm Illume of Cryo's Quarry. I've come to defeat the Dark King," he replied.

"Many have come to defeat the Dark King. All have died," she retorted. Illume noticed an accent on her lips. It was Swedish.

"I am going to be different," Illume responded with strength.

"Only when the heart of the cryomancer truly thaws will the Dark King fall," his rescued prisoner advised all the while shuffling with her equipment.

"What's your name?" Illume asked.

"I am Ingrid Ulvenstar," she replied.

Illume turned around to face her. She stood tall, nearly as tall as he was. Her blond hair draped over a frosty blue armor, which fit her well. A massive great sword hung on her back and Nordic runes were etched into the plate of her armor.

"Princess of the North," Ingrid added.

44

TRUTH COMES OUT

"INGRID, Princess of the North, it is an honor to meet you. I would like to speak with you more about this cryomancer, but right now, we need to get moving," Illume explained.

Grabbing an arrow, he notched it, poking his head out into the hallway. He glanced from one side to another. The coast was clear. Illume stepped out into the corridor, followed closely by Ingrid.

"How did you end up here?" Illume asked while backtracking the way he came.

"An ondskan had begun to taint the white of my home in the shape of a black tar. When I came to investigate, I was taken out by one of the minotaur," she replied.

"Ondskan, huh? That was a good movie," Illume whispered to himself.

"What was that?" Ingrid asked.

"We call it a corruption. Did it overtake your people and turn them into grey-skinned monsters?" Illume asked, looking back at Ingrid.

"You mean the draugr? Yes, they have begun to infest our lands, and our caves, and our strongholds," she replied.

Illume and Ingrid approached the intersection where they

were supposed to be meeting back up. Trill emerged from the darkness with a spear in hand and a few pieces of jewelry.

"Then it sounds like we are here for the same reason. Will you help us overthrow the Dark King?" Illume offered.

Nari emerged from the dark as well, several new daggers adorning her waist.

"I will," Ingrid replied.

"Who's the girl?" Trill asked.

"This is Ingrid. She's from the lands to the north. I found her strung up and being tortured the same way you were, Nari. She's agreed to help us take down the Dark King. Ingrid, this is Trillian. We call him Trill. And this is Nari. She's our blacksmith, our knife wielder, and she's pretty quick with her twin swords," Illume added, tossing a wink at her.

Nari smiled at Illume's wink.

"It is an honor to meet you both." Ingrid bowed slightly.

"The pleasure is mine," Trill flirted.

"Likewise… Illume, can I speak with you for a moment?" Nari asked.

"I'm sorry, give me a moment," Illume addressed Ingrid.

Following Nari down her corridor, Illume prepared himself for the cliché jealous "can we trust her" speech. Dreading the next thing she was about to say, Illume just followed her along in the dimly lit corridor. After about five minutes, Nari finally broke the silence while still walking.

"Do you find any of this suspicious?" Nari's question seemed rhetorical.

"Ingrid was being tortured. I couldn't just leave her there," Illume replied.

"Not that, she actually makes a lot of sense. A Dark King needs a Dark Queen, so why not torture someone into her? No, what I'm talking about is how the corridor I was given just happened to be littered with weapons that seem meant specifically for me," Nari whispered so her voice didn't carry.

Illume paused for a moment. He did manage to find the second volume of God of Ice. But no one knew about the first one, not even Trill. It was typical game mechanics to offer the player exactly what they would need right before a big fight like this. Perhaps that was why they were given their perfect items.

Illume shrugged.

"Honestly, if this were a movie, or a book, or hell, even real life, I would be inclined to agree with you. But this isn't any of those things. This is... this is different," Illume concluded, not wanting to have to explain the concept of video games to an NPC.

"Okay then, what about this?" Nari asked as she reached the end of her hallway.

Placing her hand on the door, she shoved it open. Inside, a sea of gold, jewels, and polis rose high from the pit they had been dumped in. The room was massive, the size of a hangar, Illume would guess, and it was filled with all sorts of precious items. This would put the Cave of Wonders to shame.

"Why the Scrooge McDuckian vault?" Nari asked.

Illume's heart stopped. His thoughts of the Dark King, of Trill, Ingrid, hell, even every single piece of riches that was before him all vanish. A tingling numbness overtook his entire body as he turned to Nari. Had anything been in his hands, it would have hit the ground, and should even the slightest breeze come through the vaults, he would have surely fallen over.

"How..." Illume managed to whisper after several seconds.

"How what?" Nari replied.

"How do you know about Scrooge McDuck?" Illume managed to squeeze out.

Nari didn't respond. She did, however, turn a deep red. Taking a few steps back, Illume felt the room start to spin.

"You... you're human," Illume whispered as he staggered into a wall. "Your avatar's not, but you, you ARE human. H-how was that possible? I was the first to test the system!" Illume stammered.

Trying to make sense of everything, his head swimming, Illume slid to the ground, placing his head into his hands. Nari quickly moved to his side, placing her hand on his back.

"I was the lead engineer on the project. My real name is Nariani Petrovic. When I came here, I changed it to Nari for short," she explained.

"How did you enter the game?" Illume asked. "Why are you still here? Why not go home? That's why you knew so much about the lives!" Illume exclaimed.

Nari's demeanor changed. She bowed her head and nodded in shame.

"That IS how I knew about the lives. And all I wanted to do was be the first person to experience my creation. I assume the same thing that happened to me happened to you," Nari explained. "When I integrated with our neural network, there was some sort of malfunction. I don't know what it was. Long story short, my mind was uploaded here, but an explosion that killed my body made it so that I can never leave the game," Nari added.

Illume's heart fluttered, his mind warped as he heard the screams of the lab technicians talking about a neural feedback loop. His body trembled uncontrollably as a sense of terror gripped his gut. He was dead; for all intents and purposes, he died on a live stream, blown to bits.

"What if we defeat the Dark King?" Illume asked, denial rippling through his voice.

"I thought that way too, had some friends log in to help me with him. I went against him twice, and I lost twice. I became a forger, because if I die again… my consciousness will be deleted from the server." Nari's voice softened.

As she spoke of her past failures, the scars on her body made sense, which meant the mark on her shoulder had to have been her life counter. Illume retreated into himself, his own little defense mechanism. Nari tried to speak to him, shaking him even, to little avail.

"Think about Kassandra, about Victor and their children!" Nari's words managed to break through after a few moments.

The faces of his niece and nephew flashed in his mind. They might not have been his actual niece and nephew, but they were still in trouble.

"This may be a game, but they still have lives here and they are still in grave danger. The sooner we deal with the Dark King, the better. He's programmed to level a percentage ahead of you," Nari explained.

"Who is he?" Illume asked with a growl.

"I don't know. He's procedurally generated. For me, he was a mindless beast in the woods outside. I've never gotten in the castle before. Right now, you're what, level ten or eleven?" she asked. Illume nodded. "Good, then we have a chance! I played around on level ground, so when I faced him, he was leagues ahead of me," Nari explained.

Illume did not move. Sitting on the cold floor, he took in the trivial nature of his surroundings. They were cold, they were dark, and to his left was a literal ocean of riches. In the end, it didn't even matter, as everything was a digital projection. What was the point?

Nari, clearly tired of waiting for Illume to step up, crouched down to his level and delivered a painful slap to his face. Admittedly, the stinging sensation snapped Illume out of his rut. He raised his eyes to Nari's, burning with a passion he'd never seen before. It was no wonder she seemed so real.

"We have fought for months to get this far. You have scratched, tooth and nail, to build Cryo's Quarry, make more allies than I have EVER seen, and end up here. We are a stone's throw away from the Dark King and I believe that you can defeat him. I believe in it so much that I am betting my final life on it!" Nari pulled at Illume's breastplate.

Her pull brought Illume to his feet as her words stoked the fire in him once again. Illume always had been one to put his needs aside for those of family and friends. Now he had to put his own petty grievances aside to save what he now assumed was his new home.

It wasn't anything he could be terribly upset about; he'd always wanted to know what a fantasy world was like, and now he was halfway to becoming a god of ice. Nari continued to talk, but Illume admittedly hadn't heard much else of what she'd said.

The fire she re-ignited quickly engulfed him as he thought of all the people who'd moved to Cryo's Quarry, who would have likely died if he hadn't come along to rescue them or give them a place to stay.

Illume's heart raced, his adrenaline surged, and with one swift movement, almost as if his body was controlling itself, Illume grabbed Nari by the waist and pulled her close to him. Pressing his lips hard against hers as his free hand ran through her hair, Illume felt Nari sink into him. Returning his passionate kiss, she softly moaned against his lips.

Illume broke the kiss and released Nari while readying his bow. He fired her a smirk noticing her deep blush and inability to stop smiling. Nodding back down the hallway, Illume arched one of his brows.

"Let's go kick some Dark King butt," he exclaimed.

Illume headed back down the hallway with Nari close behind. She drew her twin swords and gave them a quick bang together to hear the resonant sound they gave off. A sturdy clang rang through the air, and within a few more minutes, Illume and Nari had returned to Ingrid and Trill.

"Hope you two had a lot of fun," Trill teased.

Illume tossed Trill a sarcastic smirk.

"We're ready to go. Lead the way!" Illume commanded.

Trill nodded, drawing his sword, followed shortly by Ingrid before they both started up the stairs they'd descended. Nari and Illume followed closely behind. Reaching the top of the stairs, Nari and Illume noticed Trill and Ingrid were frozen in their tracks. Illume followed their gaze to see the once empty grand hall now filled with imps.

Illume slung his bow over his back before drawing his sword. He enjoyed ripping through imps with his bastard sword. Illume's hand grew blue and frosted over. A dark smile tugged at his lips as every imp turned to face them.

"Kill 'em all," Illume commanded.

45

FORWARD

ILLUME SLICED through imps left and right with ease. Each attack lowered his stamina but he was cutting down more than one of those creepy grey creatures. Dozens of imps, armored, winged, and grey, descended on Ingrid, Trill, Nari, and Illume. Trill sliced through the beasts with nearly as much ease as Illume while Nari and Ingrid struggled fighting multiple targets at once.

"Cover the girls!" Illume yelled to Trill as an imp slashed across Ingrid's back.

The imps attacked with axes, daggers, and claws. Illume and Nari's armor held up against the sharp attacks. Each blow that caused blunt-force trauma, however, did damage their health, chipping away little by little. Illume looked over at Nari, yelling over the clashing of metal and roaring of imps.

"Matrix?" Illume shouted.

"Matrix!" Nari confirmed.

Reaching out, Illume grabbed Nari's forearm and spun her in a circle. She ran, kicking imps in the face as she did. Illume extended his hand, unleashing a wall of frosted spikes that shot through the nearest imps like a fifty-caliber bullet. The second row froze solid, shattering as Nari ran over them. Lowering Nari, Illume noticed that Ingrid and Trill were being overrun.

"INGRID!" Illume yelled.

The Nordic warrior looked at him. Using all his stamina, Illume threw his sword to her, slicing through any imp that got in the way. Ingrid snatched his sword, and with a single swipe, cut down three with much more ease than with her sword.

Illume formed an ice spear in his hand, summoning his frost impale spell. The edge of the spear was sharp as a razor with a hook on the end. Its head came to a point so fine, obsidian seemed dull. Illume jabbed and sliced, each imp taking two hits to kill now instead of one. When he glanced back to Nari, she seemed to be keeping up just fine.

Illume sidestepped a flying imp. Grabbing it by one of its spinal frills, Illume slammed it to the ground, and with three hard stamps, killed the beast. Their numbers were beginning to thin. Illume tossed his spear to change his grip and threw it as hard as he could into an imp that had found its way onto Ingrid's back.

With his mana and stamina gone, Illume fell back to his bow as he and Nari moved toward Ingrid and Trill. Illume notched arrow after arrow and fired as quickly as he could into as many imps as possible. Any that didn't fall immediately were run through swiftly by Ingrid and Trill.

"How are you doing back there?!" Illume yelled back to Nari.

"Okay, but they're not going to stop coming until we get farther up!" she replied, slashing and hacking where she could.

Illume grabbed Trill, pulling him close before stabbing an imp in the eye with one of his arrows, pulling it out and shooting the same arrow straight through another imp. Illume positioned everyone so they were back to back. The imps seemed to be just flooding out of the darkness at all sides.

"Trill, how do we get out of here?" Illume yelled as an imp leaped onto him.

Pulling one of his daggers, Illume stabbed the imp in its side. Each stab made its health drop bit by bit while its claws attempted to dig into Illume's helmet, but its claws were unable to penetrate Illume's chimera hybrid helmet. With four more jabs, the imp fell to the ground lifelessly, twitching as the last vestige of its blood spurted onto the floor.

"This way!" Trill yelled, pointing to one of the corners.

Illume checked his mana; it was a little over halfway full now. Sheathing his dagger and hooping his bow over his back, Illume spun between his party. As he did, Illume charged a flaming impale spell with both hands.

Getting clear of his team, Illume threw his hands out. A bright flash of white-hot light erupted from his hands and incinerated the imps before him.

As the light faded, a path of corpses pointed Illume and his team to a stairwell in the corner of the room. Grabbing Nari's hand, Illume led them through the smoldering corpses. Upon making it to the stairwell, Illume turned, drawing his bow in preparation to cover their ascent.

Ingrid pulled a scroll of paper from her belt. Unfurling it, she slammed it into the ground. A blue tint took over the paper before a frosty blue light erupted into concentric circles.

Another flash of light and a wall of ice roughly four feet thick completely blocked the stairwell. Ingrid turned to everyone, obviously proud of herself.

"Scroll of Ice Wall," Ingrid bragged.

Approaching Illume, she handed him his sword back, inspecting it for several seconds before she did. Illume graciously received his sword. Placing it back in its sheath, he offered her a friendly nod.

"That is a very well made weapon," Ingrid complimented.

"Thank you, I made it specifically for this," Nari replied. Illume nodded in agreement.

"It is a good weapon. Now, Trill, what can we expect on our way? Any more rooms full of endless waves of enemies?" Illume asked as he watched his bars refill.

"There is just one more level between us and the Dark King… But a troll guards that floor. You should be able to take it out no problem," Trill replied.

"If I go berserk, there is only a percent chance that I'll be able to control it. If I let it take over, I may hurt the three of you," Illume protested the idea.

Notching the last two arrows of his first quiver, Illume led the team up the stairs. He intentionally moved slower so he could try to come up with a strategy to kill the beast lying in wait. Illume could hear its breathing echoing down the spiral staircase. Stopping near the top, Illume pressed himself against the wall.

Peering around the corner, Illume saw the massive grey-skinned troll pacing on a clearing that was hardly large enough for two more people. Illume glanced around, looking for environmental takedowns to use before he noticed three massive iron chandeliers hanging above its head. Illume had played enough games to recognize those.

Turning back to his team, Illume studied them for several moments. Nari was quick with her hands, and on the battlefield, she was faster with her hands than on her feet. Ingrid had donned heavy armor, thicker and heavier than even Illume's. This left Trill. Trill was a lightning bolt on his feet. Should he have chosen to be, this would have been perfect.

"Trill, it's going to be just you and me, okay? You distract him and get him to move under the chandeliers. Leave the rest to me," Illume whispered.

Trill nodded, sheathing his sword. He stepped forward, joining Illume in front of the ladies. Nari gave Illume a pleading look to let her join. He shook his head.

"There won't be room to maneuver with more than two people there," Illume whispered.

As he drew his bow, it gave a soft groan as Illume placed it under strain. Trill glanced back at Illume, who nodded for him to continue. In the blink of an eye, Trill sprinted across the platform. The troll turned and huffed. It slammed its massive fists down violently at Trill, who slid right past him. Illume looked up. He was almost under one of the chandeliers.

Illume aimed an arrow at the base of the chandelier and the

chain that held it. Trill lured the troll toward him with another blow. The beast took several seconds to recover back to its standing position, which was more than enough time for Illume.

As he released the arrow, it found its mark, causing the chain to shatter. The chandelier fell, striking the troll in the head with enough force to take out a third of his health.

"One down, three to go. Keep up the good work," Illume stated to Trill.

That was a mistake, as it brought the troll's attention to Illume. It turned, snarling at Illume, who managed to fire off two more arrows, both of which found their place in the troll's chest. They did next to nothing to its health. The troll roared, charging Illume, who fired several more rounds into it before diving out of the way.

The troll's fists narrowly missed Illume as they hit the ground and he rolled to his feet. Turning, his entire field of view was overtaken by the troll's fists. Dropping, Illume managed to hit the ground just as the fists passed over him.

The momentum brought the troll under the second chandelier. Illume watched Trill's sword slice through the chain and the fixture fell on the troll, taking another third of its health.

Unable to stick to a target, the troll turned to Trill and tried to assault the swift smooth talker. Trill dodged as quickly as he could, avoiding all of the troll's kicks and punches. Fortunately for them, the room was too small for the beast to have a weapon. Otherwise, they'd have been done for.

Trill attempted to get the troll under the final chandelier. Illume fired at the chain like he did with the first. His arrow found its mark. The final heavy chandelier fell. It merely clipped the troll, taking away only a fraction of the health it had left.

"Come on," Illume mumbled to himself.

The troll turned once again to Illume, who fired two arrows at its face, trying to blind it. The troll lifted its hands, blocking the arrows before swiping them away without so much as a drop of blood. The troll leaned forward, letting out a roar, and charged Illume.

Nocking another arrow, Illume was about to fire a frost shot at it when both of Nari's chimera daggers slammed into its shoulder, followed by Ingrid's great sword.

A sliver of its health dropped, but nowhere near enough to slow it down. The troll then, predictably, turned its attention to Nari and Ingrid. As it charged at them, Illume swore he saw a soft yellow glint under its chin.

Of course, a weak spot! Illume thought to himself as he charged the troll. Falling behind, Illume dropped and slid between the troll's legs before firing an arrow directly into the slightly glowing spot.

The arrow penetrated to its feathers as the troll's health dropped to zero. It let out a low growl before falling backward. Hitting the ground, it emitted a castle-trembling "thud."

Illume looked at Nari with a wide grin on his face.

"Weak spot?" she asked.

"Weak spot," Illume responded with a nod. "You okay over there, Trillian?"

"I'm good!" he yelled.

Trill threw one of the chains to knock down his sword. The first time he tossed it, he missed. The second managed to hook but then slid free. Third time was the charm. His sword fell free, embedding itself into the troll's forehead with no problem.

"Oh, now you want to get in on the kill," Illume teased.

Trill offered Illume a taunting laugh before giving him the middle finger while he retrieved his sword. Nari and Ingrid retrieved their weapons as well. Sheathing them, Illume took a step back from their joint, rather clumsy kill. Scattered all over the place were potions of every kind. Illume noticed the small save circle rotating in the corner of his field of view.

"He's right up there, isn't he?" Illume asked Trill.

"To the best of my knowledge, yes," Trill replied.

"Gather what you can. Something tells me we will have use of every single one of these potions. I don't know what we are going to be facing, so just remember, stay spread out and keep your mana and stamina in check," Illume instructed.

Splitting up, everyone gathered their own healing items. Trill offered each member a restoration item he thought they'd like or need. More often than not, he's right, and the potion was accepted. Illume retrieved all his arrows save the one buried under the troll's chin. He attempted to dig it out, but after about ten minutes, he surrendered. Looking around, Illume noticed that everyone was geared up and looking at him.

"Are you ready?" Illume asked.

All three nodded, each appearing fidgety. Trill seemed slightly sad.

"As ready as I'll ever be," Ingrid spoke first.

"I'll follow you to the end," Nari replied.

"Let's get this over with," Trill whispered.

"Okay, then,... on to the final boss," Illume said softly before walking toward the final stairwell.

46

THE DARK KING

ILLUME LED his team up the final flight of stairs. Sweat beading on his brow, hands clammy, heart racing, Illume had never felt anything like this before. The literal weight of this cyber world rested on his shoulders, and without a body to go back to, the price for failure was death. That concept helped make him have cotton mouth.

Illume drew his sword, holding it in a reverse grip while having a tight handle on his bow. Illume approached a massive black door. In the center of the door was a circle with a line carved across it steeped in blood. The very sight of the door sent a chill through Illume's veins that was colder than his own ice.

Illume looked back at his team, nodding at them. They nodded back. Taking several deep breaths, building his nerve, Illume delivered a powerful kick to the door, causing it to burst open. Illume rushed in, scanning the large, open space. Aside from bones and armor scattered along the wall and a single black helmet sitting in the center, the room was empty. Illume lowered his bow, looking back at Nari, shaking his head.

"I-I don't get it," he said in confusion. "The Dark King isn't here."

"I've never seen this before," Nari responded.

"Is there even a Dark King at all?" Illume's tone had a hint of frustration.

"Yes, there is." Illume froze as he recognized the voice.

Turning to the source of the voice, a shock rattled Illume's system. His bow and sword fell from his hands and he heard Nari whisper a heart broken "no" behind him.

"Not you, it can't be you," Illume pled, his words breathless.

"I'm sorry, Illume, I truly am. I have met countless men in my time, but none I would have considered a brother. I have been searching for a man with the strength of both character and will to put an end to my suffering. I don't want to be a plague on this land, my friend, but like the scorpion... I can't fight my nature." Trillian's voice changed, his accent disappearing as he kneeled down, lifting the black helmet. "I pray to the gods you are victorious, and if you are, all I have is yours. Just wait until you're stronger to don the armor."

Trillian lifted the helmet and placed it on his head. The moment it settled in, his form shifted. Flame and shadow overtook his handsome form, causing him to grow in size.

Standing nearly nine feet tall, the shadow and flames closed in around him, acting as protection at his armor's weak points. Reaching behind him, the Dark King drew his sword. Flames danced around it in a torrent of heat and light.

"Illume, MOVE!" Nari screamed.

The Dark King wound up and swung at Illume. Nari tackled him to the ground, causing the sword to miss. A soft sizzling could be heard as the heat from the sword caused a light scorch to form on any surface it got near.

Moving in for a second strike, Ingrid slid between the Dark King and her new teammates, a scroll open in her hand. In a bright blue flash, ice formed around the Dark King's weapon and hands, extending to the ceiling to hold him in place.

"He's not Trillian anymore; you have to fight him!" Nari roared.

Nari grabbed Illume's bow and sword and slapped them into

Illume's hands while pulling him to his feet. Illume staggered back at the sight of his friend as he twisted his hands, making flame crack the ice that held him. Nari threw her daggers at the Dark King, his life bar becoming visible for Illume to see. Illume drew his arrow and fired at the Dark King's neck, sticking in. Only a sliver of his health disappeared.

With a thunderous crack, Ingrid's ice broke, causing Illume to stagger backwards. The Dark King swung his sword at Illume so fast that had he blinked, he would have missed it. Fortunately, his staggering caused the Dark King to miss.

Illume drew several more arrows. Falling back, he shot at his old friend. Any arrow that hit the Dark King's armor bounced off. He might as well be using a Nerf gun. The arrows that did hit caused almost no damage.

Illume dropped his bow as he realized it would do no good, charging in with his sword. Nari did her best to stay behind him, but the pulses of heat that emitted from the Dark King proved too much for her and caused her to keep her distance. Ingrid smoked like a cup of hot water in the winter wind. As Illume approached, he began to steam as well. His mana dropped.

The Dark King's sword dropped on Illume. Throwing his blade at an angle, Illume deflected the blow. Illume's stamina plunged as he blocked the attack. Changing his stance, Illume slammed his sword into the Dark King's hands. The vibration from the impact reverberated through Illume's arms, causing pins and needles to overtake his extremities. The Dark King glared at Illume with fiery eyes.

"Please don't make me do this, Trillian!" Illume cried out.

Ingrid stepped forward and drove her blade in between the Dark King's armor plating. His health dropped by an eighth and he roared in pain. With a single powerful backhand, he sent Ingrid across the room. She crashed against the wall and fell to the ground. Her health dropped almost all the way to zero. The Dark King pulled Ingrid's sword from his side and marched toward her.

Nari, having run out of throwing knives, sprinted between the Dark King and Ingrid. She deflected the Dark King's attacks. Illume charged to a silver pike that lay on the ground next to one of the corpses that had been here for a centuries. Illume picked up the weapon:

Perfect Pike: Pike of Holy Light
Damage: +33 triples against the undead or unholy.
Weight: +12
Worth: 2000 polis
Pike of Holy Light was forged long ago with the intent to kill the Dark King. Too bad the man who wielded it wasn't made of better stuff.

As the words disappeared, Illume saw the Dark King pulling his sword from Ingrid's corpse, her life bar at zero. Illume felt his body temperature rise with rage. Letting out a primal roar brought the Dark King's attention away from Nari, who had been batted across the ground like a rag doll.

Illume charged the Dark King, who swung at him. Using the pike's tip to deflect the attack, Illume jabbed it into the flames between his shoulder and breast plate. A blinding white light erupted from the spear tip as the Dark King's health dropped by a third. As Illume pulled the pike away, the Dark King staggered backward, the corrupting black goo oozing from his wound as the flame disappeared, revealing the weaknesses in the Dark King's armor.

The Dark King turned and faced Illume, his eyes still glowing a fiery red, his breathing sounding like an individual unlucky enough to be placed in the ancient Greek's brass bull. Illume beat his fist into his chest to psych himself up. He was careful not to activate his berserker since Nari would certainly perish in the ensuing fight.

"BRING IT ON!" Illume roared.

His doubts about if this THING was still his friend dissipated as the Dark King charged him. Illume used the distance to his advantage. He deflected and jabbed, causing minor damage here and there, prepared to level up the moment he was struck. His stamina rapidly depleted, as the Dark King was impossibly fast, and each minor movement expended an exorbitant amount of energy, just to stay ahead of the Dark King.

Illume began to slow but managed to get a solid thrust into the Dark King's gut, dropping his life bar to a mere quarter of his health as light erupted from his wound. The Dark King grabbed Illume's pike and ripped it away from his grip, throwing it across the room. With no stamina left, Illume threw both of his hands up and fired an attack of frosted spikes at him.

With his back to a wall, Illume was unable to backpedal; he only hoped he could slow down the Dark King enough to dodge out of the way. As his mana exhausted, the Dark King swung his massive hand at Illume. Bracing himself for the blow, Illume was shoved out of the way by Nari, who was struck and sent across the room instead.

Illume watched in horror as her life bar dropped to one hit point. The Dark King lunged at her with his gleaming sword aimed directly at her chest. Using the last ounce of his energy, Illume got between Nari and the Dark King.

Trophy Earned.
Name: Self Sacrifice
Type: Gold
Greater love hath no man than this, that a man lay down his life for his friends.

Illume's vision blurred. *'You have been scorched, you have been paralyzed'* scrolled across his screen. The sensation of his internal organs starting to boil roared through his body. His vision clouded as tears well in his eyes from the agony that filled every fiber of his being. Illume could hear Nari screaming behind him as he dropped to his knees.

Illume's health bar drained. As it did, the Dark King's health raised. Illume's vision darkened and time stretched as everything started to slow down. The Dark King tilted his head to one side and leaned in, looking Illume directly in the eyes. Through the warping effect of death, Illume could almost swear he heard the Dark King apologize for killing him.

Illume attempted to look up and activate his leveling screen. He was unable to, as his body would not obey his commands due to the paralysis. The Dark King ripped his sword out of Illume's chest, causing him to fall to the ground. Illume fell facing Nari, who had tears streaming down her face as she reached out to him, taking his hand.

As his vision grew darker by the second, Illume's heart dropped between Nari and himself. Finally, everything went black as Illume's life bar dropped to zero.

You Died!
Would you like to respawn?

Yes | No

A rogue thought entered his mind, making him wonder what would happen if he were to choose the No option on the screen in front of him. If everything Nari had told him was true, then he had no physical body to go back to.

If he said No, then did he die right now?

Suddenly trying to win this level or even the game didn't mean much at all. If he couldn't get back to the real world, then what was his purpose now?

Nari, Illume thought to himself. *She's real, just like you, and she has only a single life left like you now. If you're not fighting to get back to the real world then fight for her. Fight for a chance to find out if there is even a way to get back at all.*

Illume hovered over the no prompt before deciding against it. He focused on the yes prompt instead.

You have three level ups available. Might we suggest you use them?

Illume was automatically brought to the leveling screen, where he had seventeen attribute points and seven skill points to use. Illume replayed the fight he'd just had over in his mind. He was outclassed in speed and strength while he didn't seem to have any offensive magical abilities.

Cycling through, Illume selected *Dexterity* and threw ten points into that, placing two in *Strength* and dumping the last five into *Wisdom.*

New Attributes:
Health: 200 regenerates 1% of max health a second while not in battle.
Mana: 250 regenerates 3% of max mana a second while not in battle.
Stamina: 230 regenerates 5% of max stamina a second while not in battle.
Weight Capacity: 40/590, +10 per skill point added to stamina.
Survival: Unique skill, player has 70% resistance to cold attacks.
Charisma: +28, drops to +19 when in the presence of women.
Strength: +30 average for male humans.
Dexterity: +40 average for a human.
Intelligence: +20 average for a human.
Constitution: +27 without armor rating, average for a human.
Wisdom: +38 +10 mana

ILLUME TRANSITIONED to his skill tree. Focusing to his destruction magic tree, he selected to pay three of his seven skill points to unlock *'Like a Hammer.'* Moving to armor, Illume placed three more points into *'Tank'* before using his last point to activate *'Deflector.'*

New Skills:
+100% Heavy Armor effectiveness
75% Chance of staggering an opponent
15% chance of deflecting physical damage back on caster.

Illume closed his leveling screen, selecting to respawn. Illume felt a ripping backwards as the darkness faded into light.

47

RESPAWN

ILLUME FOUND himself standing just outside the Dark King's door once again, that bloody circle with a line etched through it staring him in the face. Glancing back, Illume noticed Nari looking around as if she were experiencing déjà vu.

Ingrid stood behind her, alive and well, but Trillian was nowhere to be seen. Nari ran her fingers over her stomach as if she'd been expecting to be run through there.

"Did you just…?" Nari started in a whisper, unable to finish.

"I did what I had to do," Illume responded softly.

Nari pursed her lips, tilting her head to the side as if to say he shouldn't have done that.

"Where is the black-armored man?" Ingrid asked, looking around in confusion.

"Yeah, where is Trillian?" Nari echoed.

Illume pointed to the door. On the far side, monstrous huffs could be heard as well as massive footsteps.

"He's right on the other side of that door waiting to kill us," Illume explained.

"Oh no," Nari instinctively whispered.

"Yes," Illume replied.

Turning his attention fully to Ingrid and Nari, Illume looked both women up and down, assessing them. Ingrid had her one scroll left still attached to her hip. All of Nari's daggers were in their places.

Closing his eyes for a minute, Illume played back the fight he'd just had, mentally locating where the pike was lying.

"Okay, this is the new plan. Nari, the Dark King is giving off a lot of heat. It's going to burn you if you get close. On the far side of the room at..." Illume pointed with an open palm. "...about one o'clock, there is a pike on the ground. It's called the Pike of Holy Light. Last time, it hurt him pretty badly. I want you to get it."

Nari nodded in agreement. Illume turned to Ingrid, who was itching for a fight.

"Ingrid, he's extremely fast. I want you to stay back and use that scroll of yours on his feet, lock him in place. He's incalculably strong and his weapons are a one-hit kill. He's quick, but big. You'll be faster; just keep out of his way and leave the rest to me," Illume ordered.

"One more time, I guess," Nari huffed under her breath.

"One more time is as much as either of us gets," Illume said, remembering their life count. He didn't want to think what happened to them if they died now.

"Let's do this," Ingrid confirmed.

Illume pressed his shoulder against the door, arrow notched and halfway drawn. Illume could feel his hands frost over. Illume took several deep breaths before shoving against the door and charging into the room as it gave way. Illume drew his bow and fired an arrow at the Dark King, who stood in the center of the room glaring at the door as if waiting for them.

Illume's arrow bounced off the Dark King's helmet as Illume took off left. Nari broke away and headed right while Ingrid stayed in the center. The Dark King ignored Illume, his head following Nari. He went to charge at her when Ingrid's frost scroll locked his legs in place.

The Dark King swung at Nari, but his sword was just barely

too short to reach her. Illume drew an arrow, ice formed around his bow, then over his arrow. Taking aim, Illume aligned his shot with the Dark King's hand.

"Herregud!" Illume heard Ingrid whisper.

"Trillian!" Illume roared.

The Dark King turned his head to look at Illume. He paused, stunned at the sight of Illume imbuing his bow with frost magic. When he released the arrow, it flew through the air with the rumbling of shattering ice.

Slamming into the Dark King's hand results in him dropping his sword and letting out a roar of pain. Illume watched as the Dark King's health dropped slightly.

On the far side of the room, Nari slid and grabbed the pike. Illume noticed she looked at it as if reading its stats before giving Illume a thumbs-up. Illume notched another arrow and drew. The Dark King shattered the ice that held him in place. Retrieving his sword, he lunged at Illume while swinging.

Illume blind-fired his arrow as the Dark King closed the gap. It bounced off his armor like a pebble against a wall, dealing no damage. Illume moved to dash out of the way. As he did, the world seemed to blur around him. A split second later, he slid to a stop as he collided with the far wall. Illume looked back to see the Dark King finishing his swipe.

Illume glanced at Nari, who had a wide smile on her face and held out the pike. Illume took it, ignoring the stats this time while handing his bow and arrows to Nari.

"What the hell did I just do?" Illume asked.

"Your dexterity hit forty, didn't it? Your stats hit what could be considered low level superhuman at forty," Nari explained.

"Call me Barry Allen, then," Illume huffed. "Get Ingrid and get out of here. I can handle the rest."

The Dark King turned to face Illume, Nari notched an arrow and passed behind Illume. Illume gripped the pike as hard as he could and was about to lunge at him when the Dark King moved against Nari.

Illume dropped the pike and instinctively threw out both hands. A spear of ice slammed into the Dark King with so much force, it knocked him back several feet.

His health bar hardly moved, but that didn't matter to Illume. Nari continued to fire arrows as she moved toward Ingrid. Illume shot long spikes of ice out of both hands, staggering the Dark King about 75 percent of the time, preventing him from attacking Nari.

Illume popped the cork to one of his mana potions and guzzled it, watching his mana refill before firing several more barrages at the Dark King, keeping him from her. Nari eventually reached Ingrid and pulled her out the door, closing it behind her. Illume picked the pike back up as the Dark King's attention was brought back to him.

"It's just you and me. Let's end this," Illume growled.

The Dark King nodded, leaping at Illume, who dashed out of the way before thrusting his spear at the Dark King. Illume's first jab was deflected and he used that momentum to spin the pike and thrust its other end into the Dark King with enough force to make him stagger.

The Dark King rolled with the attack. Gracefully, he transitioned into another swipe. Illume held up his pike, blocking his opponent's blow. Spinning the pike, Illume broke their lock.

Using his speed, he stabbed the Dark King's shoulder. Just like before, a bright light erupted, burning off the Dark King's magical barrier and dropping a significant portion of his health.

The Dark King roared in agony, once again, and kicked Illume as hard as he could. Illume flew back and plowed into a back wall, pike still in hand. A blow that would have nearly completely removed his health only dropped it by a quarter. Illume was thankful he put in for tank.

Pushing off the wall, Illume dashed at the Dark King, bashing his pike so hard into the Dark King's sword, a shockwave erupted within the tower, making both men stagger.

At this point, Illume's stamina was at about half while his

magic was filling back up past the halfway mark. The Dark King swung down at Illume, who sidestepped the attack and fired a blast of ice into the Dark King's sword, freezing it to the stone it had run into.

Illume stabbed at the Dark King, sparks flew, and he was staggered back as he released his sword. No damage occurred to his health. Illume jabbed at his disarmed places. He would do minimal damage if he ever managed to land a strike.

The Dark King knocked Illume's pike to the side before delivering a powerful punch to his face. The attack dropped Illume's health to a quarter while draining his stamina as well.

Illume spun through the air like a top. The entire time, he refused to release the pike. Crashing to the ground, Illume groaned in pain. Pulling himself to his feet, Illume cast a healing spell on himself, restoring his lost health as he stood tall once more.

The Dark King retrieved his sword once more. Letting out a roar, he lunged at Illume, who, once again, used his speed to outmaneuver the Dark King. Both men held nothing back as they struck and parried each other's attacks. One had the advantage of speed; the other had strength.

Knowing his odds of winning were slim to none and that he was just delaying the inevitable if he didn't do something quickly, Illume imbued the pike with his new frost abilities. This increases the strength of his blows, allowing him to stand against the might of the Dark King for several more seconds. That was all he needed.

The Dark King slashed downward at Illume, and he deflected the blow, spinning. Illume thrust the sharp end of his frosted pike into the Dark King's gut, bypassing his armor. *Critical Hit* scrolled across the screen. The Dark King's grip on his sword loosened as it clanged to the ground. His life bar dropped rapidly.

The Dark King shrank in size, and he pulled off his helmet as he returned to his Trillian form. Blood pouring from his mouth,

Trillian yanked the pike from his gut. Illume slid under his friend, placing his hand on Trillian's wound.

Illume's gut wrenched harder than any blow that could have been delivered by the Dark King. His best friend slumped down into his arms, trembling as his life ebbed away.

"I got you, buddy, I got you. I'm right here," Illume whispered as he choked back tears. "Why, why did you make me do it?"

Trillian's trembling hand reached for Illume's. Grabbing it, he held Illume's hand close. His face twitched with agony as tears filled his eyes too, but they seemed to be tears of joy, not pain. Trillian gazed at Illume. Clenching his jaw, he nodded approvingly at Illume's actions.

"Thank you, my brother," he managed to stammer out from behind the pain. "You had to be the one to do it. No one will dispute your claim to the throne now. Thank you for bringing me peace."

Trillian's life bar hit zero as his body relaxed in Illume's arms and his blood-soaked hand slowly slid out of Illume's. The pain he felt from being run through was nothing compared to that of Trillian's death. His final words echoed within Illume's mind. Those words would haunt him for the rest of his days.

Illume let out a primal roar, manifesting his internal agony the only way he knew how. Tears streamed down his cheeks as the body of the only friend he'd ever truly had turned to ash in his arms.

Level Up Available x3
Quest Complete
Kill the Dark King

48

NEXT STEP

LEGENDARY ARMOR FOUND

Name: Armor of the Dark King
Must be level seventy to wield.

THE WOULD-BE stat page scrolled across Illume's field of view as he gathered Trillian's armor and weapon. Holding them for several minutes before rising to his feet, Illume staggered steps, catching himself as he was off-balanced. Across from Illume was a chest tucked behind several corpses.

Illume walked over to the chest, Trillian's equipment in hand, before kneeling and observing a massive lock holding the lid shut. Illume set Trillian's armor down before rummaging for the key he found on Balathor. Removing the Skeleton Key, Illume slid it into the lock. With a gentle twist, the arched lock popped open.

Removing the heavily enchanted lock, Illume lifted the chest's lid. Within the chest was a single item. An oval ball of ice sat perched upright among some hay. Illume reverently placed Trillian's armor into the trunk. His hand brushed the oval of ice. He felt it jiggle against his touch, as if reacting to him.

Releasing Trillian's armor, Illume turned his attention to the piece of ice. Illume gently picked it up, lifting it out of the chest and holding up to a beam of light that poured in through a hole made in the roof by the battle.

The light shined in, revealing the outline of an animal inside. Illume's mind went back to the letter he found on the Order of Light individual. The Dark King had been looking for dragons. Perhaps he'd found one.

Illume tucked the egg into the crook of his left arm while shutting and locking the chest with his right hand. As Illume removed the key from the chest, all the darkness that surrounded him lightening. The black marble morphed to grey, then to white as the driven snow as Illume rose to his feet.

A hollowness sank in as Illume exited Trillian's "throne room." Shutting the now brown door, whose symbol was no longer red but a soft blue, Illume used the Skeleton Key on it, locking it for everyone except himself. Nari stood with a look of concern on her face as he passed her. Ingrid appeared overjoyed at his emergence.

"Are you okay?" Nari asked, gently reaching out to touch the nape of Illume's neck.

"No one learns about this," Illume forced himself to speak, holding back tears as he did. He moved to descend the steps. "Trillian died helping us kill the Dark King and he's buried, with honor, here."

Each step seemed harder now. Even though he was going down stairs, each step he took away from his friend might as well have held the weight of the world. Illume approached the bottom of the stairs. Ingrid's ice wall was still present, but it had already begun to melt.

Illume pressed his hand against the ice, cursing the cold it gave, the cold he gave. Summoning his fiery magic, Illume burned through her wall as if it wasn't even there. It turned into water, cascading down the rest of the steps and into a room full of ankle-deep ash.

Pushing past the ash remains of the imps, Illume forced his breath to be slow and even. Feeling like a cracked piece of glass, he was only a single tap away from completely shattering, and that tap could have come from anywhere. Although it took nowhere near this long, Illume felt as if exiting the castle took an entire day. He heard Nari and Ingrid behind him, yet neither of them said anything.

Exiting the snow white castle's front gate, Illume looked at the moat that was now full of crystal clear water. Putting his hand out, Illume froze the entire moat solid before walking across. Keeping silent, Illume passed both the minotaur. He heard Nari tell them to go find their families, that they were free. Apparently, being unable to understand one another was a one-way street.

As Illume walked through, the dense fog blanketing the forest lifted. As the fog lifted, the trees rapidly returned to life. It was like watching a Discovery Channel special on fast forward, only happening right in front of Illume's eyes. He didn't care; the hollowness that filled him removed that opportunity for joy.

Eventually arriving at the horses, Illume untied them, offering Horson to Nari, taking Neighthan himself, and offering the third to Ingrid. She initially refused, but Illume insisted, resulting in her accepting. Illume climbed on the back of his horse, the egg tucked away in his elbow still.

"You are free to come with us to Cryo's Quarry, Ingrid. Your assistance has earned you a place of honor amongst my city. Or should you choose, you may return home, happy in the knowledge that you helped bring peace and security to your lands." Illume was being sincere yet he was unsure how sincere he sounded.

"I must return home and share the good news at once. When my people know, then I will come and find you. Thank you, both of you. The Jotuns will ever be in your debt," Ingrid explained.

Turning her horse around, Ingrid gave it a kick, and it took off to the north at full speed. Illume offered Nari a forced smile before turning his horse south and riding away. Passing through the cloaking spell, Illume and Nari rode for days. They didn't sprint or trot, just rode at a slow saunter.

Nari tried to comfort Illume and he appreciated it, but none of her attempts helped close that hole made by running his friend through with a frosted pike. It might have been only be a game, but the reality of the blood slick and hot on his hands was forever burned into his skull.

It took almost a month to return to Cryo's Quarry. News about the fall of the Dark King spread far and wide and often had already reached a destination before they'd arrived. Each day, Illume's egg moved and wiggled just a little more. There were times he swore he could hear something cooing inside.

One day, as the sun rose, Illume could see Cryo's Quarry in the distance. A soft bit of relief filled him, remembering why he had to act. It was not for himself, but for his people. The city had grown nearly twice in size since he'd left it last, and from the looks of it, people had flooded in from all over the land to greet Illume and Nari upon their return.

Illume reached out. He took Nari's hand, and for the first time in almost a month, he spoke. His words were whispered, as his throat was weary from lack of use.

"Thank you," he croaked.

Nari gave Illume's hand a gentle squeeze. Her soft, warm skin on his caused his heart to speed up for the first time in weeks. He has begun to no longer feel hollow.

"You're welcome," she responded.

From where they were, it took nearly a full day to finish riding to Cryo's Quarry, but upon reaching the now small city, Nari and Illume were greeted with praise and cheering. Rose petals fell from the battlements and children were hoisted onto their parents' shoulders offering roses and waves.

Seeing the faces of those he'd helped brought Illume's smile all the way back. He waved as Nari accepted flowers. People parted like the Red Sea for them as they rode toward the city and up the land bridge before finally making it past the gates. Within the walls, Illume recognized the faces of the friends he'd made. Urtan had his new axe strapped to his back. Uthrandir and Stark stood side by side and nodded to Illume. He nodded back.

Standing in the center of Cryo's Quarry was Kassandra, Victor, and their children. Illume dismounted, his egg still in hand. Approaching them, Illume gave Kassandra a gentle hug and greeted Victor with a powerful handshake.

"Your family is safe!" Illume called out over the roars of the crowd.

"Thank you. Where is Trillian?" Victor asked as he looked at Nari.

"He did what he needed to make sure the Dark King fell," Illume replied.

"Then he's a hero, and will be remembered as such. I will have a memorial made for him right away," Kassandra replied.

"It can wait. Right now, we all should enjoy peace!" Illume said.

With that, Kassandra and Victor branched off, Kassandra barking orders for the feast that was to occur this evening, and Victor yelling about setting up games.

Illume pushed through the crowd to the structure that was obviously meant to be his home. Reaching the door, he looked back at Nari, nodding for her to come in. She offered him a loving smile but shook her head.

Entering his home, Illume noted how much warmer it was in both temperature and atmosphere. Moving to the other room that he had not gone into, Illume was stunned to see a bed with intricate wood carving on its posts. Bookshelves rested against his walls and were lined with books, as were shelves with potions and forging materials.

Approaching his bed, Illume set the egg down in the center. Taking a step away, Illume walks to a warm bath that had been waiting for him. Removing his armor and weapons, Illume climbed into his little piece of comfort. Closing his eyes, Illume leaned his head back, the weariness of his journey finally taking hold as he passed out cold.

A soft crackling woke Illume from his slumber. He was unsure how long he'd been asleep, but his bath water was now cold. Wiping the drool from his chin, he sat up and looked to his bed. The egg shook, pieces cracked off and fell to the bed, instantly turning to water.

Illume leaped out of the tub, grabbing a towel that hung on the edge. He wrapped it around himself and kneeled by his bed. The egg continued to rock as soft high-pitched roars echoed from inside the egg. A larger piece of the shell was kicked away, causing the egg to fall to its side. From the egg, a baby creature tumbled out, no larger than a house cat. With big icy blue eyes, the creature looked directly into Illume's and let off a soft purr.

Dragon Found
Baby Dragon Level 1
Attack: +1
Defense: 0
Mana: 10
Special Attack: Frost Breath
Weight: +15
Worth: Do you really want to sell this cute bastard?

Illume reached out to the baby dragon, his heart racing. With a soft roar, the dragon nestled Illume's hand with the top of its head. The spiny frills that decorated its scalp were soft and flexible. Illume ran his hand behind its large pointed ears and gave them a gentle scratch, causing the dragon to purr. Soft fluffy fur sprouted from around its neck, which felt like rabbit fur, surrounding its head like a collar with a matching poof of fur at the tip of its tail.

Two tiny wings stretched out from behind the tuft of fur, revealing scaled membraned wings that appeared to be made out of living ice. The dragon stood on its wobbly legs. Four tiny white claws protruded from its paws, like a cat, and dug into Illume's new bed in an attempt to keep its balance. Illume laughed a little as the baby sneezed, causing a blast of ice to freeze part of his bed and proceeded to knock the baby over.

"I think I'm going to call you Trillian," Illume whispered.

Illume gently lifted the baby dragon. It was only then he noticed tiny little horns tucked under the frills on its head. Illume set the dragon down next to his dresser. Opening the drawers, he selected something to wear.

Getting dressed in a pair of finely made clothes, Illume felt a tug at his leg, then his hip, followed by across his back before resting on his shoulder. Illume looked up to see the baby dragon perched on his shoulder with a big smile on its face, showing off its tiny sharp teeth.

Illume headed to his front door, opening it. Night had fallen, but the celebrations had just begun. Illume took in the sight of countless people enjoying themselves and celebrating their freedom from the fear that had begun to grip them once again. Grabbing a flagon, Illume held it into the air as he looked at a constellation that glistened above him, that oddly enough looked a lot like Trillian.

"This one's for you, Trillian," he whispered before taking a massive swig.

THE END

EPILOGUE

ILLUME ATTEMPTED to quit the game several times, only to finally believe that he was stuck, just like Nari. As several months had passed since the fall of the Dark King, Cryo's Quarry had grown immensely, with its population now near five hundred. Trade had been established with every city and farmer this side of the mountains and there had even been talk about turning the Dark King's old fortress into an outpost to start trade with the Jotuns of the north.

Trillian had become a mascot of the city, having doubled in size. It became clear that Trillian was actually a he, and he had grown to the size of a small husky. He couldn't quite fly, but he was stronger than most of the horses and very playful. The children loved him. The soft fur that covered his body fell off, revealing the icy blue scales underneath, but the puffs around his neck and on the tip of his tail remained.

Uthrandir had taken any dwarf that would follow him and returned to Strang, claiming it for his people and being named King of the Mountains. His metal and precious gems flowed freely in trade to both Cryo's Quarry and all the way to Mobrebalku. There were rumors he had even begun trade to the swamp and marshlands beyond his borders.

Because of the decisions Illume made, the allies he fostered and the rights he wronged, the entire Plains Kingdom, as he found out WAY too late, was at peace and prospering. Illume had numerous conversations with Nari about the world of the game.

She said she only helped program this portion, but there were four other teams that focused on different aspects of the map. She also mentioned more than once that this was the best ending she'd ever seen someone get, referencing once when her old co-worker actually caused the world's destruction so completely that it crashed his game.

Nari and Illume pursued one another but very slowly. Illume was the lord of a city and his responsibilities often had him busy for weeks. When they could steal time, they escaped to what was left of Tanner's Folly and lay in the ruins of her forge and looked at the sky and talked for hours. Trillian stayed by Illume's side every step of the way, and more times than not, nosed his way in for more attention.

One day, in the security of his own home, Illume got to leveling up, dropping three points into *Constitution*, two points into *Charisma*, and two points went into *Wisdom*. Just for the hell of it, he put the final ten into *Intelligence*. Illume placed all three of his skill points into *Sneak* as well, having no use for much else at the moment.

New Stats:
Health: 220 regenerates 1% of max health a second while not in battle.
Mana: 300 regenerates 3% of max mana a second while not in battle.
Stamina: 230 regenerates 5% of max stamina a second while not in battle.
Weight Capacity: 0/610, +10 per skill point added to strength.
Survival: Unique skill, player has 70% resistance to cold attacks.
Charisma: +30, +an additional 5 when speaking to pretty women
Strength: +30 above average for male humans.

Dexterity: +40 near superhuman.
Intelligence: +30 above average for a human.
Constitution: +30 without armor rating, average for a human
Wisdom: +40 +10 mana
Getting close to Solomon

New Skills:
Sneak x4 You are now 80% more difficult to detect while sneaking.

Illume saw that boosting his intelligence not only got rid of his deficit, but enhanced his ability to speak in front of women. *ARE YOU KIDDING ME!* he screamed, thankful that he was the only one inside his house except for Trillian.

Trillian jumped at the sudden outburst, his eyes went wide, his ears pinned back against his head, and his frills stuck up on end like a scared cat's hair did. The front door burst open and Nari stepped in wearing her armor and armed to the teeth, a sight he hadn't seen since the day they returned.

"Illume, you'd better get dressed and come see this." Nari's voice was tense as her words were more of a demand than anything.

Illume moved to his bedroom, rubbing Trillian behind the ears as he did. Inside his room, he had a mannequin he purchased to store his armor. Donning his protective gear and arming himself with his sword, bow/arrows, and two daggers, Illume exited his house with Trillian hot on his heels.

As Illume marched through the main streets, he saw Halfdan and Abe yelling orders to men on the wall and the small contingent that were armed within the city. There aren't many, but their weapons and armor were second to none in the Plain Kingdom. An order was roared to open the gates as Victor, in human form, leaped from the battlements and landed beside the massive doors.

"What's going on?" Illume demanded.

"We saw them marching an hour ago. They are making good time and are headed this way," Victor informed Illume.

"Who?!" Illume barked.

"Them!" Nari stated coldly.

Nari made her way to the land bridge while Illume was getting ready. She pointed at the horizon. Illume followed her finger to see an army marching their way.

Banners flew above them and the sounds of drums filled the air. Illume whistled, and Horson and Neighthan both trotted up to Illume. He mounted Neighthan while Nari got on Horson.

"Victor, you feel like intimidating a commander today?" Illume asked.

"Always!" Victor snarled.

Riding down the land bridge, Victor moved to Nari's left side. Illume was on her right and Trillian trotted along next to Illume. They rode out to meet this oncoming army as Victor took his beast form and Illume drew his bow.

I WOULD LIKE to thank everyone for strapping in on the amazing adventure that is Legends Online. I had so much fun working on this for you all and I look forward to bringing you more adventures. If you would like to keep informed on upcoming releases, re-releases or just staying in the loop I have a private Facebook group I'd be honored for you to join.

Ross' O.W.S (Out of this World Subscribers) can be found at this link:

https://www.facebook.com/groups/168282640553429/

I hope you have an awesome day and I'll see you in the next one!

-Ross

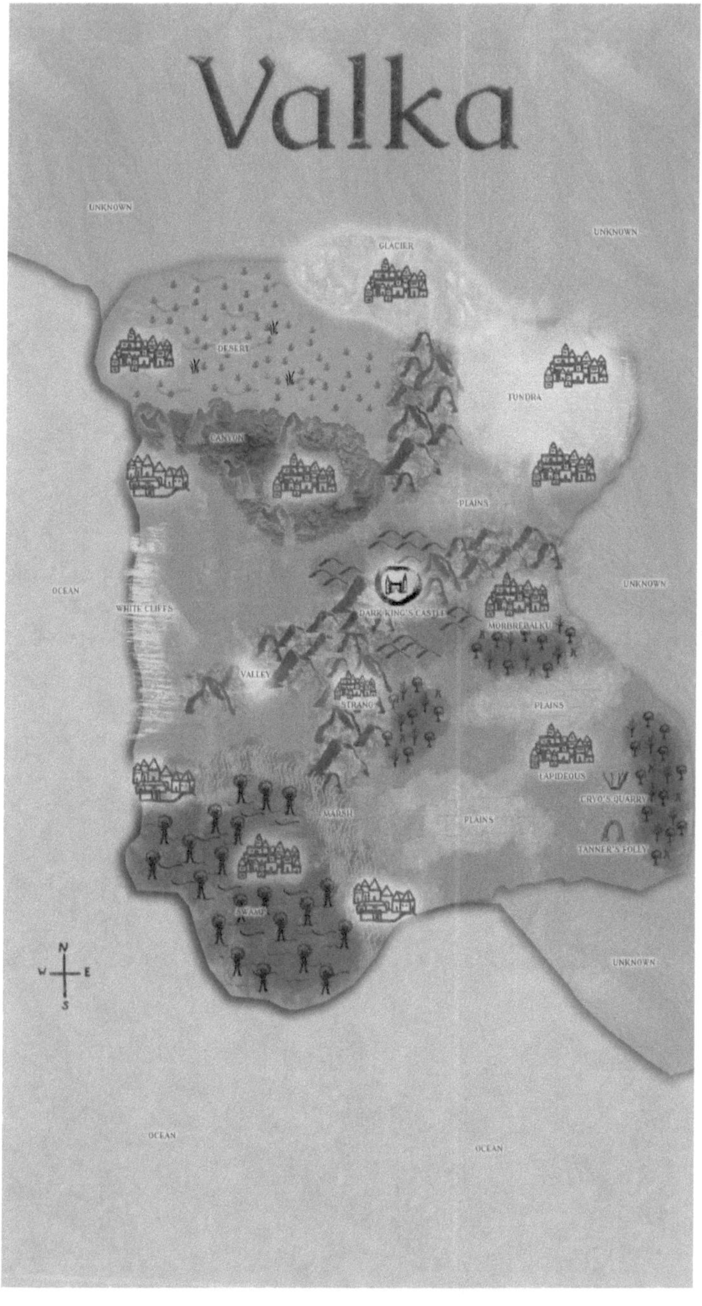
Valka
UNKNOWN
UNKNOWN
GLACIER
DESERT
TUNDRA
CANYON
PLAINS
OCEAN
WHITE CLIFFS
DARK KING'S CASTLE
UNKNOWN
MORBREBALKU
VALLEY
STRANG
PLAINS
LAPIDEOUS
CRYO'S QUARRY
MARSH
PLAINS
TANNER'S FOLLY
SWAMP
N
W
E
S
UNKNOWN
OCEAN
OCEAN

STAY INFORMED

Get A Free Book by visiting Jonathan Yanez' website. You can email me at jonathan.alan.yanez@gmail.com or find me on Amazon, and Instagram (@author_jonathan_yanez). I also created a special Facebook group called "Jonathan's Reading Wolves" specifically for readers, where I show new cover art, do give-aways, and run contests. Please check it out and join whenever you get the chance!

For updates about new releases, as well as exclusive promotions, visit my website and sign up for the VIP mailing list. Head there now to receive a free copy of *Shall We Begin*.

http://jonathan-yanez.com

Enjoying the series? Help others discover *Legends Online* by sharing with a friend.